CONSUMED BY RAGE

ZARA TELEG

Consumed by Rage is entirely a work of fiction. All names, characters, organizations, events,
and places portrayed in this novel are of the author's imagination. Any resemblance to
actual events, localities, or persons, living or dead, is entirely coincidental.

First edition

Editing by Ritchelle Buensuceso
Cover design by Raelleen Diaz
Cover photo by Shutterstock

For my husband. You never tell me my dreams are too big or too crazy. Thank you for all your support.

CONTENTS

PROLOGUE

Juliet

*F*reedom. It was something I had seldom thought about… until four years ago. I had taken for granted living life every day without looking over my shoulder. Never feeling any real peace, a tiny part of me was always on high alert. I feared that at any moment, I would be discovered. I had spent the past four years trying to cope with intense, crippling anxiety, and everything I had done was still no match against the nightmares that visited me often.

I thought fate would deal me a better hand. I believed I could escape him. Now the effects of my mistakes had spread. I feared not only for my life but also those of people I love who were put in danger because of me. I was no longer free. Now, at twenty-seven years old, my time had run out.

My eyes began to open. I blinked slowly, trying to get them to adjust to the darkness. I used my shoulder to wipe the dampness from my face. Blackness cloaked the room, making it impossible to see anything around me. The musty air blasting through the vent was frigid. My fingers and toes were numb, making them hard to move. An intense headache competed with the throbbing pain in my face. The tiniest bit of warmth against my back made me aware of the body next to mine. I tried opening my mouth; the tape that had sealed it

1

shut had been removed. My lips felt swollen, and I tasted dried blood on them. I nudged the body next to mine. I hoped that it was Paige, that they hadn't separated us.

A soft whisper came from my cracked lips. "Paigey..." I croaked her childhood nickname.

Nothing.

"Paige, please answer me," panicking, I whispered louder, waiting for an answer.

A small groan escaped her as she moved just centimeters. "Ana..." a low voice struggled to whisper back.

I let out the breath I was holding, relieved that hers was the body next to mine. "Oh, Paige..." I leaned into her as close as I could, "I'm so sorry you got dragged into this." My voice hitched and my eyes welled, but no tears came. Dehydration left nothing for my body to spare. We leaned into each other. The friction caused my broken body to ache. "I will find a way to get us out of here," I promised her.

A door opened. It creaked loudly, breaking the silence. Light streamed down the staircase. It was dim yet blinding in the blackness of the basement. We both jumped and huddled our bodies even closer with our hands tied behind our backs.

We stayed silent. The only sound came from the shoes that clanked heavily down each step. The stairs moaned under the weight of the man. A large shadow appeared, then the massive body that belonged to it. It was him—the monster. The man with all the scars. The slight limp in his step gave him away.

He turned on a small flashlight and aimed it around, highlighting areas of the basement before finding us. The light so shocking when it hit me, I squeezed my eyes shut. I could feel the tremors rolling off Paige's small body. *God, please. Please send someone to rescue us before it's too late.* I had pushed away everyone who cared; now there might be no one left who could save us.

With my eyes still closed I listened to the clicking of his fancy shoes on the damp concrete as they got closer and closer. I braced myself as the large body loomed over us.

RAGE

Six months earlier…

I tucked my head down further behind the shield as I picked up the pace. My bike pushed forward faster, anxiety building in my chest as I passed the small road sign with the arrow: Sugar Maple 15 miles.

That little sign surged adrenaline through every part of my body as I got closer to home. My bike sped through the warm night, covering the distance as fast as possible. Miles of trees, bushes, and mountains were blurred in my peripheral vision over the last five and a half hours until I finally crossed Georgia from Tennessee.

The sound of my pipes cutting through the night was all that filled my ears, the mountain air leaving a light mist on my partially exposed face. I tried to stretch my back. I felt tight everywhere from not stopping. When I was a kid, I couldn't wait to grow up so I could leave this place. After four long years of exile, I couldn't get back fast enough.

It was Monday night—I was five days early. The idea of surprising my brothers in the Stained Souls MC came to me last night when I tossed and turned trying to sleep. Friday seemed too far away. At first light, I packed my shit and left behind everything that couldn't fit on my bike. I knew my club brothers weren't expecting me until the weekend so they could throw me a huge homecoming bash. As much as that sounded great, I wanted some time to reacquaint myself with my newly renovated hometown. Besides, I knew that the party would leave me hungover for days, and that wasn't how I wanted to start my homecoming.

Last time I talked to Hawk, he said that the Stained Souls were raking in cash with all the new people in town. The club owned several buildings on the main strip, so naturally, they had done pretty well with the renovations. I hadn't decided, even with the influx of income, how I felt about returning to a town full of strangers. I was once a well-known and feared man in this town. Now I would be the stranger. The thought had my stomach turning.

My forearms tightened as the needle pushed further toward one hundred on the desolate road. The blackness of night was the perfect backdrop for the slideshow that was running in my head. All the people, places, and friends I left behind...the good times with my brothers and the bad times that destroyed my soul. I shouldn't have wanted to go back. I should have embraced my new life. But no matter how much darkness and anger Sugar Maple triggered, it was still home.

I shook my head, clearing the thoughts. I focused on the approaching glow of city lights that made the horizon over the mountain appear bright compared to the inky sky that surrounded it. The May heat and humidity created a haze blanketing the area.

I slowed my pace to almost a crawl just outside town. On the hillside, the moon illuminated the bright white chapel and gave it an eerie glow. It stood tall and menacing, overlooking the bridge into Sugar Maple. Its angular windows, the way they looked down the hill to the town below, reminded me of angry, judging eyes.

I tried to keep my eyes forward, but the small graveyard pulled me to it. The decaying stones of the cemetery were almost as white as the church. My eyes locked on a single headstone. I swallowed back the lump that formed in my throat. Every fucking time I entered or left town, I was forced to pass the painful reminder of what life took from me. I had said goodbye to three people I loved standing under those tall maple trees, which always seemed to mock me.

CHAPTER ONE

Rage

*H*oly shit. That was the only thought that came to mind when the condo complex came into view. It was stunning, even from a distance. Everyone kept telling me I wouldn't recognize the place. I couldn't even imagine how that was possible after only four years.

Shortly before I left, Sugar Maple Mill was demolished, leaving a pile of rubble in its place. I was in disbelief that the Ramseys sold out their legacy for some condos. I hated Richard and Deacon Ramsey ever since we were in school. They were both douches then, so I should not have expected any different when they inherited their family mill. The longtime residents were hoping that, since the boys grew up here, they would restore the mill to its former glory. Instead, they built high-rise condos where their family mill once employed over half the town. I heard that Main Street had become some kind of trendy hipster heaven. Great. My eyes rolled at the thought.

Thankfully, the bridge crossing Black Rock River looked the same, with old lantern-style street lights lining both sides. I smiled at the memory of sweltering hot summer days when my brother and I would jump off this same bridge into the deep cold water. Our grandma made us promise not to without adults, but we did it anyway, and she always seemed to know when we disobeyed. Our punishment was severe—there was no pie those nights. I took in a deep breath, inhaling the familiar smell of the river as my bike crossed. It was the nostalgic scent of home, the kind of smell that brought memories to life.

Stopped at the traffic light turning from the bridge onto Main Street, my eyes scanned all the new shops and buildings. The old cracked concrete sidewalks were now cobblestone and pavers that made intricate crisscross patterns. The centerpiece of Main Street was Sugar Maple Condominiums. My head had to tilt back to look all the way to the top of the expansive building. It stood about twelve stories high and had a huge mural on the side depicting the history of the town. The mill, the train, the old malt shop, town square, and the Baptist church the Ramsey family attended. The vibrant colors made the painting like I was looking at a photo album. The front of the building was a mix of modern glass and balconies, while the back faced the river and had all balconies. A large timber and glass awning covered the ground level where a security guard sat.

I jumped, startled by the beep behind me. I didn't even notice the light had changed as I took in my new surroundings. The town barely resembled the place where I grew up. It was now colorful and full of life with small stores lining both sides. I smiled when I came upon the well-lit sign of Stained Skyn: Tattoos & Piercing. It sat right in the middle of Main Street where the old five and dime was when we were kids. I laughed to myself as I remembered how much ten-cent hard-ass bubble gum we stole from that store. Mr. Brooks used to kick us out all the time; he would twist Hawk's ear and call his mama. The shop now sits between a coffee place and…Juiced? Whatever the hell that was. Street lamps were lighting the strip, and the train station that once had been used for lumber and workers now had sleek glass and timber arches that matched the condos. Not many people were milling around at this time. The shops were all closed except for Stained Skyn.

I came to a stop down the block, looking for somewhere out of sight to park. Since I didn't want to tip the guys off to my surprise arrival, I found a spot in the alley across the street, next to the only other vehicle—a crazy-looking pink and black Jeep. It was lifted high with big tires and a giant paddle board sticking out of the back. There were all these beads and a Buddha hanging from the rearview mirror.

When the sound of my bike silenced, my ears turned to the thump of loud music coming from the adjacent old brick building. It had the image of a woman holding her foot over her head painted on the side with the sign Fluid Yoga Studio lit below. The windows and storefront were dark. My ears followed the pounding music to its source; a dim light glowed from the second floor, where the rock music echoed out the windows.

Why would a yoga studio be blaring Disturbed's *Sound of Silence?* Maybe it was the adrenaline of being back in my hometown or maybe I was overtired and delirious from the ride, but I felt strangely compelled to follow the music. The song that got me through some rough nights led me up the fire escape to the second floor. It took a minute for my eyes to adjust to the dimly lit music-filled room.

Through the upstairs window, I saw some fabric suspended from the ceiling. Swinging and doing acrobatics from it to the thundering music was…a woman. I crept closer to the window to get a better look. The shadows hid her face, she was small and lean, wearing a sports bra and tiny cut shorts. Her long hair followed her movements in the air. I couldn't peel my eyes away. I was frozen as I watched her. She looked like a flying angel, and I was completely mesmerized. But then the music abruptly ended. *Oh, shit.* I moved from the window, crept back down the escape, and quickly made my way out toward the street.

Well, that was something…

From the alley, I spotted two Harleys in front of Stained Skyn. One was Hawk's—I'd know that Sportster anywhere. The bells chimed as I opened the glass door of the tattoo parlor. The place was fantastic, nothing like the hole in the wall it used to be. The glass counters were full of body jewelry, and artwork covered the walls. A large TV screen had a slideshow of Hawk piercing and tattooing customers, the before and afters. The music was loud, not as loud as the yoga girl's, but loud enough to distract from the pain of being tattooed or pieced.

The volume lowered, and a deep voice came from the private

rooms in the back, "Be right with you." I heard the thumping of his boots heading toward me.

As Hawk rounded the corner, snapping off his latex gloves, it took a second before a devilish grin spread across his face. "Rage? What the fuck are you doing here, man? I thought you weren't coming for a few days. I would have taken the night off." My best friend hadn't changed much. Blond hair was peeking through his signature bandana. His bright blue eyes stood out with his tan skin. His beard now hid the dimples girls loved so much.

Accepting the half bro hug, I explained my eagerness and that I wanted some time before the celebrating began. "Good call," Hawk said. "You know, Colt has big shit planned for your welcome home party." His eyebrows waggled with excitement.

Another set of boots made their way out to the front. Hack, our tech god, rushed toward me. "I thought it was my imagination when I saw you on the cameras," he said as he embraced me, slapping my back. "Rage, you've gotten even bigger!"

Man, it felt good to be home. These men—the Stained Souls—they were my family.

I spent the next two hours having a few beers, watching Hawk tattoo an elaborate back piece on a college girl. She was trying her best not to cry, holding her friend's hand while the tiny needles revealed a big colorful elephant. I winced at the pained expression the girl had as she breathed heavily, trying to keep herself calm.

JULIET

"Another! Jab left, left again! Now right, left ribs, right knee!" his deep voice commanded. The wraps on my hands began to feel like they were not even there. The sweat glistened off my abs, soaking the tops of my sweat shorts. The muscles were becoming sore with each blow. Left, then right. I'd been at this for forty-five minutes, and his intensity didn't waiver. His coaching methods were relentless. You didn't come to Leo for positive, weak reassurances that you were doing well—the man was all business. If you didn't work hard enough, he'd replace your spot in a second. There was a waitlist of men and women wanting to train with this beast.

"Juliet, focus! Come on, girl, you got this!" he barked. His deep voice still had the remainder of his Spanish accent. Leo held the paddles higher, then lower, as I punched out my frustrations.

Standing at around 6'3", the lean Brazilian mixed-martial arts master was maybe the most intimidating man I'd ever met. His fighting style was flawless and fluid even with his massive frame. Leo had tan skin adorned with tribal tattoos. He has one that covers the area between his right eye and cheekbone. His head was shaved, except for a tight mohawk, and he had the deepest, darkest brown eyes I had ever seen.

The only reason he agreed to train me was that he watched me struggle for weeks on my own, and it might have helped that I taught his girlfriend, Shelly, some tantric yoga moves. Men always seemed to appreciate that.

Shelly was his complete opposite. Porcelain skin, long, shiny platinum blond hair and pale blue eyes. She was petite, yet ripped. Shelly spent most of her day training at the gym. She used to be Leo's ring girl when he was actively fighting. I dreamt of having a relationship like theirs—now I barely dated.

"Come on, finish strong with a roundhouse to the head!" he commanded. He held his hand high for me to reach. Channeling some of my inner anger, I spun and released the last bit of power I had to give as my foot connected with the bag in front of me. I let out a grunt before I fell back to balance.

"Damn," Leo said as his eyes blinked at the height I just reached. My yoga training gave me the advantage of being able to stretch high and still keep balance.

When Leo saw how my yoga skills expanded my abilities, he decided to cut me a deal for the private lessons that I couldn't afford. I forced myself to pay because these lessons were way more helpful than any emotional therapy had ever been. No shrink could do for me what MMA had done.

Leo offered me a bargain. He suggested I teach a special type of yoga class once a week for his elite fighters to get them to stretch and balance. And I continue to help Shelly, of course. We called the class Dynamic Expansion. We knew the fighters would never go for a yoga class. Every Wednesday at 7 pm, I taught the scariest men around how to increase their range and balance to give them more power. It had been over a year, and they all loved it. Most never missed a class.

My best friend, Ivy, God bless her, loved to assist—more accurately, ogle and molest—the class. That girl was all about the bad boys—she loved them and was the consummate flirt. Bad boys they might be, but they were all super respectful. That might be because Leo would kick their asses and then kick them out of the gym if they stepped out of line.

With the last kick, my time was up. I was feeling particularly nauseated after today's workout; I must not have had enough water earlier. I was an exhausted sweaty mess.

"Great job, Juliet. Now get out of here and replenish." Leo said in his drill sergeant voice, pointing to the locker room.

"Thanks, Leo," I replied, still huffing. I squirted the cold water from my aluminum bottle into my mouth and some on my towel before wiping my face.

"See you tomorrow night." He winked and extended his rarely seen megawatt smile. The grin suited his usually stern face. I smiled back and hit the showers before meeting Ivy at Roasted.

CHAPTER TWO

Rage

I left my bike parked at Stained Skyn. The morning was beautiful; the summer sun warmed my face the few blocks I walked. What used to be unwelcoming, cracked sidewalks and boarded up storefronts were now tree-lined cobblestone, flower pots, and boutiques.

A genuine smile spread across my face as I approached the end of the block. In front of me was the only place where I felt my life had any meaning, the Pit.

Eight years ago, Leo and I rented a space, a hole in the wall, just a few blocks from the center of town. No other businesses were even close to it, certainly not the Organic Dry Cleaners that was now operating beside it. We started with a DIY cage, some heavy and speed bags, weights, and a small locker room.

Shit, we were so young then and had no idea what we were doing —just a couple of twenty-five-year-old hothead fighters who wanted to start a ring of our own. But it wasn't hard to convince the MC to invest. The club made a shitload of money running underground octagons, the potential for new fights alone was all the incentive they needed.

Leo and I became close as brothers. We fought the same circuits for years. He was there the night I got arrested—he's the one who pulled me off the little bastard. When I had taken the offer to skip town temporarily, he agreed to run the Pit without me. I still did what I could from a virtual location, books and shit, but even though I couldn't physically be there, he never missed sending me my cut. Training at other gyms in Tennessee just wasn't the same, nothing was like the Pit.

Walking in here for the first time in four years, I almost didn't recognize the place. Leo had gotten my approval for all the changes and showed me pictures now and then, but I was not prepared for this. It was way better than any picture.

The glass doors and front walls were tinted and had black and white images of all the fighters, including me, in large decals. My face was half hidden by my left arm while my right was pulled back in position to throw a powerful blow to some poor guy's face. Leo's decal of his famous Guillotine Choke was featured next to mine.

I moved toward the reception desk where a familiar blonde was behind the counter helping clients. As she turned my direction to greet me, our faces turned quickly to smiles of recognition. Shelly practically jumped over the counter to give me a bear hug. She was such a little thing. I lifted her off the ground, swinging her in a circle before placing her back down.

"Oh, my God! Rage!" She looked at me like she was seeing me for the first time. "I didn't think we would see you until next week. It's so good to see you! Leo is going to freak." She hugged me again. "We missed you. Things have not been the same since you left."

"I'm glad to be back. It's great to see you, Shell. It looks like Leo's doing something right to keep you around this long." I twisted my lips trying not to smile.

"Yeah, well, if I don't see a ring one day soon, you just may get a shot," she poked at my chest and giggled.

"Shelly," a deep voice boomed sternly from behind me, "I told you to stop molesting the fighters."

I turned to see Leo making his way to me, his smile wide. "You just couldn't wait to get back here, huh?" He grabbed me in a fighter hold. "Man, it's so great to have you back! I didn't think you were coming back to town for a few days." The man was even more ripped now than he was four years ago when I had seen him last.

"Well, I heard the guys need a break from the drill sergeant." I kept my face serious and watched his scowl form at the accusation.

"Oh, yeah?" His eyebrows furrowed together, and his large arms folded across his wide chest. "What motherfucker said that? I'm going to work him twice as hard," his deep voice bellowed, and the three of us broke into a laugh.

Leo's hand pinched the back of my neck as he veered me past the reception area. "Come on, bro, let me reacquaint you with our gym."

He gave me the grand tour and told me about the classes they offer. In the first room, a self-defense class was in session. There were about twenty people and two instructors. Women were facing each other, practicing breaking their wrists free from an attacker.

The next room was empty. When the lights flicked on, stacks of colorful rolled up mats sat in the corner, straps were hanging on the walls, and blocks were stacked on the floor. There were large mirrors on every wall. My sneakers squeaked on the freshly cleaned floor as I stepped into the spacious room. "What goes on in here?"

"All different classes, but our most popular is yoga." His finger pointed to the mats.

"Yoga?" My eyebrow went up. "Who the hell signs up for that shit?"

"We got this fine-ass yoga teacher from that place in town. She's a damn fierce fighter, and when I saw her range, I knew we needed her to teach."

I must have still looked confused. Next thing I knew, Leo was calling out for Shelly.

"Shelly, come show Rage something Juliet taught you."

"Okay," Shelly smiled brightly. She balanced on one muscular leg, then reached back and grabbed her foot from behind her and pulled it up higher and higher above her head.

"Ta-da" she squeaked, her face proud. My eyebrows met my hairline, and I must've smiled a dirty smile because Leo looked annoyed.

"I see," my head bobbed up and down, eyes wide at the sight of her.

"Not that," he growled at Shelly. "Show him your roundhouse. Girl, you have the other shit for the bedroom." His lips went tight.

"Oh, sorry," she giggled, covering her face with her hands as she blushed. When she regained her composure, she stood still and then threw a head-high power kick in complete balance.

"Whoa." My eyes widened and my mouth hung open. "I think I get it. That's amazing, Shell."

Leo punched my arm. "You should take her class. She's here every Wednesday night at seven. And Rage, she's single."

I'd been back not even an hour and already Leo is trying to fix me up. "Bro, you're already going there?" I shook my head and rolled my eyes.

Ever since he and Shelly got together a few years back, he had been on me about settling down. Not happening. Not because I liked a revolving door of ladies—I just would never put my heart, or what was left of it, through a meat grinder like that again.

After the tour, I spent some time in the office and learned all the alarms and their new opening and closing procedures. I got in a workout and promised to be back tomorrow. I hugged Shelly goodbye before I turned to Leo, who walked me to the door. "I guess I'll see you at the meeting tomorrow morning?"

His face was serious as he nodded, "Colt said it was mandatory. Some important shit on the table, so yeah, I'll be at the clubhouse tomorrow morning."

JULIET

I looked at my watch again, 9:10 am. Where the hell was Ivy? She was ten minutes late—she was never late. Ivy and I had developed a routine. She did the first yoga class of the morning while I beat the shit out of a heavy bag over at the Pit, then we met at Roasted, the local coffee shop across the street from our yoga studio.

My life had become predictable, just the way I liked it. I blew out a breath, thinking that a boring and predictable life was way better than… The thought had me instinctively shifting in my chair to check out my surroundings.

When Ivy begged me to move here with her, I never thought the studio would be successful enough to support us both. I had nothing to lose, and she was dying to move from Black Rock and couldn't stop talking about this up-and-coming little town. She took her allotted college tuition and bought the building before the real estate in the area skyrocketed. We did all of the cosmetic renovations ourselves, and Hawk hooked us up with some contractors to fix the rest of the building.

By the time we were ready to open, Roasted was also almost complete. I loved that the yoga studio smelled like coffee and Jasmine flowers. It was a surprisingly good scent. My thoughts were interrupted by the screeching of a chair being pulled back and then a tiny voice.

"Hi, Jet!" A little girl with the blond pigtails placed her sippy cup on the table as she climbed onto the vacant seat across from me. Her white eyelet bloomers showed underneath her skirt as she lifted herself. When she settled in the chair, her smile of achievement was bright. Her faced beamed with pride.

"Good morning, Lucy. Your dress is beautiful! Whatcha got in your cup today?"

"Latte," she said, proudly holding up her cup, then giggled. She looked around and whispered, "It's really almond milk, but Momma put whipped cream on it, so it's a latte." She tilted her head back, drinking its contents.

"Lucy, I need your help," her mom, Caroline, called. She mouthed "sorry" to me when she saw Lucy sitting in Ivy's usual spot. I waved her off—I loved seeing Lucy. Her silky blond hair and chubby cheeks reminded me so much of my baby sister when she was little. The only thing missing was Paige's unusual violet eyes—Lucy's were golden brown like her mom's.

Dan delivered my medium soy latte, no whip, with a dash of cinnamon, and Ivy's double shot of espresso. He placed them on the table and apologized needlessly for my adorable visitor. He and

Caroline owned Roasted, and they were just the best parents a little girl could ever have—they loved Lucy so much.

Ivy and I would have our daily mini meeting here, then we'd head back to our studio where I'd lead the 11 o'clock rock yoga class downstairs and she'd teach the kiddie class upstairs. Moms loved it— they got pumped with me while their kids relaxed with Ivy.

My sky yoga classes were becoming more popular. I ran them several times a week in between the regular classes I taught. More girls from the university were taking the train in, which helped our business grow.

I watched out the window as Hawk pulled to a stop in front of Stained Skyn, the tattoo shop of the Stained Souls MC. Hawk dismounted his bike and unlocked the front door. He came back out placing the OPEN tent sign on the sidewalk. Girls coming off the train stopped to watch him. The women who came to Fluid couldn't get enough of the eye candy across the street.

Juiced, the organic fresh pressed juice and raw food bar where I love to grab lunch, might have benefited from the view as well. Simon, the owner, was always bringing the guys treats. He might have a crush on a few of the men. I sold Simon fresh sprouts and microgreens every Saturday before I set up at the farmer's market.

I stared into my latte, stirring it while I waited for Ivy to join me. I didn't know what I would have done without her. She'd been with me through everything. She was my best friend growing up in Tallahassee, and we were inseparable. I was devastated when her dad had gotten relocated and moved them to Black Rock. We kept in touch over the years but rarely saw each other.

After Antonio had fucked up my life, I knew I had to get away from Tallahassee; it was too dangerous to stay. Then Ivy insisted I move with her here, to Sugar Maple, and help her open Fluid. I had already been instructing yoga at a small studio in Florida, so the idea seemed worth considering. Antonio had never met Ivy, so he or his brother would never be able to find her. I moved while my parents took up new residence in Arizona where my sister, Paige, was going to college. It was the perfect escape. It all made sense.

Just thinking back about it made my stomach twist. Tears

threatened to fall. It had been almost four long years since I left my old life behind. Since I became a liar. I left Anabelle Juliet Conti behind and became Juliet Russo overnight. Lost in my thoughts, I didn't even notice Ivy take the seat across from me.

"Juliet, honey, you're stirring all the foam away." I slowly blinked and brought myself back to the present. I looked into the mug's slowly disappearing foam before lifting my eyes to her. Without talking, she knew what I was thinking. She placed her hand over mine, giving it a small squeeze. I forced a smile.

Ivy's shiny blond hair was pushed behind her ear on one side and the rest of the chin-length waves framed her heart-shaped face. Her deep blue eyes stared into mine. She smiled, "You okay?"

I pushed her espresso toward her and let out a long breath. "Yeah, I'm fine." We sat in silence for a few moments, people watching. She knew when I needed space. She was my best friend, and the girl could read me like a book.

"So," Ivy began as she put down her espresso that was already half gone, "are you ready for this weekend?" She batted her eyelashes innocently. Her smile tilted to one side as she tried not to laugh. She was going to help me prepare for an event I was performing at this weekend for the MC.

"Not really," I confessed. "I don't know how the heck you and Hawk convinced me to do this. I must be crazy." There it was, the evilest grin she could muster. She might as well have rubbed her hands together and laughed maniacally, the evil genius. I gave her a light slap to her arm. "Thanks, Ivy. The things you get me into!" I shook my head. There was no getting out of it now.

CHAPTER THREE

Rage

The Stained Souls Clubhouse. God, I'd missed this place. This place was my home. I loved staying here. It was like living in a bar with your brothers. You could always find girls around, too, if you need someone to warm your bed.

The main house had a bar, a huge kitchen, a game room, and an old-school gym. We brought the old equipment from the Pit here every time we upgraded something. An adjoining building across the courtyard also had rooms where some of the boys stayed. There were also Colt's office and the large room with double-locking doors where "church"—our club meetings—was held.

I scrubbed my hand down my face to wake myself up. I had a few drinks last night, and I was in dire need of caffeine. My scruff was itchy on my face. Our Wednesday meeting was in an hour. I pulled my T-shirt over my head and stretched as I looked around my small room. Fuck, it was good to be home. I was happy to see the boys had kept my room for me. Other than Colt spending a few nights in there when he was fighting with his ex, my room was the way I had left it. I could smell the coffee coming from the kitchen and followed it to the long island, which had cream and sugar already out along with a bunch of clean mugs. I fixed myself a mug. The scent of bacon was also in the air. My stomach growled as I sat down on the tall stool.

Before I even took the first sip of the magic brew, I was interrupted by a high-pitched squeal, "Rage! Oh, my God! You're back!" Livi's fully made-up face was smiling, rushing toward me. She nearly knocked my mug out of my hand as she planted a sticky red kiss on me. "They said you weren't coming for a few more days!"

"Hi, doll. Been a long time." I said, trying to be polite. "You look good," I lied. She looked rough. She couldn't be more than twenty-eight, but I suppose this life was aging her faster. Her perfume mixed with cigarette smell was suffocating.

"I missed you. Did you miss me? I thought you'd call me." She pouted out her cherry-red bottom lip.

"Honey, my brain isn't really up for talking just yet. I need coffee and food."

"Lucky for you," she grinned and began unloading food onto the counter, an assortment of pastries and breakfast sandwiches, bagels, and spreads, "Colt sent me out to pick this up before the meeting."

I swiped a sandwich and quickly spread cream cheese on a bagel. Food and coffee, just what I needed.

The kitchen doors swung open, and a larger-than-life Kai stepped in. Pretty soon more brothers started arriving one after another.

"Rage! What's up, my brother?" Kai said, slapping my shoulder. Kai was Stained Souls' sergeant-at-arms, a job that was fit for me and my brute personality, but I preferred to be his second, staying in the shadows. Kai was tall and muscular. His good looks masked the twisted fucker he was on the inside. His dark brown hair came to his shoulders, his eyes were frequently hidden behind sunglasses, and his tattoo-sleeved arms were always on display. Most of the time, he walked around with no shirt under his cut. He reminded me of a rock star with his cigarette hanging between his lips and the permanent three-day scruff on his face. He came off to most as a jovial playboy, but he was one badass motherfucker. You did not want to fuck with him.

I nodded and held my cup up to him. He poured his brew, lit his smoke, and joined me.

"I'm glad you're back. I missed having you as backup. Because Leo is such a pussy," he said loud enough to be sure Leo could hear him as he rounded the corner.

"Fuck off, you Jared Leto wannabe," Leo grumbled. Leo's comment had the rest of the boys laughing as they entered the room. It became a frenzy of quickly disappearing food and coffee as they all loaded their plates and filled their mugs.

"Dude, you really think I look like Leto?" Kai asked Leo, a hopeful expression on his face. "No, you're a tool!" Leo retorted as he poured his coffee.

"Dick." Kai hung his head and grabbed the bourbon from the end of the counter. "What goes better with coffee than a little bourbon?" He filled the shot glasses he had set out.

Smiling, he held the bottle high in the air. "To Rage's return home." He passed out shots, and everyone raised their glasses in the air. The glasses slammed to the bar before Colt, our president, popped his head into the kitchen.

"Ladies, you can gossip later. It's time for church."

"Prez, you need to catch up." Kai passed him a large shot and poured himself another. They clinked their glasses and threw back their shots.

"I needed that," Colt said and accepted a coffee from one of the prospects.

Seconds later, we all shuffled into the boardroom, away from outsiders' ears. We took our seats around the maple table. Colt banged the gavel, silencing everyone.

"The first order of business," he announced and then turned to me, "Welcome back, Rage." Whistles and hollers sounded around the large table. "We're glad you came back a few days early. We have some issues you may be able to help with." He shuffled the papers in front of him. "Before we get into those, Hawk, Tiny, and Leo, you want to give me some updates on our numbers?" He turned to Ledger, who was pulling out his laptop. "Ledge, you ready?"

Having a member with an accounting degree was more helpful than we thought. Ledge put on his nerdy glasses, nodding to proceed.

The thick black frames took him from looking like Superman in leather to Clark Kent.

After the boring numbers shit, Colt finally delved into why we were all called into this meeting. He ran his hands through his hair, the jet black now had glimmers of white appearing. He's only in his early forties, but his hair was showing just how much stress running a club can age you. He became president in his thirties, just after he and Chyanne split—he took on a whole lot responsibility.

"You boys know how hard we have worked to be as legit as we can be around here." He cracked his tattooed knuckles. "Other than a few fights a year, we have really turned things around with our businesses. However, we got problems. The troopers agree not to bother us if we help keep the area clean of drugs. Unfortunately, we have gotten word from several sources that there has been an influx of Ecstasy and other tainted batches of drugs that have sent a few college girls to the ER."

He took a long breath, "There have been a couple of anger-induced incidents that jailed a few students. Police said it was from a form of meth they haven't seen before. Their intel said it's coming from Florida, with matching incidents there. Bad drugs have become a fast-growing problem, and now it's spreading into Sugar Maple, too. Two nights ago, The Ridge had a girl fall to the floor in a seizure. Trooper Jones said they are still waiting on test results to find out the drugs in her system, but the pressure is on to find out who is bringing in the drugs, probably because the girl was the Black Rock City Council President's daughter."

"What the fuck do they want us to do?" Ledger asked, taking off his glasses and rubbing his eyes.

Colt lit the cigarette he had been fiddling with and continued, "The girl's boyfriend admitted in custody that he bought it from his cousin, who then claimed that it came from a biker. There are only two possibilities around here, The Banshees or Devil's. My bet is on Devil's. The mother chapter of Devil's Damned is in North Florida where the intel indicated it is spreading from. They're known to push bad shit."

"I think it's time we have our annual meet and get this shit straightened out before it puts us out of business." Colt looked around for agreement. "Since we have Rage's welcome home party this weekend—" He was interrupted with hoots and hollers. Colt pounded the gavel hard. "I think we can have the club ready to host the boys from both chapters next weekend. I'll clear it with Trooper Jones, keep the townies from getting anywhere near the chaos here next weekend."

Everyone appeared agreeable. "I'm going to need you all to help make it happen next weekend, so make sure you are ready, willing, and able with your free time." All of us nodded our heads.

"Anyone else have any other business?" Colt tapped his cigarette out. He pounded the gavel, the last of his smoke streaming from his lips. He grinned wide and hit my shoulder, "Then, I guess I'll see you all Saturday night." Loud hoots and hollers came from my bothers as we stood and left the room.

"Rage," Leo hollered after me. "You still good to close for Shelly and me tonight? She's been bugging me for a date night for weeks." He shook his head and put it in his hands. "She wants me to take her Salsa dancing."

I tried hard not to laugh at the poor guy. "Yeah, I got you covered, and yes, before you remind me, I will check in on the classes, and yes, I know how to lock up and turn on the alarm."

"Good man. I will see you tonight." His hand landed heavy on my shoulder.

Before I could go on any farther, it was Hawk's turn. Geez.

"Oh, Rage," he said in a sing-song voice. That could only mean trouble. I was afraid to look. I slowly turned to face Hawk and Ledge, both of whom had shit-eating grins plastered to their up-to-no-good faces.

"Yes?"

"We wanted to introduce you to someone." Hawk smiled.

Behind them stood a tall, leggy redhead. Her shorts and tank top looked two sizes too small, showing off her curves. She gave me a flirtatious smile. Bright red lipstick stained her lips. Many men would find her sexy with her huge breasts and tiny waist. She stalked toward me swinging her hips.

"Hi, I'm Leann," she purred, pushing her breasts out. She looked at me through thick bangs. "The guys said you've just come back to town." She bit her lip as she looked me over. "I'd be happy to show you around your room again."

Behind her, Hawk and Ledge were nodding their heads and making lewd gestures.

Ah, fuck it. I could use a good time. "Sure, babe, lead the way." I looped my arm around her neck and pulled her in. Out of the corner of my eye, I saw the two clowns give each other a silent high five.

―――――

RAGE

It was 7:50 pm. I leaned against the doorway looking in through the glass pane as I observed the final ten minutes of the class. I was mesmerized as I watched the woman who was teaching yoga, or Dynamic Expansion, according to Leo.

She was stunning. The way she bent, twisted, and contorted, raising her leg high above her head while keeping perfect balance. How she was teaching these big Neanderthals how to do this was beyond me. They all seemed in sync following her instruction. It was quite a sight watching them on their colorful mats.

I couldn't take my eyes off her. She seemed so strangely familiar. Had I met her before? I was only a few feet from her, but with her attention focused on the class, she didn't even notice I was there.

She had the body of a trained athlete, tight in all the right places, with a tan and toned six-pack. She had a nice rack on her, too, a good size but not overdone like the fake girls at the club.

Her sports bra covered her cleavage and had all these sexy strings attaching the pale pink fabric. Her hair was twisted up; the golden locks had blue, pink, and purple streaks wound through the shiny waves that fell from the top.

Her hair exposed a tattoo on the back of her neck. A hand of some sort, with a heart at its center. I'd seen that before. The hand was colorful, yet the heart was black. It was a stark contrast to the bright colors surrounding it.

My focus moved to her muscular back, the curve of her spine

down to her perfectly sculpted ass and legs, which were outlined a little too well in her pink sparkle yoga pants. She had a sexy-as-hell belly ring that had a purple stone on top and the same hand as on her neck, dangling through the piercing. The woman was perfection down to her bare feet, with sparkly pink toes adorned by tiny rings.

As much as I was admiring the view, something made me not too happy to see her here looking sexy as sin in front of all these men. An inexplicable, almost possessive feeling washed over me.

I let out a breath when she finished the class in a split, holding her foot to the back of her head. My jaw dropped. The men around her stretched their best and did not appear phased by the impressive pose.

My thoughts and stare broke when the group of men started to file out from the room. "Good to see you back, man," Valentino, an old sparring partner, greeted me with a fist bump as he pushed his way past the others to the locker room. I smiled back, but my eyes never left her.

JULIET

It was Wednesday night, 8 pm, and I'd just finished my Dynamic Expansion class. Ivy came to "assist" that night. You know, making sure the boys were doing their stretches properly, at least that was what she said she was doing. As the class wrapped up, I told the boys what a great job they did and I couldn't wait to see them again next week.

Ivy and I cleaned up the mats, and as I turned off the music, I heard the door slamming from behind me. I thought someone forgot something.

"Holy shit," Ivy said under her breath, long and drawn out.

I turned around and caught my first glimpse of him. Dressed in loose black sweatpants and a tight white tank that made his tan skin stand out. A large tattoo on one shoulder. He was probably six and a half feet tall, walking toward me with authority. When I got to his face, I nearly couldn't believe my eyes. It was like Alcide, the sexy hot werewolf in my favorite show, *True Blood*, had come to life. I took in the dark curly hair on his head with shaved sides, a day-old scruff, his chiseled features, and sweet mother of God, the chocolate brown eyes that felt like they looked straight into my soul. He had to be the most attractive man I'd ever seen.

As I opened my mouth, nothing seemed to come out. I just blinked my eyes. Ivy, the eternal flirt, quickly jumped in, "Hi, handsome. Haven't seen you here before. You just missed class, but I'd be happy to help you with a private lesson," she offered, wiggling her eyebrows as she moved in front of me. I let out a low groan and covered my face with my hand, shaking my head in embarrassment.

Ivy extended her hand, "I'm Ivy." To break my obvious stare, she gave me a gentle push, "This is Juliet…"

How embarrassing. I peeked through my lashes to meet those dark eyes. I began to extend my hand and open my mouth to say something but nothing came out. What was happing to me?

"Juliet teaches the Dynamic Expansion class that you just missed," Ivy continued.

In a sexy gruff voice, he said, "Yes, Leo told me. I'm not here for the class. I just wanted to introduce myself."

A large heavily muscled arm reached out to meet mine. "I'm Rage," his voice went straight to my core. "I'm Leo's partner. I've been out of town these past few years."

I'd noticed good looking men, but no man had affected me like this with just his voice. A shudder ran through me, heat pooled in my core.

Ivy suddenly squealed, "Wait a minute! I recognize you. You're on the decal on the front windows." She pointed, waving her finger. "You're Rage Erikson!"

In that sexy-as-hell voice, he said, "Yes, I am. I'm ready to get back at helping run things here again. Leo has been telling me about some of the addition he's made and raving about your class, so I thought I'd stop in and introduce myself."

"Great to meet you, I've heard a lot about you from Leo. He's been looking forward to you coming back. I think he and Shelly can use a break from the place. He said you were going to take over some of the training again."

Those two muscled arms crossed his chest as he took in the room. And as if Ivy wasn't even standing there, he studied my body for a moment, then looked directly in my eyes.

"Do you train here?"

"Uhhh…yeah…two or three times a week with Leo."

He raked over my body with his eyes, sending a thrill and heat through me. My mouth went completely dry. I shuffled my feet as I gathered the items I was packing up.

"W-We gotta p-pack up and get going," a small stutter was in my voice. "Thanks for…for stopping in to meet us." My eyes went to the floor, trying to resist looking into his, but they were like magnets drawing me in.

"Anything I can help you ladies with?"

"Nah, we got this," I waved my hand.

"Okay, well, I guess I'll leave you to it. See you around the gym." As he turned to walk away, a blond head popped into the door.

"Hey, ladies! A few of us are going to get some drinks at The Ridge. Want to come along?" It was Joey The Weapon, smiling brightly.

The look on Rage's face changed. He seemed to be sizing Joey up as he stared at him. He almost looked annoyed. Why the hell would he be annoyed?

Before I had a chance to say no, Ivy chimed in, "Hell, yeah. Let us catch a shower and we'll meet you guys there in an hour."

"Will do!" His smile was wide. "See you two there, then." Ivy had a dumb grin on her face.

"Why did you say yes?" I asked her.

"Because I knew you'd say no. Juliet, you're twenty-seven, not seventy-two. You need to get out and have some fun. You're either working, gardening, reading, or beating the shit out of the heavy bag. It's not healthy, girl. You're not getting any younger, honey." She smacked my butt lightly.

Like I was offended, I gave her a pointed look and crossed my arms, even though I couldn't care less about what people thought of my routine and reclusive lifestyle, "I like working, gardening, reading, and beating the shit out of the bag. Besides, Lord needs me at home."

"I'm sure your dog can live without you for another few hours. Come on, just for a little while, have a little fun," she urged, giving her best pouty lip.

"Well, I guess I'm getting dragged out against my will," I huffed, eyes rolling. I looked at Rage, who was still there, watching us banter. "Rage, you're welcome to come, too."

He rubbed the back of his neck like he was considering it. "Nah, I got shit to do here. I'm closing up for Leo tonight, but thanks."

I twisted my hands together nervously. "Well, it was so nice meeting you, I guess I'll be seeing you around."

With his face furrowed, he grunted, "Yeah, you, too. See you around." He turned to walk out, and I couldn't help but look at the perfect outline of his butt in those gym pants. I watched him leave the room, almost fanning myself, shaking my head. This was not good, the last thing I needed was to be attracted to my new boss.

RAGE

I'd been in this woman's presence for only ten minutes, so why was I feeling pissed at the idea that she was going out to meet some of our boys at a bar? I usually couldn't give two shits.

I decided at nine years old never to fall in love—love made you weak, and it could be easily taken away in an instant. The wall I'd built around myself was high and impenetrable. I had sex—I did not date. Women were just distractions and caused you trouble. I wouldn't turn my life upside down for a hot piece of ass. I got the club to fill my needs. I was not getting whipped like Leo and Shelly. All they did was fight and fuck. But I guessed they were happy—it had been more than five years.

It was about twenty-five minutes later when laughter emerged from the women's locker room. Ivy and Juliet were dressed and heading out. I couldn't take my eyes off the pair. Ivy was long and lean, reminding me of a ballerina. She had chin-length bright blond hair, and she was fully made up. She was in a dressy tank top, her black jeans were so tight they looked painted on, and she had very high heels. Who brought heels to the gym?

My eyes moved to Juliet, who was trailing behind her friend. Wow. She looked unbelievable. Glowing tan, not a stitch of makeup other than her full lips being glossy. She wore a flowing white shirt that just came to the top of her jeans. It was modest but made her tits look even bigger. Her tight and ripped pale blue jeans showed off her perfect ass. Sparkling flip-flops were on her feet. On any other girl, it would have looked dull, but not on her. She looked sexy as fuck.

Juliet's hair was now down. It flowed long down her back in waves of color. Golden with pink, blue, and purple shades running through it. She had sunglasses holding it out of her face, with just a few strands falling forward. She had her bag tossed over her shoulder. The two said goodbye to just about everybody they came across, and all eyes were on them as they walked out the gym doors.

I watched through the window as Juliet threw her bag over the door and jumped into a pink and black tricked-out Jeep with the top down. As she started it, loud music blared out of the open vehicle. The June sky was beginning to darken, the pink and orange reflected off the black surface. The big spare wheel cover had the same hand that matched her tattoo, colorfully painted with the word *Namaste* and a peace sign.

Then it hit me. I remembered where I'd first seen that Jeep. Wait, is she…yoga girl? The woman I saw flying through the air to Disturbed's *Sound of Silence*? Could it be? I was dumbfounded. How could I have missed it? With my mouth gaping open, I watched her Jeep drive away to the music of Radiohead's *Creep*. Well, hot damn.

CHAPTER FOUR

Rage

The gravel crunched under my tires as I cruised through the large lot looking for a spot that would not leave my bike dusty. *What the hell am I doing here?* After I closed the Pit, I talked myself into stopping by The Ridge to say hi to some old friends. That was the big fat lie I kept telling myself as I drove my bike five miles into the darkness. Another lie was that I was looking for a spot in the lot, but what I was really looking for was a pink and black Jeep. When I didn't find it anywhere in the lot, I felt a pang of disappointment.

Going in for a beer seemed like a good idea considering I was supposed to be here to catch up with old friends. I couldn't just pull through the lot and leave now.

Thank fuck, The Ridge was the one place that had not changed at all since I left. Almost strictly a locals-only bar, it sat nestled on the outskirt of town. It had tons of parking in its stone lot and a particular area designated for bikes. I saw a few that I recognized as I climbed the steps onto the massive wraparound porch where a few people smoked.

This place had always reminded me of an old western saloon. Everything from the floors, bars, tables, doors, and ceilings was all made of local maple. Everything was stained in various colors and polished to a shiny finish. There were warm lights that made it easy to look around but not too bright. It had a down-home, welcoming feel. Even better than the ambiance was the food—the smell of it brought back memories.

My mouth watered at the thought of crawfish piled on top of fresh cut fries. They served all the basics, but when the owner's son, Johnny, had come home from New Orleans where he'd spent time as a chef, they added a Creole menu, too.

I searched out a familiar face and immediately noticed Tracy working the bar. We went to school together; she dated Hawk for most of high school. She still had that big blond hair and wore dark lipstick. I went straight to her station.

"Excuse me, miss, can I have a pink squirrel with extra cherries?"

Tracy lifted her head up from the beer she was pouring. Her eyes widened, and her mouth let out a loud screech, "Rage!"

She jumped the counter, her boobs practically bouncing out of her low-cut shirt before her arms wrapped around my body.

"Oh, my God!" Her laughter was uncontrollable as she squeezed me hard. "I was telling someone that story the other day, wow, and now you're here!" She put a hand on each side of my face.

"God, I still feel bad about puking pink all over your shirt." She wiped the laugh tears from the corners of her eyes, smudging the dark makeup at the edges. "My grandma always made those pink drinks sound so good, it made me curious to have one." She laughed, slapping at my chest.

"What can I get you, sexy? It's on the house." She winked as she wiped the counter down and set an empty pint glass in front of me, waiting for my selection.

She slid the cold Witcher's Way I ordered across the counter. I let the sweet and bitter taste dance on my tongue. Damn, I missed this. Black Rock and Sugar Maple were the only places I could get it. Stained Souls owned the microbrewery in Black Rock that produced it.

I leaned against the bar and let Tracy talk my ear off for the next ten minutes. She filled me up a second before I found a quiet table in the back. Tracy's fast-paced chatter drained the social out of me. I chose a dark table where I could get a good look around.

Scanning the room, I came across a group of women who looked like they were having a good time. I noticed a few of the guys from the gym among them. The icy cold beer met my lips as Ivy moved into view. But I couldn't see Juliet. Either she changed her mind or I missed her. Beautiful women were everywhere, but I only came for one. I looked over a few times, hoping Juliet would appear in the crowd. Ivy caught me, and I tipped my bottle in her direction. I had one beer more before heading back to the club.

JULIET

An hour spent at The Ridge was quite enough for me. The mountain lodge–type bar was busy for a Wednesday night. I loved that it was almost locals only. Most people who took the train into town stuck to the various bars on Main Street, not coming to the outskirts very often.

The guys from the Pit were fun, but bars usually were not my scene, unless a favorite band of mine was playing.

My body might have been here, but my mind was not. It kept thinking about a certain…werewolf. Every time the door swung open, my eyes darted there, just in case Rage took us up on our invite.

I had only one very pink girly drink because I had to drive home and wasn't staying long. Ivy was fine—she ran into some of the girls who take yoga at Fluid. After a few laughs with them, it was my perfect time to exit. Ivy was just happy I came at all. How we were best friends and so different was beyond me.

I beeped in the driveway—my weird habit to let my puppy, Lord, know it was me. When I opened the door, Lord flew off the couch to greet me. He stayed glued to my side from the moment I entered. I let him out before taking the long, hot shower I so desperately needed.

The hot spray pounded at my back, relieving all the built-up tension. When Rage's face appeared in my mind while I was in the shower, I knew it was time to get out. Attractive as he was, dating him was out of the question. I didn't want to drag anybody else into my mess of a life. But I did feel kind of disappointed at the idea of someone else dating Rage. What was I thinking? He probably already had someone.

I had been on a handful of dates with Sugar Maple's most eligible bachelor, Richard Ramsey, mostly to get Ivy off my back. I felt nothing. His too-perfect vibe didn't feel right to me. Ivy kept telling me that I just needed to give him a chance. Well, tonight just confirmed that I felt nothing for the guy. As for Rage, definitely not nothing. I'd probably go to bed tonight thinking of the sound of his voice.

The sheets felt cool against my bare legs. I snuggled in with my phone and Kindle. I had a few chapters of a sexy vampire romance novel I couldn't wait to finish.

Halfway through the chapter, I remembered to text Ivy to let her know I was home safe. We looked out for each other like that and always checked in. I picked up my phone and opened the message screen.

Me: Home in bed, sorry forgot to text <sleepy emoji>

Ivy: You shouldn't have left so early <sad emoji>

Me: Why?

Ivy: <video meme of wiggling eyebrows>

Ivy: Rage just walked in…and I think he's looking for you…

Me: I doubt that.

Ivy: I know you have the hots for him, I could see it on your face, besides don't tell me you didn't notice the uncanny resemblance to your favorite werewolf.

Me: <bitmoji of an eye roll>

Me: Have fun. I will see you tomorrow. Stay out of trouble.

Ivy: Goodnight, bitch. I love you <kissy face emoji>

Me: Night <kissy face emoji>

Well, how about that? Rage had come to The Ridge. Maybe Ivy had been exaggerating. Had he really hoped to run into me? I bit my lip to hold back a smile.

———

RAGE

I settled in on the back porch. It was late, and no one was around. The humidity encouraged all the insects to be a loud symphony in my quiet evening. I sipped on a whiskey piled with ice, trying to drown the memories. When the cubes clinked and the last drop was drunk, I pulled out my harmonica and fell into a blues trance. I let the sad notes take me back. My lips slid over the chrome, silencing the crickets.

I sat there like I had done a hundred times with my brother and Hawk when we were kids. Only now, loneliness replaced what was once security.

With each riff I pushed out, memories of my grandmother's passing reminded me of how I got here. After Grandma had died, it didn't take long after for my brother, Donovan, to change from being on the honor roll to a failing student. He kept to himself, whereas I became the opposite, always angry. I got in several fights in school with that little fucker Richard Ramsey, who took every chance to make fun of us. He would tease me, saying I had a dead daddy and we were poor. He once called my mama a whore—I didn't even know what the word meant, but I knew, coming from him, it wasn't good. So, I punched him in the face; he lost a tooth. Mama was not happy—she beat me good that night.

We used to come from school with no snack, no dinner, no fancy plate. My mother had a lot of love, just not for us. She loved drinking, cigarettes, drugs, and gambling. We had no encouragement, no affection, nobody to take care of us. We took care of ourselves.

Her boyfriend, Vinny, would take her to the casino in Fairmont whenever "the check came in." When I got older, I found out that that check was supposed to take care of Donovan and me. Instead, they took that check, left us for days, and then came back broke. Whenever the money had run out, Vinny got angry and beat my mother. He used to beat us kids, too, but for the most part, it was my mother he liked to focus on.

I hated guys like Vinny, guys who hurt girls. Grandma had always told me to treat a lady with respect, so even now that I was grown, I had never laid a hand on a girl and I doubt I ever would. My ten-year-old self had been convinced Vinny must not have had a grandma.

Donovan had never challenged him. He always used to say, "I will get us out of here someday, little brother." But the older he got, the more he went inside himself. The day he turned eighteen, although he was still in school and only had three months to graduation, our bitch of a mother kicked him out, knowing there would be no more checks coming. So, Donovan packed up and joined the Marines, just like our dad. He really didn't have much choice. To him, it was that or the streets, and he wanted to go to college and be something, make good on his promise to our grandma.

Whenever I had gotten a letter from Donovan, it gave me hope. I thought maybe I could do something similar, find something that would make me happy and get me the hell out of this place. But instead of returning home to start college as he'd planned, Donovan came back in a flag-covered coffin.

It was then that I began to live up to my nickname, Rage. I felt like I had nothing left to live for, the last of my real family had been taken from me. I swore then that I would never love or care about anyone again. What was the point? They ended up leaving anyway. My father, Grandma, Donovan... Anger and distance were the only way to protect yourself from getting hurt.

By the time I was sixteen, I had already been on my own, staying with Hawk most nights. Mama couldn't have cared less as long as the check still came.

Emotion poured through my tiny instrument. I often wondered whether I would have continued on the musical path my grandmother encouraged me to follow had I a supportive family. The lump that formed in my throat made it hard to push out the last notes. I took a deep breath, filling my lungs with the sticky summer air. Opening my eyes, fireflies decorated the black landscape. The small yellow lights flicked as far as I could see.

I squinted, shocked at the sudden brightness when the porch light flicked on. The squeaky door swung wide open. Someone inside yelled, "Shut the shit quick before the mosquitoes get in."

Kai was holding two glasses and had an unlit cigarette between his lips. He flicked his head to get the long brown strands out of his eyes. He placed the drinks in front of us on the thick paint-peeled railing.

"Mind if I join you?" He leaned against the wooden column, flicking his hair back again before lighting his smoke. The rings on his fingers reflected in the flame. I nodded, happy to have the company distract me from my thoughts.

"I forgot how good you are with that." He aimed the cherry of his cigarette at my harmonica. He took a long drag as he slapped a mosquito away.

"Want to tell me what has you out here by yourself when there's a line of girls in there fighting over who gets to warm your bed?"

I tried to be casual. "Uh, nothing. Just trying to find my place here again. Four years away is a long time, you know?" I gazed out toward the open field and let out a breath.

"Well," Kai said tilting his glass to me, "I'm glad to have you back, brother. It hasn't been the same without you."

I raised my glass to match his. "Thanks." I took a long swig, coughing a little as the fiery liquid burned my throat. "Are you trying to kill me before my party? What the fuck did I just drink?" I pounded at my burning chest.

His laughter carried over the sounds of the buzzing insects. "Sorry, I guess I should have warned you. It's Hack's moonshine. He has spent the last year perfecting it, watching all the videos and shit. He's a bit obsessed."

My eyes watered as I cleared my throat again. "Fuck, we could run our bikes on this."

We sat out there and talked until he was out of smokes. I got in under the radar, heading his warning about the girls. But I was not in the mood for any company unless it was a certain yoga instructor. I lay in my bed staring at the ceiling, trying not to think about Juliet. It wasn't working. She was way out of my league. I should save myself the trouble and not even consider it.

CHAPTER FIVE

Juliet

*T*he breath whooshed from my lungs. I grasped my chest and sat straight up in bed. I took a deep breath in, filling my lungs completely, then after a few seconds, let it out very slowly. I wiped the sweat from my brow, goosebumps covered my arms, and my hands were clammy. I grabbed my phone, turning off the still-beeping 5:30 am alarm. I took several more controlled breaths in an attempt to stop my body from shaking. They helped calm my quickly beating heart. I had to remind myself that it was just a dream. A nightmare. A memory that loved to play while I slept. All the fucking time.

I flung the soft bamboo sheets over my head and pulled Lord closer to me. His presence always helped calm me. My heart was still hammering. I pushed away from the intrusive thoughts that haunted me every damn day. I touched the scar on my pelvis and promised myself not to let my past affect who I was today. But I still found myself looking over my shoulder, never at peace. Today was no different.

I grew up a free spirit. My hippie parents had encouraged me to live with no regrets and find the positive in any situation. It was the part of me I cherished, the part I had almost lost, the part I was not willing to give up without a fight.

I knew my parents would be sad to know how often I let fear take over. I struggled to be the strong and confident woman people thought I was. But I was trying to do my best, doing everything I could, physically training my mind and body to be strong—I wanted to be my old self again, not the weakling who'd ignored all the red flags and failed to get out when her inner radar had been buzzing like a siren. The price I had paid for that mistake was steep—my freedom and almost my life.

I had let myself fall in love with the wrong man. And now I was alone, even among friends. Because when your life was a lie, when you were a fraud, you could never honestly connect with people.

I squeezed my eyes tight, anger bubbled through the fear. Because of my mistake, because of what my life had become, I couldn't see my parents or my sister. If Ivy weren't such a stubborn woman, I wouldn't have her either.

As much as I wanted more, I couldn't let my mistake hurt anyone else. Being an imposter left me riddled with guilt. I couldn't live with myself if anything bad happened to someone else as a result of my decisions. The truth could hurt people I cared about, and I would not put anyone in danger.

Lord yawned and stretched his white legs. His soft fur tickled my face as I kissed the top of his head. I wrapped both of my arms around my strong pup, forcing myself to remember the last time a strong man comforted me in my bed. Antonio hadn't been strong; otherwise, he would have fought for us and not have let his brother influence him.

I ran my finger along the jagged spot of missing hair on Lord's chest. The scar was a constant reminder that I could never feel safe. This little white beast had been my savior on the night I had been attacked. I would be forever grateful to the friendly stray who had come to my rescue. It was like he knew my thoughts. His innocent blue eyes looked into mine before he tucked his head under my chin and nuzzled into me further.

The sun was shining through the crystals hanging in my windows; they illuminated a prism onto the floor by my sparkly pink sneakers. Mornings that started like this required meditation and a brief run for Lord and me. A wet lick coated my cheek. "Okay, boy, let's go." He jumped up and leaped off the bed as I pulled the white sheets from under him.

Rolling out of bed, I set out to make some coffee. Caffeine was going to be my first cure this morning. As I boiled the water for my press, I stared into the flames on the stove. They reminded me of Gavin and how he told me the truth about the Cordonas.

I remembered Gavin telling me, "Juliet, you don't even know how close to the fire you were. Your life was nearly extinguished by the activities the man you loved was involved in." There had been a look of pity in his eyes as he told me all the facts I didn't want to believe. But, of course, I should have known. I'd seen the signs that something hadn't been right, but I didn't want to know. I had been utterly oblivious that the man I loved was part of the notorious Cordona crime family.

Gavin Jacobs had been the officer assigned to my case. He'd been on the scene that night. He'd spent a lot more time on my case because of who was involved, Antonio's brother, Marco.

I'd become close with Gavin over the time it had taken for me to heal and eventually go to trial. He had told me that Marco was not just some club owner who drove expensive cars and showed off in fancy clubs. He was a significant player in the Columbian cartel responsible for bringing drugs up the coast. Antonio had lied to me about the real work they were doing.

Gavin had a sister who had been brutalized and killed by the cartel, which was probably why he took such care in making sure I understood how important it was for me to disappear if I chose to press charges and put Antonio behind bars. Placing the man I loved behind bars was not easy, even though he'd nearly beaten me to death.

Marco had made it clear that he wanted revenge and that, if he ever found me, he would take it out on me and everyone I loved. Gavin had known that Marco was a sick bastard, and he did not want me on the other end of his wrath. So, he showed me evidence and took great risks just to convince me to go and leave everything behind. Gavin kept me protected until the trial. He even helped my family relocate so we wouldn't need to go into protective custody, which none of us were willing to do.

I received therapy to cope with what happened. I turned to Buddhism to learn to forgive. I did forgive Antonio for what he did to me physically. What I would never forgive was the fact that his actions made me lose my family. My mom, dad, and Paige. Calling them every once in a while on a burner phone was not enough. I wanted to have my family in my life. Until their cartel was brought down, I was not safe, and neither was anyone I loved.

When I first moved here a few years ago, I forced myself to get to know people in the town. I wanted to determine if they were trustworthy. But I soon realized my folly. No matter how much you thought you knew about a person, they might not be who you thought they were. I knew that better than anyone. No one knew the truth of who I was, except Ivy. Maybe that was why I loved animals—they don't lie to you like people do.

I pinched myself hard enough to let out a small squeal. The mark on my hand was immediately red, and I rubbed the spot softly to soothe it. Therapy taught me to use a rubber band and snap it against my wrist whenever I lost control of my thoughts and needed to bring myself back. I had to stop using a rubber band. Every time my eyes would land on the small band, my thoughts would go to what I was trying to keep myself from thinking. It was useless. Now, I just pinched myself whenever I needed to snap out of it.

RAGE

It didn't take long for me to fall back into the comfort of the Pit. I was afraid that after being away for so long, it would seem more like Leo's than ours. So many guys from way back still trained here, and they made me feel more like a celebrity than an outsider.

I was in the zone, hitting the heavy bag as I usually did when something bothered me. My fists pounded it harder and harder as I tried to keep the memories from creeping in. But it was no use, they were etched in my mind like a scar.

. . .

I was only nine at the time...

Donovan and I were spending the better part of our summer day doing one of our favorite activities, hunting honeysuckles. Grandma kept warning us about the bees, but that never stopped us. She often spent nights coating our stings with her baking soda remedy, but the sticky sweet treats were worth it. Then we heard the dinner bell ring from across the street, so we dropped everything and came tearing into the house.

"Boys, get washed up for dinner! If you clean your plates, you can have my homemade blueberry pie for dessert," my grandmother's sweet voice echoed from the kitchen.

"Is there ice cream, too, Grandma?" Donovan asked, rocking back and forth on the balls of his feet. He waited for his turn to wash his hands as I climbed down from the stool at the sink.

"Of course! Hurry up now, the pie is still warm, just like you like it," she said as she began preparing the desserts, singing along to the Elvis Presley songs she always played.

"Done!" we both yelled as we raced to eat the chicken, baked beans, and corn. We cleaned our plates. Grandma's brilliant blue eyes shone with pride as she handed us our warm pie with melting vanilla ice cream on top. She made us feel special, serving desserts on her good china that most people only used for holidays. She said that every dessert she shared with us was a special occasion. I loved the gold trim on the edges of the delicate plates. Donovan convinced me that it was made from pirates' gold, which I believed. Grandma served our milk in the fancy matching tea cups. We were super careful with them. Grandma said she got them when she and grandpa got married, a long time ago, before the war.

That night, Grandma tucked us into our beds as usual. She knelt beside us to say a bedtime prayer. My stomach hurt that night from the extra pie I'd snuck. She'd pretended not to notice the large missing piece. She came to my bedside, turned down the soft white blanket, and lay next to me. She rubbed my tummy and sang to me one of her church songs.

Lying in bed, all I could think of was how good that pie was, even though I ate too much. Turning toward her, I asked, "Grandma, will you always make us pies? Will you make them for us like you did for Daddy when we grow up?"

She pulled me in closer. I inhaled a mix of syrup and rose, together the scent was its own brand of grandma. She lifted my head to meet her blue eyes, which bored into mine, "Alexander, someday you will meet a warm and wonderful girl who will be your wife. If you are the same sweet and kind boy you are now, she will bake you blueberry pies, better than Grandma's."

My eyes grew wide, I sat up and said definitively, "That's impossible!" I put my fist in the air for emphasis. "You make the best pies in all of Hemlock County! Everyone says so. Preacher James said they're the best in the state!"

She smiled and kissed my forehead and ran her small hand through my dark curls. She took my chin in her hand and said, "Alexander, every night when you go to sleep, I want you to promise me you will pray that someday you'll meet someone who is as sweet as my pies. And when you do, I want you to promise that you'll treat her with respect and never let her go."

"I promise, Grandma."

She smiled brightly and tucked the blanket around me. "Good boy. I have leftover blueberries. You know what that means?"

My grin grew wide and I nodded. "Blueberry pancakes for breakfast!"

"Now, go to sleep, my sweet boy." She kissed my forehead again before turning off the light. She closed the door, all but a crack left open, and continued humming her church song down the hall.

I lay in my bed smiling at the thought of waking to stacks of blueberry pancakes. The only thing as good as Grandma's pies were her pancakes drowning in the sugar maple syrup. A mixture of wind chimes and the motor of the fan in the window lulled me to sleep as they did every night.

Only, instead of waking up to blueberry pancakes, I woke up to my brother's frantic screams. "Grandma, wake up! Alexander! Grandma won't wake up!"

An aneurysm had taken my sweet grandma, and my world had gone from living in a loving home to moving into a world of despair with my gambling, alcoholic, abusive mother. Twenty-four years later, I could still remember the sweet sound of my grandma's voice. My nose and eyes burned as I forced back the emotion.

As that memory played in my head, I punched the heavy bag as if I could make the past disappear. I tried to keep the lump from forming in my throat. I moved to the speed bag, using the fluid repetition as a distraction from the haunting memories.

Grandma had made me and Donovan go to Sunday service. She had thought it was important, and she had tried to put both the love and fear of God in us both. Her funeral had been the last time I ever went to church. Everyone from Grandma's parish had attended and most of the townspeople, too. Mr. Spencer had played Grandma's favorite song, *Hallelujah*, on his harmonica. The funeral had been barely over when my mother began making a drunken scene.

The speed bag nearly flew off the hook as I assaulted it. My rhythm was a strong and steady beat. I could feel the wraps on my hands coming off from scraping the bags. Blood began to tinge the white tape.

My mother and her boyfriend had raided Grandma's home, selling anything of value. I begged her not to sell the ring that Grandma had given to me to someday propose to my wife with. Grandpa had given it to her, and his mother had given it to him. Mama didn't care.

Daddy had been Grandma's only child. She had called him her miracle. She had prayed for a child for years, and when she was forty, God finally answered her prayers. She said that was why you should never give up; she swore that the Lord was always listening and would answer your prayers, even if it took a long time. So, I prayed every night for years for God to send me and my brother to someone who would love us like our Grandma did. He didn't. And eventually, I just stopped praying and believing that anything good could ever happen for me.

———

JULIET

It had been four days since I met Rage at the Pit. I had to admit, even though I didn't want to, I was hoping to run into him again there.

"How was class on Wednesday?" Leo asked. "I heard some of you went back to The Ridge. No one got out of line?" His eyebrow arched as he waited for my answer.

"No, Leo, it was fun." I kicked the side of the bag three more strikes, standing on one leg. "I only had one drink, then I headed home. Lord and my bed were calling."

He held the bag steady for me. "Good, I was hoping not to have to kick anyone's ass for hitting on you or Ivy."

After the last kick, he tied a weight around my waist and pointed to the pull-up bar. I did five, then jumped down to catch my breath.

"I met your partner, Rage, on Wednesday. He stopped by after class. I haven't seen him around again." I tried to act casual, but I swallowed hard. Did he notice?

"Rage is working mostly nights to give Shelly and me a break. He tries to get workouts in the morning." He looked at me suspiciously, or maybe I was just being paranoid.

He pointed to the bar again. I jumped up.

"Gotta say, it's great having my brother back. The fighters respect him, and it doesn't hurt that the ladies love having him around."

I jumped down again after another five and placed my hands on my knees to catch my breath. Thank God, I'm almost done.

"I wouldn't be surprised if we don't end up with a whole bunch of new ladies joining the gym." He must have noticed my unintentional eye roll because he nodded his head and twisted his lips.

"Juliet, I know that look. You interested, girl?" His eyes squinted with a knowing smile. "I thought you were dating that douche bag, Richard Ramsey?"

"Who, me?" I put my hand on my chest. "Interested? Nah, I just hate the kind of girls who would join a gym just to have a super hot trainer. Richard and I have only gone on a handful of dates and we're not exclusive." I said emphatically.

"I see." He stroked his chin. "So, you're not interested in my 'superhot trainer', then?"

"Nope, and by the way, Richard is not a douche bag—he has been nothing but respectful."

"Okay, glad to hear, cause that's not the Dick I know. And he better be respectful, cause if he gets out of line, he will have a line of fighters to deal with." He crossed his arms over his shoulders.

"What? You don't think you've trained me well enough to take care of myself?" I asked in mocked shock, hands on my chest for effect.

"Nah, I think your moves would shock the shit out of him, but that doesn't mean he wouldn't answer to us, too." His tone was now serious. "But if he fucks with you, he fucks with us."

"Aww, thanks, Leo. I appreciate you all looking out for me. However, I can take care of myself. And don't worry," I said, more to myself than to Leo, "nobody is fucking with nobody, as far as I'm concerned."

CHAPTER SIX

Juliet

I felt the burn of the liquid courage as it trickled down my throat. It was half an hour until show time. How did I get talked into this?

The MC wanted to do something special for Rage for his homecoming party. First, they begged me. Then they bribed me. With the same amount of money I needed to get my Jeep fixed. How convenient. I was sure Ivy ratted me out.

I had performed this routine in front of many crowds, but knowing that Rage was going to be in the crowd, probably the one person who was going to be paying the most attention, that had my stomach in knots.

Two weeks ago, Hawk came over to Fluid pleading with me to perform at his best friend's homecoming party. He was so excited and couldn't stop talking about the party and how important it was to him to do something special.

Two weeks ago...

"You guys know I'm not a stripper, right?" I studied his face, making sure he knew I was serious.

He laughed. "Yes, babe, we do. Those girls will be there, too, on the tables! We want something else, something that will steal the show. We've heard all about how talented you are and know that these guys will never have seen something like this before."

"Can you come up with something like the video Ivy showed me?" Hawk asked.

Ivy. That traitor. I knew she put him up to this. I crossed my arms and shook my head. "Yes, Hawk, I can."

I then asked the critical questions. "How high are those ceilings? Are the beams safe and sturdy?"

"Yes…you'll be fine." Hawk insisted.

I grinned as an idea came to me. "What song does Rage come out to when he fights?"

"Sick Puppies. You're Going Down," Hawk said.

The song began playing in my head. I could already see the show coming together. I knew what I was going to do.

"Okay, have everything ready the Friday before the show. Ivy and I will come and do the practice round." I pointed my finger and waved it back and forth in front of his handsome face. "No peeking."

He made a cross over his heart. "I promise, no peeking."

I shook the conversation out of my head, bringing myself back to my current predicament I was in. What the hell was I thinking, agreeing to this? I looked out at the fabric curtain that concealed the stage. There were easily over a hundred bikers and ladies in the crowd. I chewed on my thumb as I zeroed in on the girl stripping on the center table. Huh, Hawk wasn't lying. Was she naked? I tried to get a better look.

"You are chewing your nail." Ivy grabbed my hand and pushed it down.

"Oh, thanks." I smoothed my leotard and smiled nervously as I looked at the girl who was now panties away from being naked.

"Juliet. Do you need another shot?" Ivy asked, standing in front of my view of the stripper. "God, no. If I have another, I might get sick when I go upside down. I think two is enough."

I never did shots, but I needed them tonight because there was no way I was getting on that stage sober, especially looking like this. My eyes roamed down the tiny costume. Ivy applied one more layer of glitter.

"Ivy, I'm never going to be able to get that stuff off me. God, stop, please."

"Nope, you have to be perfect, glowing from every angle. I want you shining like the star I know you are." She smacked her bright lips and blew me a kiss as she winked.

My leotard was one I had used as a costume a few years ago when Ivy had dragged me to a party. We had gone as angels—I had been a white angel, and she had been a dark one. The material was almost transparent with a deep V going down to expose my belly ring. There was a sheer fabric between the top to keep it in place. Ivy had made my hair a work of art—the front pieces were in braids that surrounded my head like a crown, and the rest was left down and long. Tiny sequins were woven into the braids to catch the light. Iridescent body paint and loads of glitter coated my tan skin. My eyelashes were long, fake, and full of glitter, too. I had stage makeup on for full effect. I was as close to an angel as I could get. A few minor alterations to keep my boobs from popping out, and I was just about ready.

Through the mirror, I could see Hawk entering the dressing area with a microphone tucked under his arm. My back was still toward him. My long hair was hiding most of my back.

"Hey, babe, you ready?"

I turned my face toward him to indicate yes.

"I, ah—" He tried to form words through his open mouth.

"The words you are looking for are 'Hi Juliet, my, you look beautiful,'" Ivy said.

"Yes, uh, I...Juliet," he agreed, still staring, "you look more than beautiful, like a painting come to life."

"Thanks, Hawk," I said, grateful for the compliment. I patted his heavily tattooed hand, and with a nervous smile said, "I'm ready."

Ivy gave me one last look, inspecting me from head to toe, nodding with approval. "You did this perfectly in practice, and you'll be amazing." She gave me a gentle squeeze before Hawk guided me to the side of the stage where no one could see me.

"I'm going to dim the lights. Climb into place and listen for the music," Hawk said as he pointed up to the top of the silk.

"Okay." I let out a deep breath.

"Juliet, good luck, darlin'." Hawk winked and walked toward the other side of the stage.

The moment the lights were dim, I climbed the silks and waited for my cue. My heart raced with excitement as the silky fabric wound through my hands.

From here I could see the fairy lights that illuminated the area below. All the guys, old ladies, girlfriends, and even the strippers watched as the lights went out.

Everyone cheered when a small light found Rage, front and center, sitting in his throne with a beer in one hand and a shot in the other. He held his drink in the air and then tossed it back, to everyone's cheer. He looked uncomfortable from where I stood. Total darkness replaced the light as everyone quieted down from all the whistles and hollers.

RAGE

The room was packed from wall to wall with people dancing and celebrating my homecoming. I thought it was bad enough just being the guest of honor, but now I had a damn light in my face, and everyone expected me to be social. I raised my glass, which everyone seemed to love, and tossed back another whiskey, willing it to ease the anxiety. I hated attention. Thankfully, the light on me had gone and been replaced with total darkness. I set down my glass. Everything went completely black. The room quieted.

"What the hell is going on? Why did the lights go out?" I asked Colt, who was my latest shot partner. He just stretched his arm and pointed to the stage with a knowing grin. It had gone from dark to red. There was a curtain hiding most of it.

Hawk was at the DJ booth, mic in hand. He walked to the center of the stage.

"Is everyone having a good time?" he yelled, throwing his hands up to fire up the already cheering crowd. Spotlights flicked on and off quickly through the room, highlighting different areas.

"I hope so. You all know we are here tonight to celebrate my brother and best friend." More cheers ensued. "On behalf of all the brothers that missed you like hell these last few years," he turned up the mic's volume, "we thought we'd do something extraordinary to entertain everyone. So, instead of a lap dance, which we'll be getting many times tonight, we opted for what we've heard is called a sky dance." A low murmur of "what the fuck" rumbled through the crowd. "Now keep it down and enjoy the show."

The room became dark again. A loud hum of music began to vibrate as fairy lights turned on the ceiling and glitter burst from the floor, making the entire stage sparkle. The music thundered, rattling the decorations that hung around the room. It sounded familiar.

My MMA entrance music? Sick Puppies' *You're Going Down*? A slower version.

As the first verse started, two long, thin curtains tumbled from the ceiling until they almost touched the ground. The light show focused on the body twirling from the top of the curtain. It was the most sensual movement I had ever seen. My mouth gaped open. The woman at the top looked like a star shining in the darkness. The glitter coating her body bounced off the lights. It took me a few moments to realize who I was watching.

Juliet, an angel, spinning from a curtain high above me.

Everyone was silent, their eyes glued to every sensual movement going to the slow pace of the song. When the chorus started, the tempo changed to the original song version. It was fast, hard, and loud. Juliet's body rolled down the curtains, free falling in a beautiful motion. The crowd went wild. The music boomed as her body swung, flipped, and spun to the beat.

She wowed them with each flip and bend. A swing made of the same shiny fabric appeared between the other fabrics. She contorted her body to reach the swing where she hung upside down, posing her feet on her head. Each pose was perfection. When she dropped and held herself just by one foot, the sounds of cheering and the terror of her falling were heard even over the music, which echoed around the barn.

She was still as a statue for a moment, allowing the audience to catch their breath. For just a split second, she zoomed in on me and our eyes connected. The fleeting moment left me feeling struck by lightning.

The lights changed, violently flashing to the beat of the music. I was captivated, her body moved like…magic. She looked like magic.

Colt slapped my shoulder. "Ain't that something? That girl can move!"

Words would not come to my lips. I was mesmerized by the fluid movement. She was…amazing. My heartbeat quickened, catcall and whistles rung in my ears. Another pump of glitter exploded, the shiny pieces rained down as Juliet rolled her body closer to the floor and settled into the final move where she stilled. She contorted into a pose that looked impossible. Juliet was in a vertical split with her hands holding one foot behind her head, the other aimed to the floor, and the only thing holding her up was the silk she tucked under the back of her neck. A single light focused on her as the music came to an end.

The room was cloaked with darkness again as she descended the rest of the way to the floor. The stage brightened, the crowd roared, and she was gone. She vanished, like magic. I felt my own body wanting to run to the stage.

"More! More!" the crowd cheered. I pushed my way through the crowd, my head moving left and right to find her. But there was no sign of her, just piles of glitter on the floor and the silk fabric hanging from the ceiling.

A tattooed hand grabbed my arm, preventing me from going backstage. "Well, did you like the show?" Hawk's smile reached his ears, his tongue rolled his lip ring. "She was terrific, wasn't she?"

"Brother, I have to admit, I've never seen anything like it." I placed a hand on each of his shoulders. "Now, where can I find her?"

He pointed to a makeshift dressing area off to the side. I squeezed through a group of women who had rushed the space.

What the...? I couldn't even get to her with the gaggle of women all begging to learn how to do what she just did. Ivy stood next to her, passing out cards as Juliet kindly told them all that they can come for sky yoga classes at Fluid.

I wanted to wait for her to finish, but I was swept away by a group of brothers hoisting me on their shoulders, chanting my name and putting me into a large chair and onto the stage. A sexy stripper climbed onto my lap and began giving me a lap dance. The immense amount of alcohol coursing through my veins made it impossible to stand up. I leaned back and let myself enjoy the moment.

With just a red thong on, she ground her hips on my crotch, and my hands nearly touched around her small waist. I looked again to Juliet's direction, wanting to find her. The crowd around her had thinned...and there she was. Our eyes briefly locked, and I met Juliet's disappointed gaze before she quickly turned away. Juliet spun, her bag slung over her shoulder, and forced herself through the people on the dance floor. I lifted the stripper off of my lap, jumped from the stage, and tried to chase after her.

Shit! I went out the side of the barn doors just in time to see her Jeep flying out of the lot, kicking up gravel.

CHAPTER SEVEN

Rage

I locked my room and exited the clubhouse in a rush. I had to escape the chaos—men who were in all states of fucked up, the smell of piss, weed, beer, and sex that permeated the inside and outside of our compound—I had to get away from there. The guys from other clubs wandering around our place showed no respect for our property. The floors were strewn with trash. Beer cans and red cups littered our ordinarily clean courtyard. I watched a prospect filling up some bags, but he was no match for these pigs. Colt stressed the importance of hosting this meet, so I didn't complain. But when the chance to escape the madness and fill in for Hack at Stained Skyn came, I took it. The Devil's Damned was the worst; the less I have to be around those assholes, the better.

The corner where I stood leaning against the wall gave me a view of Main Street and Hawk's station. Hawk held a long needle in his hand; he examined his marks for the last time before he inserted it. My arms crossed over my chest, almost protectively, and I winced as I watched Hawk about to impale the man's nipple. Ouch.

"It'll only hurt for a second, honey," the bright blue-haired girl said as she bounced up and down, watching intently. Her frilly skirt showed the thigh-high fishnets held by garters as she leaned over to kiss his cheek.

I looked out the window—no one was around this late, just neon lights shining out of storefront windows. Fluid sat in darkness, apart from the lit wall with the mural on its side. Visions of Juliet's routine and the first time I saw her through the window made me smile. Then a high-pitched scream came from the big guy in Hawk's chair. I squeezed my lips together to suppress a laugh.

"You want me to keep the place open 'til two while you guys head out?" Joel, one of Hawk's artists, asked as he cleaned his station. He swept his purple and black hair to the side as he wiped down the adjacent counter. "I don't mind," he added, as the smell of bleach burned my nose.

"Nah, we want to keep it quiet in town with the brothers all at the club. We'll close at eleven as planned." Hawk kept his eyes focused on the nipple ring he was sliding into the freshly pierced skin. Tough Guy was on the verge of tears as Hawk tugged the long needle the rest of the way through and replaced it with the jewelry. His very tatted and pierced girlfriend clapped her hands in excitement. She had a thick bull-style ring in her septum that looked too big for her face.

Ten minutes later, after some strict instructions on caring for his new piercing, the couple left arm in arm. We all pitched in to close the place for the night. Stained Skyn could get busy late on Saturday nights, usually with a rowdy bar crowd wandering to the train station to take them back to Black Rock.

Ledger had just shut down the computer and Hawk had closed his station when the doors chimed. Standing in the lobby was a very drunk Joker, the sergeant-at-arms of Devil's Damned and one particularly nasty asshole. Vicious fights left a map of scars covering his body.

"We're closed," Hawk said, not looking up from his laptop.

"And you're not supposed to be here," I added in a deadly tone.

He ignored us as he tugged his patch-covered cut. The alcohol permeated from him. He tossed the dirty shirt he wore next to his cut on the glass counter, his Jester medallion swinging from his neck on a long chain.

Joel rolled his eyes. "I just cleaned that counter," he said under his breath, pushing the dirty clothes to the edge and squirting more cleaner over the area.

Joker ignored Joel. He pointed to the only ink-free spot of skin on his ribs. He looked around as if he had just noticed us. "Hey, shitheads. Nice fuckin' shop." His smile exposed his rotten teeth.

"I hear Hawk gives a fuckin' one-of-a-kind type of ink. I want this right here," he slurred, pushing a paper with an image of a confederate flag and a Nazi cross over it.

"Sorry, you're too late. We're closed," Ledge said. "Hawk had already cleaned his station, and we don't tat racist shit like that." He pushed the paper back at him. "Besides, you are too drunk to get ink right now, anyway." Ledge straightened to his full 6'3" height, meeting Joker's eyes. "Your club and all the others agreed to stay out of town and at our clubhouse. I'm sure there is more than enough going on there to keep you busy." Ledge took off his glasses, setting them on the counter as he leveled his gaze at Joker. His nose wrinkled at the stench that permeated from the man.

Joker let out a sinister laugh. He pounded his fist again, and the glass rattled at the force. "You girls need to lighten up. I've gotten ink while passed-out drunk." He tilted his chin up like he was proud of the fact.

Joel snorted. "Yeah, well, that's obvious," he said while appraising the man's hideous ink.

Wrong thing to say.

Joker reached across the counter and grabbed Joel's shirt. Joel was about half Joker's weight and six inches shorter. He looked like a boy compared with Joker, who was about to reach for his knife.

"Let go of the kid. Right now," I spoke low and clear. I moved closer toward him, my mouth seething. "You do not disrespect our employees, our businesses, or our rules. Go back to the fucking clubhouse before I drag you back there myself."

He must have realized that I had a good twenty-five pounds of lean muscle and three inches on him. Plus, Hawk and Ledge were behind me, each with baseball bats. He let go of Joel and grabbed his cut and shirt.

"Fuck you guys. My boys will be here soon, then we'll see how bad you are."

"Get the fuck back to the club and out of town." It took all my self-control not to beat the asshole and kick him to the curb.

He left the shop, but not before spitting in our direction. I went to lock the door and turn the sign to CLOSED.

I walked over to where Ledge was sitting with Joel, who seemed a little shaken. "Would he have really cut me?"

"Yes," Ledge said, "Joker is a special kind of asshole you don't want to mess with."

———

JULIET

It was a humid June night, warm enough to keep the top off and enjoy the glittering stars, which stood out against the black sky. Typically, I would have been curled up with Lord and a book on my porch, enjoying a glass of wine and listening to music. However, tonight I was driving into town because I stupidly forgot my bag at Fluid. It was better to pick it up now than wait 'til morning. It could ruin my early plans if I had to detour in the opposite direction and drive to Fluid before meeting Ivy at the shelter. We often spent Sunday mornings taking the shelter dogs on runs—it was a win-win, they got out in the fresh air, and we both got exercise.

It should only take a minute, I just needed to run in and grab my stuff, and I'd be back to my relaxing evening in no time. I sang along to the music thumping through my Jeep speakers. The vibration made the stars look like they were dancing to the beat.

I pulled up around the corner from Fluid. It was pretty dead around here on Saturday nights, except for Stained Skyn. Nothing else was open on this block. The bars were all a good few blocks down. There were a few bikes lined up in front Stained Skyn, but I only recognized two. I parked in the alley and leaped out of my doorless Jeep. Bobbing my head and still singing AC/DC's *You Shook Me*, I had the keys in my hand ready to unlock the door. I pushed my hand against the door to give it pressure while I tried turning the key. The damn lock was sticking again; the humidity made the old doors swell. Finally, with a little more wiggling, I tugged hard, and it opened.

I glanced again at the bikes that sat in front of the shop before stepping inside the studio. The sign on the door read CLOSED. They shut down early for a Saturday night.

Inside the dark studio, I jogged to the beeping alarm pad, tapped in the code, and turned it off. Catching my reflection in the large studio mirrors, I became suddenly aware of how little I was wearing. Shit, I probably should have changed out of my pj's before leaving the cabin. It was too hot to wear much more than the short cut-off sweat shorts and braless cropped tank I had on. Flip-flops kept my freshly painted toes from smudging. I looked down at my sparkling toes, admiring the job I had done. I had been enjoying a glass of wine and pampering myself, I had no intention of going out, and then I remembered the damn bag.

My hair was twisted high in a messy bun, with a few colorful strands that fell out on the windy drive over. I tucked the stray pieces behind my ears. I pulled my bag and sneakers out of my cubby, shoved the sneakers into the duffle, and tossed the duffle on my back before turning the alarm back on and walking out the door.

Now I could get back to my quiet evening at home. I continued to sing off key, which I did quite frequently. I pulled on the door, inserted the key into the lock, and heard it click; I was relieved it didn't stick this time.

I took a few steps toward the side alley when I felt an arm grab my wrist and pull me in. My eyes widened as I crashed into a body. I met the drunken gaze of a scary-looking biker who did not look at all familiar. His long, grimy blond faux hawk fell to the side of his face, touching the scruffy beard that framed his scarred face. His mouth showed a wicked grin of missing teeth and silver caps. His eyes were crazed as he spat out, "Where do you think you're going, pretty lady."

Fuck. I forgot to watch my surroundings like I usually did. How could I have let this happen? How could I have slipped up like this? I was frozen. I couldn't move. His grip was too tight. My stomach clenched. It was happening again.

My legs felt weak as bile rose in my throat. A callused hand now scratched at my bare stomach while the other went around my neck, pulling me back against his sweaty foul-smelling body. He began to assault me, keeping my back against his chest. His grip on me got tighter. "You smell good...and feel even better." The heavy scent of beer, stale smoke, and rotting teeth invaded my nostrils. My heart pounded so heavily, I was sure he could feel it against him.

Juliet, get it together, this is why you train. I took in a deep breath and summoned all the courage and training I had. No one will make me a victim again, *no one*. Especially not some disgusting man who had no respect for women.

"GET THE FUCK OFF!" I screamed as loud as I could. Finally! Adrenaline was coursing through me. Bending my head forward, I forcefully reared it back as fast and as hard as I could. His nose crunched on impact. Then I pushed my arms forward, and using all my force, I sent a hard elbow into his gut. I broke free! His hands went to his nose, which was pouring blood all down his chin and chest.

"Fucking bitch!" he cried.

Pain radiated through my head. Dizzy from the impact, I didn't see the hand coming straight at my face, connecting with my cheek.

"Bitch!" he yelled as he lurched toward me again. My fighter instinct kicked in as I bent down and flipped him over my small body onto the hard sidewalk, his head bouncing off the hard ground. I then delivered a devastating kick to his balls. But before I could run, I had more company.

———

RAGE

"Damn, that guy's such an asshole," Hawk said as he locked the cash in the safe. "Let's hope he and his boys get back to the farm before they start anything with a townie, or the police will be on our asses."

I fiddled with the stereo until I got it to turn off. Stone Sour's *Bother* faded into silence. That's when I heard the screams and yells from outside and ran for the door. I thought my eyes were deceiving me when I saw Juliet being manhandled by that no-good piece of shit, Joker.

My body couldn't move fast enough to unlock the door and get across the street. Hawk followed, and our boots thundered across the road as we witnessed tiny Juliet go from being held to flipping a bleeding Joker over her small frame in a matter of seconds. I got to her as she gave Joker an awesome kick to the balls. He grunted and yelled obscenities at Juliet, with his face gushing blood and his hand holding his crotch.

I kicked the fucker before turning to Juliet. "What the fuck is wrong with you, motherfucker?"

"Juliet," I grabbed her and pulled her to my side. "Are you okay?" Her eyes were wide, staring down at the asshole bleeding on the ground. Her hand was covering her already bruising cheek. I pulled her into the light, inspecting the damage; she was shaken and bruised, but she was going to be okay. What the fuck was she doing here? And half dressed? She didn't even have on a bra—I could barely tear my eyes away.

"I'm going to kill your skinny ass! You're dead! I won't leave town until you're dead, you little whore," he huffed out, his hands still between his legs when Hawk and Joel got to him.

"Fuck you, asshole!" she screamed back.

I could feel the darkness coming. My temper was going to explode on the asshole, and I wanted to leave him lying in a bloody pool. I turned to Joker, who was now being held by Hawk and Joel. I sent a punch to his gut and another to his face.

"What the fuck? Beating a girl? Are you an animal? Do your brothers stand for that? Because we don't."

"Girl?" he hissed spitting out blood. "That bitch is dead!" He yelled at Juliet, craning his neck to see her, "You hear that bitch? You are fucking dead!" The blood from his nose was dripping to his chin.

I studied Juliet's face; she's pretty tough for a little thing.

I forced my rage down as had been taught me in anger management, one breath at a time, cause right now I wanted to take Joker out. Joker was not one to forgive or forget. His threats were his word. Juliet was in trouble. Big fucking trouble.

Ledger then arrive on the scene and pulled his bike next to us. He jumped off and asked if she was okay before pulling her in for a hug.

"Get her the fuck out of here, Ledge," I growled. "Hawk and I will take care of this piece of shit."

He put his hand on Juliet's back. "We have to get out of here now," he said gently but firmly. She nodded in agreement, with a look of knowing in her eyes. Why the fuck did it seem like she was so comfortable with Ledger?

She started heading toward where her jeep was parked.

"No, babe, my bike's faster. We got to go, fast." The rumble of bikes in the distance was getting closer.

She protested, "I-I've never been on a bike…and what about my Jeep?"

"The guys are gonna take care of it and the rest of your things."

He got on his bike and roared it to life.

"Bike." He handed her his helmet. "Now, babe."

"But what are you going to wear?" she asked with concern in her eyes. She just got attacked, but she was concerned for him?

"Don't worry about me, babe. We gotta go now."

She took the helmet in one hand and used the other to pull on the knotted hair on top of her head. Golden, color-streaked locks cascaded down the middle of her back. My body stiffened with that swift action. It was the sexiest thing I'd ever seen.

As I watched her mount his bike, a primal, violent feeling suddenly came over me. Did Juliet like Ledger? Why did I even care? When her arms reached around his waist, I spun and gave Joker another fist to his face, this one knocking him out.

"Do you remember where I live?"

"Yeah, babe, can't forget. Now hold on to me, alright? Real tight." Juliet settled onto the bike and squeezed her arms around his waist.

"Be careful of the pipe near your leg, sweetheart." He ran his fingers near her ankle and up her calf, causing a surge in my already angry state. He gave us a quick salute, and then they were out of there.

Why did he know where she lived? Did they have a thing?

"Hello? Rage?" Hawk was waving at me as he gripped Joker's slumped body. "Looks like someone who says he's not interested in anyone has it bad for a certain yoga instructor." Hawk laughed as I watched the bike get smaller in the distance.

———

RAGE

I crashed at Kai's last night. I couldn't guarantee that I wouldn't have started a beef with one of the Devil's had I stayed in the clubhouse. Kai was furious after I had filled him in. Then it had been me trying to stop him from going back to the clubhouse.

After a few drinks, I crashed on his sofa. Lying on my back, I stared at the ceiling, wrestling with the idea of checking on Juliet myself. I couldn't decide if letting Ledge take her back to her home had been the best idea. Ledger as the one protecting her did not sit well with me. Why I instinctively felt that it should be me to protect her, I didn't know.

I waited until early afternoon to go to the clubhouse to change. Another day of putting up with this shit and the clubhouse would be ours again.

Just as I predicted, the odor of last night's guests greeted me. Trash was overflowing from the dumpsters, and the whole place was in disarray. Colt was not one to tolerate messes, so I hoped he got what he wanted. Although Kai's bachelor pad wasn't much better.

I stepped over passed-out bikers and thong-clad women draped over the drunk men. I recognized only a few people.

I unlocked my door and slipped in. I needed a shower and a nap. Tonight, Juliet was my responsibility. As pissed as I was over the situation, I was looking forward to spending time with her. She had consumed my thoughts since the day I met her, and after last night, I needed to unravel the mystery of Juliet. Maybe getting to know her better would lessen the strange magnetism I felt toward her.

I pulled my cut on over my T-shirt. I anchored my gun to its strap under my jeans before pulling my boots on. I studied myself in the mirror like I was going on a date. Once satisfied with my appearance, I sprayed on some cologne, grabbed the packed duffel, and locked the door behind me.

Weed and pizza wafted through the air from the kitchen. Hawk, Bodie, Hack, and Kai sat around the table, playing cards, with a stack of bills in the middle. Kai had his sunglasses on and his flavor of the day—a barely dressed blond, bouncing on his knee while playing on her phone.

"A game without Ledge, that's a first. He'll be pissed he missed it." I leaned against the doorway to listen in and watch.

Kai shook his head, tossing another bill in the middle. "Ever since he's gone high stakes, he never plays with us. He says he'd feel too guilty taking all our money. We only play when he's not around."

"You headed out to Juliet's?" Hawk said as he threw a fifty in the center of the table.

"Fuck," Kai threw his cards down, causing the girl on his lap to jump. "Geez, Kai, what the hell?" She fixed herself back on his knee and used her phone as a mirror to fix her hair.

"Yeah, I told Ledge I'd be there by six," I said, grabbing a water bottle from the fridge.

Hawk scooped up the money from the center of the table and glanced at his watch. "You got an hour. Sit in for a hand." He pointed to the empty chair.

"Nah, thanks, but I'm going to get some food before I head up there."

In unison, still staring at their cards, they said, "No."

"No?" I arched an eyebrow. "I gotta eat if I'm going to be up there all night."

Hawk laughed and said, "Not necessary, brother. That girl is a feeder."

"Yup," they all agreed.

"A what?" I was confused and hungry. I looked at the last slice of pizza in the open box.

"Every time I leave her place or she visits the club, man, I can barely make it on my bike. The girl loves cooking for people, even though it's all that healthy shit, she makes it taste so good." Hawk licked his lips. "Her eggplant parm is heaven." He laughed, rubbing his stomach.

Hack chimed in, "Oh, yeah, it is. Ooohh and her pie…" He had a shit-eating grin on his face.

I turned a heated shade as I stared him down, narrowing my eyes, daring him to make another comment.

"Woah, brother," Hack laughed placing his hands up, "she makes the best pies."

"Is cherry your favorite?" Bodie joined in, giggling like a teen. I threw the nearest plastic cup at his curly blond head.

"Looks like someone may have a crush." Hack chuckled, and the rest of them joined with laughs and kissy faces.

I blew past them, ignoring the last bit. I gave them the finger and my don't-fuck-with-me-glare and slammed the door behind me. "Fuckers."

CHAPTER EIGHT

Rage

*M*y eyes darted back and forth watching out for deer on the isolated mountain road. With steep drop-offs on each side, I didn't want one taking me by surprise on my bike doing nearly fifty. The road was winding, sharp and fast. Why the hell did she live up here by herself?

Turning in from the road, one could see behind the large canopy trees; the back was open with a panoramic view of the town and Black Rock River. It was quite breathtaking. I guess the seclusion was worth it. At least from this vantage point, we could quickly find out if Joker or any of his asshole brothers decide to seek revenge on her for kicking his ass last night.

I pulled into the lot next to Ledger's bike. The cabin looked like something from a storybook, nestled in trees with flowers everywhere. The sound of my bike must have alerted Ledger and Juliet to my arrival. Before I made it up the flower-lined path to the small porch, the door opened.

"Welcome, brother," Ledge said over the barking from inside the cabin.

"'Sup, Ledge?" I gave him a head tilt. "No signs of trouble?"

"No, only trouble here is Miss Juliet," he said and gave a little wink.

A white pit bull with floppy ears and a scarred chest ran out toward me. The pup was on alert as he cautiously checked me out, sniffing everywhere.

"Hi, bud," I said, bending down and extending my hand for him to inspect.

"This is Lord," said the voice that had been constantly on my mind. "Lord, this is Rage." She came and knelt by my side as she introduced us. With her approval, he let his guard down and allowed me to pet him. Lord's blue eyes stayed trained on Juliet.

"Nice to meet you, Lord." I rubbed the soft fur under his chin.

"I got to get going, Rage. You got this?" Ledger climbed on his bike.

"Yes, Ledge, I got this." I rolled my eyes, annoyed.

"You know, I'm fine. You don't need to watch me," Juliet said. "That asshole isn't going to come up here. He probably slept it off and forgot all about me."

Ledger and I looked at each other. "No," we said at the same time.

Ready to leave, Ledger started the engine.

"Oh, shit! Wait, Ledge. I forgot I made a bag of goodies for you to take back to the boys. Give me a second." She ran back and quickly returned with a box. "I packed a pie and some of the cinnamon rolls Kai likes." She held out the box to him, with the sweetest smile.

"Juliet, sweetie, I think I've gained five pounds since being here last night," he laughed. She tilted her head to the ground, her smile laced with guilt. She leaned into Ledge to give him a big hug. "Thanks for staying."

My eyes shot bullets into Ledge. He must have noticed because he backed off the hug. "No worries, doll. Rage will take good care of you." He started his bike and gave us both a nod before covering his eyes with his shades and took off.

"Come on in," she waved. Lord followed her every move. The small front porch had hanging plants and a welcome mat at the door; the few pairs of Converse and glittery flip-flops made me smile.

The small cabin looked much bigger inside. It was painted shades

70

of white from floor to ceiling. The furniture was white, the decor was white, and there were green plants scattered throughout, giving the place an earthy vibe. Tiny lights were strung up everywhere. They looked like fireflies.

Blues rock music filled the space, and the scent of something mouthwatering was coming from the kitchen. "I love this song." I was referring to Chris Stapleton's *Death Row*.

"Me, too." She closed her eyes as she swayed to the music. Her ankle bracelets jingled as she moved.

Her soft yellow sundress was strapless and almost reached the floor. Just her bare feet and sexy toes were visible. The long dress clung to her body, her tan shoulders showing. She looked hotter than the half-naked girls at the club. Soft curls fell around her face from the long braid hanging from her shoulder. Her face was absent of makeup, except those shiny lips again. The pale-yellow fabric made the gold in her green eyes stand out. She brushed away a curl, revealing her bruised cheek, and I nearly lost control of my temper.

I cleared my throat and tried not to stare. "You have quite a view here." The back wall was entirely made up of glass doors that overlooked the mountain. "I love your place."

A small appreciative smile crept across her face. "Thanks, I've been here for almost three years. It took some time to redo the old place, but I love it."

She pulled open one of the glass doors, the mountain air streamed in through the screen, stirring the air. Something smelled good.

"Are you staying at the club or do you live somewhere else?"

"The club for now." I inhaled. "That smells fantastic."

"Crap. I almost forgot." Flying into the kitchen, she turned the stove down. She smiled and shrugged her shoulders. "Just in time."

Leaning against the rustic wooded column, I looked around some more.

"Do you like pesto?" she yelled from her small kitchen where pans were clattering.

"Yes, I love it."

I walked toward where she was and found her fishing out a beer from the fridge. She handed me the icy cold bottle. "I hope you like craft beers, I got this one cause of the cute bunny on the label." She pointed to the image. "It's called Crazy Hops IPA. It's from that local microbrew in Black Rock. I'm not a beer girl, but I like to keep some on hand for visitors, and the label sold me."

I twisted off the lid wondering how frequent Ledge was a visitor. Did she keep beer on hand for him?

She pointed at the open glass door. "You can go out to the patio and relax. Dinner will be about fifteen more minutes."

I did as she suggested, ducking my head and swiping the wind chimes. A roof covered the large stone patio. To the left was a purple fabric swing hanging from a rafter with yoga mats below it. To the right was a heavy bag suspended from the beam. A basket of gloves and wraps sat in the corner. Everywhere I looked were plants. A small iron table was in the center of the patio. The porch extended out to four large boxed gardens. I sipped on my beer examining the vegetables that were growing in there, little signs marked each one. There was an entire box dedicated to herbs. Others were cut and hung to dry from the rafters.

She brought out another beer, some white wine, silverware, and napkins.

"Can I help?"

"Nope, just relax." She handed me an open beer.

As promised, fifteen minutes later, she came out from the kitchen carrying two plates. One with a smaller portion and the other piled high with pasta and bread. She put the large plate in front of me.

"My famous pesto pasta," she said in a fake Italian accent, which made me laugh.

"This looks amazing." I put three fingers to my lips and sent them out with a kiss.

We dug in. I'd never had homemade pesto, and I was just blown away by its flavor. Juliet baked the bread, and all the ingredients except for the pasta noodles and pine nuts came from her garden.

"I was hoping you wouldn't mind the pine-nut cheese. I am vegan and don't eat animal products," she said, waiting for my reaction.

I shook my head in confusion, lifting an eyebrow "Nut cheese?"

She laughed at the confused look on my face. It led to a long conversation about plant-based living and the environment. I drank a few more beers, and she filled a second glass of white wine. I found it odd when she cut the wine with sparkling water and lemon wedges.

"What's with the water in the wine?" I asked.

"I love wine. Red used to be my favorite, but I can't have it anymore 'cause it gives me sort of a migraine really quickly, even when cooked in food. White wine is a little bit better, but I still have to cut it with water. I'm not taking any chances with a migraine." She swirled the liquid in the glass, taking a sip.

Her face was becoming flushed. She pushed back the few wavy strands that caressed her face behind her ear, revealing more of her stunning beauty.

That's when I noticed the scars. One was in her left eyebrow, it was small and divided the hair. Another extended from the corner of her eye and went straight to her ear. It blended with her skin, you could easily miss it if you didn't know what you were looking at. I'd seen many fighters display those scars proudly, but she masked hers gently with her hair.

I reached out to touch her face, just grazing the marred skin. She froze, eyes widening.

"Sorry..." I pulled my hand back. "I just..." I cleared my throat. "What happened?"

I heard her make a small gulp. "Accident...a few years ago. It's nothing." She was nervous and uncomfortable.

"So, Rage, tell me..." She downed more of her wine and quickly changed the topic. "Not to be nosey, but what kept you away? Were you in jail or something?"

She wasn't ready to talk and I didn't want to push her. I gave a small chuckle to put her back at ease. "No, I wasn't in jail. Almost, though. It's a long story. I don't want to bore you."

She raised her almost empty goblet it in the air. "I got all night." She took a sip and waited for me to answer.

"Alright, you asked for it." I popped the top off a new bottle and stretched my legs out, crossing them at the ankles.

"Four years ago, I was with a few brothers at a dive bar, Charlie's Place. You know it?" She shook her head.

"Charlie's was a few blocks off Main Street in Sugar Maple. It was tucked in between a whole alley full of garages. Not many outsiders went there. That's why the brothers liked it. It was kind of a getaway from the clubhouse. Anyway, that night a group of college kids were in there—the kind of guys who thought they were better than everyone else and treated waitresses like crap. I recognized a few of them who trained at the Pit. This big blond asshole was hassling Mandy, our waitress. Now she was a few years behind us in school, so we all knew her. We warned him a few times to leave her alone. But the drunker the kids got, the rowdier they became. Finally, after they knocked over a table and spilled a few bottles, Charlie kicked them out."

Juliet was listening intently; she ran her finger along the rim of her glass as she waited for me to continue.

"We stayed until closing that night. I got on my bike and was two blocks away when I realized I had left my phone there, so I turned around and went back. Everyone was gone except Hawk, Leo, and Charlie. He was letting them finish their tie-breaking pool game while he closed out the register. On my way out, I heard a scream from the back parking lot. I knew it was Mandy. The blond fucker from before was roughing her up. He held her by the back of her head. His fist was full of her hair, her lip busted open."

Retelling what happened transported back to that place and time. I could almost feel my boots pounding across the lot. His fist struck her face again, I pulled him off and began beating him. In my head, he was Vinny, and I couldn't stop. I tuned out Mandy's screams. Leo and Hawk ran out and tried to pull me off the bastard. My blows were hard and fast, fists furiously making their way from his face to his gut and ribs.

"Rage?"

I blinked. "Fuck, sorry, where was I?"

"You tell me. Looks like your mind went off somewhere…Are you okay?"

"Yeah, of course…I…uh…I pulled the fucker off her and gave him what he deserved. Hawk and Leo were trying to control me when the police and ambulance arrived. As my luck would have it, he had an important father, some political guy. A month later I was offered an option: go to court or leave town for four years until Mr. Got A Rich Daddy gets his graduate degree from Black Rock University. I knew from experience that bikers don't exactly get the best shake in court, so I left. I moved to Tennessee and joined the Memphis chapter of Stained Souls."

I tipped my beer toward her and turned to look at the sun dropping in the sky.

"That's so unfair…But I'm happy you're back now, and you could put all that behind you."

I appreciated her sentiment. I'd certainly had a rough go at life, but at that moment, I was looking at a gorgeous sunset and sharing it with a gorgeous girl, I couldn't ask for more.

———

JULIET

Lord chewed on his ball in the backyard. I watched him, my arms held to my stomach, willing the nervousness to go away. After keeping an eye on me for the night, Ledger's shift was over, and Rage was now coming to take his place. Just the thought of spending the night with Rage had a swarm of butterflies taking up residence in my belly.

As comfortable as I'd become around most of the MC, Rage was different. Being in his presence for just the briefest of time had stirred up feelings in me that I'd thought were impossible ever to feel again. When I saw him getting that lap dance at his party, I bolted out of the barn. I wasn't even sure why.

Geez, half the Stained Souls looked like damn models in leather, and a few of them subtly tried to hit on me, but as sexy as they were, I felt nothing. Even being here with Ledger, who filled out his jeans and cut very nicely—still nothing. It was probably because I didn't want to feel anything. How could I bring myself to get involved with anyone? Share my life…my lies? It was impossible.

Besides, with Fluid just being across the street from the tattoo studio, I didn't want any drama if things didn't work out. My work was very important to me and I wouldn't do anything to risk screwing it up. God knows I'd sacrificed enough.

Sugar Maple was my chance to start over. I remembered making the decision to come here. It had been a dark time for me. I'd had a horrible day. I'd felt defeated and lost. I'd gone outside to find a full moon. I'd sat crying under the night sky, praying for a sign. Under the glow of the moon, as if she'd been standing next to me, my grandmother's voice had come in my head. When I was about thirteen, I had confided in her about some girls bullying me in school. She had said, "Juliet, one thing I've learned in life is you can only be a victim if you let yourself believe you are one. Never give up on choosing the life you want for yourself, no one can stop you but you." Gone for years, and she was still giving me good advice. It was her voice that had given me the courage to wipe my tears, pack my bags, and move away from Tallahassee.

I had marked the day I got to Sugar Maple as the first day of my new life. I'd even had the date tattooed inside my hamsa so I would never forget the day I had chosen freedom. Six months after I'd been attacked, I still got letters from Antonio, telling me how sorry he was and how we were meant to be together. Psycho. So, I'd taken Ivy up on her offer to move, started using my middle name, and never looked back. Well, that wasn't entirely true, because I had been looking over my shoulder every day, just waiting for it all to come crashing down. I woke up every day with the intention of living my life without fear. Frequent nightmares made it hard at times, but then I would remember how I was raised and try not to let what if's rule my decisions. I was naturally introverted with a few close friends and quite enjoyed spending time by myself. Sometimes I missed being in a relationship, but I wasn't ready to share that part of myself again. Antonio left me with trust issues, but I gotta believe that when the right person came along, he would get me over them and I would be able to share that part of me with him.

"Hello? Juliet?" Ledger waved his hand in front of my face. "Earth to Juliet," he said with a smile.

"Sorry, I was lost in thought. Sometimes it just happens, all that meditation, ya know."

"Yeah, I hear ya. Sometimes when I'm on my bike, and it's like I've gotten to where I'm going and I don't even remember the ride." He bent down and gave Lord some love. "Rage texted. He should be here soon."

There was that feeling in my stomach again. "Oh, okay."

"I feel so bad, you guys really—" Before the words could get out of my mouth, he cut me off, his hand came to my lips, finger extended to quiet the words.

"Don't even." He shook his head. He placed his finger under my chin, forcing me to look into those kind eyes.

"Joker and his boys are here because of us. You should have never been put in that situation." Turning my head slightly, he focused on the bruise on my cheek. His lips pursed and his head shook. "I'm so sorry, doll."

A motorcycle rumbled in the distance. The sound grew louder, signaling that it was getting closer and climbing the mountain. Ledge drew his gun. "I'm sure it's Rage, but can't be too careful." He stood by the door looking through the curtain and confirmed it was Rage.

The flurry of butterflies became intense when I caught a glimpse of him. Why was my body responding this way? He was just a man like any other. I took a deep breath.

I offered Rage a beer and poured myself some white wine to relax. He looked around, checking out my place before I sent him into the garden to relax. I hoped he'd like my pesto pasta.

Another beer, another wine, and our plates were wiped clean. We talked nonstop, debating and laughing. I swore Rage almost sprayed out his beer several times. I was pleasantly surprised at how easy our conversations came. I even convinced him to tell me all about why he left town. It pissed me off that he got treated that way when he had only been defending a woman.

After cleaning up from dinner, I suggested we sit at the fire pit. I grabbed him a beer, refilled my wine, and turned up the music before we headed out, Lord walking close by my side. We followed the path of solar fairy lights to the small clearing where I had a few chairs, a garden box that held cushions, and a blanket. As humid as it was inside, the mountains made it cool at night. Rage got the fire going, and it didn't take long to warm us.

I loved coming out here at night to stargaze. I even had a special spot where I could lie back and view the heavens above.

"There is a full moon tonight." I pointed to the bright light behind the trees. He turned his head toward the sky, trying to see where the moon was hiding. The clusters of trees obstructed his view.

"The best place to see the sky is right there." I pointed to the clearing. I took the blanket out of the garden box and spread it directly under the open area where I often came to mediate. Lord immediately jumped on it. "Move over," I said to my furry little bestie. I patted my hand on the blanket, inviting Rage to join me.

He sat next to me then leaned back, tucking his arm under his head. Lying back, I blinked a few times. "I think the wine is starting to hit me." I giggled and began to point out constellations and explain my love for the moon.

"Orion's belt is here," I took his hand in mine and traced the three stars and the arrow.

He twisted my wrist, examining the small symbol tattooed on the inside. "What's this mean?" His finger tickled my skin as he outlined the sideways figure eight.

"It's an infinity symbol. Ivy and I both had them tattooed on my eighteenth birthday. A symbol of our everlasting friendship and love for each other, no matter how far apart we may be." I hiccuped. Oh, boy, maybe drinking wine wasn't the best way to calm my nerves. I closed my eyes, taking in a deep breath, enjoying my completely relaxed state.

When Theory of Deadman's *Hallelujah* began to play from the cabin, I couldn't help but sing along. He sat up and pulled something from his pocket.

Within seconds, my body began to break out in chills as the sweet sound of his harmonica played along to the music. I didn't know if it was the alcohol or the beauty of the melody, but I became emotional, a single tear sliding down my cheek. When the last note quieted, I stared into his eyes. His finger came to my cheek and wiped the salty tear away.

His fingers lifted my chin, forcing my eyes to meet his. I swallowed down the lump that had formed in my throat. He was beautiful. I felt paralyzed when our eyes locked. His warm breath sent a shiver through me. My stomach rolled, and my heart beat faster. All of a sudden, I was fourteen again, scared of a kiss. His lips were so close to mine. In a flash, my senses somehow rushed back and I quickly turned my head. His scruff tickled me as his moist lips gently swiped across my cheek, sending an ache straight to my core.

Want and desire filled me. It was a spark I'd never felt, and it tore through my body. My fingers ran through the curls that fell in his face. My panties were no longer dry as his breath and lips met my ear and then my neck.

"This is not a good idea," I whispered. The heat coming from our bodies contrasted with the crisp mountain air.

I shouldn't be doing this, I barely know him. My mind was racing, but my body responded like it had a mind of its own, needs of its own. A moan escaped me as he lightly bit and sucked the most tender spot on my neck, my body humming with pleasure as tiny thrills spread through me. Giving in to the hunger, I started to turn my head to meet his luscious lips.

Suddenly, Lord began barking and sneering, fully in distress. His fur stood straight up, making a ridge on his back. Rage pulled away from me and shielded me with his body. Facing the direction of Lord's barks, he drew his gun and grabbed the flashlight next to the fire pit aiming it where Lord was running. He flashed some light in the bushes, illuminating a set of eyes.

"Lord!" I yelled sternly. A raccoon. With a deep sigh, we both were relieved to see the quickly retreating raccoon. My body shivered. Rage pulled me into his hard chest with one strong arm. "Babe, you okay?" *God, he smells fantastic.* "I'm not going to let anything happen to you." He kissed the top of my head and turned me to look at him. I stared into his deep brown eyes, but before I got lost in them again, I turned my head away. My wine buzz had gone along with the raccoon, and I was brought back to my senses.

"I-I'm so sorry, that…that shouldn't have happened." I stepped back and stumbled over my words. moving farther away from him. "I shouldn't have… I was caught up in the music and wine. I think I just got a little emotional when you played on your harmonica 'cause my dad used to play for us when we went camping as kids, and I haven't seen him in a very long time." I cleared my throat and I should have stopped there, but seeing the look of rejection on his face, I rambled on instead. "I'm so sorry. I don't know what I was thinking. That was a bad idea 'cause I'm sort of seeing someone. We've only been on a few dates, and I don't even really—"

"Juliet, save it," his voice was a mixture of anger and disappointment. "It was a moment. No big deal. Don't worry, it won't happen again."

Did I really not want that to happen again?

He motioned back to the cabin, and we made the short walk back in silence.

JULIET

A warm lick wet my nose. Lord was ready to go outside. How was it already morning? I tried opening my eyes. Light filtered in through the sheers, confirming it was indeed already morning. Lord was very aware of our routine—he's a natural alarm clock. Groaning, I rolled out of bed, pulling on a tank and my favorite white soft cut shorts.

I kept quiet as I tiptoed around the living room, not wanting to wake Rage, who was on the pullout sofa. I let Lord out to the backyard, I watered the gardens, and then put on my music for a ten-minute meditation and yoga before breakfast.

Rolling out my favorite pink mat, I sat in full lotus and closed my eyes. My hands on my knees, I began to take deep breaths…in, hold, then out. I kept my mantra silent in my head and let the music fill me.

The usually relaxing pose that gave me clarity before I start my day was invaded repeatedly with images of last night's moment under the full moon. It was as if the meditation was bringing it to life. I could feel my core warming. Soon I was thinking of what sex could be like with Rage. My whole body shivered and my eyes snapped open. That was enough meditation for today. I took a last deep breath and began to stretch.

From downward dog to handstands and back to child's pose, I prepped my body for the short but intense aerial yoga routine that always started my day. Once fully stretched, I grabbed my phone to change the music to some hard rock. I loved working out to rock—it made everything more intense. I scrolled through my phone to select the song I wanted: Guns and Roses' *November Rain*.

I had a feeling like someone was watching me. I sneaked a peek at Rage—he was still sleeping. Maybe it was just Lord?

I climbed my swing and let all thoughts slip away. I jammed out and challenged my body. The pose that completed my routine was King Cobra, which I held until the final note. I flipped off the silky swing. My body was now covered in a thin mist of morning dew mixed with sweat. God, I needed a shower. A few final sun salutations and then a hot shower…maybe it should be a cold one.

Entering the house quietly, I saw Rage was sprawled out on the bed with no shirt on. My breath hitched. His eight pack was visible even in his sleep. How much cardio did this man do? His chest was tan, with tattoos covering his defined pectoral muscles. There was a familiar tattoo of Stained Souls MC on the left side of his chest— wings over his pec and a sword, which looked like it pierced his heart where the drop of blood trailed. It almost looked sad, the way it was placed. Shit, I was staring. I tried to move along but ended up kicking the table and almost waking him. How embarrassing. *Juliet, let the poor man sleep.*

I warmed the shower water, then I sneaked back into the kitchen to prepare the French press with my favorite Dark Devil coffee from Roasted. I slowly added boiling water into the press and watched the heavenly mixture come to life. Coffee was my favorite smell, heaven.

I tossed my towel over my shoulder and headed to the bathroom. I left Lord outside. He loved it out there when the morning light warmed his favorite pillow. He was sleeping again, as deeply as Rage. I smiled to myself as I got in the shower. The warm spray of water felt good on the muscles I just exhausted.

Thoughts of Rage and the almost kiss materialized in my mind while I covered my body in suds. I tried to focus on the honeysuckle-scented shampoo as I lathered, rinsed, and conditioned. Moving my hands over my body, I couldn't help think how good it would feel if it were Rage's fingers gliding over my body, sliding up and down. Damn, those strong hands would feel so good touching my skin. I could imagine what his hard body would feel like pressed behind me in the shower. Maybe I should turn my hot water to cold before I lost my mind. How long had it been? Too long.

I tried singing to distract myself from the naughty thoughts. I rinsed the last of the conditioner from my hair. With the water turned off, I wrapped my body in a towel before stepping out of the stall filled with thick steam. The fog began to clear; my eyes grew wide, and I let out a scream as loud as I could.

RAGE

Sleep had not come easy last night, and it hadn't been the bed. The pillowy soft pullout had been more than comfortable. I'd had to do everything to keep myself from tearing back the covers and busting into Juliet's bedroom to convince her to finish what we started. I wasn't an asshole, so I'd had to just twist and turn and have a very uncomfortable aching in my boxers for most of the night.

I had kept my eyes fixed on the closed door that held untold mysteries. Questions had rolled in my mind: Who the hell was she dating, and how can I find him and destroy him? Destroy might be too strong a word—persuade him not to date her anymore. With every creak I'd heard in the old cabin, I kept wishing it was her coming to my bed. Fucking crazy.

The sun streamed its warm light into the small living room. I peeked one eye open in the direction of the muffled sound coming from outside.

Juliet had her eyes closed and appeared to be meditating. She was on a mat with folded legs, her hand on each knee, fingers together pointing toward the sky. Her tan skin appeared darker in her white tank and tiny sweat shorts. Then her eyes popped open, like she was startled. I kept one eye on her, squinting, so it would look like I was still asleep. I didn't want to be caught staring. I watched her stretch and balance on her hands, pushing straight up, before folding her body over into a backbend. Ogling her did not help the painful ache in my boxers; it stretched along with her. She bent from one side to the other, her legs set wide apart. My mouth went dry.

I snapped my eyes shut when I saw her get up and change the music. I again squinted open one eye, but I had to readjust myself so I could get a better view. I flipped on my back, and the sheets sent a wave of laundry detergent scent into the air. I inhaled the light fragrance that smelled like Juliet. I propped my body on the pillow, placing my one arm behind my head so I could easily squint both eyes.

Her beautiful movements on the fabric swing matched the beat. Using her strong arms to pull her body to the top, she wrapped her arms around the fabric while holding her body still and then performed a series of flips before settling upside down, holding onto the swing only by her hips.

So this is what she teaches at Fluid, I thought. I wondered if her students could keep this pace. Flipping her body, her stomach was face down in the middle of the swing as the song concluded. She extended her arms behind her, reaching for her feet and resting them on her head, staying perfectly still.

Lord was curled up on a pile of pillows in the sun and watched her enter the cabin. I shut my eyes, pretending to sleep. I could feel her looking at me. My eyes almost opened at the sound of her tripping. I bit the inside of my lip to keep from smiling.

Squeaky pipes came to life as the shower turned on. Padding back into the kitchen, she tiptoed around. Seconds later, the aroma of coffee woke the rest of my body.

It was a painful experience knowing that one room away, fully naked under the spray of water, was the most desirable body I had ever seen. The ache I felt intensified, I wanted to join her, claim her, make her mine. Fuck, she was like a siren calling to me and tempting me in ways no woman had. How could I feel so possessive over someone I just met? I wanted to kill Joker for putting his hands on her.

Why was she out at night by herself, dressed in that tiny little outfit? She needed to be more careful. If she were mine, that shit wouldn't happen.

A loud shriek echoed through the house. I jumped on my feet, shuffled through my pants, which were on the floor, and retrieved my gun. Lord barked frantically at Juliet's scream.

Juliet, dripping wet, sprinted from the bathroom, gripping a towel around her with one hand and holding out a paper towel with the other. "Oh, my God! Oh, my God! oh, my God! Get the door!" she shrieked.

Nearly slamming into her, I pointed my gun in the direction she ran from, flung the door open, and she tossed the paper towel to the ground.

My heart pounded as my eyes followed where the paper towel had landed. Out of it came the biggest, hairiest, most terrifying-looking spider. My eyes met hers through the veil of colorful wet hair.

I shook my head, relieved the intruder was the eight-legged kind. I started to walk out the door to do the manly thing, grab a boot and crush the invader.

"No!" she cried, tugging my arm and pulling me back. "I didn't just rescue him from the shower to have you stomp him dead under your boot!"

"What?" I say shaking my head in confusion. "Him?"

"Don't look at me like that." Her finger pointed in my face. "He didn't do anything wrong but wander into my shower." She used her body to block the door, staying there until he scurried into the garden. "Go find your family, little guy."

"Little guy?" My eyebrows drew together. "Juliet that was the biggest fucking spider I have ever seen."

She tightened her towel, probably realizing that she was naked underneath. "I try not to kill anything that is not trying to kill me!" Her words were soft as she brushed past me, practically running to her room.

I busted up laughing. This girl, every minute that passed, I wanted her more.

CHAPTER NINE

Rage

*R*obotically, I performed my arm workout standing in front of the wall of mirrors in the Pit's free-weights room. I curled the heavy weights; each time my biceps bulged, my veins filled with blood, making them appear even more substantial. To any passerby, I was working out in front of the mirror like anyone else.

The truth was, I had been getting here earlier this week, hoping to run into Juliet. I didn't want to go to Fluid and ask her out. I am not the type to seek a woman out, at least I hadn't had any desire or need to seek one out 'til now. I was here early again for the third time this week. I used the mirror to check out who was in the gym. Hopefully, I would catch a glimpse of Juliet and we could talk.

Ever since that almost kiss, all I had thought about was Juliet. I wanted her. I needed her. I had to have more of her. Maybe if we finished what we started, I would be able to get this woman out of my system.

She had me so twisted up, I even got hell from Colt for breaking the rules. Ledge and I had paid Joker a little visit before he left town. I just couldn't let it go. I regretted nothing. It had been more than fair, three of those loser scumbags against the two of us. It had made me happy to see his busted up, black and blue nose from the head-butt she had given him. Even after finishing what I started with Joker, it didn't satisfy me. Assholes like him never learned.

Colt had asked me to ride up later tonight to the Stained Souls' brewery, Black Rock Microbrew, to drop off some paperwork to Tiny, the brother who ran the place. I had promised Colt I would deliver them personally. Black Water, a great band, would to be playing there tonight on the deck, and I was planning on inviting Juliet to come and make the trip with me. Judging by her taste in music, I thought Juliet would love them.

I'd seen her leave the gym after training with Leo twice over the past two weeks. Since they trained early, I got my butt up, determined to talk to her today. I hadn't seen her here since the incident with Joker, so I was hoping she hadn't cancelled her training with Leo today.

It looked like my timing was perfect. There she was, training with Leo. I watched Leo use his drill sergeant tactics to draw out everything she had as a fighter. Woman or man, Leo didn't care. You trained with him, your ass was going to have to work, hard. She was no different.

Juliet's sweat-coated body was sexy as hell, accentuating her lean muscles. Her sports bra was athletic style and kept her large breasts in place. Her yoga pants hugged her curves but gave her mobility to perform high kicks.

I kept looking in the mirrors, waiting to see her leave the locker room. I had to keep reminding myself to switch circuits, so I wasn't standing here like a fool doing a thousand curls.

I repeatedly hit the speed bag while surveilling the locker room exit. A voice from my past called out, "So, it's true! You are back in town." Arrogance laced his tone. I hated that voice. It belonged to none other than Richard—Dick, as I preferred to call him—Ramsey.

He and his brother, Deacon, were the developers who owned a whole lot of Sugar Maple now. Both of them had been total assholes growing up. They'd flaunted daddy's money and thought they were better than everyone else. Richard had been a lumbering but lanky shithead whom I'd had more than a few run-ins with at school. I'd always ended up suspended, but his daddy had always gotten him out of everything. I think Ramsey Stadium at the high school had been a bribe to get those two shitheads out of trouble.

I turned to answer Dick, who was no longer a lanky guy but a well-developed muscular man. He must have hit the juice hard to gain that much size. His black gym pants had some stupid designer logo, and he wore no shirt to show off his chest and muscled arms. He still was not quite my size, but close.

"Dick."

"Alexander." No one had called me that since high school.

"What the hell are you doing here? Don't you have a private gym in your home?"

His face turned into a devilish grin, "Can't fight with the best unless you train with the best, and Leo will only train me here."

I rolled my eyes. "I didn't think you'd want your pretty boy ass kicked in a ring."

Changing to the heavy bag, I pounded at it, wishing it was his face.

"Since training with Leo over the past three years, I'm defending champ on this circuit," he touted. "I guess you need to catch up on things around here. Since you left and Leo no longer competes, this is my octagon now." He was holding a towel around his neck; his hands were wrapped, prepared for his session.

I stopped my assault on the bag, finally looking him in the eye. "Is that right?" I scoffed. "Well, then, I guess we'll see if you keep that title in July when I compete in the Firecracker Fights."

I enjoyed watching the drop wash over his face. "Wha...? I-I thought you retired." Grimacing like he had eaten something sour, he shook his head like I was lying.

"Nope, you thought wrong," I retorted, enjoying the confused look on his face. I resumed my rhythm on the bag. "I guess you need to catch up on things around here," I said before stopping the bag with my glove and leveling my eyes with his.

"I—" I started, but our attention was caught by Juliet leaving the locker room. Fuck, she was more beautiful every time I saw her.

Before I even had a chance to approach her to ask about tonight,

Dick made a beeline toward her. Her eyes caught mine. She quickly looked away and turned her attention to the douche.

She smiled and nodded at what he was saying. I strained to hear but couldn't over the music in the gym. Why the fuck was she smiling at him? My jaw ticked as he walked away giving me a smug look. Asshole.

The look on my face as he talked to her must have said it all. As she turned to walk away, he made a point to blatantly check out her ass, then looked at me.

I was going to kill this asshole. She threw her bag on her back as she walked away from him and toward the door.

"Hey, Juliet," I called out and jogged toward her.

She stood against the wall close to the exit. "Hi, Rage."

I loved the way my name rolled off her tongue. Her green eyes stared at me, I almost lost the words. Daggers penetrated my back from across the room as Dick watched.

I stretched my arm on the wall above her, leaning into her space.

"I...uh...I have to make a run tonight, and I was wondering if you'd like to come. I'm going to—" Before I finished, her head was shaking no.

"I'm sorry, Rage, I already have plans. Maybe another time?"

"Yeah, sure. Another time." I nodded. I rubbed the back of my neck, feeling like a rejected puppy. I'm a fierce fighter, but this girl had me wound up like a scared little boy.

"It was good to see you, Rage." She shifted nervously and pushed the silver bar to open the door. Her head snapped up when Richard called out from across the gym, apparently, so everyone could hear, "Juliet, I'll pick you up around seven. Be ready!" His evil grin was aimed directly at me.

What the fuck? Juliet was dating Dick Ramsey? Are you fucking kidding me?

Breathe, Rage. Leo wouldn't like it if I kicked his ass right here. It wouldn't be good for the gym. It would definitely be worth it, but I couldn't do that to Leo. I ground my teeth, and flames flew out my nostrils as I turned to face the asshole. I gave him a death scowl, and he returned it with a shit-eating grin. "Fucking asshole," I mumbled.

Couldn't Juliet see what a giant dick he is? She put her head down and continued walking out the door, giving me a casual wave as the door closed behind her.

————

JULIET

This was my first time training with Leo since I'd been attacked by Joker. I wasn't sure if or how much Leo knew about what happened that night. I scurried into the locker room before our session to be sure the makeup I had applied earlier was still camouflaging the bruises.

The lighting in the Pit locker room was not ideal for makeup application, but it was all I had. Blending out the edges, I could barely see the yellow skin that still had a purple hue. Satisfied with the quick job I did, I swept on one last coat of setting powder. Ivy would be proud. She had taught me how to do this a few days ago so I could return to Fluid without anyone asking questions. It was only my second time doing it myself. Unlike Ivy's, my makeup experience was limited at best.

When Leo greeted me, it was obvious that he knew what had happened. The MC was worse than girls sometimes with the way they gossiped.

"How are you, killer? I heard you sent Joker back to the meet with a broken nose. Everyone thought him and Rage just got into it, but Hawk told me what really went down and how you handled yourself." He rested a hand on my shoulder, guiding me to the heavy bag. "I'm proud of you, girl. Not a lot of men or women would be able to take down a man like Joker."

I beamed with pride. Hearing someone say they were proud of me made me feel pretty special. His words made me smile, and also a bit sad because I missed my parents who had always told me they were proud of me and cheered me on my entire life.

"All you, Leo." I winked. His hand then came up to my makeup-covered cheek. His smile was replaced with agitation, and his brows drew together as his finger gently touched the skin. Maybe my makeup job was not as good as I thought.

"That motherfucker," he said in a low growl. "Rage fucked him up, but I think he should've fucking taken his nuts for this."

I pulled my face from his gentle hold. "What do you mean? Rage just hit him a few times before Hawk dragged him away," I said, confused.

"Forget I said this, but," he looked around to make sure no one was listening, "Rage came back after he stayed with you, tracked him down before he left town, gave him a chance to be sober, and then fought him. He beat the living shit out of the bastard. Well-deserved, in my book." He looked around again. *Gossips, they were such gossips.*

"He beat him like you were his girl or his family. Ever since he was sent away, he's taken anger management and has been pretty good with keeping his temper. But Joker was not going to get away with hurting you. Rage was legit pissed. I would have been too if I had known what happened before they left. I'm not supposed to share club business, but seeing your face, I thought you should know." He looked at the area again, and my hand instinctively covered it."

"Don't say I told you. You got me?" He pointed his finger at me to make sure I understood. I nodded in complete shock as the words sank in and my brain tried to compute everything he had said.

Rage had gone back after spending the night with me. He'd beaten Joker like I was his girl? His family? I felt a connection to him after the short time we had spent together, but I didn't expect to hear that.

"Sure, Leo," I promised, twisting my fingers over my lips as if I was locking them. "I won't say a word."

"Now," he clapped his hands, "let's get to work. Show me what you got!" He steadied the heavy bag and began calling out instructions.

For the entire workout, my mind replayed my conversation with Leo over and over in my head. A piece of me was happy not only because that asshole was made to pay, but also that Rage dished out the payback. Another piece was kind of excited that Rage cared enough to go after the asshole. Needless to say, I was distracted. I kept scanning the gym, hoping to see Rage.

Even as I showered and dressed, I couldn't contain my smile. The idea of Rage defending my honor because he actually cared about me, even though he'd known me for such a brief time, was thrilling.

But my giddiness came to a complete halt when I overheard some women talking in the locker room. Some young college girls were changing and chatting about this super hot new guy at the Pit that they were determined to get to know. When they said Rage's name, my ears tuned in.

A locker door slammed. A redhead I had never seen here before, wearing way too much makeup for the gym, sauntered over to them. She got right into their faces. She pushed her ample breasts up when her arms crossed, and her eyes narrowed. "You little bitches better not be talking about my Rage. If you even approach him or touch one fine hair on his hard body, you won't be left with a single hair on either of your heads." The woman's long sharp red nail pointed from one girl to the other. Her face morphed, raging jealousy was written all over it. I acted like I wasn't watching and kept myself partly hidden behind the small red metal door.

"You two little school girls got it?" she seethed. They both nodded before nearly running out of there.

My heart dropped to my stomach. I was wrong after all. How could I have been so stupid? Rage already had someone. I should have known. The man belonged to a damn motorcycle club and adoring groupies were never in short supply. And judging by her tattoos, I'd say this woman was probably popular with the club.

I continued to watch her as she changed. My suspicions were confirmed as she threw on a Stained Souls tank, covering her sports bra. The scrap of fabric was so tight, the material stretched the words across her enormous boobs, which spilled out from the top. Her flat stomach was bare, and her tiny matching spandex shorts looked more like underwear. What the heck was she even doing here? Her attire was more for stripping than MMA workout.

I slammed the locker shut and entered the gym area. Disappointment filled me. Now I hoped I could get out of here unseen. I was hoping to avoid Rage and leave him to the red-haired bitch, who clearly thought she owned him. I thought I had caught a glimpse of him earlier while I was working out with Leo, but I wasn't sure. I must have looked like a speed walker, trying to get out the door unnoticed.

I was halfway to the exit when I saw Rage talking to Richard. I nearly froze. How awkward. I tried to avoid the two, but Richard waved at me, getting my attention. He jogged over to me, wanting to confirm our date. I was glad that the music was loud enough that Rage probably couldn't make out the conversation. A stupid part of me did not want him to know that Richard and I were dating. I don't know why I cared, considering that woman from the locker room.

"Juliet, you're running out of here pretty quick. I just wanted to make sure we're still on for tonight? I know it's been almost two weeks since we made plans. Are you still good?" Richard asked smiling a devilish grin.

I looked into his blue eyes; they were a dull color compared to Rage's rich chocolate and gold eyes. His pale blond hair was gelled in place and looked like it would cut you if you touched it. No stubble on his perfectly clean-shaven jaw. He flaunted his sculpted body.

"Juliet, are we good?" He looked into my eyes, bringing me back to the conversation. "Oh, uh, yeah, we're good." I nodded.

"Great, I'll pick you up tonight about seven." He ran his finger down my arm. I shook off the goosebumps and watched as Rage stayed trained on us and started heading this way. "I gotta run, Richard, I'll see you tonight." I smiled up at him and turned away, quickening my pace toward the exit.

Inches from the door, my stomach lurched as Rage's gruff voice called my name. "Juliet," he said. The inflection made my legs weak. What was wrong with me? I was seeing Richard, and Rage had someone. Apparently, I needed to inform my traitorous body of those facts. Every time I'm around him, I felt my resolve weakening. My core heated, remembering the almost kiss and the way he nibbled at my neck. *Oh, God.*

Was he...trying to ask me out? I was caught me off guard, especially with Big Red watching from a treadmill. I gripped the strap of my bag tightly as he talked. I needed to calm myself. I didn't want to hurt him by saying I had a date, but didn't he have someone, too?

Before I could respond, Richard acted like a dog trying to mark his territory and yelled out the details of our date. Dick move. I didn't like men speaking for me or acting like they have some ownership over me. I could see the anger in Rage's eyes as his jaw ticked and his forehead furrowed. I gave a little shrug and an awkward wave and walked away without elaborating. *What the hell was that?*

JULIET

The clock neared seven. I put the final touches on my sparse makeup and regretfully looked at the high-heeled sandals Ivy had insisted I wear tonight. I rolled my eyes at the tall, thin wedge with wraparound straps. Why she had thought my ankle boots were not good enough for this outfit was a mystery.

We were going to see a band in Black Rock, and I wouldn't possibly be able to dance in these death traps if I wanted to. I stood in front of the full-length mirror, making final adjustments before Richard arrived.

I left my hair down tonight with long loose curls. The rainbow colors peeked through the natural gold and caramel color. It was parted slightly to one side, and a violet curl fell over one eye, making the green even more intense. My lotus flower belly ring, big gold hoop earrings, matching bangle bracelets, and new toe ring completed my ensemble. I smacked my shiny pink lips and applied a final layer of gloss before spritzing some of my favorite perfume in the air around me, stepping into the fresh honeysuckle scent. I took one last look in the mirror before grabbing my sweater. I was ready.

Lord nuzzled at my legs—he knew I was leaving. He then started barking, alerting me someone was here. I opened the door to greet a perfectly polished Richard. Perfectly polished. Maybe that was why I was trying to give him a chance. I was trying to get away from the bad boys, and Richard had not given up in his pursuit since we met at Roasted two years ago. This was our fourth time going out. The first two were dinners that were nice but boring. He talked about himself a little too much. The last date was a wine tasting, which was also nice, and also boring. This time, when he mentioned we were going to see a band, I was all in.

I loved Black Water. I saw them last year with Ivy. She nearly had gotten us kicked out of the bar with her over-the-top behavior, a night I wouldn't soon forget.

I hoped tonight Richard would loosen up and we could have fun together. Otherwise, this might be our last date. I plastered on my best smile as I invited him in.

Lord was going a little crazy, even growling. "Lord, what's wrong with you, bud?" I pulled his collar, keeping him close to me. "I'm sorry, he's fine, I promise."

"No, that's cool. I'll wait outside. I'm not a big fan of dogs." He backed away from the door, shutting the screen door.

What kind of person doesn't like dogs? Lord busted past me outside onto the porch and kept growling at Richard, who had his hands up as he backed away. Weird, he'd never reacted this way to people.

I pulled him back in the house, scolding him for misbehaving. Lord's eyes got big and looked sad. How could I stay mad at that face? I leaned down to tell him that I would be home soon and that I loved him. I planted a huge kiss on his massive head. He nuzzled me as Richard looked at me with disgust and said, "Yuck! You just kissed that animal."

"Yes, so? Lord is like my child," I laughed. He gave me a disapproving look. I wondered what he would think of the fact that Lord slept in bed with me every night and sometimes shared my pillow?

"Bring a jacket," Richard reminded me. "It can get cold on the drive with the top down." He referred to the ridiculous convertible Mercedes parked next to my Jeep. So boring and predictable. I hoped he wasn't trying to impress me 'cause that car wouldn't do it. I grabbed my sweater and gave Lord one last goodbye. I patted his head and told him to be a good boy. His blue eyes begged me not to go.

The drive to Black Rock was about forty-five minutes. We didn't talk much because of the noise from the convertible. I was happy to arrive without too much damage to my hair. Parking was just about full at Black Rock Microbrew. I was looking forward to the deck after dinner. It was enormous and offered fantastic mountain views.

Being vegan, especially in the mountains, I didn't always have many food options when I went out. But I was able to order a fabulous plate of grilled veggies that were on kabobs over rice. Richard seemed to frown at my choice, which kind of pissed me off. I remembered how Rage was very interested in my being vegan; he asked a million questions and didn't mock my choices. I took in a breath, then let it out slowly. Yoga taught me, to each his own, live and let live. So, I wasn't one to frown disapprovingly all over his order of bloody steak. He also got a top-shelf Tennessee whiskey, neat, while I sipped on an amazing sweet strawberry maple ale.

After dinner, we searched out a spot on the deck. My stupid heels caught in the space between the boards. Thankfully, I got it out without anyone noticing. The outdoor area was expansive, with dark wood flooring and small tables everywhere. There were almost no seats open, but somehow, we were able to snag a small table close to the stage. It might have been the cash Richard handed the hostess.

An overfriendly waitress, Candy, came to take our order. She wore shorts that were more like underwear and her enormous fake boobs sprung out of her three-sizes-too-small tank. I found it slightly annoying that she not only seemed to know Richard but she repeatedly flirted with him and shoved her boobs in his face like I wasn't there.

I nursed my beer during the band's first set; they were even better than the last time I had seen them. I swayed to the cool blues sound, the purple sky behind them was a perfect backdrop to the stage. The mountain air began to chill when the sun went down. I drank a second beer, warming my body.

By the time the second set started, the place was wall to wall with people, and I felt loose and ready to dance. I was excited to see Charlene and two of her friends who take classes at Fluid. The girls hauled me out for a few songs. Richard wanted no part of the dance floor.

"You probably shouldn't spend so much time on the dance floor. You're going to get sweaty," he told me when I got back to our table. He placed a new beer in front of me, popping the top.

"I'm not sweaty, and I'm also not ready for another beer, thanks." I pushed it back toward him. He wrinkled his nose and downed another whiskey.

"You may want to slow down on those. You have to drive me home," I said as Candy The Waitress placed another glass down. "Here you go, handsome."

"I'm fine." He took my wrist and pulled me in, the whiskey greeting me. His face was now inches from mine. "You need to finish your beer. You're too uptight, loosen up."

Oh, no, he didn't! Did he just tell me I needed to loosen up? Maybe it was the alcohol, but he was being such an ass tonight. "Oh, I'm not the one who is being uptight here, Richard."

His face softened, "You're right, I'm sorry. I just wanted to make sure you are having a good time. I thought you might want another drink to feel more relaxed, that's all." He flashed me a winning smile. I gave him a fake smile and tilted my beer to him before taking a long pull, just to get him off my case. I probably needed to drink a little more so I could tolerate his arrogance for the rest of this night.

A few sips into the beer, my body was humming, the vibrations of music were taking over. I jumped off my stool and joined the girls again. I had a small giggling fit when the girls I was dancing with told some silly joke. Feeling free, I opened my arms and spun, letting the music take over and my body move to the beat. The stupid heels held me back, but I felt sexy swinging my hips to the deep baritone that was filling my ears. The music and dancing were drawing me. But then an unease began to set in as my surroundings seemed to move a little bit more slowly than normal. I really shouldn't have had that last beer.

A large hand caught mine. "Last dance, Juliet. I'm ready to get out of here." Richard pulled on my wrist. "You're all sweaty! I told you—"

"Yeah, Richard, it's summer, we're at an outdoor bar, and I was just dancing." His lip curled, "Yeah, I know."

"Ya know, we've only heard two sets?" I protested in a sing-song voice.

He looked and his watch. "The music is too loud, and it's getting late."

I rolled my eyes. What a bore. Richard didn't look tired when

Candy The Waitress came by. But I agreed, it was probably better if we ended this date sooner than later.

"Alright, let me hit the restroom first." I huffed and made my way to the ladies' room.

"Make it fast."

What the hell was his hurry? An uncomfortable racing of my heart had me stop and take a deep breath. A little wave of nausea coursed through my body and my stomach felt sour. The line for the ladies' room was so long. I groaned and fussed with my nails in boredom. I watched our table, studying Richard, who had been on his phone until Candy bounced over.

Throughout the evening, I noticed that every time I'd left him, she'd made an appearance. As I was coming out of the restroom, I saw her hand him a paper with what I was sure was her number. Then she leaned in and whispered in his ear. He laughed as he took the paper and put it in his wallet. He grinned a devilish smile as his eyes scanned her body, finally landing on her tits. Did he just lick his lips?

Oh, hell, no! Adrenaline filled me, and my already racing heart began to hammer. I could feel it in my ears. I wasn't jealous—he could take Candy The Waitress home for all I care. Spending tonight with him made me realize that I didn't even like him 'cause he was so arrogant. But I wouldn't let this asshole disrespect me and go unscathed. A sort of dizziness started as I made my way straight toward the table to give him a piece of my mind.

———

RAGE

"Here's the paperwork." Colt slapped a large yellow envelope in my hand but didn't let go. It was sealed and marked. "Do not lose this. Make sure that it gets directly to Tiny, no one else." He released it with a nod, making sure I understood.

"I know, I got it." My cell rang just before I headed out.

"Rage," I could hardly make out Tiny's voice over the music and crowd. "Yeah, bro, I can hardly hear you."

"Have you left yet?" he shouted into the line.

"No, I was just getting ready to. Why?"

"Dude, this place is wall-to-wall people. Gold Label is on special tonight. I don't think we have enough to get through. You think you might be able to swing by the warehouse on your way up and grab ten cases?"

I looked at the clock blinking 8:45. "Yeah, I can do that."

"Man, you're a life saver! Park around back, and I'll have the guys unload it for you." There was a screaming cheer in the background. "Shit, I got to go. Thanks again."

I had planned on riding my bike, but this task would give me an excuse to take Black Betty on the road. I'd missed my sleek blacked-out 1990 4x4 Dodge Dakota convertible truck. With her six-inch lift, she's a beast.

A half hour later, I was loaded up and on the road. It was a perfect night to put her top down and enjoy the ride. I blared the blues through her speakers and sang along.

Tiny wasn't kidding. It was still early, but the place was already packed. I pulled around back and began unloading the cases in the beer storage area. The employee entrance led to the kitchen, where I saw Tiny talking to a bartender. He caught my eye and waved me over.

"Rage! Brother, thanks for coming."

The man was massive. "Damn, Tiny, it looks like the brewery is doing well. Congratulations, man!"

He put his arm around my shoulder. "Let's go somewhere we don't have to yell to talk." He shouted over the music and ushered me toward his office, where we could hear each other. He shut the door and lit a smoke. He offered me one, but I declined. He poured us both a shot. We clinked our glasses together, threw it back, and slammed them empty onto the desk. "You got those papers?" He wiped his mouth with the back of his hand.

I nodded and pulled the folded envelope from inside my cut. Tiny stroked the long dark goatee on his chin as he studied the documents.

"Another?" He pointed to my empty glass.

"Yeah, thanks." The Kentucky bourbon went down smooth. He

kept the good stuff in the office. He leaned on the desk, the stacks of paper and a huge monitor not giving him much room.

"It's great to see you, man. You happy to be back?" The smoke he exhaled came out in a large white cloud. I waved it out of my face. Tiny smiled. "Sorry."

"It's great to be back. I missed a lot, but I'm catching up fast."

"When are you getting in the ring again?" He took another long drag, blowing out the smoke as he spoke. "The last event, I had to watch that asshole Ramsey kick Lorenzo Montana's ass. I thought Enzo would put up a better fight, but Ramsey killed him in the ring."

Just the reminder of Ramsey made my blood boil over again. I cracked my knuckles. "Fourth of July, the Firecracker Fights."

He slapped the side of my arm. "Damn! Good man, I love the Firecracker Fights! It hasn't been the same without you in the ring, but I heard you gave the Tennessee boys a good whopping." He whistled.

Our conversation was interrupted by tapping, then the door to the office swung open. The bartender warned, "Tiny, I think you better get out there. Some hot piece of ass is reaming out her man, and the bouncers already have their hands full."

"What else is new?" he rolled his eyes. "C'mon, Rage, back me up, and I'll buy you a beer."

We entered the dance area from the bar. A sea of people swayed their bodies and sang along to the cover of *Free Bird*. I pushed through the crowd, trying not to knock into anyone. The woman's arms were flailing as she argued with a man.

"No fucking way."

I pulled Tiny's shoulder back to get his attention. "I got this," I told him, pointing to Ramsey. Tiny nodded and moved out of my way.

"Keep it clean, Rage. I got a business to run," he warned, hollering over the loud music.

There, on the side of the dance floor, was an angry Juliet. Waving her hand in Richard's face, obviously giving him a piece of her mind. She was pointing from him to a very well-stacked waitress.

Juliet looked so fucking hot even when angry. Her black shorts showed off those lean muscular legs and her thick ass. The heels tied around her ankles were sexy as fuck and matched the pink and gold top that swayed loosely on her thin frame. A small band of her defined abs was showing as she moved. Her colorful curls bounced as she yelled.

Just looking at her made me hard. She was one beautiful woman.

I came to a stop behind her, crossing my arms, towering over her small frame. "Is there a problem here?" I asked, grinning at that asshole Ramsey over her head.

Just give me an excuse, I thought. *Go ahead, give me an excuse to punch your lights out.*

"No, no problem." He tried dismissing me and grabbed Juliet. "We were just leaving. We'll finish our night somewhere else."

She pulled away from him. Backing up, she bumped into me but still didn't turn around, continuing her rant. "The hell we are, maybe you and Big Boobs, but I'm not leaving, not with you, anyway." She shooed him with her hand. "Go have a good night, Richard," Juliet yelled over the music. Her body began to sway a little. *How much had she had to drink?*

"Dick," I said loudly. I folded my arms across my chest. "I think the lady wants you to leave." I smiled at him again, trying to antagonize him after the stunt he pulled earlier at the Pit. Juliet slowly turned around as she recognized my voice.

"Rage? What the hell are you doing here?"

"Babe, this is the run I was trying to invite you to 'cause I thought you'd like the band. But you said you already had plans."

She smiled and looked up at me with glassy eyes. Then she turned to Richard and said, "Yes, Dick, the lady wants you to leave," smiling and batting her lashes for emphasis.

Richard's face contorted, red rising up his neck from the crisp white shirt he wore. "Yeah, I don't think so," he answered in a cruel tone aimed at me. He wasn't even looking at her; he was just glaring at me.

"Juliet," I took her hand and pulled her around my back, "I would be happy to take you home now, unless you want to stay here with me and finish listening to the band a little longer."

"Why, yes, Rage, that sounds like a fantastic idea." Juliet smiled, giving Richard a pointed look.

"The fuck you are," Richard growled at Juliet. His jugular pulsed.

It took all I had not to pound his arrogant face into the bar. I ground my teeth, "Don't fucking ever talk to her disrespectfully again." I felt the muscles in my body tensing. My jaw was tight. I didn't want to start a fight in the brother's bar; Tiny wouldn't be happy if this ruined his night. There were a few more hours to rake in money.

"Want to take it outside?" I clenched my fists at my sides.

"Juliet, you want to stay here with this lowlife biker?" he spat.

She nodded, yes, moving her body closer to mine.

"Fucking whore! I can't believe I wasted time on you," he said, narrowing his eyes at Juliet. Her mouth gaped open, taken back by his words.

The surprise was apparent on his face when I spun him around and jacked him up against the wall. Anger surged through my body. We were nose to nose. "Is that how you talk to women?" I balled his shirt in my fists, holding him in place. He pushed back off the wall. I sent a punch straight to his gut. Bent over, he clutched his stomach, catching his breath. I leaned close to him.

"We can finish this," I hissed his ear, "outside." I let him go. "I won't disrespect my brother's place, and if you do, you will have a lot more to deal with than me."

Richard kicked the table over as he straightened up. "Oh, we will finish this," he said and spat, "but not tonight."

"I need to get my dick wet, and since Juliet wants to stay with the trash, I guess Candy will do." He looked toward the bosomy waitress. Her smile was large, not recognizing the insult. She dropped her tray and took his hand. "Chelsea offered to finish my shift, so what the hell," she said in a sugar-sweet southern drawl.

"Good!" Juliet yelled to him, "As if you had a chance with me tonight, or any night, you arrogant asshole!"

The bouncers led Richard out as I stood with Juliet, who was not looking so good. "You okay, babe?"

Her eyes rolled. "I'm not feeling very well...How could I actually have thought that asshole was a nice guy?" She shook and rubbed her head. "I should have known the minute he said he didn't like dogs and Lord went crazy on him."

I chuckled. "Lord didn't like him? Well, there you go, you should have sent him packing and called me." She bowed her head in defeat.

"I'm sorry, Rage. Thanks for defending me." She offered a weak smile.

"Forget it, Juliet. You are a person who sees the best in people. Don't change. Richard isn't worth it," I said as I gently pushed her toward the bar. I flagged down the bartender, ordering her a glass of water and me a beer.

"Thanks for offering to take me home," she said looking at her feet before her eyes met mine.

I nodded. "Sorry that your date turned out so bad."

She smiled, smacking my arm. "No, you are not."

"What?" I held back my smile. "I mean it, I didn't want you to have a bad night…Okay, maybe you're right." I took a swig of my beer. "I guess I'm not."

All of a sudden, she stood up. "Rage, I think I need the restroom. I'm not feeling great."

I pointed to the line around the corner, and her eyes got big. She turned and headed instead to the exit, flying out the doors. I followed her to the parking lot, where I saw her heaving behind the dumpster.

"Stay away," she said in between violent heaves.

I gave her a few moments. "Are you okay?" She didn't answer. "Juliet?"

"Rage, I'm okay. I'm going to call Ivy to get me."

"No, Juliet, I can take you home," I said while I peeked around the dumpster to make sure she was okay.

"Rage, thanks, but there is no way in hell I'm getting on a bike right now," she said coming from around the dumpster, looking unsteady.

"Babe, I have my truck. I'll take you home."

"I'm a little dizzy…my body feels strange…something's not right." She held her hand over her face.

"How much did you drink?"

"I was halfway through my third beer." Juliet moved her hand over her chest. "My heart is hammering, and I feel woozy like I'm going to pass out. Even my fingers are tingly." She looked at her hands.

"I…I…" She began to sway, and as her knees buckled. I scooped her up and carried her to my truck.

I gently placed her in the passenger side, buckling her seatbelt. I folded some paper towels, poured some bottled water on them, and placed it against her forehead.

My head was going crazy with thoughts. I clenched my jaw and fists as I rounded the truck. My ears pulsed to match my heartbeat. I slammed the door shut.

If that son of a bitch did what I thought he did, I was going to kill him. Before I even pulled out of the lot and onto the street, Juliet was out cold. She had her head on my lap and the rest of her curled up in a ball.

CHAPTER TEN

Rage

*T*he clock blinked ten. My head began to pound from lack of caffeine. I didn't know how to use that coffee thing I'd seen her use. It was time to call for backup. Ivy should be up and about by now.

I was happy Juliet didn't have her phone screen locked, yet it bothered me at the same time. She needed to think more about her safety. She was too trusting. I scrolled through her phone until I saw Ivy's name. When I pressed the number, a picture of two smiling teens appeared as the phone rang. Both wore sunglasses, embracing, heads leaned together, smiling with peace signs and matching BFF necklaces.

On the third ring, the photo vanished and Ivy's voice came on, "Hey slut, it took you long enough to call. You are supposed to call or text when you get home!" She let out a deep sigh. "Now, give me all the dirty details."

"Uh, Ivy?" I said, my deep voice catching her off guard.

"Richard?"

"No," I said sharply.

"Who's this, and why do you have my best friend's phone?" She was nervous.

"Ivy, this is Rage."

Silence.

"Ivy?"

"Umm, Rage? From the Pit?" Her voice was high.

"Yes, Rage from the Pit." I could hear her tiny squeals in the background. "Ivy... Ivy... Do you think you can come over to Juliet's? She's not feeling well, that's why I called."

"W-Wait, what? What happened to her? Is she in trouble again? What do you mean she doesn't feel well? What's wrong?" she asked with deep concern in her voice.

"Slow down, Ivy, she's okay. Just hungover, I guess you could say. I'm sure she'll fill you in when she's awake. Can you come over? I think she might need some of that green miracle juice she was telling me about, and coffee, too. I can't figure out how to use that little thing in her kitchen."

"I'm on my way. I'm leaving Fluid now. I'll stop and get juices and a vat of coffee, please don't leave my girl." I could hear her keys jingling and the keypad beeping as she activated the alarm.

"I'm not going anywhere."

"I'll be there in twenty minutes." A door slammed shut. "Call me back if you think of anything else."

While waiting for Ivy, I sent a text to Hawk letting him know that I would be at the club as soon as I could and that we needed a meeting. I had a suspicion that Richard spiked Juliet's beer with tainted X. And if I was right, he'd be fucking dead.

I quietly entered Juliet's room. Lord's head popped up, on guard. Once he saw it was me, he put his head back on Juliet's stomach and curled into her. The mattress dipped as I sat back on the bed, trying not to disturb her. A few minutes later, with her eyes shut, she began to pull at the blankets. "Lord, move over," she said in a husky sleep-filled voice.

When the blankets wouldn't cooperate, she got out of bed, and Lord jumped off, following her. She brought her hand to her forehead, squeezing her temples. Her eyes were barely open as she fumbled toward the bedroom door.

"Hold on, let me help." She must have forgotten I was here. Her head slowly turned to me, and then she looked at her tiny panties—

white and lace-topped with tiny cherries. She covered her face with her hands in embarrassment. "Rage. Oh, God. I...I don't feel so good."

"Babe, don't be shy, let me help you." I guided her the few more steps down the hall to the bathroom, and then she shut the door. I heard water running. I softly knocked on the door after a few minutes. "Juliet, are you okay?" I asked.

A soft yes came through the door.

"Ivy is on her way. She's bringing some things for you to feel better."

"Shit, I never called her last night. She must have been worried." She opened the door with a towel wrapped around her. She emerged with a washed face, hair pulled up, she smelled of mint and had an aspirin in one hand.

She disappeared into her room. A few minutes later, she appeared in a short cotton sundress. Her feet were bare, her hair was piled on her head. I was waiting in the living room when she came out holding an ice pack to her forehead.

"Rage, uh, I don't know how to ask this, but what happened when we left the Brewery? I remember you putting me in the truck...did anything...else...happen?"

"Juliet, if you're asking if something happened between us, the answer is no." I smiled to make her feel less embarrassed. "I know you haven't known me all that long, so I should tell you that I'm not the type of guy who would push himself on unconscious women."

"No, I know. Even though I've only known you for a little while, I know you're not like that. I just had to ask, you know, cause I...I just don't remember anything... nothing like this has ever happened to me before. I keep going over it in my mind, and I can't understand how I got drunk and passed out until after ten, from drinking two and a half beers.

"I don't think it was the beer," I emphasized the words hoping they would penetrate.

A puzzled look crossed her face, then it clicked.

"Motherfucker!" It came out of her mouth slowly as her arms crossed her chest. Then her anger morphed into something else, fear. In a flash, she crashed her body into mine, placing her head on my chest and her arms around my waist. "Oh, my God! Rage, what would have happened if you weren't there?" Tears began to form in her eyes.

That inner rage that earned me my name crept its way up my spine and my jaw tightened. Her embrace was so tight. I wrapped my arms around her and kissed her head. I controlled my temper, trying to calm her. I whispered into her hair, "Babe, he will pay for this."

She immediately backed away, breaking our embrace. In a shaky voice, she said, "No, Rage, please don't risk getting yourself in trouble over me. I will handle Richard. Nothing happened. I'm okay, thanks to you." Her eyes pleaded with me.

My body tensed, the fury turning my face red. "Babe, I think I should also tell you, that I'm not the type of man who would let something like this go. He could have done anything to you." I said with an even tone.

Juliet jumped as her front door swung open.

JULIET

Ivy barreled through the door, drink holders in each hand and a bag tucked to her side. One tray held four juices—two greens, a red, and an orange—and the second tray had three coffees from Roasted. The smell of coffee immediately made me feel better. Her eyes landed on me. Anger and sadness riddled her usually smiling face.

She placed everything on the table, swiping one green juice from the tray. She turned to me and hugged me tightly. She pulled back, studying my face a moment, inspecting me, before she shoved a juice in my face. "Spill. Tell me everything."

I looked at Rage, who was stirring his coffee from behind the counter. He returned my gaze and said, "Juliet, I'm going to leave you in Ivy's hands."

I nodded and was on the verge of tears again. "Don't say anything about this to anyone, except Ivy, until I figure out what to do. Understand?" I nodded again. My eyes burned as tears filled them.

Rage came around the counter, pulled me in, and gave me another big hug before kissing my head. "Shh…It's gonna be fine. You'll be alright." The comfort I felt in his embrace made me never want to let go.

"I'll be back," he said, holding one of my hands and giving it a small squeeze. "I'll text you later." He looked at Ivy, "Take good care of her. And what I said goes for you, too, Ivy. Don't say anything to nobody. No one knows about this." Ivy's face scrunched up at the order. Grabbing his coffee, he gave Lord a pat on the head before walking out the door.

When his truck's muffler was out of earshot, Ivy started with her questions. "What the hell happened last night?" She grabbed both of my hands, leading me to sit.

Ivy was the only person who knew about my past. When my eyes met hers, she knew the events of last night stirred something up. We curled up on my bed with coffee and juice. She held me and stroked my hair as I told her everything I remembered about last night.

"That bastard!" She jumped off the bed and balled her fists as she paced. "Oh, Richard is going to pay. What a fucking asshole! I cannot believe this!" Her hands were flailing dramatically. "I am so sorry I ever pushed you to date the fucker. I'm going to kill him myself," she said with an exhausted breath.

"Ivy, thank you. I love you and I know how much you want to do something, but Rage and I are going to handle this." Skepticism was written all over her face. "I just don't know what would have happened if Rage wasn't there. I'm so embarrassed." I put my head down looking away from her. I played with the strings that edged my favorite blanket.

"Embarrassed? Why the fuck would you be in embarrassed?" She crossed her arms and narrowed her eyes. "This was not your fault. That asshole is the one who should be embarrassed."

"Thanks, girl. I think I'm just going to take a hot bath and drown in essential oils to calm me right now. I have a horrible headache," I said, rubbing my temples. "Thank you so much for coming and bringing me everything to make me feel better and for being the best friend a girl could ever have."

"You would do the same for me." Ivy smiled. "Now, take your bath, and I'll make you something to eat when you get out."

Filling the tub, I heard the soft blues coming through the speakers over clanging pots and pans in the kitchen. I didn't deserve such a beautiful and fierce friend. I inhaled the bath oils rising from the steam and submerged myself in the barely tolerable water. I leaned back, covering my eyes with a mask. From the moment they closed, Rage was all I could see. The hot water could not temper the goosebumps that spread over my skin.

RAGE

I called a club meeting and asked anyone who could attend to be there. I was so angry I could barely think straight. Juliet was in such a vulnerable situation last night. My mind was racing, wondering what the hell that asshole would have done to her if I hadn't shown up. He had to have drugged her. The club had been looking into someone who had been supplying Ecstasy to the Sugar Maple and Black Rock area. This stuff was nasty. I'd already heard of two cases of women ending up hospitalized.

We sat around the large woodgrain table that had the Stained Souls MC logo etched into it. Colt pounded the gavel; its deep thump brought everyone's chatter to silence.

"I'm glad you all got your asses over here. It seems we have some information that we need to hear." He pointed at me. "Rage, you want to share what happened?"

I nodded and looked around the table, making sure I had everyone's attention. "As you all know, we have been having issues with drugs coming into Sugar Maple and Black Rock. Ecstasy and meth in particular. There were a few college girls who ended up in the hospital."

"Yeah, we know, Rage. So, what happened?" Hack asked looking tired and a bit hungover.

"I was getting to it." I snapped back. "Last night, I went to help out Tiny. While I was there, Tiny and I were called to break up an argument between a couple—it was Juliet and that fuckface Richard Ramsey," I said with more disdain than I knew I had. A few of my brothers grimaced. No one liked the guy.

"After a minor scuffle with Richard, I had Juliet back at the bar for some water. She seemed off. She only had a few drinks, but she was sick. Dizzy, heart pounding, nausea. She said she only had two beers and just started her third." Before I continued, I could already see their faces changing as the conclusion was forming. "Anyway, she said she didn't feel right and took off like a bat out hell for the door, where she began getting sick behind the dumpster." I let out a deep sigh. "A few minutes later she was in my truck out cold, dead to the world. It was ten hours before she woke up. I'm sure her drink had been spiked, by Ramsey or someone else. She said he was trying to force-feed her the last beer."

"Fuck," Ledger growled, his eyebrows drawing together as his fist pounded so hard on the table, it made the ashtray jump. That got my attention. I knew he and Juliet were friends, but he seemed extra pissed.

Hawk stood, both hands rested on the table as he leaned his big body, looking straight at Colt. Anger filled his voice as he spoke. "If that motherfucker drugged our Juliet and thought he could get away with it, he's fucked."

Hack rubbed his eyes and piped up, "It makes sense. He could have something to do with the influx of drugs. When I was asking around, I found out that few members of the Devil's had some dealings with Ramsey. Big Jake, the mechanic at A&G Garage, said Ramsey met with some bikers, and Big Jake thought it was one of us at first, until he saw their cuts. He said Ramsey acted all skittish after that meeting. He wouldn't say any more, said he didn't want to be involved in anything the Devil's Damned had going on. I also discovered that Ramsey had been supplying steroids to some of the athletes at the university."

A grumble sounded around the table. Men were talking over each other in heated conversations. Colt slammed the gavel down, its vibrations silencing everyone.

"Enough!" Lighting a smoke, he continued, squeezing the cigarette between his tattooed fingers, "Sounds like we have a big problem on our hands. If he is working with the Devil's, then we need to know. They are distributors down the line for a major Columbian cartel. I thought the only chapters they had involved were in Florida. It looks like they could be expanding their territory."

He took a long drag, exhaling the cloud of white smoke away from the table. "If we want to keep this shit from our door, we have to act fast. We need proof and real intel. I know you all have a soft spot for Juliet, but we have to be smart about this."

He pointed around the table and spoke in a slow, threatening tone. "No one is to go after Ramsey, you all understand?" Colt's dark blue eyes fixed on mine and then on Ledger's. He pointed at us, making sure we got the message.

"We can't go at this blind. As hard as it is, you all have to act like nothing is suspicious. If Ramsey is involved with a cartel, then he has no idea he's in some deep shit. Keeping them out of Sugar Maple won't be easy, but our three closest chapters should be more than willing to step in if need be."

My inner rage swelled in my chest as I stood crossing my arms over my chest. "I'm supposed to let go what Ramsey fuckin' did to her? Or could have done to her? So I see him at the Pit and I act like nothing? What about other girls he could do this to or did this to? Ivy or any of your baby sisters?" Hawk's face twisted when Ivy's name came out of my mouth.

Colt stood and got right in my face. "Rage, I know you have been in Tennessee for a long time. I'm not sure how they run things over there, but around here, I am your Pres, and you will respect that and do as I say." His face was now only inches from mine. His graying facial hair reminded me of how long he had been at this and that he was right. He was the president, and I had to respect that, even when I didn't agree with him.

"Fine, but come the Fourth of July fights, he will feel my wrath. I'll make him fuckin' pay." The group of men all cheered, and Hawk patted my back.

"Fuckin' right," Leo agreed. "You two will be the main event: Rage versus Ramsey. Wipe the floor with him. Revenge is best served in the octagon." Another round of cheers from the men.

Colt hit the gavel. "Alright, we are going to get to the bottom of this. Hack, you and I need to do some homework before we go any further. Anyone hears anything, you bring it here to church, got it?"

With nods around the room, he banged the gavel for the last time, dismissing us.

CHAPTER ELEVEN

Rage

"*D*anny, hand me a wrench from the bench over there."

"What?" he shouted. "The wrench," I yelled over the music vibrating the through the garage. I had been working on Black Betty for the past few weeks as a distraction to keep myself from constantly wanting to spend time with Juliet. Agreeing to be friends had been proving difficult. I had hoped that by now I would have convinced her to at least go on one date with me. How she got me so twisted up, I didn't know. She had stirred things in me I didn't know existed.

It had been entertaining having her around and spending time with her and Lord. I'd even come to appreciate Ivy and her smartass mouth. We spent most nights hanging out at Juliet's house. She didn't like leaving Lord. I didn't blame her. He always seemed so sad when she left him.

I'd been a loner for so long, I'd forgotten what it felt like to have someone else to think about other than myself. The quiet evenings we spent together at her home had been the best nights of my life. She always made something unbelievable in her small kitchen. Pots, pans, and veggies sprawled from counter to counter as she made her creations. Most meals, I forgot that I was eating meat-free. I even enjoyed our debates about that. When she'd explained her views about Earth and meat consumption and their effect on the environment, it made me look at everything a little differently.

After tightening the last few bolts, I shoved all the tools back in their places and cleaned my station. I wiped the area down with the new washable towels I bought so that I wouldn't use so many disposable paper towels. I got the guys these bins to keep the clean and dirty ones separate; we washed them all once a week.

Juliet had been rubbing off on me. I'd been telling the guys to recycle, and I'd been picking through the trash when I noticed bottles in it. I knew I was fucked when my energy was zapped mid-afternoon at the Pit, and instead of guzzling an energy drink, I found myself at Juiced. I didn't even think about it, I just went. I ordered this gross-looking green drink that Juliet always got. It looked like glowing green slime, but it tasted amazing, like lime and pineapple. It wasn't the drink that had me scratching my head—I left there with a veggie burger and kombucha, and I wasn't entirely sure how that happened.

The boys thought I'd grown a pussy. Fuck, I never thought I'd see the day. They would laugh at me, but when she brought dark chocolate peanut butter protein brownies to the Pit, they all begged for more.

I would have bet my life that no woman could ever have that kind of influence over me. Juliet's goodness shined so brightly, and I couldn't help but want to be around her and be part of her passions.

I glanced at the dust-coated clock on the garage wall. Shit, I had to get out of here if I wanted to get to the Pit. Leo and Shelly wanted to have the night off. I hoped Juliet was still there.

———

JULIET

I rolled out my mat, stretched, and did several sun salutations. I moved into some deep leg stretches, preparing my body for kicks. The Pit was pretty quiet, so I turned up my music and began my private practice.

I thought of Rage with every kick I threw. Over the past month, Rage had wormed his way into my life, and I was so glad he had. We had enjoyed many nights laughing, talking, and eating. I didn't think he would agree to be just friends. I hadn't yet come to terms with how much I had come to like him. I'd found myself dropping by the Pit at the times I thought he would have been here. I'd been wrestling with my feelings. I knew I wanted him. There was no denying the sexual tension between us. I had never felt so attracted to someone. All it took was a whiff of his aftershave, and I'd find myself needing a new pair of panties. God, how did this happen? No matter how much I wanted him in my bed or in my life, I couldn't let this…thing…between us go on any farther. I couldn't let myself fall. I couldn't take that risk. I couldn't drag Rage into my bullshit.

Maybe I should go out on a date with someone fun and put some needed distance between Rage and me. I could do that. Perhaps if I were dating someone else, it would lessen the tension between us. Yes, I could do that. I'd go out with the next decent guy who'd ask me. That would make Ivy happy even though she thought I should give Rage a chance. After her advice on Richard, I thought I should hold off on looking to her for advice.

The empty room at the Pit was perfect and I tried to focus on my kicks. I had been trying to perfect a butterfly kick for the past few weeks. It was way more complicated than I thought. With my gymnastics background and all the yoga, I thought I could get this quickly. Wrong.

Stretching my body, I tried it again. Lowering down, swinging my body around, I moved my other leg straight up before throwing the kick.

"Fuck yeah!" I yelled when I landed the kick perfectly. I did a happy dance, bouncing up and down at my accomplishment. I beamed with pride with a smile I couldn't contain. Four freaking weeks of practice and I finally got it!

A loud, slow clap came from the doorway. I swiveled around to see who my spectator was. My eyes met Joey. The Weapon is what they called him, and I extended him a playful bow.

"Juliet, that was freakin' awesome! Not many people can perform a butterfly kick like that," he said, smiling.

"Why, thank you, Joey. I've been practicing for weeks. I think my foot could be a little straighter, but I'm getting there," I said with a super cheesy grin, trying not to seem too excited. "My next attempt will be takedowns," I declared emphatically.

"Well, you will need a partner for those, you know?" He grinned, his white teeth gleamed.

"Yeah, I guess you're right. I'm sure Leo could teach me if he could squeeze me in another slot."

"Ow, I'm hurt," he said, holding his hand over his heart, his bicep bulging. "Juliet, haven't you seen me fight? I'm a takedown expert. Why do you think they call me The Weapon?" he said in a not-so-humble tone.

"I don't want to take up your gym time, Joey, but I appreciate the offer," I said, smiling at his hopeful look. His blue eyes met mine with warmth. He flipped his long blond hair away from his face, which featured some light blond stubble covering his sharp jawline. I'd never really looked at him before, but he sure was handsome.

He took one of my hands, placed it in his gigantic palm, and kissed the top, "It would be my pleasure." I blushed. What should I say? I opened my mouth and managed to stutter out, "Oh…uh…O-Okay, if you're sure."

He smiled at me in a way that seemed to say I've no idea what I've gotten myself into. "Well, since you are dishing out yeses, maybe you will say yes to a drink with me on Wednesday after class?"

I was surprised, but I thought maybe it was a sign. "Ah, yeah, okay, Wednesday after class."

"You have time for a lesson now?" he asked.

"I have another twenty minutes in this private room."

"Okay, then. Let's get to work. Have you ever done a clinch hold?"

"No, I can't say I have. How does it work?"

He moved his body close to mine, showing me as he explained, "A clinch is a position where competitors try to control each other's bodies by wrapping their arms around one another, fighting for good arm and hip position." He placed his hands on my hips. "It's a good way to take down someone who's bigger than you."

We began working in a position that felt like a hug but without affection.

He explained each step thoroughly as we moved our bodies. The scent of his cologne was subtle, light and sexy. I laughed once when his stubble tickled my arm. His massive arms pulsed with muscles, and he had a vein that ran from his shoulder to his wrist.

As we got to our closest position yet, the music suddenly died, and then a booming voice, "What is going on in here?"

Fuck. Rage.

———

RAGE

I took the shortest route possible to get to the Pit. I did not want to miss Juliet. I had been paying more attention to her habits, and if I was correct, she would be there practicing right now.

As I drove, my mind flashed back to her small body curled in her bed next to me while I watched her drug-induced sleep wear off. She looked so vulnerable. Stripped away was her usual bravado of acting like she didn't need anyone.

Since the night I first met her, I'd not been able to get her out of my mind. The more time we spent together, the stronger the pull had become. Like a movie replaying in my mind, I'd been seeing her smiling face all the time. I felt like such a pussy. She was wearing down the walls I had spent years carefully building. Before her, I didn't care about anyone. I had fun, no attachments.

Juliet made me want to say fuck it and risk a chance at happiness. She made me laugh, not many people do. Her caring nature, her attitude, her looks, everything about her drew me in. The more I knew her, the harder it was to stay away. When I saw Ledger get as angry as he did over what happened, I wanted to attack my brother. I knew that look, that feeling. She was an extraordinary woman, and he knew it, too.

I didn't know if there was any history there, but I didn't think I could take knowing she was with a brother. Every part of me wanted her. I'd be damned if I was going to let anyone get in the way. Richard was now out, thank fuck.

I looked at my watch as I made my way through the Pit. I followed the music—I'd recognize her music anywhere, even with the door closed, the pounding beat of her playlist floated down the hall.

I was feet away from the door, and I could see through the window. The vein on my neck pulsed. My fists clenched at my sides, sending blood surging through my veins.

Fucking Joey, teaching Juliet the clinch. What the fuck? No. Fucking. Way. I stormed into the room. Both their heads were in a lock facing the floor. The music kept them from hearing me. My feet pounded across the floor to the speaker. I twisted the volume knob hard, cutting the music off. All that was left was my voice, booming across the room.

"What's going on in here?"

Shocked, Juliet and Joey abruptly broke apart. My eyes moved from him to her. Juliet was in those second-skin yoga pants that make her ass look like a juicy fucking peach. Her tank top barely contained her cleavage, it had me wondering how Joey wasn't supporting a fucking tent in his shorts.

They both looked at me saying different things at the same time. Juliet's shoes squeaked on the wood floor as she took a few steps toward me. "Rage," she smiled, "Joey offered to help me learn some takedown moves."

"We were practicing the clinch," she said, looking at Joey for confirmation that she said the word right. My jaw ticked as my eyes went to Joey.

"She's a quick study," Joey said winking at her.

"I'm sure she is, but that isn't happening," I said sternly.

Her eyebrows shot up, and she opened her mouth, but before she could speak, I began tearing Joey a new one. "You are not certified as a trainer here. Our insurance doesn't cover people who aren't certified to instruct."

"But you never seemed to care before, us guys do it all the time." He looked confused.

"Am I not being clear? *You* are not training *her*."

"Juliet, if you want to learn, you have to follow the rules. Leo or I can instruct you."

She bit her lip and nodded. Her eyes shot daggers at me, but she kept quiet. She turned to Joey. Her hand grasped his bicep, running her hand over it. "Joey, thanks so much for the offer. I appreciate the help. Maybe we can train another time, outside the gym."

She said that last part looking at me, not Joey. My face hardened as I ground down on my teeth. Joey stood there smiling, under her spell, agreeing. "Anytime, doll."

She kept her hand on his arm as she walked him to the door and thanked him again. "So, I'll see you Wednesday night for class and dinner after?" He flicked his finger under her chin like they were the only two in the room.

She nodded, "Yep." She closed the door, turning her angry attention my way. She stomped the twenty feet to where I stood. She looked so damn hot mad.

My arms folded across my chest. "What?" I asked. "It's true. There's a rule against training without being certified."

"Since when?" Her eyes squinted. "You are acting like a big possessive asshole. You have no right. Rage, we are only friends, remember?"

"And, Wednesday night ain't happening either, so you should cancel your plans." Possession laced my tone.

"Oh, yeah? And why not?" She folded her arms across her chest. The move pushed her perfect breasts up even further out of her sports bra. I watched the fabric as it stretched, and I almost forgot my words. She waved her hand in my face. "My face is up here, Rage!" she said pointing to her nose.

I cleared my throat, embarrassed she caught me, but who could blame me?

"We are having a Pit meeting. All instructors are required to attend. That is what I was coming to tell you."

I wondered whether she was buying this. I tried to read her expression. Her eyes squinted as she tilted her head, looking skeptical.

Taking a deep breath, I said, "Look, Juliet, I'm not going to lie, I don't want anyone's hands on you. Here or on a date. You may not be able to admit it yet, but something is happening here." I wagged my finger between us. I tried to grab her hand, but she stepped back. "We really do have a meeting, though. It's mandatory." Fuck, Leo was going to kill me. I hoped he and Shelly didn't have plans and they could back me up on this.

"Rage," she poked her finger on my chest, "not you," she poked harder, "or anyone else is going to tell me what to do, got it?" She huffed spinning on her heel.

Even though she was acting mad, I saw through her. She loved knowing I didn't want her with someone else, I could see it in her eyes.

"See you at the 'meeting' on Wednesday," she said with air quotes. She gathered her things and walked right past me out the door. Like I wasn't even standing there.

CHAPTER TWELVE

Juliet

I wiped the beads of water that collected against the pane of glass. All my windows were fogged up from the past four days of rain. Through the smudged finger trails, I saw my gardens were drowning. Streams of water spilled over and ran down onto the ground, creating large puddles.

I had already battened down everything that threatened to run its way down the mountain. My yoga swing and mats and all cushions from outside were stacked inside, cluttering up the tiny mudroom.

A blue light flashed through the room, causing me to jump. Moments like these were a little lonely and scary being up here by myself. Lord helped me feel not alone. Though, at times, it would be nice to have strong arms holding me instead of just paws.

Throwing the remote at the couch, I turned off the news, annoyed when the weatherman said two more days of rain with severe winds and flash floods. Storms were frequent this time of year, but this had been downright depressing. You couldn't get out of the house without being soaked; trees were down, and debris was carried by the wind. I needed to bathe in the sun's golden rays to keep me balanced. Extended periods of gloomy weather made feel depleted and sad.

Yesterday, I braved the weather and stocked up on snacks for the weekend. I bought loads of binge-watching goodies. Popcorn, nuts, nachos, pizza, and a few bottles of wine. The organic vineyard that had a stand at the farmer's market was running a special at the grocery store because the farmer's market had closed due to the weather. Wine sale! I guess I should be that happy about that.

I planned to curl up with Lord and watch *Vikings*. Ivy had been harassing me to watch it. She seemed to have an obsession with big, scary men. That reminded me of someone...Ugh!

Get him out of your head! Just friends—that is what you told him. It's for the good of you both.

I hadn't spoken to Rage since that impromptu meeting he called at the Pit, which caused me to cancel my date with Joey.

I pulled my knees to my chest, trying not to freak out as banshee winds pounded the rain against the side of the house. The tin roof absorbed no sound; the drops pecked at it with nonstop tapping.

The lights flickered. *Damn*. It looked more like night than late morning. All my solar lights were dark after the past four days with no sun. I scrambled around the house searching for candles and flashlights. *Shit*. I flinched as lightning cracked and illuminated in jagged spears. Thunder vibrated through the house, rattling the old windows. Lord came to my side, looking nervously at me. "It's okay, boy." I kneeled and squeezed him. Thank God he's not afraid of storms. My house went dark for several seconds, two flashes, then the lights came back on. I had just set my phone to charge when it lit up and chimed with a text from Ivy.

Ivy: Are you okay up there?

Me: Yes, but I'm not going to lie, it's getting pretty scary. The lights keep going out.

Ivy: I lost power, I'm at Stained, luckily their side of the street still has power.

Me: Good idea. I was going to check on you.

Ivy: Want me to send a hot biker up to get you and Lord?

Me: Haha funny! I have a date with Vikings...and wine.

Ivy: Yes! You better text me after each episode <cheesy grin emoji>

Me: K. Be safe. If the power doesn't come back to the building, let me know where you are staying. I'd invite you here, but I don't know how the road up the mountain is.

Ivy: K. Have fun watching. Try not to lick your TV lol <tongue emoji>

Me: You are awful. Going to take a nap and then binge.

Ivy: Love you! Have hot dreams!

Me: <eye roll emoji>

RAGE

I'd been hunkering down these past few days, working in the garage, trying to keep out of the nonstop rain. All the brothers around here were miserable when they couldn't ride their bikes. I'd had enough of everyone. I'd been holed up in my room since last night. Been staring at the ceiling for so long, I had every crack memorized. I felt stir crazy. A whole brotherhood, girls, and booze were outside my door, yet I didn't feel like bothering with any them.

The blues softly played, the melody mixing with the wind. I was just about to drift off when a knock tapped at the door.

"Yeah," I yelled, not bothering to move from my bed.

A sugar-sweet voice came through the thick wooden door. "Rage," clearing her throat, speaking louder, "sweetie, do you want some company?"

Leann. She and I had spent a few nights together since I'd been back. Hell, I might be crazy about Juliet, but she had told me on several occasions that we could only be friends. *A man has needs*, I reasoned. Did I close my eyes and wished it was Juliet? Every fucking time. Maybe that was wrong and unfair to Leann, but I couldn't exactly control where my thoughts went. Since the day I laid eyes on Juliet, she had consumed my thoughts.

Even though I had agreed to only friendship, I still wanted her. I wanted that girl so bad it took everything I had some days not to go to her and make her mine. Juliet may have insisted on wanting to be friends, but her lips told lies. Her eyes held the truth—they were filled with the same need and desire that filled mine.

"Rage," Leann called again, my name lingering in her southern drawl. I took a deep breath as I contemplated whether to let her in. Maybe I did need to keep Juliet out of my head. Leann could make me forget a least for a little while, or at least pretend. I could hear her nails tapping against the wood, waiting for me to invite her in. Lighting flashed and the lights flickered. Fuck it. "Come in."

The door opened, revealing the red-haired beauty. As far as biker hang-arounds go, Leann was hot. She was no club whore, but I knew she had been with a few of the guys. She had been after me since I'd come home. She wanted to be some biker's "old lady," that part was obvious. The problem was, Leann wasn't Juliet.

I waved her in. She closed the door behind her and leaned her back against it, clicking the lock. Her gaze devoured me, her smile was predatory.

I smiled at her, admiring her easy-access short skirt and knee-high boots. They were shiny black leather with a spiked heel that clicked as she walked. She swayed her hips seductively as she came and stood at the foot of my bed. Lust filled her eyes.

Her white shirt was tied up under her massive fake tits. It was unbuttoned to display her ample cleavage. Her makeup was heavy. Her eyes looked like a cat's, outlined in thick black. Her long lashes were as fake as her tits, and her lips were an unnatural shade of cherry. She looked more like she belonged on a pole than in my bed.

Leann took a few more steps and came up beside me. She placed her hand on my bare chest, her long pointed red nails matching her lips. Her finger traced its way down, stopping at the waistband of my growing sweatpants. "Missed you, handsome," she purred.

She sat beside me on the bed, crossing her thin legs, giving me a peek of red lace under her skirt. "Why are you hiding out in here?" she pouted. "I haven't seen you in over a week." She ran her finger back and forth across my waistband. She placed her lips against my stomach, leaving a red print behind.

Then my phone vibrated. I sat up and saw Hawk's name on the screen. "Sorry, sugar, I gotta take this." Leann looked annoyed, but whatever.

"What's up Hawk? I'm kind of busy." My hand skimmed up and down Leann's thigh. She placed her hand under my waistband and walked her fingers down at a slow pace.

"Ooohhh, and who are you busy with?" he asked like a fucking schoolboy.

The lights flickered again as the thunder boomed through the room. Leann jumped, acting scared.

"None of your damn business," I said back sternly.

"Okay, okay, geez."

"Did you need something?" I was getting impatient.

"Oh, right, I was calling to see if you wanted to take Black Betty for a ride up to check on Juliet. Ivy said her power kept going out and she's all alone in this storm. But it's okay, I'll send Ledger up to do it."

My hand pulled away from Leann like I just touched a hot stove.

"The fuck you will," I growled. *Did I just growl at him?*

"Did you just growl at me?" Hawk asked with a chuckle. "Oh, so you want to check in on her? I don't want to disturb you, being busy and all."

I stood up, moving away from Leann, who still had her hand in my pants. I looked out the window, bright blue and white spiders of lightning flashing through it.

"I'm on my way," I said, then hung up. Ledger? Fuck no, he wasn't sending him.

"Leann, sorry, sweetheart, I gotta go. Club business." I pulled on a tight black Stained Souls T-shirt, wiping the lipstick from my stomach.

"You have to go? Right now?" she protested, "But there's a horrible storm out there. You would be safer here, with me, in bed." She batted her eyes and puffed out her bottom lip, patting her hand on the mattress. "Maybe a quickie?"

There had been a time when I would have begged to be with someone as sexy as Leann. But somehow messy buns, loose sweats, tight white tanks, and Converse had become way more seductive to me now. Even hotter were Juliet's dark pink eyeglasses that made her look like a sexy librarian.

"I said, I have business," I stressed, hurrying around my room pulling out jeans and socks.

Her head hung in defeat, but only for a second before her inner bitch came out. "Fine, I guess I'll find someone else who needs some company."

"That would be great, actually," I said. With a deep huff, she straightened her skirt and tossed her hair over her shoulder. Nose in the air, she trotted out of the room, slamming the door behind her.

It took only seconds to change into my favorite worn-style jeans, apply my favorite aftershave, and head out the door.

The rain relentlessly spattered on the windshield. I could barely make out the narrow road. I drove slowly up the mountain. Trees were bending in the wind, looking like they were about to snap. The drive, which usually took me ten minutes on my bike, had taken almost thirty minutes before the small cabin came into view.

———

JULIET

Lord was barking crazy next to me and woke me from my nap. I sat up groggy. How long was I out?

"Lord, calm down. What's wrong?" The headlights streamed through my bedroom window, breaking through the darkness. What the...? Who could be here now? In this weather? I pushed the sheer back. A black truck with big fat tires and a lift, Black Betty. Warmth immediately spread through me. I sprung up from the bed, sprinting to the door.

I caught my reflection in the hall mirror. Ugh, I was a mess. I threw on my glasses and then tugged the swollen door open. A gust of wind nearly pulled the door from its hinges, but luckily a big strong hand stopped it.

"Get in!" I yelled as the rain blew into the house. Running the short distance from the driveway to the cabin had him soaked to the bone.

"Rage, what are you doing here? You're drenched." I took off to the bathroom and grabbed a clean towel from the closet. When I returned with it, I found him kneeling on the floor, Lord licking the drips from his face.

"I heard you were having power issues and Hawk suggested, since I have a truck with meaty tires that can get through anything, I should check on you." He ran the towel over his face and his head. I inhaled the scent of his cologne mixed with the organic smell of summer rain.

"Oh, thanks, but you didn't have to do that." I felt a little stupid and disappointed that he was here only because Hawk had made him come.

He looked edible. Dripping. Delicious. His dark hair formed a damp curl on his forehead. Devastatingly sexy. Kicking off his boots at the door, he draped the towel around his neck. I couldn't help but watch him. His eyes caught mine, and I quickly looked away and moved into the living room.

"Make yourself comfortable. Want a beer?"

"Sure," he said, looking around the place. "You get everything in okay? Need me to do anything?"

"It's sweet of you to ask, but I got it all, thanks." I smiled, grateful for the offer.

"Are you really okay living up here by yourself even in this kind of weather?" He leaned back on the sofa, putting both his hand behind his head.

"Yes, Rage, I'm a big girl. Lord and I have made it through plenty of storms up here. The worst part is the mud that Lord tracks in. Having white everything can be an issue." I pointed to the towels on the floor near the back door.

"Rage, I appreciate your checking on me, but I'm fine. I don't want to keep you from things you have to do." A crack of lightning struck a nearby tree, which made me jump and splash him with the beer I was trying to hand him.

"Really? You seem just fine." He said wiping the liquid from his jeans.

"Sorry." I shrugged my shoulders. A deep baritone of thunder rumbled followed by the lights blinking on and off again.

"Well, maybe you could stay for another beer?" I huddled on the couch close to him as the sky flashed like a laser show.

———

RAGE

Juliet looked so fucking cute trying to act all tough behind those sexy little glasses. When she opened the door, I could tell she was relieved to have someone here. Like always, she looked gorgeous even with her hair in a messy bun, her little glasses, and no makeup. Her oversized sweats fell loose on her hip bones and looked sexy paired with the tiny cropped shirt that said, "Save a Horse. Ride a Cowboy."

A burst of wind carried her scent of fresh laundry with a hint of honeysuckle, which was better than any expensive perfume if you asked me. Her feet were bare, except for her painted toes and gold toe rings. I don't know how she made ordinary clothes look so damn sexy.

She seemed disappointed when I said Hawk suggested I check on her. The truth was, I had planned on coming up later this afternoon when the worst of the storm was due to come through. There was no way I was leaving Juliet by herself, but she didn't need to know that.

Candles burned around the small home, giving a cozy feel. When the lights went out, it was a perfect excuse for her to let me stay longer.

"Is my being here ruining your plans for riding out the storm?" I noticed the bottles of wine on the counter and the stack of DVDs.

"No, I'm glad to have the company," she said. "I bought loads of food and wine. Lord and I were going to binge-watch a series." She moved around the counter, sliding the bottle of Moscato in front of her. She reached up and pulled the bottle opener from a hook, exposing most of her stomach. The jewel in her belly button sparkled from the candle in front of her.

"You're welcome to stay and hang out if you don't have anywhere to be." She placed two glasses in front of her, filling one with wine and one with a beer.

Great. I was going to be in for a chick flick marathon. But she did say food, so maybe it wouldn't be so bad, plus there was Juliet in candlelight.

"What are you going to watch?" I asked, preparing for the worst.

"Ivy has been bugging me nonstop to watch…" Oh, boy, here it comes. "*Vikings.*"

"*Vikings?*" I loved that show. I saw the first few episodes before my cable was cut.

"I hear it's somewhat violent but the fight scenes are supposed to be good." My relief must have shown on my face.

"You thought I was going to say *Gilmore Girls*, didn't you? Don't lie." She gave me a sideways smile and poked my chest playfully.

"Something like that," I said, smiling.

"Well, I hope you like beer, wine, nachos, popcorn, and homemade pizza, 'cause I had planned on eating and watching a lot. I got nothing until Monday other than staying out of this rain."

That sounded fucking perfect. "Count me in."

"I'll make popcorn. You get comfy."

She popped a DVD in the player and turned on the large flat screen, which seemed out of place in her earthy cabin. She placed our glasses and a massive bowl of popcorn on the handmade wooden coffee table. We put on the first episode. Lord jumped between us on the sofa.

We watched one episode after another. After five episodes, we were practically cuddling as she tucked her head in my chest during the many gruesome scenes. I could see myself doing more of this. I knew I was falling for her, and this friendship I had agreed to was killing me.

"You cheating bastard!" she yelled at the screen, "I cannot believe him! Lagertha should kick her ass and his!"

"Well, Lagertha is a badass and could definitely kick her ass, but she couldn't take Ragnar."

"Oh, really?" She pursed her lips and narrowed her eyes. "Maybe sometime we will test your theory."

We were a few episodes into the second season and had finished way too many nachos. Pausing the TV between episodes, Juliet was up and down refilling our drinks and making giant plates of nachos. An episode in the second season ended, "We have to stop" she said, "it's getting late."

I shook my head no. "One more." The rain was still falling at a considerable rate. We had a few more blinks but never actually lost power.

"You're welcome to stay here if you don't have to be back. We can watch until we can't anymore," she suggested, pulling out a soft fuzzy blanket and covering us.

She didn't need to ask me twice. Maybe a little too eagerly, I said, "I can stay." I slid the blanket up further. "As long as you're making me an amazing breakfast."

"Of course, I will," she said, smiling, then she pointed to the remote. "Now hit play!"

We pulled an all-nighter watching a few seasons and fell asleep together on the sofa.

JULIET

I woke up with my legs tangled under a massive thigh. I twisted slightly, maneuvering my body from under his weight. Rage looked so at peace sleeping, not like the weight of the world was on his shoulders. The usual crease in his brow was smooth, and his ruggedly beautiful face was relaxed. Realizing that Lord needed to go out, I unwrapped my body from his and snuck around the room.

Still freaking raining. Ugh. What the hell? I ushered Lord out and back in quickly. How late were we up last night? I had a bit of a headache from the wine. Coffee, it was the perfect remedy. It only took moments for the aroma to permeate the room.

I inventoried the ingredients for pancakes. Yep, got everything. And vegan sausage, too. I was folding the blueberries into the batter when a sleepy-eyed Rage entered the kitchen. My mouth went dry and my spoon stopped. He was shirtless. His eight pack was on full display. He stretched his arms above his head grasping the doorway in a stretch. How could any man look that delicious when he'd just woken up? Before he said anything, I handed him a cup of the sweet, creamy liquid gold exactly the way I knew he liked it. Appreciation spread across his face as he took a sip, humming in pleasure. The sound he made had me crossing my legs. He pushed back the long curls behind his ears, taming them. Smiling, he looked at the batter and preheating griddle.

"Are we having pancakes?" His grin reminded me of a little boy.

I pointed to the maple syrup and plates on the table. Green juice shots and fruit set beside them. "I hope you don't mind blueberry? I have tons of my wild berries in the freezer."

He yawned, pulling the antique wooden chair from the table and sat down. "Blueberry is my favorite," he confirmed in a sexy sleep-filled rasp and took another sip of his coffee.

He pointed at the small shot glasses filled with dark green liquid. "What are those?"

"It's my 'I drank too much wine last night' remedy," I explained with a laugh. "Trust me, it's good, you don't even taste the green, I swear." I crossed my heart.

"Okay, since you are making me blueberry pancakes and coffee—"

"And vegan sausage," I added.

"And vegan sausage?" he repeated.

"You will love it all, I promise." I poured a second cup from my press and placed it on the small table.

When the stacks of pancakes were done, I plated it all up, and we sat down clinking our green shots together—juiced kale and fruit, blended with cayenne pepper and lemon.

"Cheers."

As the glasses smacked the table, he said, "That was good, and you totally could not taste the green, but should I ask why my mouth is on fire?" He raised an eyebrow.

I started choking from uncontrollable laughter. Tears ran down my cheeks. "Cayenne. It's the secret hangover ingredient. I guess I should have mentioned it." Now we were both laughing.

I watched as he dug into the fluffy cakes, his eyes closed when he took the second bite. The whole stack was gone in minutes.

"That was amazing, even the sausage and green poison, I mean juice." I threw the kitchen towel at him.

―――――

RAGE

When I walked into the kitchen, Juliet was stirring batter, sipping coffee, and singing quietly to the low music she had playing. I had never seen a sight so beautiful. I didn't want to be anywhere else in the world. Then she handed me the heavenly cup of coffee, exactly the way I liked it. She remembered. Fuck, I loved that.

Memories came hard and fast at the smell of sugar maple syrup and wild blueberry pancakes. For a moment, I was nine again.

When she broke out in hysterical laughter after we had our juice shots, I made a decision. I didn't care how fucking long I had to wait, she was going to be mine. Her laughter had lit a fire in me that I thought had long been smothered out. A tiny ember had been stoked and nourished by Juliet. It was like being brought back to life. If being her friend felt this amazing, how would it feel to be with her? I was determined to find out. I knew she felt it, too. I could see the way she looked at me.

We took turns showering and then met in the living room for another round of binge-watching. Juliet emerged from her room in fuzzy slippers and an oversized Stained Skyn shirt that hid her cut-off jean shorts. Her hair was wet and piled on her head, and her golden legs were shimmering. I breathed in her signature honeysuckle scent. As for me, well, I always carried an overnight bag in my truck and bike, just in case I needed to land somewhere a few days.

I joined her on the sofa. "We only have two episodes left in this season. Do you want to watch them now?" she asked.

"Fuck yeah, I want to watch them now." I pulled the fuzzy blanket over us. Lord sat on Juliet's feet, curled in a ball.

She covered her eyes and hid her face during a few particularly violent scenes. But then we got to some fight scenes that we just had to scrutinize, both of us being trained MMA fighters after all. After much pausing and rewinding, she again insisted that Lagertha could beat Ragnar, resuming an earlier argument.

"No fucking way," I told her.

"Oh, really?" She jumped up, and placing her hands on both her hips, she scanned the space. "Let's see."

I stood up, accepting her challenge. I had to hold back my laughter; she had such a serious expression. Juliet used her small frame to push the sofa, leaving just her big soft area rug. She moved in the middle of the carpet, opening and closing her hands, urging me to join her.

She kicked off her fuzzy slippers. The long shirt she was wearing made her look naked underneath.

I gave her a questioning look as I met her in the center. She said, "This is why Lagertha could have easily been able to win that fight." She positioned us the way the characters were in the show. She had her back toward me and was holding a candle as a knife. She then quickly pulled her back to face my front, twisting and getting at my knee, pinpointing the weak spot and exploiting the pressure point as she made her move, wielding the candle, stabbing my heart.

Well, I'll be damned. She was right. I held my hand over my heart, stumbling back, faking my death and pulling her to the floor with me. Both of us were laughing as she landed on top of me. Her giggling stopped as she became aware of our position. She froze and just stared into my eyes.

My body responded to our closeness. Our eyes locked in a momentary gaze. I stroked the silky strands of her hair, twisting it in my fingers before my mouth found her ear and breathed into it lightly. I snagged the lobe with my teeth, she shuddered, moaning in response. I flipped her on her back and caged her with my arms on both sides of her head and the weight of my body on her. I stared into her gold and green eyes, hoping for a signal to keep going.

Lust filled her eyes. "You aren't playing fair," she whispered, her voice raspy. I felt her take a deep breath before pushing herself forward, rolling away from the closeness of our bodies. Her face looked conflicted as she got to her feet.

"Rage," she swallowed hard, "I'm sorry, I-I can't. It's not that I don't find you incredibly attractive, because I do." Juliet sat on the sofa. She drew her knees to her chest and blew the wayward pink lock of hair from her eyes. "I love our friendship, and I have so much fun with you...but this cannot happen between us. I just can't. It's me, I just, I'm not ready to talk about it." She placed her head sideways on her knees, still hugging them to her chest.

"Can't we be friends?" She asked almost like she was asking herself as much as she was asking me. "I mean, Ivy and Hawk are practically best friends, aren't they?"

I laced my hands together and placed them on top of my head in defeat. I knew she meant it. God, I was going home with blue balls again, but I respected her decision, and I knew I needed to give her more time.

"I'm sorry, Juliet. Really. I shouldn't have. You are an incredibly attractive woman, and I do want to be your friend, that is, until I see you with someone else. I don't know how I feel about that." I began gathering my things from the room. Lord followed me around like he didn't want me to leave.

"Rage, I know. I'm just, I'm—" Before Juliet found the words, I held up my hand.

"Juliet, I'm gonna be straight with you. After last night and this morning, I know I said I was good with being friends, and I am, for now. But, in here," I grabbed her hand and placed her palm over my heart, "you are already mine."

"You may not be ready to admit there is something between us, but fuck, I'm done pretending that there isn't. Being around you is like being home. It's something I haven't felt since I was a kid. I never thought I'd ever let anyone in again." I kneeled before her, brushed the stray hair from her cheek and kissed it.

"Now," I cleared my throat, "I'm getting out here before I do something you're not ready for." My finger swept across her chin. I put on my cut, threw my bag over my shoulder as I walked out the door. She stood just a few feet behind me, following as I hurried out.

"Maybe we can finish what we started another day?" I sent her my best bad boy evil grin and gave her a wink.

Her eyes widened at my words, and a smile sneaked across her face as she bit her lip to stop it. That move almost had me undone. I was about to throw her over my shoulder and show her how mine she was. But I didn't, because I wanted her to want it just as bad. And she would, I knew it.

"Rage," she said in a shaky voice, stopping me with the door half open and letting the rain blow inside. She looked at her feet before bringing her eyes back to mine. "Thanks for riding out the storm with me."

I started to shut the door, then popped my head back in. "Are you coming to the picnic next Saturday after our charity run?"

She smirked. "It would take a miracle for Ivy not to drag me there." She shook her head like she was giving in. "So yes, I'll be there."

"Good. I'll see you then." I pulled the door closed and walked painfully to my truck, feeling like I was thirteen again.

———

JULIET

The door closed, silencing the rain. I rubbed my hands over my face. *What the hell am I doing?* I wanted him with every cell in my body, maybe even more than he thought he wanted me. But if I give in, I knew he would undo me. Rage was not the sort of man you could just walk away from. And I knew I was going to have to walk away, if not now, then someday soon. I was on borrowed time.

I leaned my back against the door, listening to the sound of his engine. I slid down, falling to my knees on the wet floor. I wanted to fling the door open, run to him, and pull him back inside and beg him to make me his. But I knew I couldn't. I shouldn't.

The sound of wet brakes leaving the driveway stabbed me in the gut. Loneliness tore a hole through me. The sting of holding back tears made my nostrils burn.

I thought the life I had rebuilt here was enough. I believed having Ivy and a few friends was enough. I was wrong. The pain of watching Rage walk out was searing, knowing he was going back to a clubhouse filled with girls ready to take care of him. I remembered the redhead at the gym staking her claim. I felt nauseated. An all too familiar knot balling up in my stomach. I allowed myself to cry. It wasn't fair! That fucking god of a man wanted me, and I was going to lose him to some bitch who didn't deserve him, all because of my lies and secrets.

CHAPTER THIRTEEN

Juliet

I'd changed three times. Examining myself in the mirror, I looked at my reflection from the front and then the back. I guessed this would have to do. I glanced at my watch and then around my small bedroom, which was now covered in discarded clothes, on the bed, on the floor, and any other flat surface. Oh, well, I would clean up tomorrow.

Ivy was on her way here to pick me up and the pies. She would be driving us to the annual barbeque at the Stained Souls clubhouse. Last year's was fun; it was a different atmosphere there when all the wives and kids were around. I liked their family days, but today was more like a festival than a party.

Rage being there had me checking myself out in the hall mirror one more time. My stomach rolled with a nervousness that I hadn't felt since I was a teen. Was this too much? Too little? I sighed. Why did I care about how good I looked? I kept saying no to any advances Rage had made, but my body had other ideas every time I was around the man. It was an attraction neither of us could ignore. I had been so close to giving in last week. When his breath and soft moist tongue had touched my neck and ear, I almost lost it. If I kept thinking about it now, I would need to change again.

I put the lip gloss down and filled up Lord's food and water, promising him a day all to him tomorrow. He turned his head like he knew what I was saying. He hopped up on the couch and gave me big sad eyes. It was too hot to bring him today. "I'm sorry, boy. Next time." I squeezed his face, kissing the top of his head, the pink print of my lips staining his white fur.

He started barking at the sound of music coming from the driveway. I knew Ivy was here before she even beeped. The door swung open. Lord jumped off the couch nearly knocking me over to greet her.

"Let's go! It's party time!" Ivy chanted, her arms pumping in the air. I began questioning my choice of clothing as soon as I set eyes on her. She had on tiny red cut shorts, black heeled boots that made her legs look even longer, and a tie-up black and red corset style tank top. Her cherry red lipstick stuck out against her pale skin. She had sunglasses on her head holding back the pale blond strands; black wings outlined her bright blue eyes that stood out against her thick black eyelashes.

She looked hot. She was totally biker chic, while I was kind of boho hippie style with my cut-offs and Converse. I bit my nail, contemplating a change of clothes.

"Juliet, stop. You look gorgeous like you always do." Ivy kissed my head and pulled me to her. We loaded up her car, said bye to Lord, and sang out of tune the whole way to the clubhouse.

––––––

RAGE

The Annual BBQ and Charity Run took place the last weekend of June, something I had missed over the previous four years. The Stained Souls had been participating in the event for as long as I could remember. Hawk's dad used to let us tag along for the ride when we were little kids.

The Fourth fell on a Thursday so we were celebrating nearly a week early this year. Sugar Maple Run was set to begin at 10 am on Main

Street. From there, we'd make our way to Black Rock, arriving at the Children's Hospital with a generous donation. In addition to raising the money, we provided the fireworks for the display. The boys from Stained Skyn did face painting for the kids at the hospital, turning them into princesses and superheroes, or the occasional villain. The event made the club look like real assets to the community. After the ride, we celebrated with our annual barbeque at the clubhouse.

Since I was a kid, my favorite part had always been the bonfire. I remembered Hawk's dad taking us every year. Children were welcome, at least until the fireworks. As kids, we used to gorge ourselves on hamburgers, hot dogs, beans, pies and s'mores until we were sick. We used to spend an hour looking for the sticks long enough to reach the bonfire to toast our marshmallows. All the kids would run around chasing fireflies and playing kick the can. It was the one day of the year I felt like part of a family. The sun wouldn't set until after nine. Hawk's mom used to cover us in sunscreen all day and then drown us in OFF lotion as soon as the sun went down. They were the best memories of my childhood other than my time with my grandma.

When we were teenagers, we rode our bikes to Black Rock. We thought we were the shit. Stealing smokes and beer while admiring all the pretty girls the members had around. We used to sit around the fire talking about how we would do things someday when we were club members. Little did we know what that really meant.

Ivy and Juliet were meeting us at the clubhouse after the run. The barbeque began at two, so they promised to help the women set up, and they were bringing some food as well. Even though I looked forward to the run, knowing Juliet would be at the club made me want to get back there sooner. Brothers from chapters all over came to be a part of the event. Hundreds of people would be at the club all weekend celebrating. Rebellion, a band I knew from Memphis, had agreed to play this year.

The line of bikes stretched four blocks down Main Street. All in a single file with a truck ending the line. Red, white, and blue decorations covered the truck that was full of all the fireworks we were donating. Someone always sat in the back, throwing candy at the spectators, and songs about America echoed from its speakers.

All the bikes were polished and gleaming in the hot sun. The temperature had already reached over ninety degrees by 9 am. Haze rose from the blacktop. My boots felt like they were melting into it as we waited for the run to begin. At once all the engines started. Children on their dad's shoulders cheered as the bikes took off, out of town, over the bridge, one by one in a perfect line. Even with the wind in my face, it was hard to stay cool.

Three hours later, we headed back to Sugar Maple. The run was a success. The kids at the hospital were happy, and the donation was large. A few of the brothers talked some of the cute nurses into coming back to the clubhouse barbeque later. Until the kids leave, everyone would be on their best behavior.

———

JULIET

Ivy and I spent the last three hours setting up with the member's wives and some prospects who stayed behind. My hair didn't last long down in this humidity. I felt a slight burn from the morning sun on my nose after moving some of the tables.

The sound of kids' laughter was soon drowned out by the bikes returning from the run. Everyone came to a halt, gazing at the incoming men entering the long path to the clubhouse.

One by one, the shiny bikes filed into the lot with Colt at the helm. He looked so intimidating leading the pack of bikers. Colt's salt-and-pepper hair was slicked back. Black sunglasses covered his eyes, and a cigarette was pressed between his lips. Authority rolled off him.

I was sure they all needed showers after riding in this scorching heat. The blue sky offered no cloud for cover today. They must have baked with the slow pace of the parade to the hospital. I knew how much their donations helped the Children's Hospital, and I thought it was so sweet that they did this.

The food was almost ready by the time the boys were off their bikes and in the clubhouse to change. A line of smokers around the courtyard scented the air with barbeque. After setting up the plates and silverware station, we filled the buffet with large bowls of different salads and fruit. I lit the Sternos under the water-filled aluminum trays and waited for Ivy to tell me when to bring out the hot food to set on top.

I felt eyes penetrating me. I turned, and it was exactly who I hoped it would be. Rage. In all his gorgeous masculine glory. He looked beyond sexy in his jeans, boots, and a white tank top that glowed against his tan and red shoulders.

RAGE

All the guys made a big deal for the families coming. They wanted everyone to feel welcome.

It took us three days to set up the yard with gigantic tents and tables and the stage for the band. We also rented a bounce house and water slide for the kids. When Hawk and I were kids, the only things we had were a hose and water guns. Every child begged Hawk to paint a tattoo on them. He was great with the little ones.

After a much-needed cold shower, I peeked out my window at the club to see all the action in the yard. My stomach growled, the smell of the food was overpowering as it came through my closed window. The a/c was not keeping up with this heat. I started sweating again before I even pulled on my white tank and jeans. I massaged in some aloe onto my burnt shoulders before making my way to the yard.

I was thankful the clubhouse was in the valley and was a little cooler than the town. The large trees that surrounded the property gave it shade and privacy.

There were already groups of people under the tented areas, anxiously waiting for food. My eyes roamed the lot until they landed on the tan legs I was scouting for. I'd know those legs anywhere. The sparkly Converse was a giveaway, too. Most of the girls that hung around the club wore heels or boots, not sparkly Converse. Faded ripped jean shorts with pockets hanging through barely covered her ass. Her hair was twisted on her head, exposing the tattoo on her neck.

Her loose pink top was sheer enough to show her belly piercing and some cleavage. I licked my lips in approval. Her eyes found mine, and her plump pink glossy lips smiled. Mirrored aviator sunglasses hid her green eyes. Her large earrings met her collarbone, swaying as she sent a wave my way.

"Hey," I said, giving her a chin lift as I unloaded some more of the chairs that were stacked next to the door.

"Hey yourself," she said. "How was the run? You guys must have melted." She used a paper plate to fan herself.

Small beads of sweat slid to her cleavage. I wanted to follow the trail and lick each bead off her honeysuckle-scented skin.

"Yeah, it was…sweltering on the road, but it was worth it," I said, trying not to stare.

"Tiny just loaded up cases in the coolers. Can I get you a Witcher's Way?" she asked, gesturing to the giant coolers lined along the wall.

"That'd be great," I accepted with a smile. *Juliet remembered.* She handed me a frigid bottle and popped off the top using a bottle opener on her key ring.

"Wow, you carry an opener. I like that." I grinned in approval as I watched her shove her keys back into her tiny shorts pocket.

"I don't have it just to run around and open beers," she laughed. "My favorite ginger Kombucha from the farmer's market has a pop top, and too many times I had to wait until I got home to drink it. I'm very impatient."

"Good to know," I nodded before our conversation was interrupted.

"Juliet, I need help!" Ivy, who had a full-on biker chick outfit, called as she rounded the corner.

Ivy was quite the opposite of her best friend. She ran her long red, white, and blue nails through her hair as she complained about the heat wearing off her makeup, which would have been a good thing, in my opinion. She played with the small piercing in her eyebrow, which glinted in the sun. When she turned around, her tank revealed her wing tattoos, which covered most of her back. These two were total opposites.

"Hey, sweetie," Juliet replied to her friend, "how can I help?" After

Ivy blurted out several instructions, Juliet nodded and turned to me. "Well, I guess I'll see you later?" she said, hopeful. Ivy took her hand and dragged her into the clubhouse where large foil-covered trays were brought out to a makeshift buffet. The girls made trip after trip and soon there was food on all the tables lined up.

After a while, when most people had had their fill, I made my way to the buffet where Ivy and Juliet were in line. I asked about the...food on her plate. "Veggie burger," she answered with a grin. She added corn on the cob and roasted potatoes to her plate. I watched as she piled the burger high with all the fixing before sitting down at one of the picnic tables. Ivy, Hawk, Leo, and Shelly were already seated there.

"Rage, are we partners again in the horseshoe tournament?" Hawk asked. "You know we can take 'em all again this year. I heard Kai invited a ringer to team up with him. He was so pissed at Ledge last year when he got too drunk to even hit the pin." He laughed as he remembered that fiasco.

"Wow, you guys take this stuff seriously," Ivy said.

"Hundred bucks and the trophy that gets passed down each year. Our dads started it way back, and it's been a tradition ever since." Hawk explained. "Rage and I used to play in the weekly league at The Ridge before he relocated. Shit, we should totally do that again."

Taking a long draw from my beer, I nodded. "Sounds good," I said, still watching Juliet digging around her plate.

Ivy began to get up from the bench, but Hawk pulled her back down in between his legs. She giggled, "I was only getting dessert." He pouted his bottom lip. "Could you get me more potato salad?"

Hawk's next words got my attention. "Juliet, you still coming into the studio this week?" He asked, sticking his fork into the large portion of potato salad that Ivy just put in front of him. "Thanks, doll."

"Yes, as long as Thursday is still good for you." Juliet licked the barbeque sauce from her fingers. I almost grabbed her hand and did it for her.

"You know, I'll always make time for you, babe. Drop the sketch off Monday."

I interrupted, "You're having work done?" I turned to Juliet.

145

"Yeah. A few years ago, I had my sister draw me a Tree of Life. I have always wanted to get it tattooed, so I showed Hawk a picture and he said he would do it."

"Fucking right I did, and it's going to be amazing. Just like your hamsa!" He smiled, proud of his work. I just glared at him.

"And," I cleared my throat, not liking the thought of his hands on Juliet, "where is this new ink going?" I asked, sounding more annoyed than I wanted it to.

Her words were low, practically a whisper, "Uh…on my pelvic bone." She fiddled with a napkin, tearing at it as she spoke.

"Your pelvic bone?" I said slowly, my eyebrows were probably on top of my head. I could not believe what I just heard, probably because of the steam that must have been coming out of my ears. The thought of Hawk inking her, with her pants down, showing him all that beautiful skin.

"I had an accident a few years ago, and I want to cover up the scar."

"No," I said flatly. The word just came out.

All sets of eyes looked at me as the conversations stopped.

"Did you say no?" she asked, but I could tell, what she really wanted to ask was, "Who the hell do you think you are?"

I shrugged my shoulders. "I just think, you know, you should… think about it longer, so you're sure you won't regret it someday." *Smooth. Nice save, jackass.*

"Dude, not cool." That's all Hawk said as he shook his head and threw a cherry tomato at me.

Thankfully, that was the exact moment Kai joined us. I was relieved to change the subject, although I would be talking to Hawk later. There was no way he was touching her skin without me present.

Kai set his plate on the table while he made room for himself to sit. He straddled the bench, squeezing into the last spot next to me at the end. Kai's plate was covered in pie with only enough room for the scoop of ice cream on the side.

"Geez, big enough piece of pie?" I said to him as he shoveled a large bite into his mouth.

He licked his fork seductively. "It's Juliet's pie," he said with a devilish grin. Ivy smacked his shoulder.

I shot him with a deadly look. He raised his hands in the air, surrendering. "What? She made the pie." He turned to her and said, "Babe, it's the best blueberry pie I've ever tasted." He winked at her as he shoveled another bite.

Shelly agreed as she tried hers, "Wow, this has a flavor I can't quite figure out. Damn, it's amazing, girl. You need to share the recipe."

Juliet looked appreciative of all the compliments. "Thanks, guys. The secret is just a little freshly grated nutmeg. Not many people use it, but that's how my grandmother taught me." Juliet smiled, happy they were enjoying it.

My stomach leaped at her words. My mind flashed back to Preacher James' bake-off when I was a kid. Preacher James loved Grandma's blueberry pie; he used to keep it for himself and say, "I bought it and it's just for me."

"Stella, you have to tell me. What do you put in this that makes it so special?" Preacher James asked Grandma, but she just shook her head no.

"Please," he begged.

Her finger went to her lips, the universal sign for "be quiet." She looked around, making sure no one could overhear, and continued in a hushed voice, "Don't give away my secret, but, it's the freshly grated nutmeg."

I shook my head, clearing the memory before a grabbed a fork. I looked at Shelly's dish.

"One bite?" I asked.

She narrowed her eyes at me. "A small one. If you want some, better hurry. There's a line forming. It will be gone soon."

"What?" Juliet craned her neck. "I made six. Last year I made three, and they went so fast, so I thought six would be enough this year."

I slid Shelly's plate across the red, white, and blue tablecloth. I dug my fork into the crumbly top crust, through the thick layer of blueberry filling, and then into the flaky bottom crust. My mouth watered as the fork came to my lips.

Memories were like sparklers firing off in my head as the single bite took me back to my childhood. It was exactly like I remembered. I tried to be casual as I turned to the group, waiting for my verdict. I just smiled and said, "Yeah, it's amazing. Where did you say the desserts are? I'm going to get some before they're gone."

Great, just great, as if I needed another reason to fall a little deeper into the web that was Juliet.

JULIET

I smiled and waved as soon as I saw Rage enter the pavilion. He licked his lips, running his hand through the damp dark curls as he took me in, his eyes traveling up and down like he'd never seen me before. I could feel the heat traveling through my body as I went near him. I gave him a cold beer, but we weren't more than a few sentences in before Ivy was calling for my help.

I saw him a few times before we finally took a break to eat, noting the number of women who flocked around him, asking him for help with something. When Rage joined us at the table, I couldn't help but watch him the whole time. His cheeks were stained red from the sun. I tried to keep up with conversations around me, but I was quite distracted by the massive man who was taking up more space in my brain than I wanted him to. I nearly choked when Kai teased about my pie and Rage got pissed. It made me feel good that he was a little jealous.

Something came over his face when he tried the pie I made. At first, I thought he didn't like it all that much, but then there he was, pushing his way through the line to steal the last pie plate. He got almost half a pie! He added a scoop of vanilla ice cream to it before digging in. He probably would have licked the plate had we not been there in front of him. I squeezed my legs together when he used his finger to swipe up the last of the blueberry and cream and licked it off.

I spent a few hours between getting to know some of the girls while the guys were in a competitive horseshoe tournament. I kept looking at the flat area that had four pits and a canopy with a keg surrounded by men. The clanking of the shoe hitting the pin could be heard between songs as the DJ played music and called out game results. The band was due to play at seven, so when everyone began to clean up the food area at six, I volunteered to help.

I enjoyed the afternoon, the kids bouncing, screaming, and running around everywhere. I got squirted with water guns twice. Ledge teased me about the screech I let out when the cold water met my flesh. It broke the grumpy mood he was in after Hawk and Rage kicked his ass in horseshoes.

The guys had put a lot of effort into making sure the club was super family friendly today. Everyone was at ease and just enjoying a day of fun. I always felt safe here among the MC. It was nice having a feeling of complete safety, like nothing could hurt you when you were around them.

Hawk and Rage were at a distance, next to the DJ, accepting their trophy as the other guys grumbled about their losses. When the DJ announced them as winners, a few women ran straight to them offering their congratulations, bouncing around and pulling on their arms.

Unbelievable. I shook my head and got back to folding the last two tablecloths and clearing away trash. I was looking forward to hearing the band. I was planning on heading to the area near the stage to set up a spot after cleaning up.

I held two large heavy green bags in my hands, ready to discard them. I felt his presence before the deep voice behind me asked if I wanted help. Rage took the bags from me, and we walked them to the overflowing dumpsters behind the kitchen.

I leaned against the tall white fence, kicking my leg back while I watched him organize some of the boxes and bags.

"Congratulations on winning the tournament. I hear you guys didn't lose a game."

"Nope. We've always played great together. I could never find a partner as good as him in Tennessee."

"Hey, do you happen to have a blanket we can put on the lawn for the band? I left mine in my jeep. I meant to get it before we left and forgot."

"Yeah, I have something. Give me ten minutes to clean up, and I will meet you down on the lawn by the band."

"Okay, I'll grab some beers and find us a good spot." I bent down under his arm as he held the heavy door open.

I was glad I had chosen to wear my Chucks and not the wedge sandals that Ivy had wanted me to. "Suffer for beauty" was her motto. That and "fashion first." The hill was full of divots that would have certainly had me twisting an ankle. Groups of people had already scattered across the lawn in chairs and on blankets. Farthest from the stage, a large pile of wood looked ready for the bonfire. There was a table set under a tent with boxes of graham crackers, marshmallows, and a cooler marked Chocolate. In front of the tent was a large sign that read Smores. Attached to the table was another sign that said Find Your Own Stick. I smiled watching the kids that were scouring the area, running back and forth with twigs and branches, asking their moms if they were good ones.

Distracted, I didn't see the man next to me. My arm bumped him, spilling a little of his beer from his red plastic cup.

"Excuse me, I'm so sorry," I said, slightly embarrassed.

The man stepped back and whistled as he took me in. A pair of ocean blue eyes met mine; a smile appeared on his sun-kissed face. He reminded me of a surfer, with his dark blond hair cropped close to his head, the sides shaved short, and light blond highlights filtering through. His shell necklace and shark tooth that dangled between his pecs completed the look. He wore his cut over a bare chest; it matched his black jeans.

Where the heck did they find these guys? Did they have ads at modeling agencies? Hot bikers wanted, call Stained Souls MC today! I laughed to myself as he extended his hand.

"I'm Ace, darlin'." He extended his hand out. "What's so funny?"

"Sorry, I just remembered something," I blushed. "Nice to meet you, Ace. I'm Juliet." I accepted his hand, and being the charmer he was, he took my hand and kissed it.

"Pleased to make your acquaintance."

Reading his cut, I noticed it was different from Rage's. Ace's read Tallahassee Chapter under the Stained Souls logo. I felt a tiny bit of panic to see Tallahassee.

I stumbled for words, "So…You're all the way here from Florida?"

"Yes, ma'am, a few of the brothers from my chapter come to the run every year. I couldn't make it last year, but happy to be a part of it today." His eyes roamed over my body as he spoke, then he sent me a flirtatious smile.

"So, Juliet," he said, tilting his head with a sexy southern drawl, "are you looking for a seat?" He pointed to a blanket and empty chairs between some men surrounding a cooler, all wearing the same Tallahassee rocker on their cuts. They tipped their drinks toward me when I looked over to them.

"I would be happy to have you join me." He winked and offered a wide smile of straight white teeth.

A large shadow fell from behind me, blocking the late afternoon sun. "She has a seat," grumbled the deep voice that belonged to the shadow. I winced when I heard the annoyance lacing his tone.

"Rage, hey, man," Ace extended his fist. Rage seemed irritated but still extended his arm to meet Ace's fist. "It's been a long time, how ya doing?"

"Ace, I see you've met Juliet." He pulled me to his side.

I bit my lip, feeling somewhat uncomfortable. Ace looked from Rage to me and back again. He gave him a chin lift. "Can't blame a guy for trying," he said with a wink.

Rage handed me the blanket, pointing to an open space. I began laying it out as the two men caught up.

I placed the small cooler I filled with drinks down on the corner of the blanket. We had a great view of the stage that wasn't so close to enormous speakers.

I couldn't contain my smile. I was so excited to see Rebellion play again. Live music in the open air was one of my favorite things. How did they get these guys to play at such a small venue compared to where they usually play? It must have cost the club a fortune. As if reading my mind, Rage sat on the blanket crossing his long legs, watching the stage.

"Lucky for us, one of the guys in Rebellion has a brother in the MC," he aimed his beer to the stage, pointing out the man with the cowboy hat behind the drums. "Grayson, the lead singer, and his baby brother, Blake, and I became good friends in Tennessee. We even jammed together a few times at the local bars."

I could picture him on stage handling his harmonica and making all the girls swoon. A pang of jealousy formed in my chest at the thought.

"Ivy and I went to see them in Black Rock two years ago; they were fantas—"

The tuner made a loud screech, bringing everything to a halt as people covered their ears.

Grayson's gravelly voice was heard on the mic, "Sorry, folks. Y'all ready for a good time?" He held his guitar in the air as people cheered.

The first set lasted an hour. My body was dying to get up and dance, but I didn't want to abandon Rage. I was enjoying the feel of him playing with my hair, twisting it around his big fingers. The last of the blazing sun was setting over the stage, the sky full of red and pink streaks with deep purple clouds separating the colors. I held my hand in my face blocking the intense light as a slightly drunk Ivy came and stood before me, holding a tray of fancy shots. She pushed two my way.

"Drink these," she slurred. "Tropical Sunrise. They taste like Florida! They are refreshing," she yelled over the music, holding one of the shots high in the air.

I looked at Rage, who seemed annoyed. Screw it, I thought, as I downed the drinks. It's been a long, hot day.

The band was performing a mix of covers and originals. We sat enjoying the music and laughing for the next half hour. Ivy had her head resting on my lap and her eyes closed as she hummed along, tapping her foot to the beat.

The sky was almost completely dark when the band came back from a short break and began their next set. Lights flooded the stage, making it glow in colors. Grayson came out and introduced a woman on stage for the next song. The music started, and Ivy jumped up screaming as the woman began singing one of her favorite songs. Carrie Underwood's *Un-do it*. She was up on her feet, dragging me up along with her.

"Jules, come on, we gotta dance." I laughed at her as I accepted her hand and we both nearly fell over. It was not often that I got out to see bands and I was growing envious of the sea of women dancing. I waved a small bye to Rage as we ran through blankets and chairs to reach the stage.

It didn't take long before nearly every woman there filled the grassy area, dancing and singing along with the woman's powerful voice. We all repeated the words in the chorus as she turned the mic toward the crowd.

CHAPTER FOURTEEN

Rage

I went to get a damn blanket and within minutes, "pretty boy" Ace was hitting on her. I couldn't leave Juliet alone for a minute. Ace was the Kai of the Tallahassee chapter. A real charmer that all the girls loved. When I saw the two of them chatting, I wanted to toss her over my shoulder and scream MINE! I knew she wouldn't appreciate that, so I made it known by giving Ace death looks as I pulled her into my side. While she set up our seats, I had a chance to catch up with the brother. Before the short conversation was over, I noticed his eyes on Juliet's ass as she spread the blanket on the ground. She was crawling around the blue and red flannel when her shorts rode up as she smoothed the corners and placed the cooler on it to keep it down. "Easy, brother," I grunted. My eyes narrowed where he was looking.

"Woah, Rage." His hands went up. "Sorry, man. So, are you two a thing?" he asked, fiddling with his shark-tooth necklace that dangled from his neck.

"Not yet," I said, annoyed.

He sucked his teeth, grabbed his chin, and nodded. "Good to know," he said, still staring at her ass.

I sent him the evilest stare I could, squeezing my lips in a tight line and grinding my jaw. I abruptly turned my back to him and stomped straight for the blanket.

She was smiling at me from her spot, one hand shielding the sun while the other clutched the beer she'd just opened for me. We made ourselves comfortable listening to the band. She sang along to the songs she knew. Juliet made it so easy to relax and be me. I didn't feel like I'm a time bomb, always on edge, except when men kept hitting on her.

She dug through her bag, pulling out the organic sunscreen that smelled like her. I watched the motion of her hands massaging the cream into her thighs; I had to look away to keep from attacking her on the spot. She applied it to my arms, running her slender fingers up and down my skin, making sure it was all rubbed in. I was a masterclass in self-control.

I played with the color steaks that fell from her hair as she lay flat on her stomach, legs in the air and crossed at the ankles, her fists under her chin, entranced entirely by music. We sat by ourselves almost the whole first set before Ivy found us. I liked the girl, but it seemed like she was always causing some kind of stir. Hawk always said, "Where Ivy goes, trouble follows." She forced a few shots onto Juliet before the band introduced Becca on stage.

When a Carrie Underwood song came on, Ivy, who looked exhausted with her head on Juliet's lap, suddenly stood and ripped Juliet off the ground. She pulled her to the grassy area in front of the stage. They spent the next hour dancing, while Grayson had Colt get me between the second and third sets.

"Rage," Grayson said, tipping his hat. Blake and the other guys also extended hellos.

"We got to talking about that time you played with us in that little dive bar when you first moved to Tennessee. Remember the rendition of *Hallelujah* we did?" Grayson asked.

I shook my head and smiled at the memory. That night I knew my time in Tennessee was going to be all right. We jammed in the little bar 'til four in the morning. "I remember."

"Well, we were thinking, being a special night, you might want to do it again?" Grayson asked, hoping.

I shook my head. "Nah, I think you guys can do it without me."

"Come on," Blake insisted, "don't let those sick harmonica skills go to waste."

"Fine," I agreed, thinking maybe this would get to Juliet.

We spent the next ten minutes going over the plan. I wasn't shy, but it felt a little awkward performing in front of my brothers. When I was in my early twenties, I would whip out my harmonica whenever I got the chance. Panties dropped easily, not that I needed any help.

The stage was dark as I sat on the stool in front of the drums. Grayson stood to my left, smoking his last cigarette before the set began. I scanned the crowd, looking for Juliet. She wasn't where our blanket was set up. In the field below, the bonfire began to blaze. Small groups were making their way down there when Grayson got on the mic.

The light was only aimed at him and the rest of us were shadows in the background. When he said my name, the entire place cheered. A small bundle of nerves rolled through me. I had been performing this song since I was a boy, I must have played it thousands of times. There was no reason I should be nervous.

Everything faded away as the lights went out, then a single pale-yellow light was only on me. Screams, whistles, and catcalls came from the area below, followed by a silence so deafening that I could hear the crackling of the bonfire.

Adjusting the mic one more time, I took a deep breath before I bowed my head and brought my harmonica to my lips. A few whistles came from the otherwise quiet crowd. I began the song by myself, blowing into the chrome. With each sad note I played, I hoped Juliet was listening, somewhere in the crowd, recognizing the plea through my sound. I played like it was only for her. The bright fire that burned down the hill glowed in the sky, reminding me of the night I first played for her. The image of Juliet on the blanket and me wiping the stray tear from her eye made the emotion I felt shine through each verse.

Grayson joined in halfway through the first verse. His gravelly voice was a perfect match for the song, and Blake finally came in with his acoustic guitar and brought it all together. Lighters and phones swayed in the air back and forth in perfect motion, the crowd moving to the slow beat. Grayson sang the final lyrics, and I finished the song the same way I started, alone. The last rift flowed out of my small instrument, creating an emotional stir. The audience went crazy as the final note ended. I looked at Grayson and then at Blake, who were smiling proudly.

Unexpectedly, I had not yet taken three steps off the stage when women rushed at me. The crowd was still applauding as I got pulled from one girl to the next in a frenzy. I only had eyes for one woman, but she wasn't among any of the faces pulling and tugging at me. A good head taller than everyone, I scanned the area, looking for the only face I wanted to see.

Two thin arms pulled me into a huge set of tits covered by only a tiny piece of fabric that resembled a bra. Her red hair flamed under the lights. Leann. Without saying a word. Her nails scraped down my cut before she grabbed both sides and slammed her lips into mine.

———

JULIET

Ivy and I danced for almost the whole set. I was exhausted and quite thirsty. Walking back, I noticed there weren't many kids left running around. Now, the real party would begin. I didn't see Rage anywhere, so Ivy and I headed to the newly lit bonfire, hoping to escape the mosquitoes.

We stopped in our tracks when Grayson's voice boomed through the speakers. "Can I have everyone's attention?" he asked. The stage was dark except for the light that illuminated his stool. "The boys would like to welcome an old friend on stage to play along with his harmonica." My ears perked up. "Rage," the lead singer called out as the crowd of bikers cheered.

Grabbing Ivy's arm, I dragged her to where everyone else was heading. We couldn't get any closer, so I stood at the back, watching from behind the women, as the stage went black. One spotlight dimly illuminated Rage. He sat quietly for a moment. Suddenly, breaking through the silence, the sweetest sound filled my ears.

Hallelujah began to flow through the speakers. Rage poured emotion into each note. It was like a beacon calling out to me. I wondered if he remembered the night he played for me. Women rushed the stage, waving their phones in the air. The deep smoky voice of the lead singer began, with an acoustic guitar joining in next. My whole body felt a tremble as the sweet sound took over. Goosebumps covered my arms. Tears pricked at my eyes. I was so enthralled by the music, I felt like I was alone for a moment, the rest of the party and the world were blocked out.

Everyone went wild as Rage blew out the final sad note. Immediately, half-naked women were throwing themselves at him. I didn't know if it was the sun or the alcohol, but I felt like a fool watching him. He had women like that every night. Why the hell would he even want me? Was I just another to add to his collection? Jealousy burned my cheeks as my temper flared. I stomped toward the next tray of shots I saw being passed around and took one. The liquid burned my throat. Then I took another. My eyes locked on the women still pawing at him. My legs were moving me closer to them when I was stopped just a few feet before reaching the harem.

Ivy grabbed at my wrist. "Whoa, you never do shots like that. What's eating you?" My head swiveled to the familiar redhead who had her ginormous boobs pressed up against Rage. When their lips met in a kiss, a knife plunged straight into my heart. I spun around quickly— I didn't need to see them run off into the sunset together.

Ivy stopped me again, placing both hands on my chest. "Wait, Juliet, stop." I pushed her hands off and marched down the hill back to the bonfire. In my haste to get away from there, I slammed into a wall—someone's solid bare chest, with a shark tooth between his pecs. Ace. *Fuck, not again.*

"Whoa, you okay?" I looked up through my lashes into his glassy blue eyes. "Well, well, well, we meet again. You better stop running into me, or I may think you are doing it on purpose." A huge grin covered his face, accentuating his dimples.

Ivy finally caught up. "Holy dimples, who is this?"

"Ace, darlin', nice to meet you." The panty-dropping smile almost left Ivy wordless.

"Ivy," she said staring at him, swooning.

He politely kissed her hand, making her blush, then turned to me. "Miss Juliet," he bowed, "may I walk you to wherever you are going?"

"Yes," Ivy said for me, pushing me toward him. I looked to see if Rage and the redhead were still there. They were gone. They probably went back to his room. Liquor fueled my imagination. Anger surged through me, and lava flowed through my veins. I turned to look at Ace and took his hand.

"You know what, Ace? Yeah, let's go."

RAGE

It took ten minutes to get the hell away from Leann and the other half-naked women pulling at my jeans. These girls were crazy.

I wandered around looking for Juliet or Ivy. I would have asked Kai, but he was busy with a girl on each knee who took turns kissing him and each other. It was the same almost everywhere I looked.

I was relieved when I found Shelly. "Hey, Shell, have you seen Juliet or Ivy?"

She gave me a look and shook her head at me. She obviously didn't want to tell me something.

"Why are you looking at me like that, Shell?" I stood in front of her, blocking her way.

The petite blond tucked her hair behind her ear before blowing out air. Her eyes deflected to the ground to avoid eye contact with me.

"Spill it, Shell," I demanded.

"Well," she said in a high-pitched voice as she twirled her hair, "after your beautiful performance—I loved it, by the way. I think Leo needs to learn to play the harmonica. It's fucking sexy as hell—"

"Shelly…" I was about to lose my shit. "What happened with Juliet?"

"I was near her and Ivy when you finished. She looked pretty pissed when you got off stage and swapped spit with that hoe, Leann."

I took a big deep breath and exhaled slowly, pinching the bridge of my nose. "Where is Juliet now?" I asked, defeated.

She sucked in a breath and quietly said, "I think I saw her near the bonfire...with Ace. Sorry, Rage, that boy's a real charmer."

Red. I felt red. I didn't know it was even possible to feel a color, but I felt it—heat, rising from my boots all the way to the top of my head, the vein in my neck pulsed. "That little..."

A small hand pulled on my arm, bringing me back. I looked down at Shelly's pleading face. "Rage she only went with him because she was pissed at you and thought you and Leann were together. I saw you and Leann both disappear, I didn't know if she was wrong, so I couldn't say anything."

Doesn't Juliet know me by now?

I thanked Shelly, then off I went toward the towering flames. My strides were long and heavy as my boots thumped through the damp grass. I ignored anyone who tried to talk to me as I passed. My eyes only focused on the light of the bonfire glowing from below.

My head swiveled around from person to person; the area was lit only by the ember flames. Then I heard a familiar giggling. When my eyes adjusted to the light, the outline of Juliet with Ace standing behind her came to my view.

She held a long branch into the flames. When she pulled it out, the marshmallow on its end was still on fire. Her laughter stopped as she blew out the flame. She pulled the charred marshmallow from the stick and popped it into her mouth.

"That is the third one. Come on, darlin', I want to make actual s'mores before they start the fireworks. You need to stop stealing the marshmallows," Ace teased, holding the graham crackers and chocolate in one hand as he added a new marshmallow to the stick.

"Juliet, do not eat it." Ivy stood next to her, licking her fingers and laughing along as she took the long stick from Juliet.

Ace leaned into Juliet, making his move on her, no doubt to brush off some of the sticky marshmallow that was on her mouth, the little shit. But he wasn't quick enough—I was there to pull Juliet back. She crashed into my chest, and I cupped her startled face and sucked away the sticky residue from her lips. Juliet's eyes widened in shock and then anger.

"What the fuck, Rage!"

I didn't answer her. Instead, I kissed her again before I savagely picked her up off the ground, threw her over my shoulder, and carried her away. I looked back to Ace and extended to him my middle finger and mouthed "MINE."

Whistles and catcalls chased us as I claimed Juliet in front of my brothers. I carried her the entire way to my truck, which was parked on the opposite field. She pounded my back, insisting I put her down. "Nope" was all I said.

"Rage, you had no right. We're just friends, remember? You agreed."

"Yeah, we are friends, so why did you run off, friend?"

I threw the tailgate down with one hand, sitting her on its edge. I parted her legs and stood between them as I cupped her face once again, but she refused to meet my gaze.

"Fuck friendship. You know how I feel. Fuck, the whole fucking club and visiting chapters know how I feel." Her eyes finally met mine, the pools of green looked almost black under the moonlight. I said emphatically, "You are mine. You're lying to yourself if you think we are just friends."

"Yeah? Well, from the looks of it, you have a lot of 'friends' around here." She pushed me back and crossed her arms. "Looked like you were some redhead's 'friend' only a half hour ago."

"Babe," I stepped closer to her again and lightly held her chin. "I want *you*. I don't know how much clearer I can make it." Again, she attempted to turn away.

"If Ace would have touched you," my nostrils flared, "I would have broken the brothers' code and beaten the fuck out of him. His brothers would have taken him home on a stretcher."

"Nothing was going to happen between Ace and me," she said, pushing my hand from the light grip that held her chin.

"Good."

I pulled her in, kissing her and gently biting her lip until she began returning the kiss. I knew her enough by now that she would start getting in her head about this, so every time she opened her mouth to speak, I would pull her in further and rougher until moans of pleasure formed instead of sentences.

I pulled her hair back, exposing her neck. My tongue traced her jawline to her ear, licking, sucking. I kissed her neck and throat until her one hand was grabbing my curls and the other was scratching my back. "Don't fight this, Juliet. I need you."

She wrapped her legs around my waist, molding her body to mine, squeezing them tightly. "I, I shouldn't..." My hands ran over her smooth, strong thighs before grabbing her perfect ass.

"Oh, God, Rage." She tugged at my shirt, bringing it over my head, and her hands ran over my pecs and down my stomach before moving quickly to remove her shirt and bra in one swift action.

Moans of pleasure escaped her as my mouth took in her breasts, tasting them one at a time. Her head leaned all the way back. She tasted sweet as honeysuckles.

Our hands roamed over each other. I kissed her long, deep, and hard. Two months of sexual tension exploded in a moment of frenzy. Juliet unbuttoned the top button of my jeans, her hand finding its way in my boxers. My eyes rolled back as her warm fingers gripped me. I felt like I was going to explode just from her touch. I deepened the kiss, and she gripped me harder pulling herself as close to me as she could get. I kissed along her stomach, reaching the top of her panties before making my way back up to her mouth. This was just the beginning and I didn't want it to end. I could stay pressed against her body like this forever.

Fireworks began shooting over the horizon, exploding beautiful colors into the black sky.

"It's a sign," she whispered in my ear, giving me chills.

I pushed her back and kissed her inner thighs, then ran my tongue along the sensitive flesh. She squealed, grasping my hair.

"Oh, God, Rage" her plea mixed with the loud pops and whistles that filled the air. Just as I unbuttoned her shorts and began pulling them down, louder, closer pops rang out. My head snapped up in realization. I knew that sound. Gunshots!

ZARA TELEG

"Lay back!" I shouted, covering her body with mine. I pushed her down the bed of the truck. Terrified screams replaced the sounds of cheers from the field below.

"What's happening? What's going on, Rage?" Juliet looked scared and confused.

"It's gunshots." I could see her face change as fear took over. "Juliet, it's going to be okay." I grabbed my gun from its holster in my jeans. "Get dressed. Lock yourself in the truck and stay on the floor until I come back for you."

"Wait, Rage, it's not safe. Don't go down there," she pleaded, trying to grab onto me.

"It's gonna be fine, babe. Just get in the truck right now. I'll be back." I said, calm but firm so as not to scare her further. "Lock the doors and keep your phone on. Stay low on the floor. I promise, I'll be fine. Just stay down."

164

CHAPTER FIFTEEN

Juliet

*R*estless, I held Lord close to me as I checked the bedroom clock again. Hawk had made one of the prospects drive me and Ivy home; he'd thought it would be best if we stayed together. I was terrified when I realized the fireworks had turned into gunfire. After Rage left me in the truck, I kept peeking up, looking around for any sign of him. It wasn't long before Brody, the prospect, came to get me. He assured me that Rage was fine and he was to take me and Ivy home. Thank God no one had been hurt. Rage had called about two hours later and said it had been a rival MC sending a message. They had shot at the few bikes closest to the road.

I gazed over the mountain of blankets to see Ivy was still sleeping. As tired as I was, my adrenaline kept me awake most of the night. I worried about the guys. Were they all okay? Who was this other MC and what did they want? Would they try something at one of the Stained Souls businesses next?

On my mind, more than anything, was Rage. My finger ran over my lips a thousand times as I lay in my bed struggling to fall asleep. All rational thoughts left me as dawn began to light the sky.

Since sleep refused to come, I thought a shower might make me feel better and relax me. Stepping into the steam-filled room, my body welcomed the lavender scent and the hot spray that gently pelted my back.

I had always been a hopeless romantic. I kept it to myself mostly. My Kindle was full of romance novels, mostly paranormal. My DVD collection consisted of cheesy vampire romances: *True Blood, Vampire Diaries, Originals, Twilight, Moonlight,* and if that wasn't embarrassing enough, the full collections of *Buffy* and *Angel*.

The independent woman I was turned to a pile of mush when the strong woman lead gets swept away by the sexy bad boy. For the first time in my life, the passion I had thought to only exist between the pages of books or on screen had become my reality. It made my four years of celibacy almost worth it.

My mind replayed the night as I washed yesterday from my skin. When Rage's mouth had stolen mine in front of the whole MC, and when he'd thrown me over his shoulder, all beast and savage-like, I'd melted. All the questions in my head had been answered: He did want me and I knew I wanted him.

His brute strength and possessive nature made my inner feminist cringe in disapproval. My body, on the other hand, reacted as if it had been set on fire and he was the only one who could put me out and relieve the ache that consumed me.

There was nothing about Rage that was not all man. The way he had handled my body, his kisses had been tender and rough. I squeezed my legs together, inhaling deeply. I kept my eyes closed, letting the water run over me as I tried to recall every moment on the back of his truck. The way his hands had caressed the length of my legs and grabbed my ass. The way he had kissed me everywhere. I thought I was going to burst.

Lord's bark startled me, bringing me back to the present. I needed to get this built-up frustration out somehow. A visit to the Pit to beat a bag would do the trick. It was too hot and humid here to get a workout. I knew if I got there early enough, I could get in and out without running into anybody, especially Rage. He and I needed to talk about last night, but I wasn't ready yet.

I checked my phone, no word from Rage. He had told me that he would call today after sorting things out at the club. Gathering my gym bag quietly, I exited the bedroom, trying not to wake Ivy. A shoe flew at me, missing my head by an inch. Then a raspy voice asked, "What the hell are you doing up?" Ivy's blond hair splayed every which way, her eyes shut as she spoke.

"Nice shot, but you missed." Giggling, I dove onto the bed, jumping on her sheet-covered body. She tucked her head under the pillow. Lord joined me when he saw her moving.

"Go away," her hand pointed out from under the sheet. "Both of you early birds need to leave."

"I'm heading to the Pit for a workout, then I'll pick us up something from Juiced. You are welcome to hold down the bed, and feel free to shower when you get up. You know where everything is."

"The Pit? Now?" She rolled over, tugging the pillow down hard over her. "Isn't it closed?" she mumbled from under it.

"Yes, but Leo gave me a key." I jingled the set in the air. "I'll be back in an hour or two. Hopefully, you'll be less of a monster by then." I joked.

———

JULIET

"Juliet, thank you so much. I appreciate you making extra time for me." Jenny was making significant progress through our private lessons. Thankfully, Ivy didn't mind if I used the studio for private clients before or after classes.

"Are you kidding me? I'm thrilled seeing your progress." I walked her to the door. The damn phone was ringing again. It rang in the office through our whole session, over and over again. I glanced at the phone that still had a green light, so no message was left. Even telemarketers didn't call repeatedly.

I hugged Jenny and shut the door behind her when I heard it ring again. In my hurry to catch the call, I didn't bother locking the door. My bare feet flew across the newly polished hardwood floors, tripping over Ivy's weights and skidding to a stop at the reception desk. I lifted the receiver entirely out of breath. NO CALLER ID, FLORIDA was still lit up on the small screen. I hesitated before I spoke, "Fluid, this is Juliet, how can I help you?"

"Anabelle, I'm so glad you answered," said a familiar voice.

My stomach dropped, a cold chill ran through me. I couldn't speak.

"Ana?" he paused. "I mean, Juliet?"

"Gavin?" I whispered back.

"I'm so sorry to call you at work, but I thought it was the safest place to reach you. I first called your friend, Ivy, as you've asked me to if I ever needed to get in touch with you. She said you were there."

I felt nauseated. "W-What is it? What's wrong?"

"Everything is okay, well, for now."

I tried to control my breathing. My legs were unsteady. I reached for Ivy's fuzzy white chair to sit down.

"I need to talk to you. I'm sure you are well aware of what is coming around the corner."

My mind spun, I closed my eyes tightly, acknowledgment in my silence. I let out the deep breath I was holding.

"Probation," I said. I knew it was going to happen one day. "How long?"

"Antonio is up for a hearing by the end of October. If it goes well, he will be out by November." Marco had spared no expense to get Antonio the short sentence and a chance at an early release.

"Juliet, please don't panic. I think you've kept your cover safe, but you need to be aware and know that this is not the time to let your guard down. These are not forgiving men."

My stomach soured as he spoke.

"My sources have told me you and Paige have made Marco's radar in anticipation of his brother's return."

"Paige?" My heart was hammering, and my hands began to tremble. I gripped the desk to try and keep myself steady.

"I really shouldn't be telling you this." Gavin took a deep breath. "I have a source in the cartel who provides me with intel. Marco has someone trying to locate your sister, to press her for info on you."

I tried to keep listening, my mind and emotions in a thousand directions. "The source told me they didn't have leads on Paige since she moved. You were lucky that they were engaged in a war with another cartel when you and your sister relocated. You should know, Marco has been rapidly expanding his territory and his drug reach. He's trying to move farther up the coast. Looks like has big plans for Antonio upon his return."

I was staring at the picture on Ivy's desk. It was us, about ten years old. We were putting bunny ears on each other's heads. Sadness overwhelmed me. I knew I was going to lose her again when I left. I picked up the frame and clutched it to my chest.

"I could lose my badge if anyone found out I told you any of this, but I couldn't live with myself if I hadn't warned you and something happened."

Gavin took in a sharp breath after my silence. "Juliet," he whispered, "how are you?" He breathed, waiting for a response that I did not give. "There is not a day that goes by that I don't think of you...I miss you more than you could know. I wish I could be there with you, to protect you."

I stayed silent for a moment. Gavin always had a way of making me feel guilty that I could not return the feelings he had for me. I cared about him so much, but not in the way he cared for me. No matter how many times I told him, he still believed I would change my mind.

"Juliet, are you still there?"

"Gavin, thank you for calling me. Please let me know if you hear anything more. I have a burner, so if you call Ivy, I will get in touch with you. I think it's better if you don't call here again."

"Juliet, wait, I'm sorry. I shouldn't have said that. It's just that... hearing your voice stirred up things. I'm really sorry."

He had done a lot for me over the years, and I owed him a lot, even my life. Not a day had gone by that he hadn't been there for me since my attack. He'd always been looking out for me and my family, even until now. I treasured his friendship so much, but I had never been able to look at him as something beyond that. It always made my heart break a little every time I had to break his.

"Gavin," I said more warmly this time, "thanks for the warning. I promise, I'll be on the lookout, but I'm more concerned about Paige than myself. She just got done with school and is interning in Austin, Texas. Our parents are due for a yearlong trip around the world helping various missionaries. They've been planning it for years. They cannot find out, or it could ruin everything they had worked for."

"Paige's safety and yours are my priority. I won't let either of you end up like Sophie."

And there it was. The dagger that sliced my heart. Images of Sophie's battered body flashed in my mind. Gavin, devastated over his baby sister, who was killed by the cartel. My finger ran over the scar on my brow.

I sighed, "Gavin, I know. I'm sorry, I just, this is all overwhelming." My words were not enough to express the emotions I felt.

I could hear the plea in his voice. "I know, I just want you aware. You know, my best friend from the academy is a detective in Austin. I could have him check in on Paige if I get wind of anything else."

A small bit of relief filled me. "That would be great. I would really appreciate it. Don't worry about me. I'm in a small town with many friends. I'll notice if anything is out of place here. I don't want to alarm her if I don't have to. She had nothing to do with any of this."

It was then that I noticed someone heading toward the studio. It was hard to make out who it was in the dark until the street light made him visible. Rage was crossing the street and was headed this way. I swallowed hard. I had been avoiding him the last few days.

"Gavin, uh, I have to go. Leave Ivy a number so I can reach you back. And Gavin, thanks." He hung up just in time as the bells jingled and the door opened.

"Okay, thank you, it was my pleasure." I faked, then hung up.

My eyes now fell on the large man in front of me. He was frowning. He closed the door, leaned against it, and just looked at me. I wondered if he could sense my panic from the phone call.

"Why are you here by yourself without the door locked?" he asked in an authoritative tone, crossing his muscled arms. "It's not safe."

God, if he only knew.

I stood from behind the desk, pushing the chair out. "Well, if you have to know, I just walked my last private client out, and the phone kept ringing. In my hurry to catch it, I just forgot to lock it behind her." His frown was still there.

"Look, I am okay and safe, Mr. Overprotective." I waved my hands at him, sweeping them from my head to my feet. "My dad didn't bug me as much as you do," I said, rolling my eyes. His mere presence made the unease I felt moments ago dissipate. But from the stern look on his face, he didn't find my comment funny.

"It's just never a good idea to be alone and not have the doors locked. You never know who could walk in. It might even be someone you've been avoiding for a few days." He crossed his arms and tapped his fingers against a bulging bicep.

I could feel blood rushing to my face, which was probably turning bright red. He freaking called me straight out on it. He was right. I had been avoiding him.

His eyes now bored into mine, looking for an answer. So, I tried to be cute. I covered my face with my hands, peeked at him through my fingers, and squeaked a tiny "Sorry."

He pulled my hands away from my face. His hands were huge compared to mine. He slid his hands up and down from my shoulders to my wrists before depositing one hand on each shoulder and staring directly into my eyes. He left me no escape.

"I saw your Jeep hidden far back in the alley where you never park, and you haven't been at the gym during your usual time. I was going to wait until tomorrow and catch you at Roasted, but I was lucky to have to stop at Stained Skyn and saw you. If you're trying to play a game here, Juliet, I am not that kind of man. I won't chase you. You know how I feel about you. I want to see you."

His finger covered my mouth as my protest was about to begin.

"As much as I like you, and I know we have become friends, I got to tell you, I will not be able to see you with anyone else after the other night. So, I want it straight from you. Why the fuck have you been avoiding me? Because I know," his finger now trailing from my lips to under my chin, he lifted it to have my eyes meet his, "you were just as into it as I was."

Desire flooded me. I hated demanding men, but damn, he made it hot. He was so controlled and to the point. I loved his no-nonsense way.

I gave him my best sexy smile and placed a small kiss on his lips before drawing back. I looked at him intently, my eyes hooded as they took him in.

"I..." I swallowed, then tried again. "The other night was—" I cleared my throat, trying to control how my body was responding to the memory of the back of his truck. "It was amazing."

"Short of getting shot at, I would not have wanted to be anywhere but with you at that moment." I took a deep breath and pushed a wayward pink strand from my face. "You," I pointed to him circling my index finger at his chest, "are a lot to take in. I didn't know what to do the next day, so I thought it would be best to hide until I figured it out." I bit the side of my lip and shrugged my shoulders.

"I'm sorry. I'm just not good at this. I have a bad history of falling for the wrong person." I swallowed, waiting for him to respond.

He blinked at my words and appeared uncertain. "Juliet, I'm not asking you to marry me. I don't even date. But, you and I, I think there is something between us that's worth exploring. Juliet, I care about you. I have never been so fucking attracted to someone, but I won't let you play with me, so you need to figure out what you want." His thumb ran across my lips.

"Saturday night is my fight. I heard you, Ivy, and Shelly are going to be my ring girls." A huge smile lit up his face. It was contagious.

"Ugh, you have no idea what Ivy has planned," I groaned, remembering the outfits she ordered up.

"I'll let you have some time to give what I just said some thought. I don't want to pressure you, so you have to let me know after the fight if I'm wasting my time."

I placed my hands on both sides of his chiseled cheeks, then kissed him lightly before pulling away.

"Thanks, Rage. I'm just a little confused right now," I said, shaking my head with my eyes closed. "I'm not playing a game." *I'm just a fucking damaged mess*, I thought. A mess he might one day regret.

What chance could I give him? A chance to get killed by the cartel? Every fiber of me wanted this man, body and soul. But I couldn't allow myself that. What I needed to do was finish out the season, let Paige finish her internship, and get us the hell out of Marco's grasp. I needed to make sure that the people I cared about were safe, including most of all, Rage.

Then he kissed me. No, he devoured me, taking me out of my swirling thoughts until all I could think about was him and me and this kiss. My body weakened when his hand tangled into my hair, my core aching for him. I returned the kiss with just as much passion, and then suddenly he pulled back.

"You can add that when you're deciding on what you want." He turned to walk out the door. "See you Saturday. And Juliet, lock the door behind me."

I was left standing there, my body unable to move for a few seconds. I made it to the door to lock it, then leaned into it to support my melting body.

JULIET

Gavin's phone call had shaken me to the core. For three days in a row, every time I had laid my head down to sleep, my subconscious replayed that night like a movie. That night was a permanent tattoo on my brain, there was no detail that I couldn't recall.

Four years ago...
It was a typical day at our home on Juniper Street. I had gone to school, taught a yoga class, and then came home to cook dinner. Antonio said he would be back no later than five. I had the table set and his favorite meal waiting. Ever since he began working with his control freak brother, Marco, being late and putting me on the back burner had become common.

I slammed a few pots and pans, cursing to myself at six, watching our dinner get cold, again. Frustrated there was no sign of Antonio, I figured it was a good time to feed my new pal.

Walking to the back alley, I put two fingers in my mouth and let out a sharp whistle. I placed the bowl of kibble down and the second bowl with water. I had to keep them hidden in my potting bench. Within a matter of seconds, I saw his floppy ears and pit bull smile rounding the corner. He ran to me, knocking me back with wet kisses. He dropped to the ground and rolled onto his back, begging for a belly rub. I granted his wish and gave the sweet pup some love and comfort. I'd found him sleeping on the porch the past week, and every morning I had been waking up early to feed him in the alley.

The skinny white pit bull was constantly hanging around. I had taken him to the vet a few weeks back and gotten him hooked up with some shots and flea and tick meds. Even though Antonio had repeatedly said no, I still hoped the sweet boy would grow on him and that he would let me give him a home. I'd had dogs my whole life. Antonio was not a fan. Dog hair, muddy paws, blah blah blah. So he was my secret pet, for now.

I looked at the now-ruined dinner on the beautifully set table. Annoyed, I cleaned up the kitchen and made a plate for our neighbor. Mr. Dipetroni was always so appreciative when I brought him meals, and he loved my cooking. Ever since Mrs. Dipetroni passed away two years ago, his kids hadn't been around much, and I liked to know he had a home-cooked meal once in a while. The sweet old man would always say something like "Enjoy with your dinner, Anabelle" or "Antonio is blessed to have you" or he'd hand me a bottle of his homemade red wine.

The clock now read 6:49. No calls. I had sent four texts that Antonio didn't bother to answer. I decided to take a bath upstairs rather than continue to wait for nothing.

Ever since Antonio started working for Marco, he had slowly been turning into a different person. Before Marco came along, we'd spent so much time together, talking, laughing, or just watching movies. After two years of being pretty happy, the last four months had me questioning whether I should still be with him. He had become very secretive, possessive, and unreasonably short-tempered. I was not too fond of the influence Marco had on him.

I was not too fond of Marco, period. Rolling into town with his fancy car, flaunting his money and upscale lifestyle, insisting Antonio drop his job and work for him. I'd always dreamed of living on a farm, and now

Antonio kept talking about moving to the city in a high-rise to be closer to Marco. I could tell by Marco's passive-aggressive comments that he wasn't too fond of me either and preferred that I wasn't a part of his brother's life.

Submerging myself in a hot bath, I tried to inhale the lavender and let my anger go. My phone rested on the edge of the tub, playing my favorite music, and I allowed the sound to take me away. I stayed that way until the water had become cold and I shriveled.

I wrapped myself in a towel and heard a crash coming from downstairs. Glass shattering, yelling and screaming, furniture turning over. I was about to dial 911 when everything suddenly went quiet. I slowly made my way out of the bathroom, and then he saw me. My blood turned to ice and I froze.

I realized it was Antonio, and relief washed over me. "Oh, my God! Baby, you scared me." I was shocked by his disheveled appearance, blood dripping down his hand. I barely recognized him. This was a stranger, a maniac that stood before me, his eyes tracking my movement like a predator.

"Baby," I said again, looking at the trail of blood coming from his knuckles, "what happened to your hand? And what was all that noise?"

He pointed a shaky hand at me. "You..." he slurred. His eyes were crazed, and he was sweating profusely. "You..." he said again, spitting as he spoke. I took two steps back. I could smell the cheap perfume and alcohol on him.

"You are a little bitch who's holding me back. I'm doing important work with Marco, and your whiny little texts kept coming in and bothering us. You don't want me to be successful. You want me to fail. Not like Sophia. She helps Marco."

Sophia? He wasn't making any sense. I clutched the towel and started backing up.

"Okay, baby, just calm down. I'm sorry about the texts, I was just a little worried, that's all. I'll try to be more support—"

A swift backhand struck my cheek. I didn't see it coming and I screamed as the throbbing pain began to radiate through my face.

"You are holding me back," his words slurred.

He sat me up from the floor, grabbing me by the shoulders, and screamed at my face, "Why? Why can't you support me?"

"I-I do. I do support you, baby. Just tell me…what do you want me to do? I'll do it." I sobbed, shaking. Hot liquid was trailing down my face, the pain unbearable.

He then let go of me and sat beside me. "Marco…Marco needs me," he cried. He put his face on his hands, pulled on his hair, and started rocking back and forth.

It was my chance. I made my escape and ran out of the bathroom. I made my way down the steps, gripping the towel tightly as I ran.

He lunged at me, almost getting a hold of the towel. My thumping heart pounded in my ears as a wave of heat rose through my body. I almost made it to the bottom of the steps. The impact of a kick to my back knocked the wind out of me. I tumbled down the last few steps, landing on the floor, slicing my hand on a sliver of glass. My bleeding hand felt around for something to defend myself with. I scanned the room, it had been destroyed. I focused on the overturned table, the meal I prepared mixed with glass and broken dishes on the floor. I spotted the chef's knife about two feet from me. I lunged forward. Before I could grab it, a fist connected with my face.

I almost lost consciousness. I wished I had. But he was still there. It wasn't over.

"Stop! Antonio! Don't do this!" But deep down, I knew he wouldn't. "Help! Somebody! Help!"

I was grabbing at anything I could. I threw a plate at him, hitting the side of his head.

"Bitch!" Disoriented, he slowed.

I shuffled across the floor, grabbing for the knife. I ran out the door, but a push to my back threw me down, skidding across the concrete. Pain seared through my hip. He jumped on top of me, flipping me over, punching me in the face over and over, blow after devastating blow.

"No…" I tried to scream but nothing came out. I was barely holding on. A bloody hand came around my neck, tighter and tighter, crushing my throat.

Saliva pooled in the sides of his mouth as he yelled, "Where the fuck do you think you're going?" With my weakened arms, I used all my strength to push against his wrists to loosen his grip on my neck. "You can't leave me!" he spat.

I was no match for his psychotic power. He squeezed my neck with one hand as he grabbed the knife. Spots began to form as the darkness took me. The blade held in the air was the last thing I saw.

wo days after my attack, I woke up in the hospital. My parents, Paige, and Officer Gavin Jacobs were by my side. From the moment Gavin arrived on the scene, he had made me his priority. He had been there through all my surgeries and rehab. Gavin had made sure I got out and helped me change my name and start a new life. He had developed feelings for me that I wished I could return, but I had been too damaged, too broken, even now.

"Fuck!" I screamed it so loud that Lord began to bark. I ran out to my patio and beat my heavy bag, screaming and crying until I had nothing left except purple bleeding knuckles.

CHAPTER SIXTEEN

Rage

The door to the small locker room slammed behind Leo. He held a medical kit in one hand and a roll of wraps in the other.

"You feeling ready, champ?" He asked with a slight amount of concern in his voice.

"Yeah, man, I am. I can't wait to get my hands on that little fucker."

He just nodded and began to prepare to tape my hands. I hadn't been in the octagon in over a year. I might not have been running the circuit, but with all the training I'd been doing, I know I'm stronger and more prepared than I'd ever been. I geared up by focusing on the thoughts of the night that Richard drugged Juliet. I felt it in my bones. I just wanted to rip him to shreds. Richard Ramsey had been tormenting me since I was a boy, but nothing he'd ever done set me off like that night.

We didn't know what he'd been up to yet, but judging from some of the characters here tonight, he must've been in deep. Ledge had told Leo that there were several clubs along with a few different mafia fighters. I knew he was involved in something.

Tonight was the Firecracker Fights. There were several clubs here with guys in the tournament, but most were here to see us in the main event. Two champions, Richard Ramsey and Rage Erickson, fighting for the title. But if you asked me, the only reason Ramsey even became a champion was that I wasn't in the fight. There was only one champ here tonight.

I don't know how the hell I was supposed to focus on a fight with Juliet being one of my ring girls along with Ivy and Shelly. The girls at the club were pissed, most especially Leann. They thought their skinny asses should represent us. When the three of them came strutting out of the dressing room, I didn't know who wanted to cover them up first, me, Hawk, or Leo.

Ivy had bought them these tiny ring-girl outfits. Even though I liked Juliet in her soft sweat shorts, tight tanks, and no makeup, I nearly fell to my knees at the sight of her. My eyes roved over her, from her red painted toes sticking out of fuck-me heels, to her shiny, tan, muscular legs, and to her little red shorts that hung low on her hips. When my eyes reached her chest, I wanted to say fuck the fight, scoop her up, and spend the next three days in bed worshipping her body. The shirt squeezed her perfect tits together, pushing them up and out if not for a string to hold them in. She had thick lashes and lipstick on those full plump lips that matched her shorts. I wanted those lips wrapped around me.

Then they spun around. Fuck me. The only word that came to my head was *mine*. Juliet's perfect ass had my name across it in big white letters: RAGE. She had no idea what she'd done. I wasn't waiting any longer. Tonight she was going to find out what it meant to be mine.

The girls were giggling at our reactions; however, Leo was not happy. He growled and almost made Shelly change, but Ivy would have none of it. We asked them to get their boards while I had my hands wrapped and went over strategy with Leo.

When the door shut, I looked up to see that Juliet had stayed with us. I couldn't take my eyes off her. She stood across the small room, biting her nail with a terrified look on her face. Juliet's body language was powerful. It was a mix of fear and dread. Leo was talking about... something, and what I agreed to, I had no clue...it might have been to turn over my first born if I lost. Then the crowd made a daunting sound, and all three of us ran to the door.

———

JULIET

Millions of tiny butterflies swarmed inside my stomach. The small locker room seemed to be closing in. Outside the room, the crowd was going crazy over the bloodbath that was happening now. It had been one slaughter after another.

I'd taken a peek at the action several times, attempting to prepare myself for what Rage would participate in tonight. Terrified did not begin to describe the gnawing in my gut.

My eyes shifted to Rage, who didn't seem to share my concern. He stood calm and collected. The muscles in his chest were pumped up; his veins were pronounced, stretching from his shoulder to his wrists. He didn't acknowledge Leo as he approached him with tape in his hands. Rage must have been in the zone. He was still as a statue.

The room was stuffy. Small beads of sweat were glistening from his chest down his eight-pack to the low-slung shorts he had tied tight around his waist. His chiseled face showed nothing but intensity.

I'd been told that the rules in the underground octagon were much more lax than in a sanctioned fight. I couldn't imagine that sleazeball Richard fighting fair. Not when he didn't even believe rules of basic human decency applied to him. I prayed that Rage would kick the shit out of the arrogant asshole. The night he spiked my drink I wanted to fight him myself. Anger surged through my veins every time the thought of that night crept into my mind. I kept my promise and acted as if nothing had happened to me that night, but I seethed every time I saw him.

Leo wrapped Rage's hands and reminded him of the plan of attack. He was speaking all kinds of technical stuff that I couldn't focus on, my mind overwhelmed by anxiety. I could feel my back tightening with tension.

Rage should have been concentrating on Leo. He nodded at Leo's instructions, but his dark brown eyes stayed focused on me. My cheeks heated with the hungry look he gave me, melting away some of my nerves.

I already felt self-conscious dressed in the small ring-girl outfit that Ivy had picked up for us. The bright red booty shorts rode up, exposing my oiled legs and maybe the round of my butt cheeks. They also rode down low on my hip bones, exposing my entire stomach. Where the fuck did she even find these? The plunging top squeezed my cleavage together and up, making my C cups look more like full D's. The tiny straps holding the red material went around my neck and tied at the back. She also somehow arranged to have Rage's name appear in big letters across our asses. She had been so excited when she got them, screaming at Fluid, forcing us to try them on between classes. I thought Hawk's eyeballs were going to fall out of his head when he saw her. He might have a thing for her.

A loud collective "ooohh" came from the crowd that broke me out of my thoughts. The three of us all jumped to our feet and peeked our heads out of the room to look at the octagon where the fight had stopped. Two medics were already making their way to the man. Damn. One medic waved to another to bring a stretcher.

When I expressed to Rage how concerned I was about this, he told me about the military medics they kept on the cash payroll to assist ringside. That didn't make me feel any better, especially as I watched the downed fighter get carried away, his body jerking. A man hopped into the ring, mopping up blood as the winner's arm was held up in victory. Bile rose up my throat at the sight of the drenched red mop.

The crowd went wild, chanting "Cobra" as the winner's entrance music, Metallica's *Enter Sandman*, began playing again. Lights strobed as he held his arms up to the crowd, encouraging them.

I didn't know what I was expecting by *underground* and *unsanctioned*. I guessed some basement with a bunch of people in a circle. Not a full-blown event with a DJ, music, seating, locker rooms, medics, and a real octagon. It took an hour drive to the old warehouse turned arena. There were easily over a thousand people here tonight. I saw several MCs and other men in suits who looked like mobsters. The event was high class. There was a mix of motorcycles and limos in the parking lot. Security was all over. I wondered how they put together something this size.

Two more fights before Rage and Richard. I thought the last fight would have lasted longer, but the smaller fighter took the big guy down. For the third time in ten minutes, I looked at the time on my phone. It was 11:30. I felt nauseated. I took a deep breath in, holding it for a few seconds before letting it out. Ivy would kill me if I ruin the hours' worth of makeup and fake lashes she had put on me with my head in a bucket.

As if reading my mind, Rage called, "Juliet."

I turned to face him. He smiled that devastating, panty-dropping smile of his as he waved me toward him. "Leo, could you give us a minute?"

"Yeah, man, I gotta find Shelly, anyway. I hope she's not running around with Ivy in that fucking outfit," he grumbled as he looked at mine again and shook his head. "Ivy may not be welcome at the Pit anymore."

That made me laugh for a second. Once Leo had left the room, Rage pulled me close to him. The sound of the speakers announcing the next match made me jump. "Babe, you okay?" He was smiling, enjoying that I was a bundle of nerves.

"Yes, of course, why wouldn't I be?"

His sexy dimple deepened. "Yeah, right, you just jumped out of your skin at the announcer. What, you think I can't take your ex?" he asked, the cheeky bastard. He was clearly enjoying this.

"What? I went out on a few dates with the fucking asshole. I would hardly call him an ex. Just try not to get knocked out in the first round, okay? 'Cause I was planning on parading in this little number for at least five rounds." That had him belly laughing.

Taking his wrapped hand into mine, I looked straight into his eyes. "Rage, please promise to be careful. You have become one of my closest friends, and I just couldn't take it if something happened to you." I turned my gaze away, willing my eyes to not well up. I couldn't lose another person I cared about.

He put his hand under my chin, forcing me to look back into his eyes. "Babe," he said softly, "I'm glad to know you consider me one of your closest friends, but as I'd told you before, you are mine, and I think you should start accepting that."

He put a hand on each side of my hips and squeezed. "You look sexy as fuck in that." His hand swept up and down. "When you walked in, I wanted you. When you turned around, I nearly kicked everyone out to take you right here. So, I'm going to beat that fucker fast and hard to make it back to you as soon as I can and rip those clothes off you."

His words made my legs weak. We stood face to face, so close, our lips almost touched. I wasn't sure what came over me, but emboldened by his desire, I leaned into him and whispered in his ear, "You better."

Before either of us could do anything more, the door slammed against the wall, making us jump apart. Leo was back with Ivy and Shelly. Our moment was gone.

Ivy was bouncing up and down, "Juliet, did you see that guy? Oh, my God! Blood splattered all over the first row. It was awesome!" Her eyes were wild with excitement. "He scissor-kicked him right to the face and I literally heard his face crunch!" She shook her head closing her eyes. "Rage, please be careful, we all like you in one piece."

That commentary did nothing for my nerves and had me looking at the bucket again. *Deep breaths*, I told myself, *in and out*. Rage squeezed my hand.

"Thanks for the update, Ivy," Rage groaned, "but I think it's time you girls go and get ready for the announcer."

Leo's deep voice instructed, "Remember, start down the path the second you hear Rage's music start. Richard is entering first so he will already be in the ring."

As we exited the room, a hand grasped my wrist, tugging me back. Spinning me around, Rage held onto my arm, but he didn't say a word. His mouth opened, then closed with a quiet huff. I smiled at him, placing my hand over his and said, "I know." I stood on my tiptoes, kissing his cheek.

"Good luck, I'll be right by the side sending you good vibes so you'll crush that asshole." With a wink, I left him in the room. The crowd became rowdier with every minute that passed in anticipation of the main event.

JULIET

Rage stood at the entrance to the arena. His long curls were pulled back into a tight ponytail that just reached the shaved part of his head. A menacing look etched on his face. The crowd was still roaring for their last champion, Richard. He kept encouraging the audience as his entrance music, *Power* by Kanye West, came to a close. Richard stalked around the ring with his nose in the air, flexing his biceps, making a show of his body. Gross. *Somebody needs his ego stroked.* I knew we didn't fit. I felt disgusted just knowing I ever dated the sleazeball.

The lights dimmed as the emcee began Rage's introduction. "Let's introduce tonight's challenger..."

Silence filled the arena when the lights went completely black. Vibrations rumbled through the crowd as the large speakers began to play Rage's music. The song's base had everyone to their feet chanting Rage's name. The three of us girls were placed midway down the ramp, waiting for Rage to start walking down.

I looked up to see a single light illuminating Rage's figure at the top the ramp, giving him a larger-than-life appearance. The shadows and light effects defined every muscle. Like a comic hero come to life, his hulking arms, expansive chest, and lean abs were on full display against the stark white and red gym shorts that clung to his body and grazed just above his knees. He raised his arms, and the already outrageous crowd went out of their minds.

Excitement and anticipation replaced my fear as I took in the crowd's reaction to Rage. They knew him. They adored him.

He entered the octagon. He spun slowly, pointing to the crowd. As the words about the guy's fist making the other guy's face hit the floor bellowed from the speakers, his finger stopped and pointed directly at a fuming Richard. The crowd made it no secret, they favored Rage.

As the announcer let out, "Twelve-time champion, R-AAAAAAG-E Erickson," Rage pumped his fists a final time, and the three of us ring girls held our signs high, circling the octagon.

The two huge men resembled tigers in a jungle, ready to attack and defend their territory. Rage turned his gaze to me when the stare down came to an end. Flexing his biceps, Richard looked to see where Rage's attention had gone. An evil sneer crossed his face when he saw me. The asshole then made a show of licking his lips and blowing me a kiss. Immediately, Rage charged at him. The ref had to keep them apart before the fight even began.

Both of them were now on their respective sides of the cage waiting for the go, their eyes never leaving each other. I looked at Rage, a warrior in all respects, from his head down to his bare feet. Feet that were on a mat with crimson spatter from the previous contenders.

A boulder formed in my gut, just as the men were called to the center to start the fight. Rage found my eyes one last time. I mouthed, "FUCK HIM UP." His eyes then went back to the large man in front of him, matching his stare. Oh, my God! I swallowed the rock in my throat. How could I watch this? I silently prayed. The bell rang.

———

RAGE

The words Juliet had mouthed to me were clear as day. Fuck him up. I didn't need the instruction to know what fate awaited the man who had tormented me through my life and then had the fucking nerve to think he could look at Juliet that way. My usual reaction to taunts was no reaction. The moment his tongue gestured to her, all my common sense left. I just wanted to tear him apart. I felt like a hungry lion and wanted to devour the bastard.

I was a big man, much bigger than most men, but I wasn't clumsy or slow. Trained in mixed martial arts, wrestling, and boxing, I was a lethal street fighter with fluid range and deadly moves. My speed matched my strength. In size, Richard and I were perfectly matched, but in skill, we were miles apart. I heard he'd won his last fight only because he cheated. This poor loser didn't stand a chance against me. And now, he'd gone and thrown fuel into my fury. Maybe he was baiting me. He should have learned to never poke the bear.

The ref brought us to the center. Head to head. Under my breath, I growled, "Ramsey, you're a fucking dead man." His eyes bore straight into mine, like lasers searing through me. Twenty years of built-up hatred toward each other brought us to this moment. Tonight was payback for what he did to Juliet. I finally had free rein to fuck his world up, and that was what I planned on doing.

The bell rang, and we split apart. Our eyes still engaged, we were dancing and circling each other, moving like animals. For the first few moments, I studied his weaknesses. I easily moved around the fists that cut the air, blowing past my face. I couldn't help but smile to agitate his offensive strategy.

Fighting was in my bones, like how a musician feels the music and learns the rhythm. I could feel the tempo in a man's maneuvers, easily revealing his weaknesses. I watched his cadence, letting him expose his flaws. There it was.

I measured the steps...three, two, one. My fist tightened and landed on the right side of his jaw, knocking him off balance. Surprising me, he was back to his stance, recovering quickly. Spitting blood, he smiled, "Is that all you got, biker trash?" He then came at me with a leg to my side, and I felt the piercing pain of a cracked rib. And just like that, the fight was on.

I advanced several paces, sending out a fake-out punch to his right. He leaned into my left hook, catching him under his chin. The crowd that was white noise in the background was now cheering me on. Richard charged me, swinging violently, his white shorts were now stained red. We embraced, leaning on one another, our sweat mixing and running off our bodies. We were both vying for a chance to get the other down to the mat for submission. Locked together, neither of us yielded.

Our faces were so close, Richard whispered, "I can't wait for another chance to get in those pants and touch that tight ass when Juliet realizes what a loser you are, lying knocked out on the mat, and I know that bitch has some ass."

A new strength shot through me with that mental image of Juliet with Richard. I pushed out and forced him back far enough to make a space. I landed a hard kick to his gut. He stumbled and fell on his ass. From his back, he jumped to his feet.

Bobbing and weaving, we came at one another. Each of us landing as many jabs as we missed. Richard swiped my left eye, connecting with a sharp slice. Blood gushed from the wound, filling my vision. He used the momentary blindness to get a few shots to my already cracked rib. There had to be something on his wrapped hand that made the cut; it was impossible to have it come from his fist alone.

My right eye found Juliet on the side, covering her face. I would not disappoint her. I mustered all that I had. I stood still in a wide stance in the middle of the cage. Our eyes locked, and I waved him to come at me. The crowded roared, forcing him to take the challenge.

Richard bent his head from side to side, cracking his neck. I waved him in again, four fingers close together in a sharp invitation. He advanced. Three, two, one. I jumped into the air, moving to the side in a jumping scissor kick, knocking him down on his face and bouncing off the mat. The crowd made a thunderous noise.

I was now over his body, delivering several punches. His one hand got free and punched my already blood-filled eye. A scream tore through my throat with the pain of skin splitting further. I let go and he was to his feet throwing down a punch, but I rolled away, leaving him to hit the bloodied mat.

"You fucking cheater." I spat, wet blood coating my face as I got to my feet.

"Yeah, when Juliet's moaning my name, I'll remember that."

I wiped away the blood that streamed down my face like tears. Richard began to charge with a smug look. I backed up two paces, remembering the tempo. Three, two, one. I leaped up and landed a furious Superman punch with all my power, hitting his smug ugly face. *Knock down!* I climbed on top of him, finishing him off with continued punches until he was out cold.

The ref pulled me off his body, inserting himself between me and Richard's limp body, protecting it from further damage, before raising my arm in victory.

Screams, oohs, and aahs were rumbling from the crowd. The cheering continued as money exchanged hands. Richard's entourage of assholes carried him off. I loved the rush of a fight and even more of a win, but tonight, it was more than that. I searched out Juliet with my one good eye. I couldn't find her in the sea of people scattering in all directions. All my brothers were entering the ring holding me up on their shoulders. As I rose above the crowd, her colorful streaks became visible. The girls were behind me on the inner part of the ring. The moment my feet touched the floor, I beelined to her.

Juliet's hand covered her mouth; tears filled her green eyes. "Are you—" I crashed my mouth over hers, not letting her finish.

The crowd was screaming, encouraging us. I pressed Juliet's body more tightly to mine, lifting her with one arm. When our kiss finally broke, she buried her head in the crook of my neck. My nostrils were filled with her scent, making the pain more bearable. Her arms wrapped around my neck, then her body was jerking as she sobbed, tears flowing down her cheeks. She embraced me even tighter, still attempting to catch her breath.

"I got you," I whispered in her hair.

"I got you, too," she hiccupped through tears.

CHAPTER SEVENTEEN

Juliet

*S*ardines had more room than I had in the hallway. We stood outside the small room where Rage was being attended to. I knew Rage's left eye was in need of several stitches.

Sweat coated my body from the heat of all the people and the adrenaline that still coursed through my veins. I fiddled with my hands as I nervously waited for Rage to make his way out.

I was sure the boys in the club have some celebrating to do. I overheard conversations; they had made a small fortune on this fight.

I couldn't lie to myself any longer. I could no longer deny my feelings for Rage. It was like a slap in my face. I'd been pushing down my feelings since the first night he played his harmonica for me, when we almost kissed, but they just kept on growing. I held my breath for so long during his fight, I thought I was going to blackout. When he won, overwhelming relief washed over me.

I was losing the battle to stop myself from giving in to him completely. The moment his lips met mine in front of the whole arena, that made me realize that not only do I care for Rage, but I, too, deserve happiness. Rage made me happy, happier than I had felt in years. I still had some time left here before I had to get Paige, before I disappear. I would no longer deny myself the pleasure of caring about Rage or being in his arms. As long as he didn't know what's going on, as long as I didn't tell him the truth, he wouldn't be at risk.

He would be fine when I leave. He was a biker. Bikers didn't get involved in long-term relationships, anyway. They had club women around to always keep them content. He and I would be fine. We were both adults. We had survived before without each other, we could do it again. One day at a time. Maybe Marco would die, and I would be free. Fate could be kind, too, couldn't it?

My thoughts were disrupted by the woman who tried to bust into the room where Rage was getting fixed up. Her flaming red curls were sprayed tight, her makeup was heavy but perfect. She wore a tight black catsuit with knee-high boots, showing off her every curve.

She attempted to pass Hawk, who guarded the room, his hand clasped around her wrist, stopping her. "Leann, you are not going back there."

Wait a second. That was the bitch from the picnic. So, Leann was the mystery woman.

"But my man is hurt, and I need to help him," she whined.

Excuse me? Her man? Now it was my turn to fume. Hawk must have noticed how loud she was being. His head towered over her and found me. My fists balled at my sides, fire shot out my nose as I huffed. My body became tight and stiff.

She spoke again, this time in a sing-song southern accent, "But Hawk…"

"Go the fuck away. You shouldn't even be here. Who the fuck let you come?"

"I got one of the prospects," she said with a devilish grin, licking her lips and batting her fake lashes.

My blood boiled, remembering her lips on Rage. My body began to move before I even realized I was taking steps, squeezing my way through people.

"Oh, fuck." Hawk rolled his eyes as he watched me approaching, then Rage's door began to open.

I froze for a second, taking in his swollen face, stitched eye, and bandaged ribs. The dark curls on the top of his head were now ringing wet and falling over his forehead. Gingerly, he took two steps out the room.

Leann pushed past Hawk and grabbed Rage's hand. "Oh, baby." She raised her hand to his face, but before she could touch him, my hand grabbed hers.

I ground down on my jaw and squeezed Leann's wrist. "Baby," I repeated, pushing her arm down, "I don't think so."

I didn't know what the hell possession took over my body. I was usually passive, not aggressive. But I grabbed her hair and yanked her back.

"Oh, my God! Bitch, get off!" she screamed, struggling against my hold. With her hair still firmly in my hand, I turned her to face me, my eyes even with hers. Slowly and clearly, I said, "Don't ever put your fucking dirty hands on my man again, or I will rip every fake red hair right out of your head."

I gave her another hard yank, which caused her to lose her balance and fall to her knees. I shoved past and gently put my arms around Rage, the pain on his face was replaced by a stupid smile. Even in five-inch heels standing on tiptoes, I found it hard to reach his lips. He leaned down, and with lips locked and eyes wide open, it was my turn to claim him. All the noise and people faded away. We were the only two standing there, for just a moment.

———

RAGE

Everything in my body ached as I sat in the small room, waiting to have my eye stitched and ribs wrapped. The young Army medic shuffled in with a black bag in hand.

"Rage, nice to meet you. I'm Derek, and I will be fixing you up." He extended his hand and I extended mine. He was as big as any of the fighters here tonight.

"That was quite a show you put on," he said, turning my face to inspect my eye. The raw wound throbbed, but it was nothing compared to the cracked rib, which made it hurt to breathe.

"Looks like you need at least fifteen stitches." He pulled a fluid-filled needle from the bag, tapping the vial a few times. Oh, fuck. I hated needles. I'd broken more bones than I could count over the years, pushing them back into place was never fun, but the tiniest needle freaked me out.

"This may sting, but in a few minutes, it will be numb. I will wrap your ribs while it works." He turned his head to examine the already purpling area. I stared at the very long silver point making its way to my eye. I held my breath for a second so Derek wouldn't know what a pussy I was as he inserted it in the split flesh.

As he cleaned the wounds with a saturated cotton ball, I asked him a few questions about his station and military life. Listening to his story reminded me of Donovan. I never shared his story with anyone; I kept that pain to myself.

I remained still, not giving away an inkling of the searing ache that tore through my abdomen as he tightened the wrap. After he was done with the last stitch, snipping the end, he shot off several instructions and gave me a few pain pills.

"Thanks, for the handy work." I nodded, as I looked in a mirror at my perfectly wrapped rib cage and the clean, neat stitching.

"My pleasure. Keep the sutures clean and you should have minimal scarring."

Derek exited the room, leaving the door wide enough for me to see and hear the group waiting for me, but I only wanted one face. One small step at a time, I dragged myself to the door. It swung wide open. Hawk turned and grinned, seeing me approach.

A squealing voice carried above the rest, "I want to see my man." That sure as shit was not the voice of my angel. What the fuck? Leann? She was trying to push her way past Hawk when a very angry-looking Juliet beelined to Leann. And as Leann reached out for me, Juliet was there to stop her.

Holy shit. I couldn't help but smile when she grabbed Leann by the hair and told her whose man I was. I had repeatedly explained to Leann for the last two weeks, we were done. The girl had her head on twisted.

After dropping Leann to her knees, Juliet pressed against me to give me the hottest claiming kiss, letting everyone know we were together. My need to claim her with more than my mouth shot blood straight to my shorts. Our eyes never left each other.

———

JULIET

The ride back to Sugar Maple seemed twice as long as it did to get there. We stopped for takeout, which Rage devoured in seconds. Hawk didn't mind dropping us off at my cabin after I promised to care for his best friend. Ivy fell asleep mid-sentence, leaning her head on Hawk as he drove. I appreciated Hawk taking off his jacket at a traffic light to cover Ivy with it. I guessed we were both taking care of each other's best friends.

I had to keep Lord from jumping on Rage as we made our way inside. I took him straight to my bedroom. Handling his battered body with care, I gently took control, removing his clothes one item at a time until only his shorts were left. I was careful not to touch his tightly wrapped ribs where I could see violet and red showing up below the bandages, all the way down to his hip bone. He tried not to make a noise when I lightly grazed several areas as I pulled the tank over his head.

Inspecting his stitches, I pushed back the curls that covered his forehead, careful not to touch his eye. One eye had many stitches, and the other was a shade of lilac that was growing darker by the minute. I leaned over him as softly as possible and touched my lips to the injuries on his face. A small lump formed in my throat, my eyes blurred as they fought back the tears that were threatening to spill. I swallowed hard, and my chest clenched when the images of tonight's fight flashed through my mind. I turned on one of our favorite playlists, letting the music fill the space, giving me the courage to take what I wanted.

I moved to the bed feeling a little anxious as he watched me. My fingers softly touched his face. I could feel the pulse of his heart against my lips as I trailed kisses from his neck, his well-defined pectorals, and down the line of abs to the sexy V where the top of his shorts slung low on his hips. He jerked on the first touch.

"Sorry," I whispered.

When he opened his mouth to speak, I placed a finger over it. "No. Don't say anything. Let me take care of you." I whispered. Heat flared in his eyes.

"Just lie back, relax." I nipped at his ear, kissing my way down his neck, inhaling his soapy scent. My lips dragged down his chest oh so gently. The change in his breathing had my body weeping for his touch. When I got to the top of his shorts, I could see how ready he was. I looked up at him. He was staring at me, his arm above his head as he just watched my actions.

I began guiding his shorts down his strong legs. My eyes grew wide at the beautiful sight of his naked body. He was a fucking Adonis. A shudder ran through me, my core heated, the little tingles letting me know how ready I was for him. Wanting these feeling to last, I kissed up and down his length, loving the groan that he made at the warmth of my mouth. I kissed my way back to his lips.

I pulled my thin tank top over my head, revealing my bare breasts. The lust in his eyes nearly brought me to an orgasm. He reached out, smiling as he touched the boxing glove belly ring, the small diamond chips in the gloves glinted under the soft light in the room. My body flamed at his reaction to me.

I removed the sweat shorts I had on, revealing the pink lace boy shorts that cupped my ass. His fingers extended, touching me softly, making me moan. I was so wound up I could barely hold on. I rocked over his fingers aching to know what he would feel like inside me.

"Look at me," he said, and my eyes met his. "You are so fucking beautiful. Come here, kiss me."

I crawled up his body, careful not to apply pressure to any injured areas. I leaned forward and his lips captured mine in the most intense kiss, before his fingers reached down, moving my panties to the side and began working their magic. I reached around, gripping him and massaging him as our mouths continued long, devouring kisses.

Rage tugged at my drenched panties, assisting me in removing them. I rode his fingers greedily and let my mouth move at the same rhythm over his. It was only seconds later that he touched the spot that had me soaring over the edge and crying out in pure pleasure.

"Oh, my God, Rage." I squeezed him tightly as my orgasm exploded. When I came down from my high, I was desperate to feel him inside me. "Do you have a—"

"In my bag, inside pocket."

After rolling the condom on him, I placed my body over his, trying not to hurt his ribs. "Are you okay," I asked as I began sliding on top of him.

"Oh, fuck yeah," he groaned. "There's no injury that could stop me from having you now." Rage looked at me so intently as he guided me up and down. He grabbed my hair gently and began nipping at my throat. Sparks flew through my whole body with each thrust. His breath was in my ear, and his fingers were digging in my back as I rocked back and forth. It was almost too much. My orgasm began building again, and I gripped his shoulders and kissed him furiously. I could feel his body begin to jerk. I pulled away from his mouth and rolled my head back, crying out as we rode out our orgasms together, into oblivion, where it was just him and me and nothing else mattered.

CHAPTER EIGHTEEN

Rage

*I*n my palm sat the two painkillers that Derek gave me earlier. I had refused to take them before, but I underestimated the amount of discomfort there would be in my face and ribs as they competed for which hurt worse. I swallowed them down with water, the cold liquid coating my throat felt good as the pills disappeared with a promise to ease the suffering.

I didn't expect, given my current condition, that Juliet and I would be able to spend so much time giving each other pleasure, but now I was feeling everything from the fight to the much-needed release she gave me. Before the pills even took effect, she had fallen into deep asleep. Minutes later I followed, smiling at the memories that we made tonight.

A warm light shone through my heavy lids. I blinked a few times and then I squinted at the sudden brightness hitting me in the face. I groaned slightly. The aches brought by the morning didn't allow me to sleep any longer.

Lord lay in a ball at the bottom of Juliet's side of the bed. His ears moved when I stirred, but his eyes remained shut as he breathed. Juliet's back was to me, half covered by the sheets. Her perfect ass was aimed right at me, begging for another round. Even in this state of pain, the image of her had me ready again. I couldn't help but stare at the goddess who lay next to me. I wanted to memorize every part of her. Juliet's tan legs were smooth and shiny. Her skin felt like silk against my finger as it softly trailed the curve of her back, her body twitching at the light touch.

I continued moving farther up her back to her neck. I swept her long multicolored strands to the side of her shoulder to get a better look at her tattoo. The bold splashes of watercolor ink acted as a vivid background against the black and white tattoo over them. The hand had fine detailing with an intricate lace pattern woven through it. All kinds of small symbols made up the hand. From far away, it was just one of those things you could see on yoga stuff. But when you got close, all the small symbols that made up the artwork were revealed. The piece must have taken several sessions to capture all that detail. White ink filled the center of the hand. Inside the circle were numbers, maybe a date—6.2.14. I wondered what it meant. If she had it permanently tattooed on her perfect skin, it must have been pretty significant.

She seemed so guarded sometimes, with walls even taller than mine. I wanted to know everything about her. She might not know it yet, but she bonded us last night, she was mine. Fuck my rules. There was no way I was not taking a chance on her. She was too damn special. Besides, I'd been a goner long before—she'd had me since that night I spent with her in the storm.

I could feel she was awake. She turned her head, peering over her shoulder at me. Her eyes grew wide when she saw that mine were open. She saw my body's way of saying good morning and happy to see you, and a sexy smile took over her lips.

"How are you feeling?" she asked, now lying on her back. Her voice was raspy with sleep.

"Like I was in a fight," I smirked at her.

"Can I get you some more meds?" She examined my face and winced at my purple ribs.

"I'll get them." I started to get up, but two fingers pressed my shoulder back onto the mattress.

"No, Rage, you need to rest. I'll get us some coffee and you something for the pain." As she rose from the bed, the blanket fell down, exposing her beautiful breasts and pink panties that stood out against her tan skin. She must have read my mind because she said, "Don't even think about it, you need to heal. There is plenty of time for that. Don't worry, I promise, I will make sure you are well taken care of during your recovery." She waggled her eyebrows and laughed as she put on a loose white tank and tiny shorts.

"I'm going to hold you to that," I promised.

It wasn't long before she returned with some coffee, her "miracle" healing juice, warm berry muffins, and something to take the edge off the pain. We sat in her bed, devouring everything.

I pushed a piece of hair from her face and tucked it behind her ear before running a finger down her jawline. She smiled weakly at the gesture. "I've been meaning to ask you, what does your tattoo mean?"

"It's a hamsa. It's a symbol of an ancient amulet meaning the hand of God. It's a protective sign. It's supposed to bring the wearer luck, good fortune, health, and happiness. It can have an eye at its center as well, like the eye of God. The fingers represent the senses and chakras in Hindu. I love its meaning. My mom gave me one when I was young, and I used to always wear it around my neck and felt close to her, like she was watching over me even when we weren't together. I lost it snowboarding when I was eighteen, so I had it tattooed so I could never lose its protection. I had the artist do the watercolors behind it so I could have all the colors of the chakras in it."

"What about the date inside?" I asked, finding it odd that she didn't mention it. She swallowed hard. Her eyes were looking at the floor. "Oh, uh, I had Hawk add that for me. It, uh, well, you know, I had an accident and recovered." She breathed a heavy sigh, "Well, it was pretty bad, and I almost didn't make it. I had a long recovery. And when I was at my lowest, my grandmother gave me some advice. I took it and I decided I would move with Ivy and start a new life. That is the date my old life ended." Her eyes never lifted from the floor.

Another long breath, "Rage, I'm not sure what this is," she pointed between us, "but I have a hard time talking about my past. I want to, but I'm not there yet. Please don't be mad. It's just," she blew out a

201

hard breath, "not something I like to remember. I hope you understand."

A sense of sadness took over her, which I hoped never to see again. I lifted Juliet's chin. "Look, I wasn't trying to pry. I was curious. I didn't mean to upset you. I hope someday you can trust me and open up, but I get it, my past isn't filled with rainbows and unicorns, either." I kissed the top of her head and gently pushed through the burning in my side to pull her into my chest.

It should have bothered me that she wouldn't open up, but with her pressed against me like this, it was very hard to care about anything else. She erased each question from my mind with every touch, kiss, and orgasm. She gave herself to me, and my body was insatiable. It was more than sex, more than passion. It was all-consuming, life-altering kind of sex that I had never experienced before.

———

JULIET

I did not expect that to be our "after" pillow talk. My stomach did backflips as the subject of my past was brought to light. I felt like such a lying piece of shit. Rage didn't deserve this. I was protecting him, but why did it feel so wrong?

I spent two days caring for Rage in my bed. Today was the first morning I woke up to an empty bed. I already missed him.

I was aware that it was selfish of me to want this time with him. When he pulled me to his side, I nearly lost it. I wanted to cry and confess everything and beg him to never let me go. But that wasn't fair to him. I knew that. Rage deserved someone who could be there for him. My head felt heavy in my hands. My eyes were covered by my fingers, elbows on my knees. I let my neck drop, so overwhelmed that I could not even pick my head up.

How could I have been so selfish? How could I have given in to my desire? I had wanted him so badly that every part of my body ached and wept for his touch. I knew now that I had deluded myself into thinking that it would be easy to walk away from him. And every moment we spend together would only make it more painful.

Could I come clean and tell him the truth? No, I couldn't. He would hate me for sure. And in the small chance that he would forgive and accept me, his life would be put in danger. No, I couldn't do that. I had no choice but to keep my secrets. He couldn't know.

I just had to accept once and for all what my life had become—a fortress that cannot let anybody in. Rage had been slowly tearing down the walls I had carefully built for so long, but I couldn't let him no matter how much I wanted to. I was going to have to leave him.

I tried to swallow the pain down. My head fell back to the pillow, the headache pounding so hard even my jaw ached. I hugged my pillow and prayed that someday he would forgive me.

CHAPTER NINETEEN

Rage

The smell of coffee coaxed me awake. The rich aroma can drag even the most hungover of men to their feet. It was the scent that signified the promise of a new day, a new beginning. And it was a new beginning, I woke up in Juliet's bed again, and not for any other reason but that she wanted me here. For the past two weeks, we had spent most of our time together.

Last night, we took my bike on a long cruise. I loved the feel of her body pressed against my back, her arms around me, holding on tight. It was torture having her that close for so long. She laid her head against my back, shielding herself from the wind. Every move she made drove me wild. I thought I was going to burst by the time we got back to her place. She felt the same, and we spent the rest of the evening showing each other just how turned on we were.

Even now, in my half-asleep state, my body was ready to take her. I never wanted a woman so badly. A smile crept on my face as I began to feel around for her. Juliet wasn't in bed. She had made a habit out of sneaking out to make coffee and crawling back into bed next to me. I tried to avoid the light streaming through the white sheers. What pathetic excuse for curtains. Who could sleep with this much sun in their face? What time was it anyway?

I retrieved my phone from the crumpled jeans on the floor. Six missed calls from Hawk and Colt. I checked the time, 6:35 am. What could they want? It was practically the middle of the night to most of my brothers. *Where was Juliet?*

I followed the smell of the ground beans through the kitchen and into the garden. There, I quietly peered out to see Juliet sitting on a big pillow with Lord wrapped around her, laying as close as possible. Her eyes were closed, her arms stretched out in front of her. Candles lit the area. The soft music playing was no match to the tinkling of the wind chimes that drowned it out.

Juliet remained focused on her prayer? Meditation? Whatever she was doing, she didn't hear me approach, but Lord did. He picked up his head and gave me a look that said, "Don't even think about it buddy, this is our time." She must have felt his movement because her eyes snapped open and found me watching her.

She smiled. The green and yellow in her eyes appeared vibrant in the sun; her dark lashes gave them an exotic frame. Her wild hair was half twisted in a knot on her head while the rest streamed down her back in gentle waves. Juliet rose from her seat, and I realized she was only wearing a loose-fitting white tank that was showing the chill in the morning air.

As much as I didn't want to disturb her ritual, I couldn't help but want to scoop her up, throw her over my shoulder, and go back to the bedroom. So, that's what I did.

"Rage," she giggled, "put me down." Lord didn't like it and began to growl, but her laughter calmed him as I carried her, wriggling around, before I threw her on the bed.

We ended up in the shower. Afterward, Juliet twisted her wet hair on top of her head and made her way to the kitchen while I stepped outside to call Hawk back. What the hell could he want, calling so many times?

"Rage, where the fuck have you been? Colt has been going crazy looking for you. There was some vandalism at Stained Skyn. We need you, man. We're meeting there in an hour."

"Yeah, okay, I will see you there."

"Rage, one more thing."

"What?"

"Tell Juliet I said hi." He busted out laughing.

"Fucker." I hung up on him.

On the small table sat a French press with two cups and some very dark green liquid in shot glasses. Cut up fruit was overflowing out of bowls, and one plate with a lid over it sat on one side of the table. Juliet gestured for me to sit. She lifted the lid and steam escaped, revealing a stack of golden pancakes. *Damn, this girl.*

"Is that all you're eating?" I asked, looking at only fruit on her plate.

"Yes. I can't practice a routine hanging upside down with pancakes in my belly. I'll grab a smoothie at Juiced after my class."

I nodded, but not quite agreeing.

After cleaning up from breakfast, I had to head back to my place to get a few things before meeting Hawk.

I turned to Juliet, who was putting away the last of the dishes. I pulled her in for a kiss before asking about her plans for the day.

"I'm heading to the Pit for a few rounds and some training. Then I'll teach the one o'clock class at Fluid. Big Jake needs some help at the shelter later, so I promised him that Ivy and I would help him with a litter of pups that arrived late last night. Ivy suggested we have dinner and drinks over at Stallions after we finish at the shelter. I should be home by nine, maybe."

"Stallions? You two, alone? I don't think so." I huffed as I put on my boots.

"Um, last I checked I was a grown-ass woman who can decide where I'm having dinner. I'm pretty sure I didn't tell you not to go to the Cave and have a meeting with the strippers the other night."

"That was different. It was a club meeting." I grinned.

"And this is dinner with a friend."

"A lot of dangerous men go to that bar."

"Like who, your brothers?" Her hands were now firmly on her hips.

"How about I meet you here after dinner, then I can prove that I am home safe?" she asked as she leaned against my back and lightly bit the side of my neck.

207

I'm not going to win with her. "Fine, but I still don't like it," I grumbled. "Text me when you're there and when you leave."

"Yes, Dad."

———

RAGE

I turned into the stone driveway leading to Juliet's cabin. When I cut the engine, her music was so loud, she didn't even hear me coming. Usually, as soon as I pulled in, Lord and Juliet were both waiting to greet me.

Rounding the garage, I could hear Juliet's off-key singing. She was belting out vintage Metallica. I spotted her Jeep. A bright pink yoga mat and two sparkly Converse high tops were under it, tapping to the beat. There were dirty oil rags and containers by the tire. Is she…? Surprising me again, there she was, changing the oil of her pride and joy, Athena.

Working my way up her sexy legs, she began to wiggle her way out from under the Jeep, still singing. I stood back to watch without her noticing. She flipped over onto her knees, wearing tiny shredded jean shorts. I could see the curve of her perfect ass as she pulled the tray from under the vehicle.

Once her head was clear from the vehicle, I made my presence known. I yelled over the music, "Need any help?"

Juliet jumped two feet, placing her hand over her heart and getting oil on herself. "Rage, you scared me." She let out a deep breath as she snapped off a glove and leaned into the vehicle to turn down the volume.

She looked fucking adorable. Her shorts were overalls, which were even sexier. Underneath, she had a pink strapless bikini top. Her hair was in two long braids peeking out of her pink glittery Namaste baseball cap that matched her Chucks. She had a smudge of oil on her face. There was a long old T-shirt rag tied to one of the loopholes.

"What are you doing?" I asked with an eyebrow cocked.

"What does it look like I'm doing?"

"It looks like you're changing your oil."

She pointed a latex glove covered index finger at me and said, "Bingo! You win a prize." She snapped off the other glove.

Juliet walked around the side of the Jeep to a small cooler and offered me a beer and got herself water.

My smile widened as she handed me one of my favorite icy brews. "White Wolf from Blackrock Brewery?"

"You said you might drop by, and I remembered you were drinking it at the picnic, I didn't want to go in the house all oily, so I prepared," she said smiling.

"Thanks, babe, you're the best." I kissed her clean cheek. "Now, can I help you?" I offered as I picked up the new jug of oil and inspected the bottle. "Full synthetic," I noted.

"Yep, nothing but the best for Athena. It's okay, I'm just about done, and you're clean." She laughed.

"Or," I suggested, "I could get dirty, too, then we could get clean together." I wiggled my eyebrows. Juliet threw a dirty rag at me before asking me to open the bottles.

I spent the next few minutes watching her work as she told me how she had always helped her dad when he changed the oil and how he had wanted both his girls to know how to do things themselves.

Her whole body language changed when she spoke about her family. I couldn't understand why someone who seemed to care so much and miss their family would move so far away from them. Every time I brought up the subject, somehow she got out of answering.

Then Juliet went into a whole rant about synthetic oil and how essential it was. Even though I agreed with her, I pretended not to know, just because her talking engine care elevated her to a whole 'nother level of hotness. She had me wanting her so bad, I barely let her get out of the shower before attacking her for the first of several times. The last round left us exhausted, falling asleep in her bed again before it was even 10 pm.

The constant chirps of all the damn birds Juliet insists on feeding woke me. Willing myself back to sleep, I placed my head under the pillow, trying to avoid the bright light streaming into the room again. I was going to beg her to get shades. Jesus, I couldn't take it every morning. I might need to stay at the clubhouse to get some decent sleep in my dead black room. Although, it was nice wrapping my body around hers. I would either wake her or fall back to sleep, whichever happened first. The silkiness of her body had me ready for her again, but judging from the soft murmurs that were coming from her, she was still fast asleep. This girl was turning my world on its axis. The more I told myself that it was okay to care, just not too much, she would do something or say something to push me in further.

I was dozing back to sleep, holding her close under the light sheets, when her body tensed. Juliet started mumbling and then screaming. Her body thrashed and fought.

"Noooooo!" she yelled.

Not again. A few days ago, she woke up screaming. She said she had dreamed that something happened to Lord. I didn't believe it. Her face went pale, and she zoned out the whole morning.

I shook her gently. "Juliet, it's okay. Babe, you're dreaming."

Nothing.

"Juliet," I said louder, gently shaking her again.

Her eyes popped open. She shot up on the bed. Small beads of sweat appeared on her brow. It took a moment for her body to settle and her eyes to focus on me. I pulled her into a tight hug, rocking her. "Rage," she whispered in relief.

"Babe, it was just a dream." I kissed her head. "It's okay."

I pulled her back enough to see her face. Wet streaks stained her flushed cheeks. *What the hell is going on?* I looked into her fear-filled eyes; they held something back, I just didn't know what.

——————

JULIET

"Nooooo!" I screamed, trying to push Antonio off me. "Nooooo!" Using all my strength, I pushed harder. This time, he was shaking me. "Juliet," he said gently.

"Babe, wake up, you're dreaming." The voice was louder this time.

Startled, my eyes opened from a vivid dream to find Rage holding me, shaking me gently, calling my name. A muscled arm pulled me in, keeping me tight to his chest, making me feel safe. Rage placed a soft kiss on my head as I tried not to breakdown. He tilted my head up examining my face, which must have revealed too much.

He didn't say anything right away. Comforting me with his body, I felt his hard chest and could hear the steady rhythm of his beating heart. It strangely calmed me as my breath and heart slowed to match his. My body relaxed as the signature scent of his body wash and lingering aftershave filled my nose. When had I become this familiar with him? I pushed the thoughts of Antonio away as I took comfort in the moment. I knew the questions would come. I had an awful feeling Rage knew it was more than just a nightmare. He studied my face.

With my head resting on his chest, I whispered, "Thanks for waking me from the nightmare. I've had them since I was a kid," I lied.

He pulled me back to look at him. Studying my face again, his square jaw was ticking. Did he know I was lying? My eyes could barely meet his.

In that raw, sleep voice, he said, "Juliet, want to tell me what that was really about?"

Shit. Shit. Triple shit. I am a terrible faker. I blew out a long breath.

"Uh, it's fine, just a nightmare. I'm not even sure. Someone was chasing me, then the person caught me, and I was fighting them off."

Rage's brown eyes narrowed at me, his lips tightened. Large arms crossed his chest making him look intimidating.

Uh-oh.

"Babe, I have been patient. One of these days, you are going to spill whatever the fuck you think I can't handle. I told you how hard it has been for me to even consider getting close to a woman. And you've changed all that. You know that I'll move mountains for you, but you won't even move an inch to let me in."

He turned away from me and started to get up. I reached out to pull him back into bed. The sheet I had wrapped around my naked body slid to my waist exposing my breasts. I could see the heat flare in his eyes. He stared a moment before he turned away again, picking up his jeans off the floor.

"Rage," I started.

He put his hand up, telling me to stop. "No, Juliet." He pulled his white T-shirt over his head. "I may not have known you your whole life, but I know you well enough now to recognize when you are hiding something."

His boots were on his feet and cut over his shirt before I could even respond.

"I'm going to give you some space," he said as he picked up his keys.

He opened the bedroom door, and Lord flew into the room and onto the bed. Rage gave me one more glance over his shoulder, then he shut the door behind him. His bike started before I could put on my robe and make it to the door.

Fuck! I hit the door with my open palm.

He was right. I was going to lose him...and I didn't want to. I had fallen in love with him. A scream tore from my throat as I pounded the anger out on the door. I needed to talk to Ivy.

––––––––

RAGE

I felt like shit. I'd confronted Juliet about her night terrors, and I'd been too hard on her. I remembered how difficult it had been for me to open up to anyone. But this thing with Juliet made me feel as if she couldn't trust me, like she was holding back.

I gave it a day and then just acted as if nothing had happened. I sent her a text letting her know I wanted to see her. Neither of us brought it up again. I hoped she would confide in me because it was becoming a wedge between us. I hated knowing she was keeping something from me.

Summer was dwindling. It was hard to believe Labor Day was only a week away. Since the first night I spent in her bed, Juliet had made time fly by. We had spent as much time together as we possibly could.

For so many years, I had sworn never to get close to anyone. But I'd never known anyone like Juliet. She was as beautiful inside as out.

She cared so much about…everything. Even the damn environment. I loved the way she frowned at using plastic, her crazy recycling routine, and how she composted anything she could. I loved how she teared up whenever that heartbreaking commercial came on that showed all the animals that needed help. She had me seeing the world differently. She had inspired me to do better. Become a better man.

Before Juliet, my dates had been going to a bar, dinner, or maybe a movie. Last week, we took her Jeep up to Boulder Lake for a paddle boarding date. How she'd convinced me, I didn't know—oh, yeah, she'd promised a special night if I tried it. Hawk thought I was whipped. Yeah, well, I didn't give a fuck.

Juliet had snuck out of bed before dawn and packed a whole cooler full of food and drinks. She'd had an entire breakfast spread on the table when I woke up, including homemade cinnamon rolls. Then after breakfast, we packed our gear into her Jeep and hit the road.

It had taken us an hour to get to the lake. I had planned on taking us to a good swimming and kayaking spot where I always used to go as a kid, but she said, "Keep driving another mile and turn left."

I did as she asked, wondering where the hell she was taking me. She directed us to a small turnaround where we parked and unloaded all our gear before hiking down a wooded path. "Trust me" was all she said with a grin that lit up her angelic face. She must have taken Lord there before because he led the way right to the small creek inlet off the lake. The landscape was breathtaking, high trees where the sun streamed through. The private inlet was shallow, yet deep enough to get on the boards and paddle out.

Lord was with us all the way in this little adventure. Who knew dogs liked paddle boarding? Juliet put a life vest on him, and he proudly sat at the front of the board.

Juliet laughed at my wobbly start when I stood on my board— well, Ivy's board, which she didn't mind me borrowing—but I got the hang of it quickly. We paddled down into a remote area of the lake, about an hour out.

There were small islands scattered through Boulder Lake. Juliet had taken me to one I had never been to. She explained that there was

---

shallow water for about half a mile, and boats didn't come out this far for fear of getting stuck.

I threw the ball into the lake, entertaining Lord, while she laid out a whole picnic for us. The amount of gear in the backpack she had was startling. She had a small speaker playing music on her phone. I had the cooler of beer and food strapped to my board. We lay on the blanket laughing, telling stories, and feeding each other strawberries. I had my head on her lap while she played with my hair when I decided to open up about losing my brother.

I felt her body stiffen and her hands stopped. She was listening intently, letting me spill things I had never told anyone. Then a single tear slid down her sun-kissed cheek. She tried to wipe it away without me noticing it. It touched me deeply, knowing that she cared that much.

I tilted her face and brushed her lips with mine. The kiss we shared was so sweet, so pure—it was more profound than just lust. The connection I had with her at that moment was deeper than I had with anyone my whole life.

Thankfully, the island she chose was deserted, the only sounds were the splashing water against the shoreline and the birds. Behind large boulders, I spent the next hour worshipping her body. For the first time in my life, I didn't have sex—I made love. I knew I was not just falling for her—I was already in love with her. I felt like such a girl having feelings like that. I didn't care. I never felt this before, and all I knew was I never wanted to let it go.

CHAPTER TWENTY

Rage

$\mathcal{W}$e strolled through the produce section of the grocery store. Juliet explored the vast amounts of fruits and vegetables, grabbing anything that she didn't forge in her garden. She wandered the aisle like some women did jewelry stores. She had a look of pure bliss on her face as she found the perfect papaya, holding it up high in the air and shouting, "Oh, my God! It's perfect! Have you ever tried this?"

I felt eyes on me the whole time. A little boy was following my every move. The only time he peeled his eyes away from me was when making a big decision between an apple and a banana. He was as bad as Juliet.

The boy was there with his mama and baby sister. His mom had on her hip the little girl with a way-too-full diaper. Juliet and I ended up in the same check-out line as the family. There was only one cashier, and the woman in front had a huge cart full. Juliet seemed oblivious to the boy and his family as she organized all the fruit in the basket while waiting for our turn in line.

"Come on, Jacob," his mother snapped, pushing him forward as he examined the apple he held in one hand and the banana he had in the other. When we took our place in line behind them, the boy turned and looked at me from my feet all the way up to my face. He took a step back and smiled at me.

"Are you a wrestler?"

"No, little man, I'm not," I answered with a grin. I noticed his faded WWE shirt that was a little too small.

"Well, you look just like the wrestlers we watch on TV." I didn't think the kid believed me.

"I'm going to be a big wrestler someday," he said, popping out his chest.

His mom was paying no attention; she placed her bottle of liquor and a couple of bags of Ramen noodles on the belt and asked the clerk for a pack of cigarettes.

"Who is your favorite wrestler?" I asked. His big brown eyes grew wide, and without hesitation, he yelled, "John Cena!"

"He's a good choice." He smiled big with several missing teeth. He then gestured for me to come close.

"Is she your girlfriend?" he whispered loudly, staring at Juliet.

I squeezed my lips together, trying not to laugh at his attempt to ask quietly. I smiled at him and whispered back, "Yes."

His eyes widened and mouth gaped open. "Wow! She's really pretty." Juliet smiled, hearing his innocent appraisal.

He turned back around, his brown hair flopped in his face. He stretched out his arms, reaching up to the conveyor. "Mama, don't forget my apple and banana, you promised me. I've been good and did all my chores," he reminded.

I smiled down at him, admiring his purchase. "You know, if you want to be a wrestler, it's really important to eat your fruits and veggies." Juliet agreed, smiling at the boy and then at me.

"I'm sorry, ma'am, you're going to have to put something back. You're a few dollars short." The clerk said, leaning close to the boy's mother. She examined the items and looked at the boy. "Jacob, you can get an apple and banana next time."

A sad look that was all too familiar crossed the boy's face. "We don't need those things right now," she snapped.

"But Mama, you promised. We haven't had apples or bananas in forever."

"Jacob," she scolded. "I said, no."

It was like hearing my mother's voice. Anger torched through me. Poor little guy, all he wanted was fruit. His mom had a pack of cigarettes and liquor but couldn't afford an apple and banana? I reached down in my pocket, pulling out a few dollar bills. I slammed them down on the counter. "Please pay for the apple and banana for my little friend here," I told the clerk.

His mother gave me an unappreciative look and said, "That's not necessary."

"But ma'am, it is," I said coldly. I leaned in close, the smell of smoke and booze was overpowering. "What's not necessary are cigarettes and liquor," I whispered in her ear so not to let the little boy hear.

Still smiling his toothless smile, the boy said, "Thanks, Mister," grinning as if I gave him a million dollars.

I kneeled beside him. "You are very welcome. Now, you be good for your mama, keep eating your veggies, and you will be big like me."

Hugging the fruit to his chest with one arm, he agreed enthusiastically. He looked at me like he was memorizing me. His other hand reached out to touch the logo with my name on the patch. "Rage," he said.

I nodded.

"I'm Jacob," he held out his hand, "and my baby sister is Sara."

"Jacob, let's go, now." His mother pushed him toward the exit. She looked over her shoulder, giving me a nasty gaze.

"Have a good day, buddy," I waved.

"Thank you, Mr. Rage," he yelled over his shoulder.

When they were out of earshot, Juliet turned to me and said, "Rage that was super sweet of you." She got on her tiptoes and kissed my cheek.

"Yeah, well, I'd had an awful mother, who drank and smoked and couldn't care less if my brother or I ate. I recognized that kid. Shit, I was that kid."

JULIET

With every week that went by, the idea of leaving Rage became harder. It had been less than three months since we became a couple, yet it seemed like we had been together for years. It was almost like the world was a million-piece puzzle and our two pieces came together in a perfect fit. We had developed a routine and often finished each other's sentences. Rage made me laugh harder than anyone ever had, which his brothers found strange because he was the brooding one of the bunch.

I set the table outside and carried out two huge plates of pasta with grilled veggies. Rage should be here any minute. I had made dinner almost every night; he had supplied the ingredients many of those nights. Not once had he complained about eating a plant-based meal. I even offered to included meat in his. I know he thought as much as he worked out that he needed it. But he had declined and said if I looked this ripped on a plant-based diet then he would be happy to eat anything I made.

Antonio had rarely eaten my vegan meals, except my eggplant parm, but almost no one who had tried it ever turned that down. He had complained all the time about everything I did. How could I have been I blind for so long about Antonio? He had been such a controlling asshole. First loves could do that to you, I guessed.

I sipped on the sun tea I had made earlier today, its coolness made me feel a little better in this end-of-summer heat. The mint I had added from the garden was Rage's favorite.

The condensation from the glass wet my forehead as I ran the icy drink across it. I felt overheated after being in front of the stove. The cabin had gotten stuffy when I was boiling the pasta earlier.

I smiled and relaxed back in my chair as I heard the rumble of his bike getting closer to my house. I crossed my legs tightly as a naughty thought about what I wanted for dessert crossed my mind. *What has this man done to me?*

Two large hands landed on my shoulders from behind me, squeezing gently before the calloused skin tickled me as they ran their way down to my elbows and a wet kiss touched my cheek. "Dinner smells almost as good as you," he whispered in my ear before rounding the table and taking a seat.

Lord ran to greet him with his favorite drool-coated ball grasped between his teeth. "Hey, bud, how's my boy?" he said, taking the wet ball and tossing it to a grateful Lord, with ears flapping as he chased it across the yard.

A strange feeling caused me to shudder. A sense that I'd almost forgotten because it had been so long since it was part of my life— family. We felt like a family. Since my parents and Paige disappeared from my life, I had not really felt that kind of happiness and security. I took in a deep, heavy breath and stared at my plate, pushing around the food.

"Babe, you okay? What's wrong?" Rage asked. He was getting to know my sounds and sighs too well.

"It's nothing," I tried to play off the feelings with a smile. "How was your day?"

He stretched, his long arms revealed rippling muscles as he reached back. "Much better now. This pasta is, mmmm, amazing! I thought you were going to wait for me to grill the vegetables?"

"I was, then I started prepping and thought it would be nice to have everything ready for you," I raised my glass of tea and he did the same with his.

"Thanks," he pushed out a breath. "I know it has been a little crazy for me, with club business taking up a lot of my time. You know I can't discuss it, but you should know, we are so close to closing in on the men that Richard is working with."

I felt a mixture of anger and relief. My eyebrows raised, my eyes widened. "You guys are still pursuing it?" I asked cautiously. His forehead wrinkled, a scowl forming as he ground his jaw. "Of course. There's no way we're letting this go. You could have been hurt or more. Other women have been hurt already. This is not something the club takes lightly."

"I see." I straightened, surprised at the bitterness in his tone. "I'm glad you're getting somewhere. I hope anyone involved pays," I said, meaning every word.

The music filled my yard as we sat at the fire pit, watching the sun's last light fade over the mountain. I sat on Rage's lap, wrapped in his arms. We made out like teenagers. I loved the long kisses that were hard to break. I leaned my head on his shoulder as he held me. It felt like home, a place I never wanted to leave. But every time I got too comfortable and felt like I could have a chance at forever, there was that haunting voice inside my head, reminding me that it wasn't possible. I hated that voice.

The mountain chill was setting in for the evening, Rage held me tight, warming me with his body. His face reflected the glow of the warm fire, making all his deep-set features more prominent. He was beautiful.

"I never thought I could be here," he admitted.

I glanced at him, puzzled. "Not here like your house, but here like in this moment," he breathed hard, "caring about someone... For years, I've sworn I would never. I find it hard to trust people, to let them in, especially women. My mother was a liar and an abuser, now, I tolerate neither."

Pain pricked at my eyes, but I didn't want him to stop. At the same time, guilt overwhelmed me.

He took another drink of his Long Island Iced Tea. "Losing people I loved, like my brother and Grandma, caused me so much pain and anger. I never could have imagined that anyone could ever feel that raw and alone. I would gladly take a thousand beatings over the pain of losing someone you love. I was left with a hole so big, I thought it could never be filled..." He took a deep breath, and I could hear the sorrow in his voice.

"So, I spent the last decade being an angry dick that most people didn't want to be around. That's how I wanted it, no one too close. Leo and Hawk were the only two people who truly knew me. It's funny, when I first got back to town, both of them tried to give me hints about you. Like they knew. They knew you could be the person who could pull me out of the miserable life I've made for myself." He gently touched my chin, forcing me to look into his eyes.

"Juliet, you are a pure soul. So good, kind, generous, and nurturing. I don't deserve you, but you've changed everything. You've changed *me*. You are my healer." He cupped my face and covered my mouth with his before I could even say anything.

It was a kiss I would never forget. The pain and love mixed in the kiss made my toes tingle and fever rip through me. Rage stood up, lifting me in his arms and holding me to his chest like a bride.

He carried me into the bedroom and set me down onto the bed. I watched hungrily as he removed his shirt, then his jeans. My eyes roved over his glorious body. Just looking at him had me ready. I pulled the cotton dress over my head, leaving me in just my panties. I leaned back on the bed waiting for him to join me. His eyes held something I'd never seen. He was looking at me like it was the first time he saw me.

He knelt on the bed, hooked his fingers into my white lace panties, and tugged them down my legs. I could feel myself coming alive as his fingers skimmed down my thighs. He brought his body over mine, until we looked into each other's eyes. I was at a loss for words. He placed a hand on each side of my face and touched his lips to mine so gently, like a feather.

"Juliet, I've never said these words to anyone." My heart was hammering. "Juliet, I love you. Before you came into my life, I was barely getting through each day. I had no purpose; I was a fighter with nothing to fight for. But now I finally know how it feels to love." The emotions I felt slammed into me like a freight train.

"Rage, I love you, too." I told him, admitting the truth out loud. I loved Rage.

His lips crashed over mine. I could feel the warmth of his body as he pressed against me, leaving no space between us. He ran his hands up my arms, holding them above my head as his lips caressed my neck, causing me to moan. His fingers reached down to touch my flesh, making my back arch and body tingle. I could feel my orgasm building...he must have felt it too, and flipped me on top of him, straddling him. I ran my fingers over his smooth skin, his pectoral muscles were rock hard. He shivered when the tips of my fingers glided over his ribs, tickling him.

Now it was my turn to bring him to the edge. I worked my way down using my tongue and lips. I pulled back slightly every time I could feel him inching near his release. When we both could barely hang on, I crawled up his body to once more taste his lips before sinking onto him. Inch by glorious inch, my entire body shuddered as intense pleasure sparked through me. He sat up, causing me to scream in pleasure. Rage grabbed my face, kissing me as he controlled my body with his hips. I was so close. My breaths were shallow gasps. I couldn't take it any longer, I felt like I was going to explode.

"Please Rage, don't stop." I cried out in ecstasy as he moved his hips, pushing me back to hit the spot that took me straight to heaven. As he was about to climax, he gripped my hair and sucked on my lips, making me feel all his pleasure. I collapsed on his chest. His rock-hard arms wrapped around me, holding me so tight, like he thought I would disappear if he let go.

We didn't say another word to each other. We didn't need to. We just stayed there entangled in each other. His words repeated in my mind, "Juliet, I love you." They both consumed me and crushed me. Body, mind, heart, and soul, I was consumed by Rage.

RAGE

We sat around the Maple table again. The discussion was the same as last week's. How were we going to infiltrate the cartel and uncover the band of bikers that were helping them?

"There has to be a weakness," Colt said. "We have it narrowed down. Two MCs are on our radar. Devil's Damned and Cajun Kings, the two are sworn enemies, but both have increased their drug trade along the coast. It was the trafficking of women and arms that has us focusing on the Devil's. Their club has no respect for anyone. Now that Viper, their president, is temporarily out of commission, Joker and Blade are going to want to take over. Even though Viper kept things friendly between us a few months ago, we all know the others are not so inclined to play nice." He took a long breath before he continued, "We also got a lead on this Columbian, Marco Cordona. He is a drug lord who has been making his presence known in a growing number of small coastal towns. He uses MCs to move his merchandise up and down the coast. His family was primarily dealing in Florida and Louisiana. Now they are branching out."

Colt looked around the table, taking in our responses. "These are the type of men that if you let them in your town, it's impossible to get them out. Then their MC will be making a home here. It happened to a few of Outcast's chapters along the coast. Their small ones had to patch over to other clubs to stay alive. This is a threat we cannot take lightly. We also have seen Richard Ramsey with an MC contact. I know the guy is an asshole, but I didn't think his arrogant ass was that stupid. He has no idea what he has gotten himself into."

"Hack has a meet with an informant later this week. We should have all our answers then. For now, any of you," he pointed his tattooed finger around the table at each one of us, "has a run-in with another MC, you keep it calm and do not retaliate. One thing I know is, we cannot handle a cartel with only one chapter, let alone a cartel that is fully armed and dealing with other outlaw clubs. You see or hear anything, you bring it here. Don't try to take care of it yourselves, understood?" We all groan in agreement, except for Kai.

Kai cracked his knuckles and asked, "So we just sit here and let them come to our town?" He pushed his chair out roughly and stood, slapping both his hands down on the table. "Let them think they can just come in and take over our streets?" He looked at all of us. "How long are we supposed to let that happen?"

"Kai, sit the fuck down," Colt commanded. "I just said we got intel. It may take Hack a few days, but we will handle whichever club it is. There has got to be a way to put pressure on this Marco character and push him out. We just don't know what it is yet."

Kai sat down, pushing his long hair from his face. He laced his fingers through his hands, resting them on his head as he leaned back and groaned, "Fine. But you know I can't hold my temper for long. We need to get this shit under control."

I watched the exchange knowing that I was going to be a part of the plan. I had to leave town for a few days and meet with our founding chapter. I was leaving tonight and didn't have much time to spend with Juliet before I went. I was not too fond of the idea of leaving her there alone. I knew she had been fine on her own for years, but now I wanted to be there for her and protect what was mine.

She answered on the third ring. "Hey, so glad you called!" Her giggling, sweet angelic voice came through the phone and I almost forgot why I was calling. Damn, I got it fucking bad.

I shook my head and responded, "I wanted to see if you had any time to see me today. I got to go out of town tonight on club business and probably won't make it back until late tomorrow night or the next morning."

"Really, tonight? That sucks. I was going to invite you to watch a band and have a few beers at Stallions with Ivy and me."

"Aww, babe, I wish I could, but I got to take care of something. You know, I don't like the idea of you going to the bar without me, don't you?"

"Come on, Rage, I used to go there with Ivy all the time. Besides, no one will bother me. It's no secret that we are together, and I don't think anyone wants to get on your bad side," she laughed.

"Maybe I will send a prospect with you girls, just to be safe."

"Fine," she gave in more easily than I thought. "Just make sure he is eye candy for Ivy, or she will be pissed."

"I have two hours between my private lessons and the evening class I teach. I could meet you at Juiced for a late lunch."

"Yeah, that works. I have to go to Stained Skyn before I hit the road. I was hoping to be having more than just lunch since I won't see you for two days."

"Haha," she giggled. "I'll text you when I'm on my way."

JULIET

This was the second night in a row that Rage had not been in my bed. I held the pillow that still smelled of his cologne and squeezed it as I tried to sleep without him. Even though I had Lord to hug, I had gotten way too used to the security that his big, sexy body next to me had brought to my life.

Ivy and I had fun last night at the bar, laughing, singing, and torturing the poor prospect. Ivy had kept giving Bodie a hard time. The entire evening, I had felt something was missing. How pathetic was I? There I'd been, having a good time with my best friend and a few other girls we knew from Fluid and all I could think of was that I would do anything just to be sitting at my fire pit and getting bit by mosquitoes in Rage's arms.

Tonight was not any easier. I did everything I could to distract myself from thinking about Rage, to no avail. I spent the next hour in bed fighting with myself. I was torn between missing Rage and knowing that I had created this giant mess and that very soon I would have to leave him. If I missed him this much after two days, knowing he was coming back to me, how could I abandon him forever? Seeing him with that little boy at the store had melted my heart and made me fall even deeper in love with him. How was I going to do this? I never intended on falling in love. Never. It was 11 pm, and I was hugging his pillow like a pathetic teenager in love.

My phone vibrated and flashed. A goofy smile crossed my face as I threw Lord off me and leaped across the bed to grab it, knowing who it would be. My heart swelled at the sight of his name illuminating my screen.

Rage: Babe, you up?
  Me: Yes, lying in bed missing you.
  Rage: You are killing me.
  Me: I'm all alone and wearing nothing but the sheet.

I bit my nail. What the hell was I doing?

Rage: Fuck, babe, you make me want to jump on my bike right now and race home.

Me: I wish you would, I would much rather it be your hands on me than mine.

I smirked at my wit, waiting for his response.

Rage: ahhhhhhhh…I'm dying! Stop.

Me: If you promise to be back soon, maybe I'll wait for you. Maybe.

Rage: I miss you like hell, but I don't think I'll be making it back before noon tomorrow.

Me: Aww, that's too bad. I guess I'll just have to think of you…

Rage: You better wait for me. I'll make it worth every minute I was away.

Me: Maybe.

I clutched the phone, wishing I could feel his touch through it.

Rage: Babe…

Me: Where are you anyway? Can you tell me?

Rage: I had to meet a few brothers from Tallahassee. We met in the middle.

My stomach flipped at his words. Tallahassee? Why was he meeting the club from Tallahassee? Don't freak out. Just act like nothing's wrong.

Me: Oh, really, are you with Ace?

Rage: Really? <angry emoji> Yes, and no, I won't tell him you said hi.

Me: I'm just messing with you <smiling emoji>

Shit, I hoped he wasn't mad.

Me: Hurry home. I miss you.
  Rage: I will. Fuck, I want to be home with you right now. I promise I'll call you in the morning. I got to go. Sleep well.
  Me: You, too. Drive safe. I miss you.
  Rage: Babe, you better WAIT FOR ME. I'll be home soon.

Home, I thought. Did he mean home to me or home to Sugar Maple? Have I...have we...become home? I read his texts over and over. And then I read them some more. Fuck.

I set the phone down and buried my head in his pillow again, sucking up every bit of his scent that I could breathe in. My inner overthinker started again. First, I was sexting, then I was saying *home* —what the hell was I doing?

After tossing and turning for a good hour, I took some valerian root and magnesium, which usually promised a restful sleep. I couldn't figure out if the bout of insomnia was caused by Rage being away or the fear of another nightmare. I turned my phone to a Beatles playlist. My mom used to sing *Here Comes the Sun* to help Paige and me sleep. It worked, the combination had me dozing off minutes later.

CHAPTER TWENTY-ONE

Rage

I swung the door to the clubhouse open, stomping to the meeting room. My mood was apparent. It was bad enough that I had spent nearly three days away from Juliet, but as soon as I thought I could make up time, my phone rang, with a fucking club meeting. I went straight to Juliet's from my trip and hadn't been back to the clubhouse since. I had Kai deliver the info we'd collected. I needed to get a new change of clothes, but I wasn't ready to leave her yet. I could stay wrapped around her in bed forever. Everything I used to think was important now carried little meaning. Juliet had filled all the empty space in my heart. She had given me a home again. She had made my life have meaning. Now, anything that took time away from that just pissed me off.

"Wake up on the wrong side of the bed?" Hack asked.

I just narrowed my eyes, ignoring his assessment. He walked with purpose. He held a huge coffee in one hand and his laptop in the other. His hair, which was usually plastered in place, was disheveled. He looked as if he had not slept.

Once all the boys were around the table, Colt got right to it. "We have some information. I'm glad you all came. This mission is going to be all hands on deck." He rubbed both his hands over his face.

"This situation is way more dangerous than we first suspected. We are not just dealing with the cartel, but Marco Cordona and his new crew. He has been expanding fast and has his eyes on Sugar Maple and Black Rock. Infiltrating small coastal towns with little police presence is part of his plan. We need to find something we can use to get to him. Hack has been working tirelessly. We now know that Marco grew up in Columbia with his father, a cruel man, who was at the top of the cartel's food chain. He has a brother, whom we are trying to locate. This brother was raised here in the States by his mother. She has since passed away. We think the brother is the key to getting out a threat of our own. Our other chapters are ready to go to war, if necessary. The cartel has been a threat to several of them."

Moans and groans echoed around the table. I could see how exhausted Hack and Colt looked. Now I felt like a dick for being pissed that I was interrupted from my time with Juliet. They were trying to save our home from being taken over by a real threat.

"This is our home, and home to the people we care about most. I'm in. Anything the club needs. What can we do to find the brother?" I said.

Colt tilted his chin toward Hack. "Hack's on it. We just got the intel this morning. We hope to have something by tonight. We're trying to stay off the radar; we don't want anyone getting wind of what we know or that we plan on defending our territory."

Hack sat across the table just staring at the computer screen. His hand appeared to have a slight jitter as he swallowed the last of his monster coffee. He pulled a Red Bull and cigarettes from his bag. I watched him crack the can open and guzzle. I waited for the room to empty before speaking to him.

"Hack, you okay, man?" His gaze didn't move from the screen.

"Hack!" I slapped my hand on the table, causing the can to jump.

His head shook as his bloodshot eyes finally looked from the screen. "Sorry."

"Are you okay, man?" I asked again, waving my hand in front of his monitor.

"Yeah, I got to go do this from home. I don't have enough security and jammers here to cloak my presence. I got to go home." He closed the screen and began loading the laptop into his bag.

"Once I find anything, I'll have you come over." His glasses couldn't conceal the dark circles behind them. He must have been at this for a while.

"You look like you need some rest. You can't do your best work unless you have a clear head. Dude, take a fucking nap." I snagged the Red Bull from his hand.

He nodded. "Yeah, I guess an hour won't hurt. I'll text you later, man."

RAGE

Rolling out from under Black Betty, I cleaned my hands and opened my phone when it alerted me again of an incoming text.

First text from Ledger: Need you at Hacks ASAP. Text on your way.

Second text from Hack: Get your ass over here now. Important.

The third text, two minutes later, Ledger: Where the fuck are you?

Fourth text, one minute later, Ledger again: Rage, where are you?

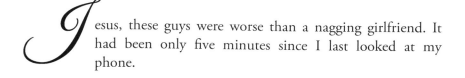esus, these guys were worse than a nagging girlfriend. It had been only five minutes since I last looked at my phone.

Me: On my way. Keep your fucking panties on. See you in twenty.

Hack lived closer to Black Rock. He always complained Sugar Maple's internet was too slow. The main feature he needed in a home was fiber optics or some shit like that. It didn't matter to him what the fuck it looked like as long as it had optimum high speed. I rolled my eyes at the thought. I could do without all this shit. I liked having a phone, but I missed the good old days before the robots took over.

I pulled up to the curb of his small suburban neighborhood. Ledger's bike took up the last space in the driveway. All the ranch-style homes looked alike. Hack's was different because he was the only one that didn't have all the fancy landscaping and shiny new exterior. He bought the worst house on the block but didn't fix it up like all the other suburbanites, at least on the outside. On the inside, however, it was a modern marvel.

I knocked twice before letting myself in. I flinched at the sound of my boots squeaking across the just-polished black marble tile floors. I walked through the kitchen before getting to his office. Fancy stainless steel appliances were bright against the black quartz counters. I stole a beer from the fridge. His stash was neatly lined up on the shelves; everything in the refrigerator stood in perfect order. I would bet that none of those appliances had ever been used.

Sleek modern furniture decorated the living room. A 75" TV with every game system known to man all sat neatly underneath on separate shelves. He had special fans installed to keep his gear from overheating. Abstract paintings only he could understand adorned the walls.

The smell of cleaning products bothered my nose. I was amazed he spent any time at the club, knowing what a clean freak OCD kind of guy he was.

I heard the voices coming from the office. I didn't announce my arrival. Hack bragged about his "smart home." He had surveillance cameras everywhere. He must have been running a pretty sick business considering all the tech gear he had here. I pushed the office door the rest of the way. Holy fuck. It looked like the fucking FBI headquarters. Monitors were everywhere. His neat desk had cans of Monster and Red Bull covering it. An open bottle of Johnnie Walker Blue Label sat on the edge of the desk with a few shot glasses around it. I pointed to the bottle. "Are we celebrating? Isn't that like a three-hundred-dollar bottle?"

Ledger poured me a shot, and another for them, judging from the remnants of amber in the bottom of the other two glasses. We raised our glasses together, before shooting them back. Smooth, I got why Hack preferred only the best.

"Not celebrating, brother. He refilled my glass and pointed to the chair. You may want to take a seat." Ledger pointed to the buttery black leather executive chair."

My eyebrows furrowed. "Sit? I think I'm okay. What the fuck is going on?"

"Sit." Ledger and Hack said together.

"Fuck, you two are bossy." I blew out a breath and sat in the chair, "Happy now?" I downed my second shot.

"Ledger, what the fuck's with all the dramatics?"

Ledger began explaining how Hack found Marco Cordona's brother in Florida State Prison.

"Okay, great, we got friends in there. The Dade County chapter should be able to help. We can get to him and use it against Marco as we planned."

"Yes, but…" Ledger stopped and took a long breath. "We did some digging to find out why he's in there." He closed his eyes, rubbing his temples, before continuing. "Antonio Cordona beat his girlfriend nearly to death."

"That's fucking tragic, but why am I sitting for this?" I leaned back in the chair, waiting to hear why they were acting so peculiar.

"His file has pictures of the girlfriend, Anabelle Conti." Ledger paced as he spoke. "She was unrecognizable after the incident, until the trial." Hack handed me the folder of the reports and the pictures.

I opened the five-year-old report, taking out the woman's photos. God, what a fucking tragedy. I found it hard to look at the girl's beaten face and body as I moved from one photo to the next.

"So, what does this have to do with…" There were close-ups of swollen, beat, and bruised body parts. It was the picture of her arm that caught my attention. The wrist was black and purple. However, under the bruising was something I recognized. A fucking sideways figure eight.

My breathing became shallow, my heart sped. I quickly flipped through the papers, getting to the trial. "What the fuck?" I growled aloud. I pulled out the close up, gripping the picture with both hands, letting the rest drop to the ground.

I could feel that familiar tingle. It started at my feet. The flush of heat rose through my body. It turned to fire as my beating heart pounded out of my chest.

Images of Juliet flashed in my mind. The scars on her face she covered with her hair. The scars on her pelvis. The nightmares. Everything became crystal clear. "Accident?" I screamed. "She told me she had a fucking accident!" I was spiraling.

Ledge handed me another shot. I drank it before hurling the glass across the room, crashing into a monitor.

"Fuck, Rage, calm the fuck down!" Hack yelled holding back my arms. "We knew you would react like this, that's why we brought it to you first, before announcing it to the rest of the club." He placed a hand on my shoulder. "She's alive and well, and now she's your girl. You need to talk to her. You got three hours before our meet tonight to go to her and sort this shit out."

I removed his hand. "What the fuck do you know?" I looked at the picture again, at the face I loved, busted and broken. My voice turned into a fractured whisper, "She said it was an accident. She wouldn't talk about it."

"Well, now, I guess she'll have to talk to you." Ledger said, picking the papers from the floor, placing them back into the folder. I snatched it from his hands, taking long strides to the door.

"Rage, wait," Ledger called after me. "calm down before you talk to her. You can't drive like this."

My knuckles were white from gripping the folder so tight. I spun at the door. "Calm down?" I spat. "She fucking lied to me! Everything about her was a fucking lie," I yelled, punching a hole in the wall next to the door.

I secured the folder under my jacket, tucked the top in my jeans, and took off on my bike faster than I ever had. The trees lining the winding mountain road were a blur of green. I was sweating, and my heartbeat was competing with the speed of my bike.

Turning into the driveway, I parked next to the Jeep. With each step toward the door, I felt like a knife was getting plunged deeper and deeper into my heart. How could she have kept this from me? Let me fall in love with her and never tell me?

I heard Lord's barking before Juliet, or Anabelle, or whatever the hell her name was, opened the door. She offered me the most beautiful smile, holding a mug in her hand with her crocheted blanket wrapped around her. The scent of apples and cinnamon welcomed me in.

"Hey, handsome, what a nice surprise. I thought you were working on your truck today?" She took a step back, looking at my face for the first time.

"Rage," her voice became shaky. "Rage, what's wrong?"

JULIET

"Rage what's wrong?" I asked, stunned by the hateful, angry look on his face.

"I don't know. You tell me, Anabelle."

My mug slipped from my hands, smashing to the floor, its contents splattering. My heart pounded. How did he know? I was speechless for a moment. I pressed my eyes closed. I could feel the tears building. I took in a shaky breath, forcing my eyes open to look into his.

"Rage, I'm sorry, I wanted to tell you." I could only force out a whisper.

He held his hand up. "Stop lying. I don't believe you had any intention of telling me." He looked directly into my eyes, waiting for an explanation.

"You don't understand. My life was in danger, is still in danger, and I will not drag another person into it. Why do you think I tried to keep us friends? I didn't plan on falling in love with you." A few tears escaped despite my attempt to hold them.

"In love with me?" he laughed. "That's hilarious. You couldn't love me and keep this from me. I shared everything with you. Things I've never shared with anyone." His face looked so full of pain.

He unzipped his jacket, pulling a folder from inside. "I had to learn the truth from my brothers. From a police report," he yelled with venom in every word. "I loved you. You filled the emptiness in me only to turn around and obliterate my heart." He tore the folder open and held up a picture of my beaten face.

I ripped the photo of my beaten face from Rage's hand. My finger touched the swollen and stitched face in the picture.

"No, Rage, you're right. This is Anabelle Juliet Conti." I said with a steely voice I wasn't sure how I summoned. "She was a trusting girl. She was weak. She lost herself in a man who wasn't who she thought he was. She had no idea what she was wrapped into until it was too late."

I brought my fingers to the faint scars on my face, the same spots shown in the photo. I ran my fingers across the small jagged lines.

"I could've had these lasered off. You know why I didn't?" I took a deep breath and squared my shoulders. "These scars," I pointed again, "remind me every day, that I was once weak. That I allowed this to happen to me. But no more."

"You're hiding from a cartel and didn't think it was important to tell me. What were you planning on doing? You must know Marco will be released soon."

My eyes went down to the floor. I stared at the scuffed motorcycle boots that were mere feet away. I couldn't bring myself to meet Rage's angry face.

"Juliet, what were you going to do?" He stepped into my space, crowding me. "Tell me, Juliet, what were you going to do?" He spoke slowly, his voice was a low growl.

"I was going to run!" I yelled. The words were out of my mouth before I could stop them.

He took a step back, recoiling as if I burned him. The angry expression was now full of hurt. "You were going to leave?" He shook his head. "You bitch. You fucking made me fall in love with you, knowing all my pain, and you were just going to leave?" His fists balled at his sides.

"You think it's going to be easy for me? You think I enjoy running around, looking over my shoulder with my whole life strapped on my back? You think I enjoy having no one in my life, leaving people I love behind? You think I want to leave you? I love you more than I ever thought it was possible. That's why I couldn't tell you all this. I didn't want you to get hurt because of me."

"So, you couldn't trust me to protect you?" He hung his head, shaking it. "I would have died protecting you." He began to turn away.

I grabbed his arm, but he pulled away. "Don't you understand? I want love, not protection. I want the freedom to be me, not be watched over or babied. I want to live life on my terms. If I had told you the truth, what would you have done? Admit it, you would have been consumed by the need to protect me and watch my every move. You would have been obsessed about hunting down the person who attacked me. You wouldn't have been able to look at me the same way, all you would have seen was a victim, a weakling you needed to shelter. And where would that have left me? I would've always wondered whether you were with me because you truly loved me or because you felt obligated to protect me."

His eyes narrowed on me as his face twisted in anger. "Well, I guess, you don't have to worry about that now, Anabelle, because I am done. You've destroyed anything I had left." His hand was holding his heart.

The lump in my throat grew painful and tight, and the river of tears I'd been holding finally flowed in streams.

I said in a whisper, "You cannot protect me all the time. No one can. The day I moved and became Juliet, I decided I would be my protector. I would live free, making my own choices. I had a second chance at life. I won't waste it. There are seven billion people in this world, I will not let two fucking assholes ruin my life. I want to live, experience, feel, love, make a difference. I can't do that with a shadow. I'm sorry if you can't understand that."

I finally allowed my eyes to find his, hoping he would hear my plea. Those soft brown eyes that had shown me love these last months were hard and narrowed as they met mine.

The tears poured over my cheeks; I could feel the warm liquid running down my neck.

"Rage, I gave up my family to get away…my mom, dad, little

sister. Losing them was more painful than anything he did to me physically. Paige is five years younger than me. I missed everything— her graduation, college, broken hearts, everything. She's my baby sister and best friend. She's not nearly as strong as me, and I had to leave her behind. I've sacrificed a whole lot, so I could start a new life and keep them safe."

With each word I spoke, the pain and heartache returned. The box where I kept it all in had been blown up, and each word was a dagger. My arms went around my body, hugging myself, attempting to find comfort.

"Rage…" My breaths had become short and staggered, practically hiccups. The words I tried to form would not come out, stuck in my throat.

For the past few weeks, I'd been thinking of how I could possibly leave him. Now I had my out. A painful one, one that would not give me the closure I wanted. The thought of never being wrapped in those arms again frightened me more than Antonio's or Marco's threats. But I had to let him go. His life being in danger if I stayed was something I couldn't bear. So, I pushed.

"Rage," I repeated, summoning all the strength I had left, "I cannot and will not let you take this on. I am sorry for lying to you. But my freedom is all I have left. Yes, I lied to you, but I had to. I'm sorry, but it's clear now that it's better for us to just go on our separate ways." I recited, hoping he wouldn't call my bluff. If he touched me, I would melt into a pool of mush and would do anything he asked of me.

"Running is not freedom." His fists relaxed as he blew out a breath, and with a low voice he said, "But if that's the way you want it, fine. You won't be a kept woman by me. I knew this was a mistake. I should have never let myself fall for you. I should have gone with my gut."

Be strong, Juliet. "I'm sorry I hurt you, but I'm not giving up the independent life I've made for myself and built for myself. I can take care of myself as I've done the past four years." I lifted my chin, trying to show him I was strong in my resolve.

With those words rolling off my tongue, he nodded and said, "I hope you'll be happy with that decision. Enjoy your independence. Goodbye, Anabelle." He turned away and stormed out the door, slamming it so hard a sconce fell from the wall and shattered on the floor, in a million pieces, just like my heart.

It took everything I had not to follow after him and tell him how much I loved him and wanted him. But I couldn't. I knew he wouldn't let my past go. This was the only way to keep him safe.

As the sound of his bike faded into the distance, my body crumbled to the floor, and I freely let the tears flow. Lord pushed against me, and I buried my face into him. It was the two of us alone again. I'd done it before, it might take time, but I would get through this. I would rather live with a hole in my heart and know Rage was alive than risk him losing his life for me.

CHAPTER TWENTY-TWO

Rage

*I*t had been the longest, loneliest, and most painful month of my life. Each day, I went through the motions like a robot. The club had been busy at work, attempting to put an end to the threat on our territory. All the brothers had taken turns going out of town on business, trying to get our connections in order. I used that as a distraction, but even the imminent danger didn't keep me from thinking of Juliet.

This morning was my Saturday shift at Stained Skyn. I stood looking out the tinted glass, watching people come and go from the farmer's market. Because of the colder weather, it was only open on holiday weekends. Halloween had everyone leaving with pumpkins and barrels of apples. I repositioned myself several times, hoping to catch a glimpse of Juliet. I knew it was self-torture, but I turned out to be a masochistic fuck up.

Juliet no longer went to the Pit. She had Ivy doing her Wednesday classes. I felt bad about that. I knew she loved her MMA workouts, and avoiding me had kept her from them. I was going to have Shelly call her and arrange a schedule that would allow her to come in without the possibility of us running into each other. She was not even at the club party two weeks ago; she used to never miss those, more to keep her eye on Ivy than to party.

Two weeks ago, I noticed her at the corner from Fluid; I almost didn't recognize her. She looked thin, tired, and her glow had disappeared. Her golden brown locks were dull, no more pink, purple, and blue peeking out. I didn't understand why she looked so miserable —*she* rejected *me*. She had lied to me, then stabbed my heart and set it on fire. She had made it clear. She wanted to be alone. After losing Donovan, I did not believe there was anything left of my heart to crush—it turned out there was.

I refused to ask anyone how she was doing. Especially Ivy, 'cause fuck her, too. This was Juliet's fault, and I wasn't asking.

I was done feeling like shit, so tonight I was determined to stop feeling sorry for myself and hauled my ass to The Ridge. Saturdays were usually busy, but tonight it was unusually packed. Brothers, townies, college kids, mostly women, made up the crowd to see the band. Blood Moon was a blues-rock band from Tennessee who made it through the area a few times a year.

Every time they played The Ridge, the women went crazy for the lead singer, Parker Wilson. The acoustic sound of the guitar filled the room, the large amps carrying Parker's deep voice over the riffs. Woman swayed and cooed on the dance floor while the men shot pool and darts.

I found myself scanning through all groups of women, assuming Juliet might be here considering the band. Not one held a candle to her. I noticed a group of women who were way overdressed for this place. They were loud even over the music. One woman was staring me down. Her barely there top was casually readjusted to give me a glimpse of her cleavage. I rolled my eyes and turned away to listen to the music and grab a beer with a few of my brothers.

Colt was the last to arrive. We did a few shots, and I felt a bit loosened up. I kicked Hawk's ass at two pool games and three games of darts, then sat back down at the bar and ordered one more shot. I made myself comfortable on my stool, relaxing to watch the band's next set. The lights dimmed on the stage.

Parker, in a smoky, deep acoustic blues version, began to sing *Ain't*

No Sunshine. With each lyric, everything else in the room stilled and silenced. It was like the words were being sung directly to me. A dull ache formed in my chest as Juliet's face flashed in my mind. The darkness of her being gone made my heart ache. With each verse, my mood darkened. I motioned to the bartender for another shot. I threw it back and walked over to the woman who had been trying to get my attention all night.

A crooked smile came across her mouth as she acknowledged my approach. "You looking to get out of here?" I asked.

Her eyebrow arched, and she licked her lips. "Oh, yes."

I grabbed her hand and pulled her through the crowd and out to my bike, not looking back. I handed her the helmet and pointed to the seat.

"My name is Sherri, by the way." Her fingers glided over the seat. "I love your bike." She giggled with a small hiccup.

"Rage," I grumbled back and nodded to her to get on.

She was cute. She wore more makeup than I liked, and she wasn't soft and natural like Juliet, and she didn't smell of summer honeysuckles. Her clothes were too tight, she had big tits and a small waist, but she lacked the tone and curves of Juliet. She wore really high heels. Juliet owned flip-flops, Converse, and boots. I remembered when she had to borrow a pair from Ivy when she needed heels. What the fuck was I doing, comparing this bar bunny to my Juliet? I was with Sarah, or was it Mary, whatever, to get my mind off Juliet.

"Where are we going, Rage?" She swayed and giggled.

"Clubhouse. You think you can hold on?" I assessed her movements.

"Oh, yeah, I can hold on. I could ride all night." She giggled.

I rubbed my eyes, shaking my head as I mounted the bike. "Get on, watch the exhaust. Hold on tight, Sally."

"Sherri, my name's Sherri."

Right. Sherri. Who fucking cares?

She wrapped her small body around mine and squeezed more tightly at every curve. I felt sick. Juliet was the last woman to ride on my bike. I had to keep reminding myself that all I needed was a night

243

with a woman and maybe tomorrow would be easier. Seeing her the other day and then hearing that damn song had my head fucked.

We made it back to the club. I walked in, grabbed a bottle from behind the bar, and pulled her back to my room. She walked around the room, looking around, asking me questions. I didn't really answer. "You're a quiet one," she giggled.

"We aren't here to talk. If that's what you want, I'll bring you back to the bar."

She smiled, not insulted at all. "No, I guess we aren't," she agreed. She removed her shirt and was just wearing a small strapless lace bra.

She walked toward me, grabbing my belt and pulling me close. She brought her lips to my mouth. I could smell the alcohol and faint smell of smoke coming from her lips. I pulled away and said, "No kissing." I turned her so her back was toward me. I didn't want to look at her. I couldn't look at her.

She wiggled out of the micro skirt, rubbing against me. I tried to get into it. But that damn song was stuck in my head, over and over. Juliet was my sunshine. She only had to gaze at me with those yellow-green eyes, one look and she had me hard.

Sherri's hand covered my denim-clad crotch. She popped the button and unzipped it. She had her hand in my boxers, rubbing up and down. Nothing. Her half-naked body or warm hand did nothing for me.

"Is this not working for you?" she noticed.

I grabbed her hand and jerked it away from me. "No," I snapped. "*You* are not working for me." She kept quiet as she looked at me, taken back at my harsh words.

"Sorry, recent breakup."

"I get it," she nodded. "If you give me a chance, I'm sure I can wipe that bitch right out of your mind."

Her strapless bra unsnapped, falling between us to reveal her huge tits. Picking up the bra, I handed it back to her. "She's not a bitch. Get dressed. I'm taking you back to the bar."

There were still quite a few people hanging out around the club. I heard Hawk's voice and the giggling of women coming from the game room.

"Rage, yo' man, want to get in on a game?" He pointed his cue at the table. "I need to earn my money back," he yelled.

"Nah, man, I'm headed out to take her home." As the words left my lips, the woman with Hawk turned, shooting me daggers. A furious Ivy, with hands on her hips. She gave Sherri a once over, then looked at me.

"I guess you've moved on, you bastard."

Hawk snapped, "Ivy, shut it."

"No, Hawk. He fucked up Juliet, and now he's out with some whore."

"Who are you calling a whore, bitch?" Sherri answered back.

"Ivy, she was the one who fucked me, so you can just shut up and mind your own business."

I took Sherri's hand and led her to my bike. Outside, Sherri was turning in circles, her chin tilted toward the full moon that lit the sky. "Look how pretty the moon is."

My eyes looked at the sky, gazing at the bright full moon and the sparkling stars surrounding it. I closed my eyes, remembering the night I almost kissed Juliet the first time. She had been under the club's protection then. We had lain on a blanket in her backyard and she had pointed out constellations and spoke of their meanings. Juliet had told me how her parents always used to say that whenever she missed them, all she had to do was look at the moon and remember that no matter how far apart they were, they were both looking at the same moon.

I missed her so fucking much, it was killing me. We were both under the moon, yet worlds apart.

———

JULIET

Halloween was usually one of my favorite holidays. I loved the crisp fall air, pumpkins, and seeing the leaves begin to change color. Despite the miserable depression I was in, I have kept up with my running. Usually, I could talk Ivy into coming. Not today, though. She was going to take a nap while went for a run. She stayed over last night. She had been doing that more often, partly because she worried about me and because she knew I was leaving soon.

I decided that I would pack up and be ready to move by the end of next week. My landlord was happy to accommodate me; he knew how well I had kept the place. Ivy and I had packed a lot the last few days.

My sneakers jogged over the yellow and orange leaves as I took advantage of the Indian summer we were having and went for a run. Unlike Ivy, I had too much anxious energy to nap. I was going to miss this place. It felt good to get out and run the trails or pound the pavement down the mountain, especially since I hadn't been going to the Pit. The ground was still a bit muddy from yesterday's rain, so I ran the main road down the mountain. I admired my neighbors' decorated houses. Bales of hay, corn stalks, and colorful mums with the occasional ghost hanging in a tree all made the holiday seem happy and not like winter was just around the corner.

Halfway down the usually deserted road, there were cars lined up about a quarter mile long. Somebody was having a party. As I approached the next house, which was on several acres, the smell of a bonfire became strong and I heard the sound of children laughing and screaming mixed in with chattering voices. Music played in the distance.

Then I heard it, the unmistakable clank that a horseshoe makes when hitting the pin. My heart clenched as I listened to the roar of men's excited voices. With each clang and cheer came another pain in my heart. The sound reminded me of the club barbeque where Rage and Hawk had won the horseshoe tournament. We shared our first kiss that night at the bonfire. I couldn't stop the images from flooding my mind. Rage's possessive move of throwing me over his shoulder and making me his made my body seize. I couldn't run another step.

The side stitch had me bending over, holding my ribs. I was panting. It took me a few minutes to catch my breath and bring my heart rate to a normal pace from the marathon it was running in my chest. My pulse still throbbed at a higher-than-average rate as I turned back to make the long walk up the hill to my cabin.

When I was back up the hill, far enough away from the party not to see any more vehicles or hear anyone around, I began to relax. I was almost home when loud rumbles of motorcycles coming up the mountain surprised me. Anyone leaving the party would be going down the hill. Mine was the last house before the Hendersons', and they never had guests, let alone bikes. The nagging gut feeling telling me to hide ate at my stomach. I ran behind a massive evergreen as the loud mufflers approached. The sound was not familiar; none of the Souls' bikes sounded that way.

A wave of nausea flipped my stomach upside down as I crouched on the ground and sharp pine needles poked into my bare knees. The bikes came into view—two of them. They began to slow as they approached. Did they see me?

For the second time today, my heart quickened and felt like it was beating straight in my throat. My eyes narrowed at their strange cuts. Theirs had large yellow rockers with bleeding skulls on the back. I couldn't make out the words.

Suddenly, the symbol became familiar. The asshole who attacked me, Joker, wore those colors. I quickly followed behind the line of trees when they drove so slowly that they practically stopped while passing my house. Fuck!

A moment later, they revved their engines and flew the rest of the way up the road. I stayed behind the biggest bush and watched, knowing that they had to come back down the same way they came. Why did I not bring my phone? Ivy was in there. *Oh, God, oh, God, oh, God.*

My breaths became short and fast as panic took over. My Jeep and Ivy's car both sat in the driveway. Maybe the second vehicle would prevent them from stopping.

I could hear them coming. I lay on my stomach, watching from under the bush. I stayed completely paralyzed. Tingling and involuntary shaking took over as I saw them slow down. Both heads covered in black bandanas, not helmets, turned their sunglass-covered eyes toward the house before nodding at each other. They looked around, every sound drowned by their motorcycles, except that of my heart. It was pounding so fast, I felt like they could hear it. I ground my body as far as I could under the bush for fear they would feel my gaze and catch me. I wanted to close my eyes, but I couldn't. Just when I thought my heart would explode in my chest, they accelerated and sped down the mountain.

My Jell-O legs could barely make the fifty yards to my door. It swung open. There was Ivy, clutching her phone. Her eyes met mine as she dropped the phone and broke into a full sprint to me. I fell onto her like I had no bones. I was sobbing, my body still convulsing. Lord ran straight to me, knowing something was wrong.

"They were looking for me," I said between hiccupping sobs.

Ivy pulled me into the living room. "Who were they? Why were they looking for you?"

"I'm not sure, but I think they're in the same MC as that Joker guy."

"I was calling Hawk." She wiped off her phone, checking to see if it still worked.

"No, you can't. It's okay, Ivy. They didn't stop."

"The fuck I'm not," she began dialing. "Hawk can and will want to help you."

"No, Ivy, I don't want Rage finding out. That's the last thing I need. I'm leaving in a few days."

Ivy forced me to sit. "What if I make Hawk promise not to tell Rage?"

Fuck, it didn't matter what I said, Ivy would tell Hawk. It would be better to give up now and lay down the rules.

I felt a sense of relief a half hour later when Hawk pulled into the gravel drive. I believed I could handle anything, that I could protect Paige. What a fool I was.

After getting Hawk to promise not to tell Rage, who might not care anyway, we explained to him what happened. He paced the floor. That couldn't be good. His cheeks were full as he blew out a heavy breath. His hands were on each side of his temple as he thought about what the hell we were going to do.

"Nobody knows this, but I am leaving," I admitted. Ivy's eyes shot to mine, surprised that I told Hawk.

"I'm leaving next week," I said somberly. Ivy came to my side, pulling me close.

"I have to go. You know about Marco. Antonio is going to get out of prison. I have to get as far away from here as I can and take my sister along before they find her, too."

Hawk shook his head in agreement. "I get it," he said, staring at the scar on my face like he had never seen it before. He pulled me against his chest for a hug. I hugged him back, squeezing him. I didn't realize how badly I needed it. He kissed my head. "I'm going to miss you, girl."

Hawk sat me down. "Rage is away on business. He isn't coming back for another few days. Where he is, I couldn't get him if I wanted to. Joker and his brothers have been spotted in several places around here. He must not have forgotten about you. I'm sending a prospect to stay with you until you leave."

I reluctantly agreed, I needed some time to get everything together and tie up loose ends, at least I had a better chance at being safe with someone else here. This was the last push I needed to go; I had dragged my feet long enough. As sad as it made me, it was time to say goodbye to Sugar Maple.

JULIET

An hour after Hawk had promised us a prospect, the vibrations of a very loud motorcycle made us aware that he was close. Hawk drew his gun until he could see it was Bodie who had arrived. Bodie was all smiles walking in. Bodie was first to volunteer when he found out about the detail. The boy couldn't be more than twenty-two. He was blonde with a baby face. I bet he got carded everywhere he went. Was Hawk sure this guy could protect us? Well, I guessed anyone was better than no one.

His duffle strap was across his chest, the big bag on his back. How long was he planning on staying? With a kiss to our hands, he winked and asked where he should put his things. I gave him the instructions and sent Ivy out for some pizza and a few other things I could whip up for our guest over the next few days. She and Hawk were just about to leave when I remembered I needed her camera. I was going to post some things on a local yard sale site.

After lighting a calming aromatherapy candle and taking a few magic anti-anxiety herbal drops, I began to get my head on straight. The shaking and nausea stopped, and I was able to form a plan. I already had a good bit packed. I needed all the money I could get, so selling the big furniture I had would really help.

When Ivy returned with the food and camera, I temporarily set my worries aside and focused on making dinner. We still had most of the kitchen intact so I allowed myself the simple pleasure of cooking, one of my favorite things to do.

After a few hours of cleaning and packing and I was ready for sleep. I just wanted this day to be over. My head hit the pillow but sleep wouldn't come. A million crazy scenarios ran through my mind. I hoped that Paige was ready to meet me. I had spoken with Paige earlier, and she seemed annoyed at the idea of moving but still agreed to it. With our parents out of the country, it just wasn't safe for her to be by herself. We would go to Colorado. There were a few small towns there I had researched. One had an ER looking for nurses, so Paige might like that.

Guilt was leaning its heavy head on my shoulder. It hung thick in the air. What if I was taking opportunities away from her? Would she understand I was trying to save her life? *From my fucking mistakes.*

Tiny needle sensations pricked my eyes. I blinked until they passed. No more damn tears. As much as I regret ever being with Antonio, it did lead me to Rage. I would never have moved to Sugar Maple if not for everything that had happened. I would never have known love, real love.

It was already 3 am, but I was still awake. My fears were keeping me awake, but also Bodie's snores. They weren't cute little snores, but big sawing-wood, vibrating-the-house snores. I had just fallen asleep when the buzzing of my alarm startled me. Fluffy bunny slippers on cold floors had me dragging myself into the kitchen to make coffee. Lots of coffee. My eyes were practically sealed shut as I went through the memorized motion of boiling water and pouring it into the press over the grounds. I made a mental note to stop by Roasted and stock up before I left town.

I quietly sat with my brew and made a list of everything I had to do. First thing was to take Lord over to the vet. He was going to stay the night. He needed minor surgery on a small lump that I had found a few weeks ago. Dr. Hennesey thought it was nothing, but I wouldn't take a chance and it might be a few weeks or longer before I could find a new vet in Colorado. Bodie said he could take him for me so I could keep packing. I had a feeling that it was really because Dr. Hennesey had a super cute nineteen-year-old daughter who worked there every morning. Kaitlyn was one of my best yoga students, and she drove most men wild. A beauty inside and out.

My phone had a crap camera so I pulled out Ivy's camera, taking photos of the items I was going to list. Bodie was still sleeping, so I was being extra careful not to make noise and wake him.

I poured a second cup and sat at my laptop to load the pics on the site. A screen popped up that it was downloading twenty-three new photos. I had only taken about seven. I guessed Ivy still had some on there. Oh, boy, I hoped there was nothing embarrassing. As the screen opened with thumbnails, my phone rang.

RAGE

After the unsuccessful night with Sherri, I was first to volunteer to go on the two-week run out in the middle of fucking nowhere to get to the bottom of the cartel-MC connection. I decided during the first few days on the road that when I got back, I was going to see Juliet. I had unfinished issues to resolve. I wasn't letting her take off without answering some of the questions in my mind.

Ivy and I had had a short conversation before I left; she had made me feel like a real asshole for letting Juliet go and not fighting for her. My ego and the part of me that wanted to protect myself had forced me into a bad decision. I knew that now. So, the minute I got back, I was going to see her, and she was going to listen to what I had to say whether she liked it or not.

So far, Kai and I were on a cold track. We had several more people and places to check out, but as of now, the intel we had did not seem to be current. These guys moved a lot.

Kai, as the sergeant-at-arms, had a twisted way of getting information out of the solo punks who relied on the MC drug dealers for their next fix. After persuading them to cooperate, it didn't take the burnouts long to give up secrets.

It took two hours to make it to the next town on our list. We'd been here since yesterday, and we hoped this would be our last stop. The bar we walked into was near Columbus, Georgia. It was close to the highway, university, mall, and airport. Out of all the places we'd been, this city made the most sense.

There was one big problem. Stained Souls MC did not have a presence in the immediate area. Not only was it Devil's territory, but it was also where their mother chapter was. We had no business being here. This bar visit had to be undercover. No cuts. No bikes. We had to act new to town, take an Uber, and act dumb. We were too old to pass as college students, so we went with two guys looking to open a gym near the university.

We had scouted it out the night before. Locals arrived around 7:30, and the members of the club and the rougher crowd came after nine. It was about two hours before the bar filled with locals. By 9 pm, we had been chatting it up with a few pretty girls when a very unwelcoming Devil's Damned member stumbled in, already halfway drunk. He noticed us as outsiders pretty quickly. He was tall and broad with a noticeable beer gut and unshaved face. The beard was not very long but gave him an unapproachable air.

The man took a seat near Kai. He pointed to the bar, and the sexy bartender set down a foamy beer and a shot of tequila in front of him without him uttering a word. He lit a cigarette, directing the smoke to our direction before turning back to the bar.

A deep, gruff smoker's voice said, "Never seen you two in here before." He looked straight ahead, watching the bartender lean under the bar to get out a bottle that was stashed low and far back.

Kai answered him—he was better with talking. "Who, us?" he said, playing dumb.

That made the big man swivel his chair and look at the both of us carefully. Another drag from his cigarette. "Yeah, I'm talking to the two of you." His eyes appraised us.

Kai was dressed in jeans and a long-sleeved white V-neck, and I wore black jeans and a black long-sleeved shirt, both of us hiding our ink. Kai extended his hand. "I'm Brian, and this is Matt," he said, pointing to me. "We're in town for a few days, scouting out some possible locations to open a boxing gym."

The man's face was expressionless as he looked at Kai's hand but did not reciprocate. He faced forward to stare at the bartender again. "If you're looking for gyms, why are you in my bar?"

Kai smiled and said, very convincingly, "You know, the best way to get to know a town is by visiting a local bar."

The man nodded one short nod. He took the shot, slammed it on the bar, before turning to us again. "You can look all you want, but don't touch. Every bitch within these walls is the property of the Devil's Damned MC. You understand?" he asked, leveling his gaze with ours.

Kai responded by getting the bartender's attention and pointing to the empty glasses in front of him, asking for a refill. "Please add his drinks to my tab." Then Kai turned to the man and said, "Appreciate you not throwing us out of your bar. We got it—look, don't touch." The man pursed his lips, raised his glass, and nodded his head up and down.

A few minutes later, when his drink was half gone, he spoke again. "You two hotshots don't look like you will fit in around here."

"And why is that?" Kai asked.

"Pretty boys and a boxing gym? The Devil's run this town. We, let's say, 'work' with any new businesses that open in town."

"You mean you take a cut of their business?"

"You're a sharp one, ain't ya?" the man said.

"So, if you take a cut," Kai continued, "would you be able to assist in finding a source for some…enhancers? We are relocating from South Florida and don't know any suppliers around these parts."

"Mmm-hmm" was all he said, slamming the second shot down after emptying its contents. The dark circles under his eyes made him look older than he probably was.

"You any good?" he asked. Picking at his nails with a toothpick that he snagged from the bar.

"At?" Kai asked.

"You said a boxing gym, aren't you boxers?"

"We were in college. Paid our tuition through the underground, then opened our first gym near the university. We built it up over five years then sold it last month. We signed a no-compete clause, so we needed to find a new location far away from where we were. We prefer being near a college, so this town was third on our list of spaces to check out."

Grizz finally introduced himself, and we ended up talking to him for two hours. All the free drinks had him spilling a little more than he intended. Kai was great at getting info out of people without them knowing. The man had a gift.

It wasn't long before he bragged about the cartel and what goods and services they could provide. Bingo! The Devil's Damned was undoubtedly the club that was working with the cartel. Joker and his crew were seen in Black Rock a few weeks ago, and now we knew why.

It looked like we were headed on a ten-hour ride home tomorrow.

CHAPTER TWENTY-THREE

Juliet

I answered the phone on the second ring, knowing from the tone that it was Ivy.

"Hey, Ivy," my voice sounded somber from all the craziness.

"Hey, Jules, how are you feeling today? Did you get any sleep?" She knew me too well.

"Not really, but the big guy is still snoring on the couch," I said looking at the two big, sock-covered feet sticking out from the blanket over the side of the sofa.

"He is going to take Lord to the vet for me at noon. I need to finish packing."

"Jules, you shouldn't be there alone. What if they come back?"

"Ivy, I'll be fine for an hour. Besides, I think Bodie would like to see Kaitlyn."

"You are so stubborn. I guess you should know, Hawk has men on the Devil's Damned. He said that last night a whole group went through town and headed down south. I'm pretty sure they're gone now, so maybe it was just a scare tactic, you know, trying to freak you out. They most likely think you and Rage are still together."

My short sigh had her saying "sorry."

"It's fine, you're probably right. I have to focus. I only have a few days to get out of here."

"Jules, I don't know how I'm going to live without you. We've always been like sisters, I…I just can't believe you're leaving me…" she sniffed.

"Please, Ivy, don't get me started again," I said, begging her to rein it in.

"It's temporary. Someday, I'll be able to stop running, and I'll return here. This place is my home, it's in my soul. But for now, until things are safe, you know I have to do this." I said emphatically.

"I knooooow, but I'm going to miss you so much," she whined.

"Come by around eight if you're not too exhausted after your class. I'll have some dinner ready, and we can pack the rest of the bedroom if I don't get it done today."

"Did you post any of the furniture yet?"

"No, I was going to do that today, though." I looked at the still-open laptop with the thumbnails I hadn't viewed yet.

I jumped what felt like three feet off the ground when Lord started barking uncontrollably. That got Bodie to his feet, pulling out a pistol, his sleepy eyes were wide, and his hair was in every direction.

"Put that away! It's okay. It's trash day. Lord always barks as soon as they get within hearing distance. He hates garbage trucks." I tried to soothe the startled biker who was on high alert in my living room. Bodie's shoulders relaxed and wiped his hands over his face, one hand over his heart as he breathed a huge sigh of relief.

"Geez, Lord, you scared the shit out of me, buddy." He laughed and gave Lord a good head rub.

I offered him a steaming mug of coffee with enough sugar, the spoon could probably stand on its own. He gave me a grateful look and "thanks, doll" before inhaling the coffee. He placed the half-empty cup down and stretched his long arms wide.

"I got some good news." He smiled, looking more awake. "Colt texted me last night. All of the Devil's are gone, out of town. You should be okay to get finished packing and get out. We have someone surveying the bridge, so if any of them come back, we will know. He said there is a massive rally in Atlanta that most clubs are attending."

Relief washed over me as I looked around the room, knowing I could finish this up over the next few days and be out without worrying about the Devil's Damned.

"I can still take Lord to the vet for you this morning so you don't have to stop what you're doing."

"That would be great. Thank you, Bodie. I'll make some breakfast and get his things ready."

Two hours later, I was saying goodbye to my boy for the night. A deep sadness crept over me as I looked into Lord's eyes. I didn't know how I would get through life without the constant love of my goofy white pit bull. He was a guardian angel if there was such a thing. I traced the scar down his chest before giving him one last hug and handing Bodie his favorite blanket.

I threw my arms over Bodie's neck and pulled him in for an appreciative hug. Bodie took two steps back. "It's fine, Juliet. You'll be okay." He patted my back.

The house was quiet. Too quiet. I had to distract myself, so I put on some decently loud music, grabbed another cup of coffee, and sat back in my chair to get to the task of listing the furniture on the yard sale site.

When I flipped back on the screen with all the thumbnails, I found out why there were extra pictures. These were from the Fourth of July fight. My eyes immediately stung. How could I go from so happy a few months ago to total despair? Ivy had promised to send me these. It had been so long, I forgot all about them.

I clicked on the first photo. Three smiling, very made-up divas stared back at me. Ivy, Shelly, and I in our ring-girl outfits. Damn, we looked smokin', I must say. No wonder the guys were having a fit. That thought made me smile. I clicked on the next. It was a candid photo of Rage and Leo. Rage's hands were being wrapped by Leo, who looked to be saying something valuable, judging from the intense look on Rage's face. The next was of Rage and me, as I wished him luck. I didn't know Ivy had been able to take this shot.

The next few were of the fight, I could tell from the thumbnails. I skipped them momentarily to click on the one of me in Rage's arms after he had been declared the winner. The picture was perfect. A perfect moment of us staring into each other's eyes and about to kiss. The next picture was of the kiss. By just looking at the photo I could recall the feel of his grip, the warmth of his body, the way his lips touched mine. He had captivated me so absolutely that I had blocked everything else out. That night, I had decided to move forward and give Rage and I a chance. How quickly he had become my everything. And now it was all gone.

The pain I felt in my chest was so much worse than any pain I had experienced before. A gaping hole was left in my heart, ripped open by my own lies. The picture I held of this happy couple was now blurry behind the tears that wouldn't stop. I was in mourning for losing Rage and the life I had built here. I blotted my eyes with tissues and took long, deep cleansing breaths until I could see again.

I clicked on an action shot next; it was stunning. Rage was throwing the Superman punch that knocked Richard out. His curled fist and predatory look stayed frozen on the screen. His body was in the air, his fist about to make contact with Richard's face. I was so proud of him for taking down Richard.

I sipped my coffee as I studied the photo more; Richard already had damage to his face, but from the photo, it looked like he knew that this punch was going to be the end of him. The next pictures were of the crowd cheering as Richard lay knocked out on the mat. I guessed I hadn't really noticed how many men in suits were mixed in with the bikers that night. I had seen a few suits that looked out of place for the setting, but the pictures really captured the mixed audience.

One photo caught my attention. There was a group that was not cheering. They sat on the third row, center. They looked like bodyguards flanking the sides of a few men who were dressed impeccably. The man in the center looked familiar. He was stoic, like a king, sunglasses covered his eyes, his black hair was slicked back, a large ring on his finger. It was odd, he wasn't looking at the fighters. He was staring somewhere to the side…at me.

The next pic was the same, only his arm was stretched out, pointing at me. The man next to him was taking a picture. What the…? I zoomed in closer, and then closer, to get a look at his face.

My mug fell from my hand, the coffee burning my feet as it spilled. Uncontrollable shaking took over my body as I zoomed into the next picture. It was Marco. He was whispering into the ear of the other man who was taking my picture. I propelled out of my chair, directly into the bathroom where I only just made it. I heaved, my stomach emptied its contents, convulsing. My head spun.

Marco had recognized me. My time was up, he was coming for me.

———

JULIET

I had to get out and leave, now. I didn't have time for goodbyes. I didn't want anyone knowing where I was going; it could only put them in danger. My mind was racing. I was hyperventilating. I was out of my mind with overwhelming fear. I couldn't breathe...

Keep it together, Juliet. You can do this. Just breathe, in and out. That's it, deep breaths, in and out.

I thought a shower might help. It didn't. I ran the hot water over me and rocked on the floor until the water went cold. I took some anxiety medicine that I had stashed away. As it kicked in, a plan formulated in my head. I would pack and then get Lord on my way out early tomorrow morning. He just had the small surgery so I called Dr. Hennessey to see if it would be okay to pick him up at the crack of dawn. He lived on the property where his clinic was, so he was always there early checking on his overnight patients.

Telling Ivy about this would just make things so much worse. I couldn't think about how angry she would be when I just took off without telling her. I needed to put distance between us; the less she knew, the better. I hoped she'd understand that I did it because I had to. I wouldn't have her in danger.

I cranked the music and reveled in the calm the little pill provided. I packed my ass off the rest of the day. I canceled dinner plans with Ivy and told her I had finished packing and was headed straight to bed. I told her we could meet for breakfast. She bought it, or she was too exhausted to argue.

I packed the essentials in my Jeep until the only space left was for Lord, leaving behind anything that was not necessary. One more little blue pill made me too tired and loopy to do anymore. Now I just had to wait 'til first light, and I could pick up Lord and be on my way. At dusk, I sat in the lawn chair by the fire pit one last time. Alone. My wine glass was my only company as I relived the memories I had made over the past four years in a place I would soon no longer call home.

RAGE

Five hours into the long journey home, we stopped for some food. Since it was close to dinner, the diner on the side of the long, deserted highway seemed like our only viable option. Serving breakfast twenty-four hours a day sounded good to me. I would never turn down pancakes for dinner.

The door chimed as we walked in. Heads turned, everyone stared at the two of us. After five hours on the road, with our cuts and bikes covered in dust, we probably looked like trouble. The place smelled like greasy food and coffee. My stomach rumbled. Kai even heard it and looked at me, shaking his head. "Hungry?" he asked.

A waitress cautiously approached our table like we were going to rob her. She instantly relaxed as Kai turned on his playboy charm. The waitress was maybe in her mid-twenties with big hair. It seemed they still went with that look around these parts. She spoke with a heavy southern accent as she took our order, she stared at Kai even while taking mine.

I was surprised the coffee was decent in the dive. Juliet got me hooked on that really dark, strong brew from Roasted, and now most anything else seemed weak. Maybe even bad coffee was tasting okay because it had been two weeks since I was home—maybe time just had a way of changing your mind.

Our orders came, and we ate in silence. We paid our bill and left

Bunny, our waitress, a generous tip. I think if Kai had asked, she would have jumped on his bike and never looked back. Now full, I would have much preferred a nap to another five hours on my bike. The sun would be long set by the time we arrived home.

Before going back on the road, I hit the restroom while Kai mentioned needing to call Hawk back. He had a couple of missed calls. When I came out, I saw Kai pacing next to his bike, his phone by his ear. It had been two days since we had decent phone service and here I still only had barely one bar.

Kai gave me a worried look. "You tell him," he said into his phone and handed it to me.

"What the fuck now?" I asked.

Hawk went over the past two days' events. When he got to the part of Bodie having to watch over Juliet because Joker's men were stalking her, I nearly lost my shit. He assured me they had all left town and that she was safe. It was then that Bodie chimed in from the background.

What the fuck? "Is that Bodie? Did you leave Juliet alone?" I yelled into the phone.

Bodie yelled from the background, "She's fine. They're gone. After I dropped Lord to the vet overnight for her, I didn't want to be in the way of her packing."

I could hear the slap and then the whisper, "Shut the fuck up!"

"Packing?"

"You heard that, huh?" Hawk said, sounding defeated.

"Packing for what? Is she going somewhere?" She couldn't be moving yet. Ivy had said she had at least another month in town, not that I was asking.

After exhaling a deep breath, he said, "I didn't want to tell you before you drove."

My voice turned into a growl, "Tell me what, Hawk?"

"Rage, she's leaving. For good. She got spooked by the Devil's and now she's hell bent on leaving right away."

Dots formed in front of my eyes, my blood pressure rose so fast I became slightly dizzy. Anger took hold of me.

I hung up the phone without saying another word, throwing it to

Kai. I was on my bike kicking up gravel and out of the parking lot before Kai even mounted his.

The speedometer couldn't keep up with my pace.

———

RAGE

I broke every traffic law known to man. With the speed I was going, I didn't think a camera or the police could have caught up to me. The bridge to Sugar Maple came into view, the home stretch. I had spent the last three and a half hours thinking about how much I fucked up with her.

I should have never listened to her—I should have been there to protect her, then maybe Juliet wouldn't be leaving. If she'd already gone, I knew I would never see her again. Never hold her in my arms again, never be inside her again.

I still loved every inch of her. The more I thought about her as I drove, the more I realized I was a fool. Now it all made sense. She was trying to get me to push her away. I just hoped I wasn't too late. I don't know how I ever thought I could live without her.

An unfamiliar sting pained my eyes as I flew over the bridge. The twists and turns going up the mountain that I usually cautiously drove up was just a dark blur until I spotted Juliet's cabin. The fairy lights still illuminated the small home, making it look like something out of a fairy tale.

My heart slowed its rapid beating when my eyes landed on her Jeep, sitting in its usual place in the driveway. Relief filled me.

I took long, quick strides to reach the door as quickly as I could. Thank fuck, Juliet hadn't left yet. I smiled as I heard the music coming from around back. My knuckles struck the door three times, hard. On the third, the door popped open. Weird, I thought that after the incident with Joker's men, she would have her door locked. Maybe she was expecting Ivy. Since Lord wasn't here to greet me, I yelled her name several times before going to the patio where the music was playing. I could see her favorite chair illuminated by the fire. I called her name again as I made my way down the path.

"Juliet," I said before realizing no one was there. Her blanket was on the ground next to a bottle that was tipped over. The stem of a glass sat among thousands of tiny pieces that glittered across the area.

My mind was racing as I looked at the spilled red wine that coated the ground. Wait, Juliet was allergic to red wine. I bent down, touching the dark liquid. My two fingers trembled as I put them to my nose. I inhaled deep, the copper essence filled my nostrils as I kicked over the table. FUCK!

Something unfamiliar under the table caught my eye. It sparkled on the ground, catching the light from the dwindling fire. A necklace? I pushed the small wooden table back further to inspect the area. A gold amulet was on the grass, the fire glinting off its shiny back and chain. I wiped it off and turned it over and angled it to the light from the fire.

My teeth ground together so hard I nearly cracked them. My hand tightened around the medallion, squeezing it hard enough for its sharp edge to draw blood.

I dug into my pocket for my phone as I raced back inside, looking around. With all the boxes and piles, it was hard to tell what if anything was out of place. I looked around every room. Hawk picked up.

"Asshole," he answered. "You fuckin' hung up on me."

"Gone, she's gone." My eyes wildly scanned the room. The open laptop caught my eye.

"What are you talking about?" Hawk asked.

Hawk was hollering something I fucking couldn't understand. I placed him on speaker and approached the laptop that was open on the table. I was speechless as the picture on the screen became clear. It was a photo from my fight. I pushed zoom on the keyboard and looked intently at the shot. A man was leaning over, speaking to another man; he was pointing. I followed the line. His finger was directed at Juliet. Zooming in more, I knew exactly whom I was looking at. Marco. I recognized him from the trial pictures. He wore the same smug look on his face.

"Dude, what the fuck is going on?" I heard Hawk, echoing out of my phone.

"Meet. We need a meet now. Call everyone in."

I grabbed her laptop and cord, tossing them into the first bag I could find. I threw it on my back and ran toward the door, shoving the medallion deep into my pocket.

RAGE

I drove past the line of bikes parked at the club before skidding to a stop. I jumped off and ran through the doors into the meeting room. My brothers were in little groups talking and became utterly silent when I barged in. I set the laptop down, plugged it in, and opened the screen.

"Hack," I yelled. He was the tech guy, not me. "Can you pull up the pictures that were on the screen, I'm not sure, I—"

"I got you, man." He turned the computer and began to work.

A stone-faced Hawk entered with a bottle and a full shot glass and handed it to me. I gulped it down and refilled before I could get anything more out.

A few minutes later, Kai stormed into the room with such force the papers that were sitting on the large wooden table scattered into the air, fanning up and onto the floor. He approached me with a scowl on his face. He fisted both sides of my cut, his face inches from mine.

"What the fuck, you asshole?" He said, almost spitting his words. "You just took off. I couldn't even keep up with you. You could have killed yourself. Every fuckin' time I came upon something on the road, I fuckin' prayed it wasn't your spattered body." He pushed off me, letting my cut go and stepping back, wiping the spit from his mouth.

"Are you done?" I asked, pointing to the empty seat around the table.

"Got it, man" Hack yelled.

I turned the huge monitor that Hack linked to the laptop so everyone could have a view. About twenty thumbnails showed up on the screen. The first photo I clicked was of me sending the Superman punch that knocked dickface Ramsey out.

"Are you showing off?" someone piped up.

My eyes glared at everyone around the table. "This is not a fucking joke," I barked.

"Zoom in here." I pointed to the group of men in suits. "And here." Hack zoomed in on Marco's face. A unanimous "fuck" made its way around the table.

I clicked on the next photo, the one where he pointed out Juliet. My stomach soured. Ledger kicked his chair out from the table. "He knew? He was fucking there."

I reached deep into my pocket and pulled out the broken chain with the gold medallion hanging from it.

I choked out, "I found her chair overturned by the fire, with glass everywhere." I swallowed hard before continuing. "Blood...blood was on the ground, and this."

I tossed it from my hands like it was burning me. It landed face up, the Devil's Damned tag had the name Joker engraved below the skull.

"She's gone," I choked out. "Joker has her."

Hawk was up, standing next to me, his arm on my back. I pushed him off.

"Fuck, man, she was leaving. You couldn't fucking keep a man on her another day until I got back?" I pushed him hard.

He stumbled backward before coming back at me. "We thought they were gone."

Others jumped to their feet and forced us apart. Colt hit the gavel. "That's enough. Rage, you ain't going to find her fighting with your brothers."

Hawk looked distraught, head in his hands, "Fuck, you think I would have let Bodie leave if I thought there was any possibility of her still being in danger?" He shook his head. "They were gone. We watched the bikes cross the bridge."

Colt yelled, "All of you, shut the fuck up. Let's get a plan to find her."

An hour later, we had all our sources on the lookout. We had learned a lot about the cartel's operation when we were on our road trip. We shared intel with several of our chapters as well as other civilians that we call in from time to time. Hack said it would take a few hours, but he would tap into some traffic cams to see what he could find.

Right before dispersing from the room, we heard heels clicking heavily, stomping across the floor in the hallway outside the room. A woman's voice became clear. Ivy.

"You can't go in," the prospect stepped in front of her, blocking her way.

"The fuck I can't." She pushed passed the two prospects that operated the door. Her mission was to get to me. Her hand went up, forcefully slapping me across the face. I could have stopped her, but I didn't. I deserved it. She kept her red hand out, shaking.

She crumbled to the floor sobbing. "You shouldn't have left her. He's going to kill her and Paige."

"Paige?" Her baby sister? "Ivy, what are you talking about?"

Her sobs made her words unintelligible. She pulled out her phone. Her finger shook as she pushed play on a voice mail.

A man's voice began speaking, "Ivy, this is Gavin, I need to speak with Anabelle. Please have her call me, it's urgent."

We all looked to each other, confused.

"I-I was teaching and didn't have m-my phone on me. G-Gavin called five m-more times b-before he left this m-message," she said between sobs. She clicked on the last message.

"Ivy, please, it's Paige. My source that has been checking on her said she's missing. Her apartment was overturned. I didn't want to tell you over voicemail, but Anabelle could be next." His voice was begging, "Please, she needs to call me immediately."

Ivy stuttered, "I-I would have been here s-sooner, but I had to t-take a taxi. Someone stole m-my car, and none of you fu-fuckers answer your phones when you're in a m-meeting." Her sobs became heavy, her tears were flooding from her eyes.

I picked up the nearest chair, putting it over my head and launching it like it was foam. It bounced against the wall; two brothers dodged out of its way.

Colt slammed the gavel. "Feel better?" He grabbed me. "Man, throwing shit isn't going to get her back here. We all have jobs to do if you want to save them. Let's get to it."

Hawk grabbed Ivy and pulled her into his chest. "We will find them." He kissed the top of her head.

"You ha-have to," she said, collapsing into him. "He will k-kill her. He'll kill them b-both."

CHAPTER TWENTY-FOUR

Juliet

A creaking floor kept trying to wake me from my deep sleep. I could feel eyes boring into me. Lord must have to go out; he always stared at me until I woke up.

I tried to blink to shake off the terrible sleepiness. Something wasn't right. Only one eye half opened, the other was so swollen it seemed sealed shut. Every moment I became more aware of the pain that radiated in my body, especially in my face. Drool pooled at the side of my lips. My throat was sore and dry. I couldn't open my mouth.

I could see from one eye a man sitting in a chair, a bat in his hand. He was staring at me. His voice echoed, "Anabelle, good, you're awake." Light fluttered in and out as the echo sounded loud in my brain.

A door slapped against the wall; my body jolted at the sound. A metal chair screeched as it was dragged against the floor. Muffled screams became loud; the chair now stopped next to me. I kept trying to force my eyes open.

"You slept much longer than your sister. I thought you'd never wake up."

Those words, the Spanish accent, my eyes snapped open as far as they could. I ignored the shooting pain. I squinted, zooming in to make out the figure screaming in the chair next to mine. Tape covered her mouth. There was no mistaking it. Paige, my baby sister.

No. No. No. It can't be. I tried to reach out. It wasn't until then that I realized my body was tied up and my mouth was covered in tape. In a span of seconds, a million scenarios went through my mind.

Paige wouldn't stop shrieking. She wailed and thrashed in the chair until it nearly fell over. Marco suddenly stood and yelled, "Shut her up!"

An enormous man then approached her. His voice was deep and disturbing, "Calm down, my sweet, I don't want to hurt you again." He touched her face, which made her muffled shrills even wilder. He placed a white cloth over her nose and mouth. Her body became limp in seconds. "Now, that's better." He stroked her hair.

It was my turn to thrash and yell, seeing his creepy hands on her. "Don't even try it," a new voice came from behind me. He took a few steps until he was right against the back of my chair.

"You aren't going to be that lucky," he said by my ear, his hot, foul breath on the side of my face. "You can imagine my delight when Marco came to the club looking to kidnap some whore who did his brother wrong. I recognized you as soon as I saw the picture." He laughed a sick, devilish sound. Chills ran up my spine. *Joker.*

"Rage's girl." He knelt in front of me as he drew out the words, smiling through his rotting teeth. "We're gonna have so much fun." A cold steel blade traced across my cheek and down my jaw. The tip rested under my chin as he forced my head up. His calloused fingers ran over my cheek. "Yep, as soon as these boys are done with you, you're mine." He said those last words in a wet whisper into my ear. "It won't be long now until I get a taste of you!" The icy blade rested against my neck, he pressed it enough so I could feel it just slicing my flesh.

Bile burned my throat as it shot up and I gagged, trying to push it down and not choke behind the tape.

He laughed, and with a quick swipe, he used his blade to slice my shirt wide open, exposing bra-covered breasts.

"I admit," he said, placing the knife's edge between my breasts, "you did put up quite a fight last night." His fingers traced the deep scratches on his face. "But it was worth it." he gyrated his hips.

Last night...

I was sitting by the fire, drinking wine, listening to soft music when I heard a car pull into the driveway. The squeaking brakes screamed over the music—it was Ivy's car. I kept telling her she had to get those fixed, they could wake the dead. She couldn't stay away. I was going to miss her bossy ass.

I didn't get up. I knew she would pour herself some wine and follow the light of the fire. It would be nice to spend one last night together. I would have to make her drink a few glasses so she wouldn't hear me sneak off in the morning. Luckily, she arrived this late—it was dark enough that she wouldn't see my jam-packed Jeep and figure out my plan.

The lights from the house cast her shadow before her as she approached the fire. I could see it from behind me. I was snuggled in my blanket, holding my knees to my chest. "Hey, girl, glad you c—"

My eyes widened when the shadow behind me grew large. Before I could scream, a hand went over my mouth and another around my waist, hauling me up and out of the chair. The wine glass next to me spilled over and crashed to the ground, shards of glass sprinkling like glitter on the stone below. "I'm glad I came, too," the deep voice gritted out.

Where I lived, it didn't matter if I screamed. I guessed he realized that, too, and he let go of my mouth and spun me to face him, cold-cocking me the minute our eyes met.

My cheek and brow took the brunt. Fuck, Joker hit hard. He loosened me up, almost inviting me to fight back. I got a few kicks and swings in, but not enough to damage him. He ground himself against me when he held me from behind. I was reaching and grabbing for anything I could. I clawed his face and ripped his medallion from his neck in the shuffle. My thin lace shirt ripped, fragments of the light pink material falling to the ground.

I kept struggling. "Keep fighting, darlin', you know I love it." He pressed his hardness roughly against my back, making sure I felt him. I kicked and screamed to no avail. He was too strong.

Daggers of pain shot down my nearly broken arm, which he held behind my back. "Sweet cheeks, come on, give me more." His free hand grabbed between my legs. "Makes me hard." The words were hot and wet in my ear. Vomit was inching its way up my throat at the thought. I stopped struggling, trying to gain my strength as he dragged me across the yard.

"Ahh, now why did you go and stop?" Jokers body odor was suffocating.

"What do you want from me?"

"Oh, sweet cheeks, you know what I want, but that will have to wait. We've had enough fun, for now. We gotta get out of here."

Out of here? Oh, no. My heart hammered against my chest. I screamed as he twisted my arm further and pushed a cloth over my face. The chemicals invaded my nose and mouth. My breathing was already so rapid I pulled them in quick. I was down in seconds.

"*E*nough," commanded Marco. "You'll have plenty of time for entertainment when your job is complete. Now, go."

"But, I—" Joker started.

"Leave now." Marco's words were sharp and unyielding.

Joker couldn't just go. No, he leaned in one last time and whispered "until later" and licked my face.

I felt vomit rising again. I jumped when the door slammed. Paige was next to me, knocked out, leaning over in her chair.

"Anabelle, look at me," Marco ordered.

I kept my head down in defiance. A sharp whistle followed. His goon's large shiny shoes clicked across the floor, stopping at my chair. My face was yanked up and turned toward Marco, the man who held my fate.

"You were not easy to find. I was shocked the moment I saw you with the group of lowlife thugs you live among; it was like a gift. You had not a clue that I was coming for you and Paige."

I tried turning my head, but the goon's cologne-scented hand kept it in place. "You are a defiant woman. I will never understand what Antonio saw in you. He nearly lost his mind when I told him he must give you up to join the family business. I knew he couldn't handle it without some pharmaceutical courage, but I had no idea it would have such an effect on him."

"Now, I was sorry he roughed you up. But then you went and testified against him…" His finger waved back and forth as he shook his head. "You really shouldn't have done that. I've lost four years with him, and this made my father very unhappy. We were to run the operation as a family. But you and that dirty cop stuck your fucking little noses where they don't belong. Not for long." A wicked grin crossed his handsome face. His half-tinted gold sunglasses covered his eyes, but he still reminded me so much of Antonio.

"It took a lot of time and money, but my brother is coming home. Your death at the hands of our enemies will be just the motivation he needs to get back in line." His elbows were on the table, fingers woven together in front of his face. "Your disappearing act made the whole plan so easy. After all, Anabelle no longer exists. No one will even bother looking."

He pointed to the man holding my face and motioned for him to remove the tape. I screamed as he roughly pulled it from across my mouth.

I then straightened, trying to act like I wasn't in pain everywhere. "What do you want?" I said, with venom in my whisper.

"Ah, yes, that is the question." His fingers now tapped together. He sucked his teeth and said, "You have nothing I want. I need you dead, but just killing you after all the trouble you caused didn't seem enough. You will atone for your deeds. You will pay with blood and your body. Oh, and of course, since it was my brother whom you wronged most, it's only fair your sister pays as well."

Those were the words that did me in. I knew he meant every word, Gavin told me what a sick twisted man he was. Through the half-open eye, I penetrated a stare and forced out the words, the dryness in my throat made them nearly a whisper, "You're a monster. She has nothing to do with this. I was the victim, not Antonio."

Incessant laughter followed. "You had your spell on Antonio. You kept him from taking his rightful place in the family empire. Your influence was poison to our family. I won't allow you to be his kryptonite. As long as you are in this world you will make him weak."

Marco took a long breath. Silence for what seemed like an eternity. "Your body will pay back a debt owed. You will be begging for death when we are through with you, and I shall grant your wish...in time."

I forced the words out through my pain, "Gavin will know, and he will find us."

"Gavin?" he asked, surprised. "You mean the ex-cop who helped you convict Antonio?"

Ex-cop? What was he talking about?

He must have read the confusion on my face and laughed maniacally. "Ahh, you thought the cop was going to rescue you? What, he didn't tell you?" He laughed again. "He was thrown off the force two and a half years ago for going rogue."

No, it couldn't be true...Gavin would have told me. Marco had to be lying. He wanted me to believe there was no hope.

"Marco, Paige had nothing to do with this."

"You took my brother from me, it's only fair. In this life, we can only count on family."

"*Familia primero, mi amor*," I said in a low whisper. Antonio used to always say, "Family first, my love."

Marco stood from his seat. "What did you say?" I clamped my mouth shut and looked at the floor. The big guy took a few steps back as Marco came to my side. He yanked on my hair forcing me to look up at him.

"I asked what you said?" At first, I didn't answer, then a stupid surge of courage mixed with anger had me spitting in his face. He froze and pulled something out of his jacket to wipe his cheek.

"Ahhh, Juliet, you still have spunk." He backhanded my face so hard my teeth chattered. I held back the scream, clenching my jaw, showing no pain on my face.

"You don't need to worry about your sister." He pointed to the goon with the large, shiny shoes. "Sebastian, will be taking care of her." Marco's grin was wicked. "You and your sister have helped me pay a few debts."

"No..." Before I could speak any more, the tape was slapped back over my mouth. I struggled in anger and squinted my half-open eye to get a look at the enormous man, the jagged scars on his face made him look like a monster. He hid a portion of it behind large glasses. He was impeccably dressed and bore no sign of humanity in his stoic stance. The first words he spoke were in a heavy Columbian accent, "Boss, where do you want her?"

Marco turned his back and made his way to the door that was being held open for him like he was royalty. He stopped and waved his hand in the air. "Put them *both* down stairs.."

"But boss, you promised—" Sebastian began as he stroked Paige's hair.

"I said, both. Now."

———

RAGE

"Man, you are going to wear a hole in the floor," Hawk groaned as I paced. My brow drew in as I stared back at him. He knew how wound up I was. He held his hands up in surrender at my glare. "Hack said it wouldn't be much longer." He passed me a shot; I shook my head. I needed a clear mind to drive out as soon as he gets a location on Ivy's car.

"I feel fucking useless and helpless just waiting here. She could be anywhere by now."

"I know, but we have to wait. You don't want to cost yourself more time by heading in the wrong direction. We'll find them. Juliet is a strong woman. She'll be okay."

I passed the rec room to find a group of brothers that just came in, prepared to ride out with us. Where? I didn't fucking know. Every member of our chapter was here now. Shelly was helping the other girls get food and drinks for them. Even though the brothers had an obligation to contribute in situations like these, this was no obligation to them—they all knew and adored Juliet. I got a wrath of shit every fucking day from them after we had broken up. I was sure they would rather have her here than me. She had sucked everyone into her world of loving-kindness. Her smile lit up every room she entered.

I spun and smashed a hole into the wall. Everyone turned to look at me. I couldn't breathe in here any longer. I had to get outside.

Colt leaned against the wall behind the building. He sucked in hard on the joint between his fingers. He offered it to me before letting out a long stream of white smoke. "It will take the edge off." I took a hit, letting the smoke fill my lungs. I tried to pass back what was left. "Finish it. You need it more than I do." He lit his smoke and gestured to Leo, who was darting straight at me.

Leo and I hadn't seen each other in a few days. He had been away with Shelly. They came back as soon as they heard what went down. Sympathy was all over his face when he pulled me in and whispered, "Juliet is one of the toughest women I know. She can handle herself." He only got a nod from me when Hawk came barreling out the door, looking around before spotting us. "Hack's got something."

"Ivy's car was tagged in the turnpike system crossing into Florida. It looked like Joker was headed to Tallahassee." Hack pointed to the screen.

Both my hands scrubbed my face. "Fuck. That's a big fucking area to cover." My pacing began again.

Colt called the Tallahassee chapter. They talked to Hack, and we set up a meet. Tomorrow morning, we would be there, and hopefully not too late.

Crossing into the city limits, my eyes took in the vast city and became painfully aware of the enormous task that finding her would be. It was the longest drive of my life. Every part of my body ached from the tension I carried as I rode.

The meet was at a dive go-go bar in the city. I'd been in the Tallahassee clubhouse before, but never the titty bar that acted as their second site. There were two girls on the small stage shaking their asses. I headed straight to the meeting room until halted with all the other guys. We were made to wait outside the room; Colt and their chapter's president, Cain, had to talk first. I felt like a caged animal waiting outside the room. I was offered several drinks, but I turned them down.

Ace, who was usually all smiles, found me immediately. He aggressively walked over with a pissed-off look on his face. "I thought

Juliet was your girl?" He pushed me. "How'd you let those bastards get her?"

"I don't owe you any explanation, brother. All you need to know is that Juliet and her baby sister need to be found." I pushed him back the same way.

"You have no idea what the fuck you are dealing with here." His expression was full of worry.

"And you do?"

"Yeah, I do. Those assholes in that cartel are cruel soulless fuckers. They deal in drugs, guns, women, and children. Do you get that? As in sell women, never to be seen again."

Another member got between us. "Ace, why don't you go get us a bottle, huh?" He pointed to the bar. "Rage, good to see you. Sorry about that. Ace had a regular at a strip club. He was real close with her." He blew out some smoke before he continued, "The girl's ex was a member the cartel, and he did not take kindly to being replaced by Ace. Word has it that he sold her to traffickers across the border." Tapping out his smoke, he hit my shoulder, "We'll find your girl."

"The cartel used to have a pipeline through Tallahassee that didn't give us any trouble. We stayed out of each other's business. Until Marco Cordona decided he was going to set up shop here," the brother explained. "Now we are in a constant battle keeping those fuckers out of our business."

Hack was set up at a table. He was using some info that Cain's guys gave him to pinpoint where the girls might be. I wanted to get a lead so we could move. I was drowning there waiting.

"I got some interesting information," Hack announced.

We all quieted.

"We aren't the only ones who are looking for Juliet. That cop, Gavin, may have a better idea. He had some good connections. Only…" he paused and let out a sharp breath, "Gavin's no longer a cop. He got suspended and then fired from the force for going after the cartel on his own, outside of his jurisdiction. He interfered with a bust and got his ass handed to him. Now he's working as a bounty hunter and a private investigator."

I was dialing the number Ivy gave me before he finished. We don't deal with cops, but a bounty hunter and defamed officer, fuck, we could do that.

A half hour later, a few of us were riding out to meet the little prick. Ivy had given me a brief history of Gavin and Juliet's relationship. I was not happy that Gavin was harboring feelings for Juliet and it pissed me off that Juliet seemed to trust this guy to protect her, but not me. No, I didn't like this guy at all.

JULIET

Rage's arms pulled me in tight, his soft lips touched mine, sending chills through my whole body. Even though he held me, I couldn't get warm. Why wouldn't he speak? I kept pulling him closer, but he just smiled down at me. Rage's face began to disappear. *No! Don't leave, please. I'm sorry, please stay.* I touched my head. Water trickled down my cheeks.

My eyes began to open. I blinked slowly, trying to get them to adjust to the darkness. I used my shoulder to wipe the dampness from my face. Blackness cloaked the room, making it impossible to see anything around me. The musty air blasting through the vent was frigid. My fingers and toes were numb, making them hard to move. An intense headache competed with the throbbing pain in my face. The tiniest bit of warmth against my back made me aware of the body next to mine. I tried opening my mouth; the tape that had sealed it shut had been removed. My lips felt swollen, and I tasted dried blood on them. I nudged the body next to mine. I hoped that it was Paige, that they hadn't separated us.

A whisper came from my cracked lips. "Paigey…" I croaked her childhood nickname.

Nothing.

"Paige, please answer me," panicking, I whispered louder, waiting for an answer.

A small groan escaped her as she moved just centimeters. "Ana…" a low voice struggled to whisper back.

I let out the breath I was holding, relieved that hers was the body next to mine. "Oh, Paige…" I leaned into her as close as I could, "I'm so sorry you got dragged into this." My voice hitched, and my eyes welled, but no tears came. Dehydration left nothing for my body to spare. We leaned into each other. The friction caused my broken body to ache. "I will find a way to get us out of here," I promised her.

A door opened. It creaked loudly, breaking the silence. Light streamed down the staircase. It was dim yet blinding in the blackness of the basement. We both jumped and huddled our bodies even closer with our hands tied behind our backs.

We stayed silent. The only sound came from the shoes that clanked heavily down each step. The stairs moaned under the weight of the man. A large shadow appeared, then the massive body that belonged to it. It was him—the monster. The man with all the scars; the slight limp in his step gave him away.

He turned on a small flashlight. He aimed it around, highlighting areas of the basement before finding us. The light was so shocking when it hit me, I squeezed my eyes shut. I could feel the tremors rolling off Paige's small body. *God, please. Please send someone to rescue us before it's too late.* I had pushed away everyone who cared, attempting to save them; now there might be no one left who could save us.

With my eyes still closed, I listened to the clicking of his fancy shoes on the damp concrete as they got closer and closer. I braced myself as the large body loomed over us.

I heard the sound of a cap twisting off plastic, and then he kneeled by Paige. "Open," he directed her. I could barely see, but he held the bottle of water to her lips. "Sip slow." He tilted the bottle allowing her to drink. He wiped the dribbles of water from her face gently.

He turned the bottle to me. I opened my mouth; my jaw was almost too painful to open. He angled the bottle to my open lips. The cool liquid felt better than anything I could remember. It put out the fire in my throat, until I choked on it. I coughed violently, and some of it came out my nose.

"Shh," he said, pulling the bottle from my lips. I caught my breath and kept silent as he instructed. Paige had a few more sips before he walked away from us, without a word, and went back up the stairs, leaving us in complete darkness again. There must have been a boarded-up window at the other end of the basement. I could see daylight through a few holes, probably from bullets, but I tried to keep my mind from going there.

My pinky found hers, and we kept them together like we did when we were children when she had nightmares. She used to hold my pinky all night. I leaned my head over hers, "We will get out of here," I promised her. A promise I hoped not to break.

A few hours later, I heard the door again. The sound of music trailed down the steps. Then a line of light appeared when the door creaked open. I heard voices, but no one came down the steps.

My body tensed. "I want what you promised to me!" Joker's angry voice echoed down the steps. It's been months. I've been patient."

The door slammed closed again, and the voices became shouts. My body trembled so hard, it was as if I was being electrocuted. Marco was going to give me to Joker and his men.

"Ana, I won't let them take you," Paige said. It was sweet, but she was in as bad of a position as me.

"I know, we'll be okay." I squeezed her pinky again. "Just try to rest and save your strength."

———

RAGE

Customers gaped as we pulled our Harleys into the busy parking lot. A gas station sat on one corner and a fast food restaurant on the other. My guess was Gavin wanted to meet in a highly populated area. He leaned against his vintage black GTO. Not at all inconspicuous. On any other occasion, I would have complimented his pristine ride, not today.

I was the first off my bike to walk toward the flashy ex-cop. I expected someone older, not a guy who looked like he could challenge one of us in the ring. Gavin was not as tall, just over six feet, but his build was all lean muscle. He watched me approach. His plain white

V-neck stretching across his chest, large ripped arms folded, his legs crossed at his boots. He flicked his cigarette, straightening his stance as I approached.

He took off his dark glasses. His blue eyes were surveilling me like he was eyeing the competition. "Colt," he said, reading his cut, and extended his hand. Colt shook it. "Rage." I ignored the gesture.

"We are here on business, now fucking spill, and if one hair on my girl's head is hurt, you are—"

Colt pushed his hand on my chest forcing me to back up. "Rage, take it down. Now."

I gave Colt a death look as Gavin began to speak.

"I had eyes on Paige. When she went missing, I knew Marco was gunning for her. I didn't think he knew where to find her, but I underestimated his sources." A growl escaped me.

"I have it narrowed down to three possible locations the cartel has been using for transport. However, they have a few safe houses that are tucked in the city and are very undercover. It could be any abandoned building." Gavin explained as he showed us a few spots on his phone. We worked on getting the info to several club members.

Colt was pacing on the phone, leaving me with the ex-cop. "So, you're the lucky bastard she finally let her guard down for?" he asked in an almost sad way.

"Are you fucking kidding me? Are you really asking me about her?" I breathed fire. "All you fucking need to know is that Juliet's mine and that ain't going to change. When I get her back, she is never leaving my sight again."

"Yeah, I get it. If I had her, I'd feel the same." He looked at his boots, kicking them like he was reliving a memory. A possessive growl escaped as I studied him.

He attempted to calm me, "You don't have to worry about me, man. After I found her beaten, almost dead, I spent close to a year by her side, and I fell in love with her. But she never wanted to be more than friends. Antonio really did a number on her, not just physically, messed with her real bad, and she built walls on top of walls around her." He sucked in a breath. "She just wanted him behind bars and Paige safe."

As my mouth opened to respond, Colt pointed to our bikes. "Rage, we gotta go, now."

"What, you're not gonna tell me anything?" Gavin was surprised when Colt didn't share intel.

"This is club business now."

Gavin grabbed Colt's arm. "Are you kidding me? These bastards killed my baby sister. They took Anabelle. You think I'm going to just back off? I'm going with you, and besides, I have connections on the force who want Marco just as bad as we do, and I can help with whatever fall out occurs."

Colt and I exchanged glances, a silent agreement that he could come. As much as I hated the fact that he had a thing for Juliet, I saw the familiar rage in his eyes, the agony when he mentioned his sister. Having him around wouldn't hurt; we'd take any help we could get to get the girls back safe.

We decided to split up, scouting out the locations until we found something. Colt and I mounted our bikes and took off to the farthest location.

JULIET

My mind spun as the hopelessness overtook me. I kept playing that moment over in my mind. I prayed Marco had been lying about Gavin. I couldn't believe that Gavin would not tell me and have me think he was still on the force.

Paige had been sleeping for what seemed like hours. I stayed quiet so she could rest. I watched as the bullet holes that had let some light in turned from bright to black. It must be night. It had been several hours since I saw any light. The musty smell was overpowering from the Florida humidity. Even the remainder of my clothes felt damp.

The door opened, waking Paige. This time it was not Sebastian bringing water. It was Marco's other thugs. Armed with automatic weapons, they looked like soldiers in suits.

They scooped us both up without a word. Placing tape over our mouths again before pulling us to our feet and dragging us up the steps.

Bound together, we were clumsily pushed down a hallway. We passed several rooms. I could see one door open where a man in a suit had a woman, hands bound behind her, by the hair down on her knees in front of him pulling her head back and forth roughly. Paige flinched, terror on her face. She looked away quickly, her eyes pleading with mine. There was nothing I could do to comfort her.

My stomach was sick. Marco's men pushed our backs against the wall, guns aimed at us as we waited outside a room where Marco was holding a meeting. I could see half of Sebastian's scarred face and large body through the ajar door.

I strained to listen to voices, hoping to hear something that would help us know our fate.

"You promised only to supply and stay out of my town. That was our agreement." A man's voice carried out of the room.

"Ahh, yes, but you were holding back on us. You neglected to say how hospitable your little town could be. The lack of police presence and the railway will be very valuable to our operation."

"That was not our deal," he said sternly to Marco. I strained to hear more.

I was shocked by the pistol whip to my face. Blood immediately gushed from my nose. Paige tried to scream, but the tape suppressed it, her eyes went wild looking at me. I ignored the stunning pain as I looked into her frightened eyes. I did not want her pushed over the edge; she had gone there before.

"You don't listen to the boss's business," the thug with a heavy Spanish accent said as he held my chin, forcing me to look at him. The blood trailed down my jaw and onto my chest in giant spatters. I forced myself to stay strong, biting my lip under the tape. I would not let these assholes break me.

The door opened the rest of the way. Sebastian gestured for his men to usher us inside the room as he escorted the other man out. Sebastian's gaze went to Paige after seeing my bloodied face. Sebastian seemed almost relieved that she had no other damage as he looked her over in a way that was almost disturbing.

The man who was meeting with Marco stepped out of the room. My eyes nearly fell out of my face when they met his. He managed to stay expressionless, but he knew it was me. He scanned my body and face in the seconds that we passed each other. I could feel his gaze even after I passed him.

"Hey, turn around and keep walking. They are not your concern," Sebastian commanded.

CHAPTER TWENTY-FIVE

Rage

Frustration took on a new meaning as the last place Gavin had told us to check came up empty. *Goddammit!* I roared out my frustration and kicked over the trash cans in the alley, sending them rolling down the block.

I hoped that Gavin and Hawk were having more luck than we were.

Colt pulled out his phone to call Cain and tell him we were on our way back. What the fuck were we going to do now?

My gut was telling me something was very wrong. I just knew it was worse than my mind could even dream up.

I was mad at myself as much as I was at the fuckers that had her. This was all my fault. I had let her go. She had tried to explain. I should have listened to her. I should have given her time and then gone back. I would have begged for her forgiveness and never fucking let her out of my sight. *What if we don't find them?*

My vision blurred as we rode back, my eyes stinging as the panic began to take hold. A few more blocks to go. Maybe Hack will come up with something. He had to. We couldn't end like this. She couldn't be taken from me the way everyone else had been.

My phone buzzed in my pocket. I was pulling into the lot on the third ring. Unknown Caller. I hit answer, "Yeah?"

"Rage, it's Ramsey."

"No time for whatever bullshit you're calling for." I hung up.

I followed my brothers back in the dive bar where we started. My phone rang again, Unknown Caller. This sonofabitch. He probably wanted to taunt me about something, as he had done a million times before. *How does this fucker keep getting my number?*

"The fuck do you want, Ramsey? I don't have time for your bullshit." The bar was loud. I was getting ready to hang up again when I thought I heard him say Juliet's name.

"What did you say?" I started to go back outside, waving the people around me to quiet down. Ramsey started to speak, but I still couldn't hear. "Wait, I can't hear you," I yelled into the phone." I stuck my two fingers in my mouth and whistled loud enough that people covered their ears. "Quiet the fuck down a minute!"

"Ramsey, start again."

"Rage, you know I don't really care for you, and you probably think I'm a prick, but I'm not a monster. So, I thought you might like to know that I just saw Juliet."

"What?" My heart stopped. I opened the door and stepped outside the dive. "What the fuck do you mean you saw her?" Each shallow breath I took mimicked the speed my heart raced as he spoke.

"Man, looks like she's in some real trouble and is in pretty bad shape. I almost didn't recognize her—"

"Where is she, Ramsey?" I growled, darkness ready to take me over. "Did you have something to do with this? 'Cause if you do, I swear to God—"

"Calm the fuck down, alright? She's in Tallahassee."

"Yeah, I know that. I'm in Tallahassee, been here two fucking days turning this city upside down looking for her. Where exactly?"

"You're here?"

"Listen to me very carefully. Tell me where the fuck she is, right now."

"Look, maybe I should meet you. Marco Cordona has her and

another girl. The place is guarded and well-armed. I can help you get in…if you help me with something."

My head tilted back. I pinched the bridge of my nose and squeezed my eyes tight. *You have got to be kidding me.*

"Fine, meet me at the…" I looked around to see where the fuck I was. "Meet me at Lips and Hips on Green and 4th Avenue. You better move your fucking ass, Ramsey. I don't have time to waste."

––––––––

RAGE

In the twenty minutes it took for Ramsey to arrive, I thought about why the fuck he didn't help her. I didn't care how much he hated her guts 'cause she ditched him, a man wouldn't leave a woman helpless among sharks. Then he had the nerve to ask for our help. He was a bigger motherfucker than I thought.

The second I saw the arrogant asshole, I wasted no time walking straight to him, jacking him up, demanding to know why he left Juliet and Paige there. Three brothers pulled me off. "How do we know this isn't a trap?" Colt asked.

"It's not a trap! Look, I can't force you lowlifes to trust me, but if you don't want Devil's Damned to be the new bikers in town, running a pipeline that goes right through Sugar Maple and up the train into Black Rock and other coastal towns, then you're just gonna have to trust me and help me out!" Concern and remorse were in his face.

"Marco Cordona is an ambitious fuck. He's breaking away from Daddy and his guns. He's running meth, X, and a whole slew of other designer drugs. He has a wealthy clientele willing to pay. He's got his network of bikers and rogue members of the cartel to do his bidding, and he's banking on his brother's release to help him with the expansion."

Ramsey looked guilty and disappointed in himself. He shook his head and said, "One day I was selling them a property along the river, but before I knew it, I was sucked in. I don't know how the fuck to get out." His face, normally filled with arrogance, now had a look of desperation.

"What does any of this have to do with Juliet? Fuck, how are we getting her? Where is she?" I spat questions out like bullets.

"They are camped out in an abandoned house on the north side as their temporary headquarters. I can show you where on a map. But, I gotta be honest, I don't know how much time Juliet has. While I was waiting to see Marco, there was a Devil's biker there. He had crazy eyes, rotten teeth, and smelled pretty bad. He wore a big ring with a jester on it. He complained that he hadn't gotten his money, and he was getting impatient. I heard him talking about the bitch promised to him. He bragged how he beat her pretty good trying to get her there. He went on and on in great detail about the disgusting vile things he had planned to do to her to make her pay. After he has his fun, she's a marked woman."

I lifted a table, tossing it across the room. I swiped the nearest bottle of whiskey, finishing it before throwing it against the wall as the last drop burned down my throat. The shards of glass spread across the floor. Two bouncers started toward me, but my brothers took care of them, knowing my current mood could leave them hospitalized.

Hack pulled up a map of the location where Juliet was being held hostage. It was an hour until midnight. We all armed ourselves inside and out. Cain had a blackout van that was perfect for getting close.

"Fuck, man, they have a camera system," Hack said.

"Great, just what we need," I grumbled.

"No, you don't understand. I can get into the system and manipulate the cameras to repeat the moment you get in. Those fuckers won't see a thing." He pushed his small glasses up his nose as he typed so fast his fingers were a blur on the keyboard.

"Amateurs," he grinned, amused at the low security. "I'm in."

We went over the plan maybe twenty times in the van. Ramsey was too much of a pussy to come. He stayed with Hack, guiding him through what he saw and where in the building. Hack gave us mini cameras and mics. Luckily, he had every gadget known to man and spent every penny he had on the latest tech gear.

1:10 am. We pulled up to the façade of an abandoned building.

JULIET

"Where do you want them, boss?" Sebastian asked.

Marco held up his finger, answering his phone. He started screaming and yelling in Spanish. He hung up, looking furious. He unbuttoned the top of his shirt; his brow was covered in a sheen of sweat.

Marco's eyes met my bloodied face, a smile of satisfaction spread across his face. He put his suit jacket on before dishing out instructions in Spanish. The only word I understood was *baño*, Spanish for bathroom.

He looked at me again. "Our fun will have to wait awhile. In the meantime, because I'm a kind guy, I am letting you use the restroom. No funny business, got it?"

We were led to a bathroom where each of us struggled to take a turn, being tied up and gagged. One man stood outside the stall. My eyes frantically looked for anything in the bathroom that could be used as a weapon. There was a loose screw in the toilet paper holder. It would have to do. I used my fingernail to twist the screw the rest of the way out.

"Let's go. What's taking you so long?" The man was yelling from outside the stall. The screw popped out, and I caught it before it fell to the floor. It was sharp and over an inch long. I was able to conceal it easily.

Stepping out the stall, he grabbed a fistful of my hair, adding to the hurt of my already throbbing head. I could feel the gun pressed against my back as Marco's men guided Paige and me back down the stairs. Paige's eyes were wild. She was prone to panic attacks and anxiety. She had almost gotten admitted to a clinic once. She had spent most of her life in and out of therapy. That look on her face told me that she was in a dark place.

When the basement door opened wide, I tried to take in everything I could about the area. I scanned it for exits. How the hell was I going to get us out of this?

The moment we were alone, I wiggled the screw through my fingers and tucked it far in my palm. I didn't have much choice with my hands behind my back. We found each other's pinky again. The tape was loose on my mouth. "Sleep," I said, as loud as I could. Paige must have understood. Her body relaxed against mine. Even with my mind racing, my body screamed for rest. I couldn't fight staying awake any longer.

I was startled by the subtle taps of boots creeping down the steps. A low "fuck" was uttered when the person knocked something over; the sound of an object rolling on concrete broke the silence. That woke up Paige, her body stiffening, and she pushed harder against me. Who the hell was sneaking around in the dark? The pungent body odor hit me next. *No, no, no, no. Not Joker.*

Shuffling footsteps were getting closer. Then a phone lit up some space, just enough for Joker to aim the light around, looking for us...or me.

"Gotcha, bitch," he spoke softly.

Joker made quick work of disconnecting the two of us, tying Paige to a pipe. "I hope you like to watch." He placed me just feet in front of her. He held her chin in his hand as she struggled. Her eyes were pleading with mine.

"The fucking Columbian ain't making me wait any longer for what's owed to me." He whispered in my ear, hauling me up roughly. His blade glinted in the light of the phone. He slid the cold sharp edge along my throat as Paige struggled and tried to make noise. He turned the knife toward her. "You make one more fucking sound, and you will be permanently silent." Paige quieted, but her eyes stayed wildly trained on me, her body shaking.

Joker turned his attention back on me. He took the long blade and ran a line from my belly button to the bra that was already exposed from our last encounter. He tucked it under the fabric and split it open, exposing my breasts. I tried to push back, but I remembered how turned on he'd been when I fought him off before.

"Perfection," he growled, shining the phone light on my body. I trembled as the knife made its way to my jeans. Cutting off each button, licking his lips as each struck the ground. He was enjoying the slow torture.

Joker placed the knife on the floor so he could use both hands to yank my jeans down, panties coming with them. I tried not to panic. I had to wait for just the right moment. I pushed the screw through my fingers, pointed it out, made it ready. I gave him a quick and hard kick to the head. I must have been weaker than I thought because he recovered quickly and punched me in the gut, the screw dropping to the floor. The blow had me gagging and gasping for air. Defeated, I could hear the metal screw bouncing on the concrete. Paige shrieked through the tape, infuriating Joker.

"I said shut the fuck up!" He grabbed the knife, pointed it at her and began marching toward her. But he abruptly stopped—a loud set of pops, followed by shouting, and pounding footsteps ran across the upstairs floor.

———

RAGE

Marco was either confident in the safety of their location or stupid. We entered quietly, following the instructions Hack spoke through our earpieces. The moment someone discovered one of our men, complete chaos broke out. There were seven of us who entered the building, four who took the outside.

I took out two men by the back entrance. My silencer was on; no one heard a thing. Colt did the same at the front. One jackass came out of the bathroom, caught sight of an intruder, and yelled in Spanish before Ace could shut him up. Guns were firing all around. Several suicidal men shielded Marco. One in particular caught my attention as he went the opposite direction. He was massive and had dark glasses and a fucked-up scarred face.

I followed him. He seemed to be on a mission. I opened doors along the way, praying to find Juliet behind one of them. I stayed at a distance, hiding behind walls and doors until, through a mirror, I saw him stop in front of a door. He looked around before opening it and then disappeared.

From the corner of my eye, I saw Gavin pointing behind me; two men were coming down the hall. I took cover, keeping an eye on the door the big man had gone through. A few seconds later, the door open, and the big man re-emerged. He wasn't alone. Lifted under his arm was Paige, tears flowing down her face. Her mouth was taped, and her hands were tied. He was dragging her down the hall toward an exit.

Gavin directed me to Kai, who was hiding behind a door in the next room. Kai followed the big man, nodding to let me know he was going after Paige. I had no doubt he would retrieve her safely. I kept watching through the mirror.

I opened the door from which the man came out. I looked down the dark stairwell. I felt around to locate a switch that turned on a single hanging bulb at the bottom of the steps. Not much light came from the old bulb. I pointed my gun as I descended.

At first, I didn't hear the muffled screams through all the noise coming from upstairs. I shone the light toward the sound.

Twenty emotions hit me at once. I didn't know where to look. Joker held Juliet in front of him as a shield. Her hands were tied behind her back, her face battered, her body naked.

There was no scenario in which Joker was coming out of this room alive. My gun pointed at him. His knife was held sharply against Juliet's throat. My pistol was too kind. I wanted to spend a long time making him painfully regret every hair on her head that he'd hurt and every tear she had shed. Blood pumped through me like lava, a heat, a level of fury that I had never experienced before. My sweet baby was trapped in his fucking arms.

"Drop the knife," I growled, my Glock aimed at Joker's head.

"You think I'm that stupid?" he spat. "She's mine now, hotshot. She's my payment. You ain't taking her. She's my ticket to getting out of here, alive."

"Not a fucking chance." My arm extended a perfect line to his forehead. Could I make the shot and not hit Juliet or chance his knife slicing her neck wide open? The knife pressed into her delicate skin. A

292

line of blood trickled down her neck. Joker laughed as he began to back away.

"Oh, yeah?" Juliet's scream pierced the air as Joker plunged the knife into her side, pulled it out and brought it back against her neck.

"Boy, you better let me pass, or she's going to bleed out right here in my arms."

Juliet's eyes found mine. I read her face as if she was speaking out loud, her eyes pleading with me to take the shot. She gave me a small nod, confirming my thoughts. Her naked body was shaking under his hold. A puncture wound in her beautiful torso, bleeding badly.

I took a breath and focused my eyes. Finding my target, I zoomed in on a mark on his forehead. There was no sound as I squeezed the trigger, just two bodies hitting the floor.

I sprinted the few feet, lifting his bloody body off hers. I gently pulled the tape from Juliet's mouth. "Rage..." my name came out broken. My beautiful wild angel was broken.

"Baby, it's going to be okay. You're going home." My eyes filled up. "I'm going to take you home," I whispered.

Using Joker's blade, I cut the ties holding her arms and hands. I pulled the black T-shirt I was wearing over my head and maneuvered it over her body. She was weak and could barely stand, the blood from her stomach was causing her to pale by the second. I pulled off my bandana, stuffing it hard against the wound to try and slow the bleeding. "We're getting you out of here, baby, just stay with me."

I scooped her up and carried her silently through the basement. She needed a hospital. I had to get her out of here, now. Panic and adrenaline were fighting over my body.

Juliet's head was cradled in the crook of my neck. She could barely speak but managed to say, "Paige..."

"Kai's on it," I whispered back. As I got to the top of the steps, I listened for gunfire before cracking open the door. I saw bodies. Then a few more. So far none were my brothers. When I thought it was clear, I pushed it open, with Juliet light in my arms. I crept down the hall. My earpiece was dead. Shit.

There was a room to my left that I needed to pass to get to the exit. If there was a God, like my Grandma had promised, I would make it out of here to get my angel help. Her lips were pale. I had to move. I took the steps toward the exit. I hiked her body over my shoulder, putting pressure on her wound, holding her tight. My head swiveled to the open room.

Fuck. A standoff.

Three of my men—Ace, Ledger, and Hawk—against three of theirs. Marco and two of his men looked to be the only ones left.

Six guns pointed at one another, six sets of eyes looking at me. Juliet limp in my arms, my gun in my waistband.

I stood frozen at the scene before me. Juliet stirred at my abrupt stop. She lifted her head off my shoulder taking in the situation. Marco laughed at the sight of a bleeding Juliet. "I told you, you won't be leaving here alive, bitch."

Then the sound of a cocking gun. "Gotcha, motherfucker." It was Gavin, fury and revenge written all over his face. His gun added to our numbers.

I felt it before I heard the shot. The movement taking me by surprise, cold metal sliding up my bare back. One perfect shot quietly discharged into Marco's head. Blood sprayed the room before anyone realized what had happened.

Marco's eyes were still open, a hole in his head, his white suit covered in his blood. "Fuck you, Marco" she whispered. The gun fell from her hand as she collapsed back in my arms.

Our boys quickly disarmed Marco's men. I blew past them and out the door. "I have to get her to the hospital. She's bleeding out." Gavin was only a step behind me, helping me load her into the van.

"Juliet, stay with me, baby. I can't lose you. Angel, I love you so much. I'm so sorry." I kept her tight to my chest, kissing her head as tears I never shed came spilling out of my eyes. The pain was more than I could bear as I watched life leaving her body one moment at a time. I screamed at the driver, "Get us to the fucking hospital now!" I couldn't lose her. If I did, I wouldn't be able to live in this cruel world any longer. I did something I hadn't done since I was ten years old—I prayed. I prayed to any god, angel, or loved one who'd listen. I bargained. I made promises. She had to survive. Her breathing was slowing by the second. She was slipping away from me.

CHAPTER TWENTY-SIX

Juliet

*F*or a nearly a month, Rage had not left my side. He had been my shadow since the moment I woke up in the hospital.

I spent a week at St. Mary's. Waking up there was like déjà vu. They told me I'd been out for several hours after the incident, and Rage had gone nearly out of his mind.

Ace and some of the other guys from the Tallahassee chapter had been in and out, checking up on me. Every time Ace smiled at me or touched my hand, I thought Rage was going to punch him. Even worse was when Richard had come by the house. Though I still didn't like the guy, I had to thank him for his part in getting us rescued.

The guilt I felt for the Stained Souls putting their lives at risk for mine and Paige's was overwhelming at first. But they kept reassuring me and telling me how relieved they were that we were safe and Marco was out of their territories.

I was temporarily a little worse for wear, but at least I was alive and surrounded by people who loved me. Rage and Ivy fought for the times I was allowed visitors.

Paige had been so attentive toward me the first two days in the hospital, then she became withdrawn and wouldn't see me. That hurt more than any injury I had sustained. I knew that I needed to give her space. I couldn't even imagine what all this had done to her already fragile mental state. She wouldn't talk to anyone about what happened. Ivy assured me that she was okay and that Kai was keeping an eye on her.

Rage had become my resident caretaker since I got home. Simon had been sending every green juice imaginable to help me heal. When I wasn't drinking juices, an assortment of Roasted brews always filled my kitchen with heavenly aroma.

I had a doctor's visit this morning to remove the remaining stitches. I got cleared for non-strenuous activities. I could think of a few strenuous activities I would like to be doing. Sleeping next to Rage every night without having him inside me had been torturous.

The Stained Souls were still waiting for the fall out of what happened. Gavin used his connections to get the mess taken care of, leaving the Souls out—the guys on the force were just happy to see Marco and his operation taken down. Now we're uncertain what the hell would happen next. They were worried about retaliation, especially from Antonio.

Today the clubhouse was helping me celebrate my all-clear status. Just a small get-together. Ivy organized it with Colt and Hawk. It was unusually warm for being so close to Thanksgiving. The view at the club was picturesque. The leaves were vibrant shades of orange, red, and yellow lighting up the sides of the mountains. There were a few tables set up around the back, and the boys started a bonfire where we sat around like a bunch of kids eating, laughing, and drinking hot chocolate and spiked cider.

Our private party was interrupted when a new prospect, Jamie, came running down the path behind the clubhouse. He was out of breath with his hands on his knees as he puffed out, "Limo, out front."

"Stay here," Colt told the women. We, of course, didn't listen. We all peeked around the corner where the guys cautiously approached the vehicle.

Jamie wasn't kidding. A long, sleek black limo parked out front. The front passenger door opened first. A tall man dressed in a black suit and shiny shoes stepped out. He stood next to the door with his hands crossed in front of him as the limo driver opened up the backseat door.

A set of black shoes hit the ground, followed by a gold cane. A salt-and-pepper-haired man, also dressed in a suit, stepped out. Another man followed, gun strapped across his chest.

The older man was dressed impeccably. My stomach flipped as he removed his glasses and I got a better look. He extended his hand toward Colt. His face was Antonio's twenty-five years in the future. I knew him immediately. This couldn't be good.

After he had introduced himself, tension rose, both sides on guard until Mr. Cordona made a gesture and spoke in Spanish. Soon everyone relaxed, and Colt and Rage joined him at a small table. His guards stayed by the limo while our guys remained a safe distance back. All eyes were fixed on the men talking. Everyone was on edge, eager to find out the reason behind the visit. Then Mr. Cordona gestured as he spoke, of what we couldn't tell.

It was more than thirty minutes before the three men stood and shook hands. Rage turned to look around. He spotted my snooping face among the others and waved for me to join them. I felt uneasy as I walked the twenty yards to where they stood.

"Ahh, so this is Anabelle. I see why my son had such a hard time letting go." His English was a little hard to understand. His eyes swiped my body from head to toe and smiled in approval. Then he offered me his palm, and I gave him my hand. "Mr. Cordona," I said respectfully.

He kissed my hand gently, sincerity was apparent in his manner. "I am truly sorry for the events that happened to you. Sebastian informed me of the unpleasant experiences you and your sister had at the hands of my sons." He covered his heart with both his hands, slightly bowing his head.

I jumped at the mention of Sebastian. "I'm sorry, dear, Sebastian worked for Marco, but he reported to me." He straightened his stance, leveling his eyes with mine.

"Marco was acting on his own. I explained to your family here," he motioned toward Colt and Rage, "that he was trying to go off on his own, getting into places and with people he had no business doing. I came today to apologize for my son's bad behavior, and I would like to make peace with those whom Marco wronged. We have no intention in taking up where he left off. And we would like a truce between our cartel and the Stained Souls MC."

He appeared sincere, but so did Antonio. I learned once not to trust the Cordonas.

Rage draped his arm over my shoulder. "Thank you, Mr. Cordona. The girls appreciate that. I hope your other son feels the same, and we won't have any further issues with him." That had Colt stiffening, the tick in his jaw prominent, but he held back, not wanting to insult the cartel's word.

"Yes, Mr. Rage, was it? Antonio will be no trouble to you or Ms. Conti again." He emphasized the words and kissed my hand again before returning to the limo.

Once the car was far enough down the drive, the whole lot of them let down their guarded posture. "What the hell was that?" Kai spoke first.

Shaking his head, Colt, lit a joint. "Fuckin' crazy." He inhaled deeply, waiting a few seconds before sending out the large cloud of smoke. "They're offering a truce. I hope it's true, but I don't fucking trust them."

RAGE

Lord's head swiveled back and forth as he watched me pace for an hour, waiting for Juliet to wake up. She usually got up earlier than I did, but last night I couldn't sleep.

I felt like a five-year-old, only I was the one waiting to give the gift, not get it. I sat petting Lord, waiting for my girl to get out of bed. It was barely 5 am, and we were out pretty late last night. The girls organized a Christmas Eve party at the clubhouse; it was something we'd never done. They decorated and had a tree and lots of food and holiday-themed drinks. They planned a big dinner for today, too. The clubhouse had become a little less wild since Shelly,

Ivy, and Juliet decided to hang around. It was more like a family now. I had not had a real Christmas since my grandmother passed away.

I was glad Juliet had the girls to keep her mind off things. I knew she struggled, especially with Paige being so close but still not responding to her. Paige's correspondences had been limited to Ivy and Kai. Ivy had offered Paige a room in her place, but she insisted on being on her own. Kai agreed to let her take an empty unit in his apartment building, knowing he could keep an eye on her.

Juliet had such a tough time giving Paige the space she asked for; this whole thing with her and Paige was eating her alive. She'd begged her to see a therapist, but since she was not a threat to herself or others, we couldn't force her to go.

I wish I could get them to talk to each other; Juliet's guilt was overwhelming her. I know Kai had been trying. Not sure what was up with that, I'd never really seen him be protective of any woman. He seemed to be the only one Paige trusted. Kai was the one who got her away from Sebastian, but neither of them was specific about what happened. All I knew was that Kai and Paige had shared something that day, but that was something Juliet would have to figure out 'cause, as a manly man, I wasn't getting involved in that mushy drama.

I studied the dancing flames as I placed a log in the fireplace in the center of the cabin. We had a small tree, which Juliet had decorated with fairy lights and pine cones, popcorn, cranberries, and a few things from her childhood. We had driven for two hours up the mountains to find this small tree lot that had a machine that pulled the tree out by the ball so you could plant it in your yard after Christmas. She loved that idea. Not only was it renewable, she said, but the small tree would mark our first Christmas and then we could watch it grow over the years.

I finally learned how to use her coffee maker, well, *our* coffee maker. I couldn't wait any longer, so I made some brew because I knew the scent would wake her.

Dawn crested over the mountains, and I could see the light dusting of snow that fell a few days ago. I remembered how we sat outside around the fire pit, drinking hot cocoa and eating smores and watched the snowflakes turn the mountain white. Juliet sometimes took the big bad biker out of me, but I loved her for it.

After what happened with the cartel and almost losing her, I realized I couldn't live without her. I needed that woman in my heart, home, and bed every damn day. I would give up my life for her—risking my heart was a small price I was glad to pay.

I heard the jingling before the fluffy elf slippers poked out from around the corner. Lord jumped up to greet his mama. "Merry Christmas," she said to us both. "The coffee smells so good. Thanks for making it." She yawned, stretching her arms above her head revealing more of her bare legs. "What are you doing up this early?"

She looked adorable in her elf slippers and one of my flannel shirts, half buttoned. I loved seeing her in my shirts. Her petite body drowned in them, and she looked sexy as hell. Her golden-brown hair was down in curls with ribbons of red and gold streaks running through them. She filled our Santa mugs and set them on the wood stump she had shellacked into a table. Juliet popped a homemade peanut butter treat into the air for Lord to catch before settling in my arms next to the fire.

I finally knew the meaning of butterflies in your stomach. This awkward, excited, nervous feeling must be that. I kissed the top of her head, inhaling the scent of honeysuckles.

Christmas music began to play through the speakers. She had been playing it since Thanksgiving. I couldn't wait any longer. I could see the box tucked under the tree with the other gifts wrapped in brown paper bags. Juliet had spent an entire night at the table with recycled bags, wrapping her gifts and then decorating them with personal designs. She refused to buy wrapping paper. Her concern for the Earth is just one of the many reasons I loved her.

The first gift was for Lord; he couldn't help but sniff out the deer antlers that we collected in the woods. He was gnawing on one as she pulled out a stack of presents. Her grin went all the way up to her ears. We promised nothing extravagant; she preferred sentimental gifts. I desperately wanted to give her mine, but she looked so cute and impatient. She handed me a box. "I hope you like it," she said and bit her lip.

I carefully pulled off the paper; I didn't want to wreck it. *Wow!* It was a shiny Hohner Super 64 Chromonica. A top-notch professional harmonica that I could never justify getting for myself. I was speechless, examining it in the light of the fire. Now I felt even more like a five-year-old. "What? How did you—" I couldn't contain my smile. "I can't believe it! I've looked at this a zillion times but could never pull the trigger. How did you know?"

Her face was full of joy. "Well, I can't take credit for knowing what it was, but I made some calls and got hold of your old band member, Grayson. I asked him what a dream harmonica would be. He spent half an hour explaining them to me before finally telling me how you've drooled over this for years."

I hugged her tight. "I love it." I immediately started playing a song I knew she loved. It took a few seconds for her eyes to be glassy as she watched me.

"There is no sound sweeter than hearing you play." Her face was flushed as she handed me a second box a little bigger than the first. The brown paper shone in hand-drawn silver and gold metallic stars with glitter sprinkled around. She pushed the present toward me.

"Another? I thought we said just one."

She flipped her hand in the air. "They go together."

Again, I carefully pulled off the paper that she worked so hard to create. Inside was a small piece of fabric that wrapped a box. I opened up the fabric. My throat closed as the choking sensation took over. Tiny needles were pricking my eyes. I held the box out, staring at it.

"It's a box for the harmonica. I made it," she said nervously. "I hope it's okay. Oh, my God, do you like it? I kept the originals and had duplicates printed for me."

I couldn't speak. I grabbed the back of her head and pulled her in, capturing her lips. The kiss made time stand still. It was what words couldn't say, it was laced with love and possession.

"This is amazing, Juliet! How did you get these?"

"Hawk's mom. I knew you grew up together and thought she might have some pictures of you from when you guys were kids. We spent half a day going through boxes in her garage. When I saw these two, I knew they were the ones. I made you an album with the rest." She pulled another box from under the tree and handed it to me.

The harmonica box was wooden with an image of me around seven years old playing my harmonica with my grandmother next to me. We were sitting on Hawk's steps. Grandma was staring at me while I played, a proud smile on her face. The inside of the box was another picture taken the same day. It was me, my brother, and a toothless Hawk smiling on the steps. My brother had an arm around each of us.

I'd never been more clear that I had made the right decision than I was at that moment. I reached under the tree and pulled out a big package. It was not decorated like hers were, but it was wrapped in recycled paper, per her request. She was giddy with excitement. I used way too much tape. She carefully opened the heavy box. She kept removing the crumpled newspaper until she got to the bottom, where she found two heavy bricks. Confused, she turned around to look at me, her mouth dropping open at the sight of me on one knee.

Her hand covered her mouth while her eyes became glassy. I took her small hand in mine. "Anabelle Juliet Conti, will you spend the rest of your life with me?"

She let out a full-on cry and jumped onto me, wrapping her legs around my waist. She cried in my arms, kissing my whole face. "Yes, yes, yes." Lord jumped up, too, not knowing what was going on. Catching her breath between tiny sobs, she held the ring up, examining the intricate pattern that held a square diamond on top.

"Wait, is this—" My smile grew wide as she recognized the antique ring she had been admiring when we visited a few antique shops on one of our day trips.

"You remembered?" She threw herself at me, hiding her tear-stained face in my neck.

"Thank you for always listening to me," she sniffed. "It means so much."

I lifted her and carried her into the bedroom. We spent the next hour making love to Christmas music. We ended our escapade in the shower before sitting down to blueberry pancakes. I caught her looking at her finger as she cooked. I couldn't believe I had done it. She was going to be mine forever.

After breakfast, we stayed in front of the fire, looking at the album she made. I laughed at the various stages Hawk and I had gone through. Mullets were our funniest photos. We finally decided to get ready to go to the clubhouse to meet everyone for Christmas dinner.

"Do you think Paige would come?" she asked, packing her sister's present in the Jeep. "Christmas has always been her favorite holiday."

"Ivy said she would." I could see the uncertainty in her face. We packed everything in the Jeep including Lord in his new red Christmas collar. Juliet said we couldn't leave him alone on Christmas.

Getting in the driver's seat, I looked at Juliet, who was leaning into the back, fussing over Lord and getting him buckled in. It made my chest swell with love and pride. They were my family. Juliet was marrying me, and someday it would be our kids and us.

I looked at the sky, remembering my Grandma's words. *If you pray, someday it will happen. You must have faith, Alexander. God always answers your prayers.* I could almost feel her soft fingers on my chin and her sparkling blue eyes looking into mine.

The sun cut through the clouds, casting a glow through the trees. On one of the branches sat the brightest red cardinal I'd ever seen. Juliet said cardinals were signs of our loved ones who had passed. I felt like my grandmother was there at that moment, watching over us.

I closed my eyes and thanked God for everything that had happened in my life, even for all the fucked-up things. I knew now that everything, even all the pain, had led me to this woman and this moment.

"What's wrong?" Juliet pushed a loose red strand of hair from her eyes as she watched me.

"Nothing." I tried to play down the emotion that was gripping my heart.

She placed my hand in hers. "Rage, I am so happy and excited to begin our life together. I cannot wait to tell everyone. Ivy's going to flip." She held out her hand, admiring the ring. "For the first time in many years, I feel safe. I feel free. I feel loved." She kissed me, her green eyes beamed into mine. "You've given me this gift. You've made me happier than I could have ever imagined. I never thought..." She stopped, holding her breath for a moment, her eyes were now glassy. "I never thought I could have this. And I hope I can give you all you have given to me. No words are good enough to express to you how much I love you. I want us to be each other's forever."

I cupped her chin, kissing her gently, "We will be. Together, forever and always."

The End

AFTERWORD

Thank you!

I hope you enjoyed Juliet and Rage's story, the first book in The Stained Souls MC Series.

I would greatly appreciate it if you'd consider leaving a review on Amazon. I read them all and thank you for taking the time to write one.

I love hearing from my fans, so please reach out on Facebook or Instagram. Also, please check out my Author Page on Amazon where you can find out more information and view book trailers.

Consumed by Rage has a complete chapter by chapter playlist that can be found at www.zarateleg.com. You can listen on spotify or youtube!

There are a lot more adventures in store for the Souls. *A New Paige* is the next book in the Stained Souls Series. Please sign up for our newsletter at www.zarateleg.com if you would like to know when upcoming books are going to be released and also be included in receiving giveaways.

- https://www.facebook.com/Zara-Teleg-Page-364304024367828/
- https://www.instagram.com/zara_teleg/

ABOUT THE AUTHOR

I live in a suburb outside Philadelphia, Pennsylvania, with my husband and daughter. I was born a tree hugger, and I just love the outdoors, fitness, and yoga. Paddle boarding with my husband and dog is my favorite activity, and I long to move somewhere I can enjoy it year-round!

I'm a serial entrepreneur and a certified health coach and holistic nutritionist, but my passion and obsession are in books. I enjoy reading and writing about alpha males and strong females the most, and I look forward to sharing many more stories with you!

I love hearing from fans so please feel free to let me know your thoughts on my books, characters, or any questions you have.

- **Facebook:** https://www.facebook.com/Zara-Teleg-Page-364304024367828/
- **Instagram:** https://www.instagram.com/zara_teleg/
- **Email:** zarateleg@gmail.com
- **Website:** www.zarateleg.com

ACKNOWLEDGMENTS

Thank you to all my beautiful friends and family who have supported me through this process. You encouraged me and believed that I could do it. Here's to finishing something I started!

Andy, thank you for believing in me and giving me the time to write. Your support made this happen. I love you and hope we can make all our dreams come true.

Mom, you have always been my cheerleader. I can't tell you how much your support of this crazy idea has meant to me. You have never doubted me. Thanks for sharing my book with everyone you know and everyone you meet!

Dad, thanks for believing in me and telling me I could do this, and everything else you support me in, too.

Mya, my beautiful daughter, thank you for listening to all my ideas and sharing them with your friends. At the beach and at home, they have also been my biggest supporters. I did this for you, to prove that you can do whatever your heart desires. That's all I want for you in life. Always do what makes your heart feel joy and never settle for anything less than happiness.

Ritchelle, thank you for holding my hand through this process. Thank you for your impeccable editing skills and your eye for detail.

You have been invaluable to me, and I could not have done this without you.

Raelleen, thank you for scouring thousands of pictures to design me an awesome cover!

Becky, thank you for proofreading and helping me improve my writing.

PJ, you have helped me keep my head on straight. Thanks for showing up every day.

Katie, thanks for being my cheerleader since we were eight!

Lisa, thanks for listening to chapters even when you did not have time.

Selena, little sister, thank you for always giving me your honest opinion and helping me with all the important choices!

Kathy, thank you for making the time to give my book baby one last set of eyes.

Ruthie, RIP my sweet angel. You said the words that put me on this journey, "write the book." Neither of us knew what that meant at the time, but I am happy I listened.

To everyone else who has been a part of this process, thank you. I appreciate each and every one of you for every bit of support you have given me.

Made in the USA
Middletown, DE
30 April 2019